Hohenstein

Hohenstein

DIDI LAWSON

Didi Lawson
12-3-2016

Xchyler Publishing, an imprint of Hamilton Springs Press, LLC
Penny Freeman, Editor-in-chief
www.xchylerpublishing.com

1st Edition: February 2015

Cover and Interior Design by D. Robert Pease, walkingstickbooks.com
Edited by Elizabeth Gilliland and McKenna Gardner

Published in the United States of America
Xchyler Publishing

To my sweetheart Laurie Linwood
who believed in me even when I doubted myself.

Chapter One

Marie-Louise, Baroness von Hohenstein, looked out the window of the hired carriage driving her from the train station, past the little farming community of Hohenstein, into the rolling hills of the southeastern tip of the Black Forest, and onto the road leading up to Castle Hohenstein. Her castle. At least, it currently belonged to her, but who knew what tomorrow would bring?

Too many years had passed since she had been home. Her mother had whisked her away to boarding school in Lausanne, Switzerland, right after her father's funeral twelve years ago. She had been seven at the time.

A bend in the road brought the castle into view, and she leaned out the window to drink in the sight. Memories of loneliness flooded her mind, when the longing for home had been so strong that her heart ached. Now, her heart constricted once more, but it was tears of joy that welled in her eyes.

The heavy two-winged oak gate was flanked by square, two-story buildings—the gate house on the right and the armory on the left, with an ornately sculpted frieze above the gate that displayed the Hohenstein coat-of-arms. The boards were painted alternately in the two Hohenstein colors, black and gold, and formed an inverted chevron pattern when the gate was closed, though now it had been left open in anticipation of her arrival.

Marie-Louise squinted to make out the coat-of-arms but could hardly see the colors that had faded over the years. She wrinkled her brow and shook her head in annoyance. It needed a fresh coat of paint, and so did the gate. Why hadn't anyone tended to that?

As the carriage stopped in the courtyard in front of the curved stone stairs, Marie-Louise remained seated for a moment. And when the driver handed her down from the carriage, the baroness stepped over weeds growing between the cobbles and along the foundation of the building. She couldn't remember ever having seen weeds in the courtyard or anywhere else on the premises, and wondered why nobody seemed to take care of the castle. Jakob never neglected his duties. Something wasn't right, and her bewilderment grew when she also noticed cracks in the stone steps and crumbling stucco on the walls.

What was the reason for such neglect? Hohenstein had always been kept immaculate. She didn't think that Tante Ambrosia, her father's sister, would be lax in managing the staff. Perhaps she had gone blind and couldn't see the disrepair. That, however, shouldn't be a reason for the staff to disregard their duty.

As she walked toward the steps, she noticed that one of the basement windows was broken and strips of newspaper were glued over the cracks to hold the glass together. She shook her head, and her joy in coming home dimmed by apprehension of what else she might discover.

As if sleepwalking through a nightmare and expecting to wake up any minute, she tried to clear her mind, but couldn't shake a feeling of alarm. She had come home to straighten out the delay of her tuition payment to Humboldt University in Berlin but was faced with an even bigger problem right there at the castle.

Could Tante Ambrosia have dementia? Other than the obligatory birthday and Christmas cards, they hadn't corresponded at all, and Marie-Louise didn't know much about her aunt's life at Hohenstein.

She looked up to see Ambrosia waiting on the terrace, regal and erect, one hand on the stone balustrade.

Marie-Louise's throat tightened and a frisson of dread crawled up her spine, the same as it had when she was a little girl and had broken one of her aunt's strict rules. She had done nothing wrong, yet the memory of past experiences brought on the old anxiety.

While she climbed the steps, she watched her aunt and tried to remember if she had ever seen her laugh. Ambrosia may have smiled, perhaps, but she never laughed out loud. That would have been considered *bourgeois*. Still a very attractive woman, her once beautiful blond hair, styled in her usual chignon at the back of her head, now showed silver highlights. A shame that such a good-looking woman never found a husband. Yet, how could she have met any eligible bachelors when she was busy raising her niece at Hohenstein and later lived as a recluse at the castle? Besides, her stern demeanor must have chased away any possible suitors. And now she still lived at the castle, all alone and surrounded only by staff.

Marie-Louise looked around, but didn't see any of the staff. Someone needed to take luggage up to her room, but other than Tante Ambrosia, she didn't see a living soul; only a dog barked somewhere in the vicinity of the stables.

When she turned to see where the barking was coming from, she stood there with open mouth, unable to believe her eyes. What she saw wasn't a dog but a sagging roof. She turned toward her aunt with an unspoken question, but Ambrosia only nodded.

A shiver ran down Marie-Louise's spine. She extended her hand. "Good afternoon, Tante Ambrosia."

She hadn't expected a hug but would have welcomed a smile. The strict and haughty paragon of the antiquated nobility greeted her instead like she would a stranger, and Marie-Louise knew then that Ambrosia hadn't mellowed with age.

"It is good that you came home, Marie-Louise," her aunt said simply.

The baroness couldn't tell if her aunt was happy to see her, or that it was about time that the heir to the castle took charge.

Marie-Louise asked, "Can someone bring my luggage upstairs?"

"I'm afraid you'll have to do that yourself. There are no servants."

"No servants?"

Her aunt stared at her. "Marie-Louise, is there a problem with your hearing?"

"No, ma'am." She hung her head.

After a moment, the older woman offered, "If you need help, I can assist you."

"Thank you. I appreciate the offer, but I think I can handle it."

"Very well," said Ambrosia. "When you are finished, you can come to the dining room where I have laid out some refreshments."

With a lift of her head, her aunt turned and entered the castle.

Ambrosia had laid refreshments and not Frau Becker. With no servants, someone had to do the work in the kitchen preparing refreshments. And if her aunt wanted to eat, she'd have to do the cooking . . . unless . . . Marie-Louise held her breath for a moment . . . Ambrosia *paid* someone to bring meals for her up to the castle.

Marie-Louise's head spun. She had looked forward to being home again, to feel the peace and serenity of the beautiful hills and forests, but instead of tranquility, she'd encountered one mystery after another, and she hadn't even been here for more than ten minutes.

Tomorrow she'd find out why her tuition hadn't been paid and why the castle was in such disrepair. She had never given much thought to the management of the estate, assuming that somehow someone would take care of things. Not until she'd received notice from the director's office that her tuition hadn't been paid did she even contemplate the source of the money for her education.

Obviously a mistake on her part.

Ambrosia served refreshments that would have put the best restaurant to shame. An assortment of mouthwatering delicacies artfully arranged on the family's Meissen porcelain raised the question in Marie-Louise's mind if her aunt had ordered these wonderful treats from a café in town. She still couldn't believe that Ambrosia would slave in the kitchen. Not her proud and proper aunt.

It wasn't until after the two women retired to the parlor that Marie-Louise cautiously asked some questions.

"Tante Ambrosia, why don't we have staff at the castle?"

The aunt pursed her lips before she answered. "There is no money for staff."

"No money for staff?"

Ambrosia gave her a stern look. "Marie-Louise, it's not becoming to repeat what the other person said. Are you sure your hearing is all it should be?"

She hasn't changed. Always correcting me, always nagging.

"I'm sorry. I didn't mean to upset you. Repeating your statement was an expression of my astonishment."

Ambrosia pursed her lips but gave a curt nod.

"What happened to Jakob and Frau Becker," asked Marie-Louise after a moment of silence.

"Jakob retired a few years ago, and I dismissed Frau Becker."

Marie-Louise caught herself just in time before she repeated Ambrosia's answer again.

The aunt twisted her hands in her lap. "A lot of work remains undone, as you can see, and I do what I can, but it is a large undertaking. A woman from town comes every other week to do the heavy cleaning."

Unbelievable. Marie-Louise tried to picture Ambrosia performing all those duties, to no avail. For all her strictness, she knew Ambrosia shouldn't have to be confined to a life of poverty. She deserved better. Marie-Louise couldn't believe there wasn't any money, and wondered who controlled the spending. She'd had no idea that her aunt lived like a pauper while she had everything she could wish for. Life certainly hadn't been fair to the older woman.

"Forgive me. I had no idea how difficult things have been."

Ambrosia jutted out her chin and pressed her lips into a thin line. "Don't fret over me. I'm quite content and have learned to live and enjoy a simpler life. I even discovered my passion for cooking, and I like to work in the garden, to plant and to see things grow."

"Don't you miss society?"

"Not really. I was never one to seek company and entertainment. I read and play the pianoforte and the flute, and I collect herbs for their medicinal properties."

"Why do you collect herbs, and what do you do with them?"

"I use them as teas or salves and poultices should the need arise."

That didn't make sense. Because Ambrosia didn't socialize, who did she want to treat with her salves and poultices? Her aunt had always appeared a little different than other people, but now Marie-Louise thought her to be quite strange. There was nobody to nurse back to health. There was only Ambrosia.

Living like a recluse with nobody to talk to, no money for staff, and no entertainment could very well change a person, and she felt sorry for her. Apparently, she was content with the life as a pauper, although she certainly had been used to a different lifestyle at one time.

There had to be money for the upkeep of the castle. Even if Ambrosia didn't complain about the cooking and house cleaning, there had to be funds for necessary repairs. The broken window, the sagging roof and the crumbling stucco needed attention. And

Marie-Louise shuddered to think of what else she might find wrong. She decided to go on an inspection tour the next day and make a list.

In the meantime, she searched for something to do, anything to pass the time before she would retire for the night. Conversation with her aunt wasn't very lively, and sitting demurely on the settee and staring into space for the better part of the evening was an uncomfortable thought.

After the sun had gone down, both women retired to the parlor. Ambrosia sat erect and motionless in her chair and didn't seem inclined to converse at all. Apparently, she was used to the quiet and enjoyed it, but Marie-Louise fidgeted in her seat. When the silence became oppressive, she asked, "Do we have a phonograph? We could listen to some music."

Ambrosia offered a disapproving look. "I don't believe in modern types of entertainment. No need to alter what has worked so well in the past."

Deciding to press her luck, Marie-Louise continued, "How do you know what's going on in the world when you stay at Hohenstein all the time?"

"I subscribe to the daily newspaper."

"Oh."

After a pause, Marie-Louise asked the question foremost on her mind. "Why isn't there any money for staff or for the upkeep of the castle?"

Ambrosia looked up, a crease between her eyes. "I wouldn't know." Sniff. "I'm not familiar with your father's will. You would have to contact the solicitor, or the executor of your father's will."

The baroness bit her lip. If she wanted to get to the bottom of Hohenstein's financial problems, she would have to do what her aunt suggested. She'd have to visit the solicitor anyway to straighten out the problem with her tuition payment.

Later, on her way to her suite, Marie-Louise detoured via the picture gallery where the portraits of all the Hohensteins looked down on her from their gilded frames. As a child, she'd often come here and hold imaginary conversations with her ancestors. She knew them well; their features were familiar to her.

She stopped in front of her father's portrait. *Papa, I wish you were here. Nothing has been the same since you passed away. I feel lost and don't know which way to turn. This is my home. I don't want to lose it. And I know you loved it, too. Please help me to know what to do.*

Baron Wolfram von Hohenstein smiled down on his daughter as if to say, '*Don't worry. Everything will work out.*'

The next portrait showed her parents together, her mother a head shorter than her father. Marie-Louise had always liked this picture because her parents looked happy. Their happiness, however, hadn't lasted long, and eventually ended with her father's death. Anique certainly was a beauty—*and still is*, Marie-Louise corrected herself. She had inherited her mother's looks, her dark hair and slender build, but was tall like her father.

Her mother never liked the castle and spent as little time as possible there, and since her father's death has never set foot here anymore. Marie-Louise was the sole heir and responsible for Hohenstein.

She sighed. One day, her portrait would join the other Hohensteins on the wall. She smiled at the thought, then sobered. Would her ancestors want her beside them should she marry a commoner? Not marrying within one's social circle was still frowned upon, although things were changing in Germany. Nobility was losing some of its superior status, and more commoners moved into higher-ranking military positions and industrial leadership roles.

Her mind to never marry someone from of her own rank had been made up years ago when she realized that her parents' marriage hadn't been a happy one, and especially, when her parents were never home to see her except for her birthday or on Christmas. If marrying someone from her own rank meant that her children would be deprived of a normal family life, she'd look elsewhere for a husband.

In her circles, a husband was chosen by someone else for his eligibility, proper upbringing, and social status. No, she decided, she wouldn't submit to the old rules and dictates of nobility. That could mean, however, that her portrait would never be among her ancestors.

No sense worrying right then whether or not her picture would hang in the gallery. She had weightier matters to deal with at the moment and needed to prepare for tomorrow's visit to her father's solicitor about her tuition payment. She also wanted to see Onkel Georg, a distant relative and the trustee and executor of her father's will. Then she'd get to the bottom of the mystery of Hohenstein.

Tomorrow would mark the beginning of Hohenstein's renaissance.

Chapter Two

The next day didn't bring the desired results. When Marie-Louise visited the Schmidt & Roth Company, her late father's solicitor, about her tuition payments, she was informed that Mr. Roth was out of town and not expected to be back until the following week, and no one else in the office was familiar with the case.

That seemed very odd to Marie-Louise. She was sure that there must be a file in the office somewhere with her information. If the tuition wouldn't be paid before the deadline, her classes would be dropped. She was especially eager to take the Art History class which always filled up quickly, according to the professor.

After receiving the letter from the director's office that her registration was on hold because of the unpaid tuition, she'd inquired at the Registration Department to find out that the Schmidt & Roth Company had been sent not one, but three reminders, but no reply had been received. And that was the reason why she had to return to Hohenstein to sort things out.

She tapped her foot while concentrating on her next move. She didn't want to wait until Mr. Roth returned. She had nothing to do, no phonograph, and nobody to talk to except her aunt, and that wasn't a viable option.

She'd go to the Wolfburg Bank and talk with Onkel Georg—Count Wolfburg to be precise—about her situation. As the trustee and executor of her father's will, he'd help her understand the legalities of the trust and tell her if there was anything she could do to reverse Hohenstein's decline.

On her way to the Wolfburg Bank, Marie-Louise still fumed when she remembered her aunt's admonition to conduct herself with the utmost decorum. She was not a little girl anymore who needed to be taught and guided, especially not with a wagging finger. Of course she knew that Count Wolfburg expected her to conduct herself appropriate to her station in life, and Tante Ambrosia didn't have to remind her with her favorite phrase *noblesse oblige*.

Marie-Louise rolled her eyes and mimicked her aunt. *And don't forget to thank the count for his time.* As if I was an ungrateful chit!

A secretary ushered Marie-Louise into a small conference room at the Wolfburg Bank. "Please have a seat, Baroness. Count Wolfburg will meet with you presently."

Marie-Louise looked around. The room's furnishings exuded warmth and tranquility. A wall unit with carved detail along the top covered the north wall, and on one of the lower shelves were several trophies. She marveled that the count still participated in such strenuous sports as sailing, skiing, and water polo.

Count Georg had been a frequent guest at Hohenstein whenever her parents were in residence, and again later, when her father had returned to the castle with an ailing heart. It was only natural for Marie-Louise to call him and the countess *uncle* and *aunt*.

On the shelf below the trophies, she noticed a picture frame and bent to look at the photograph. Upon closer inspection, she found that it contained the Knight's Code done in calligraphy, with the first letter of each stanza artistically scrolled. Picking up the frame, she read:

THE KNIGHT'S CODE

Be always ready with your armor on,
Except when you are taking your rest at night.
Defend the poor,
And help them that cannot defend themselves.
Do nothing to hurt or offend anyone else.
Be prepared to fight in the defense of your country.
At whatever you are working,
Try to win honor and a name for honesty.
Never break your promise.
Maintain the honor of your country with your life.
Rather die honest than live shamelessly.
Chivalry requireth that youth should be trained
To perform the most laborious and humble offices
With cheerfulness and grace;
And to do good unto others.

Somehow these words exemplified his life. He had always been strict but fair, she recalled. Maybe not always easy to live with since he expected much from everybody, though nothing he wouldn't expect of himself.

Would he be as aloof as Tante Ambrosia? Her aunt hadn't changed. In fact she had proved to be as stern as ever—no deviation from the standard rules and traditions that kept nobility atop their antiquated pedestals.

Marie-Louise looked at her watch and drew a deep breath. Where was Onkel Georg, and what was taking him so long? She paced the floor. Eight paces toward the window. Turn. Eight paces toward the wall. Turn. Each step seemed to chip away a fraction of her confidence. She didn't know what she'd do if the count couldn't help her with her problems.

Although she hadn't seen Onkel Georg since her father's funeral, she could still remember him as being particularly fond of her, calling her Snow White for her dark hair and delicate complexion. He would understand and explain the situation with her father's trust.

She became impatient. Eight minutes already. Of course, he hadn't known that she would come calling today and probably had every minute of the day planned.

The opening of the heavy leather-padded door interrupted her thoughts. Onkel Georg. At last. Marie-Louise turned to greet him with her most charming smile.

With her hands outstretched, she took a few steps forward, only to stop short. Smile disappearing, her hands dropped to her sides. She stared at the stranger.

Tall and lean, he appeared powerful with broad shoulders and a natural grace of movement. His thick, wavy hair looked like weathered copper, parted and feathered back at the temples. Hair of that color normally demanded a pale complexion studded with freckles, but neither was the case here. His smooth skin looked nicely tanned, telling of many hours spent outdoors, and his business suit enhanced his athletic physique, which stood in stark contrast to his professional appearance.

He certainly was the best-looking man she had seen in a long time, but who was he?

With a smile, he pointed to the settee, inviting her to have a seat before he sat on a sofa perpendicular to hers.

When he gave her an encouraging smile, she asked in a cool a voice, "Sir, would you please inform Count Wolfburg that Baroness von Hohenstein is waiting?"

At that moment, the secretary stuck her head around the door. "Please excuse me, but Herr Maier is in the office and wants to speak with you."

Two creases appeared above the bridge of his nose. "I believe I said that I didn't want to be disturbed."

"I'm sorry, but Herr Maier said that he had important news for you."

The young man turned to Marie-Louise and said, "Please excuse the interruption," before he stood up and followed his secretary.

His voice had sounded clipped and business-like, and Marie-Louise shuddered at the thought of having him for an opponent. Although his generous mouth and the fine lines around his eyes spoke of warmth and humor, his voice attested to a toughness she'd rather not experience. She resolved to speak only with Onkel Georg and not with this stranger, although he obviously held a position of considerable influence and seemed determined to find out why she had come to see the count.

Her business with the count was of a personal nature and not fit for anyone else's ears. Should Onkel Georg be unavailable, she would have to come back another time, although she had so hoped to see him today.

The young man returned presently. "Sorry for the interruption." He smiled while his eyes rested on her face.

Marie-Louise stiffened, sat bolt upright, and put as much hauteur and disdain into her expression as she possibly could. He, on the other hand, seemingly unperturbed, watched her reaction with one arm resting on the back of the settee.

Enough delaying. Clearing her throat, she looked straight at the man. "Are you in the count's confidence?"

A low chuckle emerged from deep down his throat. "Yes, I definitely am."

"You are his right hand, I presume?"

He tilted his head to one side and wrinkled his brow as if to consider her question. "Yes, I think so."

She eyed him with cold defiance. "Why did Count Wolfburg send you to talk to me? Is he unavailable?"

The young man leaned forward as his smile intensified and little devils danced in his eyes. “I guess you don’t remember me, Snow White.”

Chapter Three

Too shocked to comment, she glanced at him for a moment and lost herself in a pair of deep-set, blue eyes. To shut out their disturbing intensity, she lowered her gaze and traced the seam line on the material of her skirt.

Finally, he ended the guessing game. "I'm Ulrich. No wonder you don't remember me. It's been about fourteen or fifteen years since we saw each other."

"Ulrich?" She tried to imagine him as a young boy. Was it possible? She remembered him as a lanky and stand-offish lad with light strawberry blond hair whom she had always held in awe. Could that be him? She finally smiled, thinking that he had surely improved with age.

"Snow White has grown into a beautiful young woman," he observed, smiling. "I still remember you as a little imp with a white, flouncy dress and red sash—you must have been five or six years old at the time. Your hair was curly and you had a knack for getting into mischief."

Marie-Louise felt the tension ebb away as she relaxed against the cushions.

"Poor Tante Ambrosia," she said, smiling in remembrance, "she didn't have it easy with me." Lighthearted laughter accompanied this contrite testimony. Concentrating on him, she continued, "I remember you now. You are the older of Onkel Georg's sons, and the taller. You always distanced yourself from Peter and me and our childish pranks."

Silently, she added, '*And all I wanted was to impress you so that you would notice me, which you never did.*'

"Where is Onkel Georg? I actually expected to talk to him . . ."

"Father suffered from apoplexy about two years ago which left him partially paralyzed. He passed away a little over a year ago, and I stepped into his shoes as the head of the family."

She swallowed. "I'm sorry to hear that."

Silence.

She racked her brain and couldn't remember having been notified of the count's passing. *Oh, drat! I didn't pay much attention to news of the families in the Wolfburg clan, but I should've paid attention to Onkel Georg's obituary.*

Now, she'd have to talk to Ulrich, and she didn't know him nearly as well. As a matter of fact, he intimidated her a little, and she wasn't sure how to approach him with her questions. He probably would think her immature or unintelligent, because she had no idea about financial things. Having enough problems on his plate running the bank and overseeing his vast empire at such a young age, he may resent to having to deal with Hohenstein's problems. Although, as she now recalled, her monthly stipend checks always came from the Wolfburg Bank.

When Ulrich stepped into his father's shoes, that likely meant that he also replaced Onkel Georg as the trustee and executor of her father's will . . . as such, he would definitely be the person to approach with Hohenstein's problems.

She looked at him again and guessed that he must be in his mid-twenties.

He smiled an encouraging smile, and she bit her lip, trying to come up with an intelligent way to describe the complications she faced. Ulrich waited. His silk tie, knotted to perfection, hung straight as if its position had been determined with a ruler, and his white shirt stood in stark contrast to the color of his eyes. Those incredible eyes! Their blue intensity hit her like an electric shock every time, and she drew her gaze away to watch her restless hands instead.

She had to start somewhere, but tried to find the right words without disclosing too much of the sad state of the castle. In desperation, she asked, “How's Tante Sybilla?”

A faint smile lifted the corners of his mouth. “Mother's fine. She took residence at Falkenberg, where she's close to her friends and her beloved mountains, and she seems quite happy and content with her life there.”

“And what's Peter up to these days?”

“My brother is studying international law at the University of Heidelberg, but at the moment he's on his way to Lake Constance to go sailing with some of his friends. They're on holiday right now. You actually just missed him—he left my office about ten minutes ago.”

“Oh, then it was Peter I saw leaving the bank in white pants?”

“Yes, he was off to have fun. But let's not talk about Peter—let's talk about you. You're enrolled at Humboldt University in Berlin, I presume. What are the courses you're taking?”

She cleared her throat. “I'm taking courses in art history, but haven't decided yet what direction I want to go.”

“You have time to make up your mind. In the meantime, Tante Ambrosia will be happy to have you home.”

“I'm not so sure about that.”

“What do you mean?”

“We don't see eye-to-eye on certain issues,” she confessed.

Ulrich leaned forward. “May I ask what issues, or would you rather not talk about it?”

“Well, ah . . .” Marie-Louise shifted. “It's actually my fault. There was always friction between us, and I suppose there always will be. As long as I can remember, she's been strict and stuck in her ways, and it hasn't gotten any better. Or maybe I'm more pigheaded than ever."

"How long have you been home, Marie-Louise?"

"I arrived on Monday."

"Give yourself—and her—time to readjust. She has been alone for so many years . . . She's set in her ways and has to get used to having a young person around again."

Marie-Louise sighed and rolled her eyes, which made him laugh.

"You don't think the problem is that simple?"

She shook her head, trying to think hard of how best to broach the subject of Hohenstein's problem. It had seemed so easy to talk to Onkel Georg about it as she had rehearsed her speech on the way to Wolfburg, but now she needed to discuss her problems with *Ulrich* and couldn't even come up with a good beginning.

Finally, she decided to just plunge in. "Actually, I came here today to discuss a problem concerning Hohenstein with your father."

He stretched his long legs out in front of him. "I didn't think it was a social visit that brought you to Wolfburg." He smiled and looked with genuine concern into her eyes.

Still not quite sure how to start, she twisted her hands in her lap. "I don't know if you have been to Hohenstein lately . . ."

He shook his head.

"The castle is in sad need of repair. The stable roof caved in, probably quite some years ago."

At his nod, she continued, "I actually returned to Hohenstein because my tuition hasn't been paid, and Mr. Roth, my father's solicitor, never responded to the university's letters."

"I know that your father took out an insurance policy with you as beneficiary to pay for your education, but I don't know if the funds have been depleted or not. I doubt it, but you'll have to find out from Mr. Roth. If the funds are exhausted, they should have informed you."

Marie-Louise agreed.

"Have you spoken with the solicitor since you arrived?"

"I visited the office yesterday but was informed that he was out of town until next week."

Ulrich raised an eyebrow but didn't say anything.

"Are you familiar with my father's trust?" she asked.

"Yes, of course. I looked it over a couple of weeks ago."

Marie-Louise tucked a wisp of hair behind her ear. "We're . . . having problems at Hohenstein."

"What problems other than a sagging roof?"

Marie-Louise related her amazement at Ambrosia's dismissal of all the staff and her need to fend for herself, that she couldn't afford modern amenities, and that she tended a garden and performed household duties like a servant. "I don't understand how there are no funds to maintain the castle and the grounds and to allow Tante Ambrosia a lifestyle befitting her status."

Ulrich leaned forward. "You're talking about two different problems here. Ambrosia's father, your grandfather, set up an annuity for your aunt to secure a living for her. She receives an annual distribution. I assume that your aunt has set the amount quite low because she doesn't want to spend more than absolutely necessary and is probably overly cautious to make the money last."

"Is there any danger that the money might run out?"

"That depends on how many years she'll need to draw on the annuity."

"How much money is in the account?"

Ulrich smiled. "Sorry. That's something I'm not at liberty to divulge."

All right, Tante Ambrosia was more or less taken care of. At least, her living expenses. "What about the upkeep of the castle?"

Ulrich steepled his hands. "Here lies the real problem: when your father created the trust, he didn't allow any flexibility on how the funds could be used. This is highly unusual, and was either an error on the part of the lawyer, or intended by your father to safeguard the funds from being abused by others."

The baroness wrinkled her brow, confused. "Who pays my stipend? I mean, is there a separate account?"

"Yes. Your father opened a special account and designated the money to be paid to you in monthly stipends until you have access to your inheritance at age twenty-five, or on the day of your wedding, whichever occurs first."

"Yes, I know." She sighed.

Ulrich smiled. "Your father made sure that you're well taken care of, at least financially."

"Yes, and I appreciate that, but in the meantime, my hands are tied and Hohenstein will decay further because I can't get to the money to restore the castle." *Of course, Papa couldn't have foreseen the deterioration over the years.*

Marie-Louise looked at Ulrich. "Do you think that my father purposely set up the trust so that nobody could use the funds?"

"That would make sense, but I assume that it was the lawyer's error rather than your father's intent."

"If my father set up the trust the way it is worded, who did he think could misuse the trust?"

"Your aunt? Your mother? I, myself?"

Marie-Louise shook her head. "Tante Ambrosia would never touch anything that doesn't belong to her, and you wouldn't because you're the trustee and executor. My mother? Well, she doesn't need any money. She married Philip Didier, and he is quite wealthy."

She remembered how upset she had been when her mother told her that she would marry Philip so soon after her husband's funeral, but Anique had only shrugged and said that she didn't want to lose Philip to someone else. Some other gold-digger, probably. That had been the first time that Marie-Louise guessed her parents' marriage hadn't been a love match, and she was so dismayed that she cried herself to sleep that night.

She closed her eyes for a moment.

Ulrich tore her out of her musings. "Are you going to spend the summer at Hohenstein?"

"Yes, I want to stay at the castle and see what I can do to beautify it, even without money."

"What do you have in mind?"

She gnawed on her lower lip. "The gatehouse and armory need a fresh coat of paint, and the courtyard requires some attention, too."

"Who will do the work?"

"I guess I'll have to do it since we can't afford to hire help."

Ulrich reached for the pencil on the corner table and twirled it between his fingers a few times. "Won't you miss your friends when you stay at the castle with only Tante Ambrosia for company?"

"I can find entertainment in town, I suppose."

"Among commoners?"

Marie-Louise looked at him, scarcely believing what he had just said. He was a snob! A very handsome snob, but still a snob, and he reminded her of her aunt's elitist demeanor. This was the twentieth century, for heaven's sake and nobility was losing its allure slowly but surely, or hadn't he noticed?

She gave him a sideways glance. True, he looked regal, and no one would ever consider him a commoner. Not with his imperial air. Perhaps it wasn't so much nobility that kept their distance, but the commoners themselves that set them upon pedestals. Could it be that people wanted to hold on to their fairy tales? Hmmm. That thought had never occurred to her before.

"Why shouldn't I find entertainment among commoners?"

"You may not fit in."

"I adjust easily."

"That's good to know," he returned dryly.

Marie-Louise didn't know what else to say and stood up, preparing to leave. She remembered her aunt's admonition to thank the count and extended her hand.

"Thank you so much for taking the time to explain the ramifications of my father's trust. Of course, I had hoped for better news, but will have to find another way to bring Hohenstein back to its original beauty."

Ulrich had risen, too. Taking her hand in his, he smiled into her eyes. "It was a pleasure to speak with you, Marie-Louise. I hope we'll see each other more, now that you are staying at Hohenstein. I wish you luck with your undertaking, Snow White."

She felt heat flood her cheeks at his use of the nickname his father had given her those many years ago.

His eyes danced with merriment. "You're adorable when you blush." Her brows drew together. Was he making fun of her?

"And you're cute when you glare at me with your big brown eyes."

She pouted. "You're making fun of me."

He laughed as he walked her to the door. Before he opened it, he lifted a wayward tendril of her hair and tucked it behind her ear. "Please give my regards to Tante Ambrosia."

All she could do was incline her head as she walked past him. She was baffled by his change in behavior from businessman to *charmeur*. He had totally confused her.

Silly goose, she chided herself. He was only trying to be nice. That was all. Trying to take the sting off the dismal news. She'd go home, assess the situation with the castle, come up with an alternative plan, and get to work. If she couldn't tackle the major renovation projects, she'd start with the little things, like painting the gatehouse, the armory, and the coat-of-arms above the gate.

Yes, she could do that.

Chapter Four

Marie-Louise was disappointed that her visit to Wolfburg hadn't brought the desired results. On the contrary. Her father's trust didn't allow any digression of funds for the upkeep of the castle, which meant that her beautification plans would have to progress at a snail's pace. The little money she could spare from her allowance would only buy some paint and tools or whatever would be needed for minor repairs.

Ulrich's hands were tied, and her inheritance remained untouched.

The count had seemed as stuffy and unbending as Tante Ambrosia, for all his pleasant manners. She knew he could have helped her somehow. He could have offered her a loan, being a banker. If he had truly wanted to help her.

To rid herself of her disappointment, she decided to explore the land around the castle and whistled for Kaiser, her aunt's German Shepherd. He seemed to have been the only extravagant expense her aunt splurged on, but being alone in the castle with no staff, she doubtless had felt the necessity to have at least a big dog for protection. His deep bark would discourage anybody from unlawfully entering and alert her should anyone venture into the courtyard.

On the trail, Marie-Louise walked at a sedate pace and touched every rock or root that lay in her path with the tip of her shoe while Kaiser trotted ahead, stopping frequently to sniff out a particularly interesting tree or plant along the way. The dog seemed ecstatic at the unexpected treat of running free.

The baroness strolled along, seeing and yet unseeing. When Kaiser came prancing toward her, tail wagging, eyes begging, she bent to pat the animal. "Sorry I'm such a poor sport, but I have a lot on my mind. Just run along and find yourself a rabbit to chase."

She came to a small stand of trees in the middle of a clearing, once her favorite playground. Here she had dreamed up all sorts of stories: monsters invading the castle, capturing the beautiful princess, locking her up in a tower. Then a handsome prince would come and rescue her. She closed her eyes. If only a prince in shining armor would come along right now.

Of course, she corrected herself, it wouldn't be a prince, but some handsome and honest young commoner.

Standing still, she embellished her dream with deep blue eyes, rusty hair and a quirk at the corner of his mouth. She smiled.

When she realized, however, who the man of her fantasy was, her eyes flew open and she shook her head. How silly to imagine Ulrich as her rescuer! He hadn't even so much as offered his help.

She picked up a pebble and hurled it along the path. Should she ask her aunt about the count's character? Better not. Ambrosia would call Marie-Louise's question blasphemy, to doubt the integrity of the head of the House of Wolfburg. No, her aunt wouldn't understand or share her worries in that respect.

Marie-Louise resumed her walk. A few steps further brought her to the grove of trees where she also used to play her childhood games. Sometimes, children from the town below would sneak up the hill and play with her here. That didn't happen too often, though, because Tante Ambrosia never looked favorably upon her mixing with common folk.

On those Sundays when Onkel Georg and Tante Sybilla had visited the castle and the weather had proved halfway decent,

Marie-Louise and Peter had always managed to steal away and come to this spot to play unobserved while proper Ulrich stayed behind. Even then, he had been stuffy.

Marie-Louise sighed. Her thoughts persistently returned to the count and her fruitless visit to Wolfburg. Other than the knowledge she'd gained that she couldn't tap into her inheritance before her twenty-fifth birthday, her visit to the bank had been a complete waste of time.

Squaring her shoulders, she stepped into the grove and looked around until she found the makeshift ladder that led up the sleek trunk of a birch tree into the treehouse Jakob had built for her so many years ago. The ladder still stood firm, but the wooden planks overhead looked weathered and unsafe in some places.

Good old Jakob, the factotum of the castle, had been around forever and had always found ways to do nice things for her. She needed to get him back to Hohenstein if she wanted to restore the castle. She also would like to have Frau Becker back, but, of course, there was no money for staff.

Disheartened, Marie-Louise returned to the castle, where Ambrosia met her in the foyer. "How was the visit with the count?"

"Disappointing. I can't touch my inheritance, not even for the upkeep of the castle."

"I hope you weren't rude to the count when he couldn't help you?"

Marie-Louise rolled her eyes. "Of course not."

Ambrosia sighed with relief. "I'm sorry things didn't work out the way you had hoped. Sit down and rest awhile. You look exhausted."

"I think I'm not used to the warm temperatures yet."

"I'm not surprised. It's unseasonably warm for this time of year."

The baroness nodded and walked toward the stairs when Ambrosia lectured, "Walk straight, head high, chin up, long neck."

Marie-Louise frowned. *Why does she have to censure every move I make?*

"By the way," Ambrosia added, "the mayor of Hohenstein called in your absence. He wanted to personally welcome you back."

Marie-Louise turned in surprise. "How does he know that I'm in town?"

"I don't know. Someone must have seen you, or the coach driver noised the news abroad."

"What did the mayor want?"

"To know if he could visit tomorrow afternoon at three-thirty."

She shrugged. "Well, since I don't have any particular plans for tomorrow afternoon, he is welcome to pay a visit."

And at three-thirty sharp the next day, the mayor's carriage rolled over the drawbridge and into the courtyard. Dressed in a dark business suit, he produced a huge flower arrangement in a basket, which almost obscured his vision as he proceeded to walk up the curving steps to the front entrance of the castle and ring the brass bell.

Marie-Louise opened the door and greeted him with a smile. Still a little out of breath after climbing the stairs, he extended his free hand.

"Baroness von Hohenstein, thank you for allowing me to visit you in your home." He set the flower arrangement on a nearby side table and turned to her. "On behalf of the town council, I want to formally welcome you home and present you with this small token of our heartfelt pleasure at having you back."

"Thank you very much, *Herr Bűrgermeister,* and thank you for the lovely arrangement."

She seated herself on a delicate white Louis XVI armchair with petit point cushion and invited the mayor to take a seat opposite her.

"Baroness, it must feel good to be home again."

She nodded.

"Your aunt is probably happy to have you back, too. It must be awfully lonely for her in this big castle all by herself."

"Yes, it is lonely, but she has hobbies and interests that occupy her time."

The mayor looked around, admiring the chandelier and the ceiling fresco, and let his gaze follow the gracefully curved staircases to the second floor.

"What a magnificent place you have here, Baroness! You are the envy of every girl in Hohenstein who dreams to look and live like a princess. My granddaughters surely love everything to do with princesses—the stories, the gowns, the tiaras."

Marie-Louise laughed. "It's not all that glamorous to live in a castle. It's a lot more spacious than most homes, to be sure, but then it takes more upkeep, too."

"That's true enough. It probably takes an army of staff to keep everything functioning smoothly."

The baroness only inclined her head and smiled. *If he only knew.*

The mayor entertained her with some of Hohenstein's events and happenings until it was time for him to leave.

"Is there anything the town can do to be of assistance?"

"Thank you for your kind offer, *Herr Bürgermeister,* but I can't think of anything that we need at the moment." She smiled and accompanied him to the door.

In parting, he said, "Baroness, may I express my hope to see you at some of our town functions in the future?"

"Yes," she said, "I will try to be a good citizen, Herr Schmidt."

"Wonderful. I was hoping you might be available to represent the town at some of our special events, like the upcoming dedication of the new hospital." He smiled and winked at her before continuing, "Having a beautiful, young baroness there to cut the ribbon would give us excellent publicity."

She nodded. "You can count on me."

"Excellent. The town council will be pleased to hear that." He took a few steps toward the door, and then turned to her again. "It's a real pleasure to have you back at Hohenstein, Baroness, and I hope that we will have the pleasure to see each other frequently. You will certainly be an asset to our town."

She inclined her head in acknowledgment, although she had to suppress a smile at the man's eagerness.

"Baroness," he said in a more serious tone, "if there's anything I or the town can do for you, please don't hesitate to let me know. You're alone here and probably need some help once in a while. Please promise that you'll call on me anytime."

"Thank you for your kind words, *Herr Bűrgermeister*. I will certainly let you know when I need your assistance. And please, relay my sincere appreciation to the town council for the beautiful flowers."

After the mayor left, Marie-Louise wondered if all the towns with resident nobility invited them to participate in the local affairs. She didn't know, and she assumed that Ambrosia didn't know either, but she had to admit that she felt honored. It might be interesting to learn more about the workings of the town, and perhaps she'd even meet a nice man who'd accompany her to the theater or other social events once in a while.

Eventually, she would need to get married, and because she wanted her future husband to be a commoner, this might be as good an opportunity as any to meet a nice gentleman. Besides, being involved with the town gave her a good excuse to be away from the castle without raising Tante Ambrosia's suspicions. Yes, it was the perfect scenario, and Marie-Louise was quite satisfied with the outcome of the mayor's visit.

She walked over to the pianoforte and played a few chords, and marveled that the instrument was tuned to perfection. Oh, yes—Ambrosia said that she had her music to occupy her, and that's why she had the instrument serviced. One of her few luxuries. Perhaps they could play a duet together one evening. It would be nice to have something relaxing to do after working on beautification projects all day.

She looked at her manicured hands, turned them palm-side up and sighed. If Ambrosia could do menial work, so could she. Painting the gatehouse and armory was first on her list of projects, and the courtyard needed a transformation also, but there was only so much she could do by herself. She needed Jakob. Could he possibly repair the stable roof? No, probably not. He'd be in his late sixties or early seventies by now, and she couldn't allow him to climb up on that roof. Besides, she didn't have the funds for the materials anyway.

First, she had to find out if Jakob was still alive; and if so, if he still lived in town and was willing to come back and work for next to nothing. Yes, paying him was a problem she needed to address, but first things first. She'd try to find him.

Better not tell Ambrosia that she wanted to find Jakob, because her aunt might discourage her.

Marie-Louise found a lady's bicycle in the carriage house and set out the next morning to talk to Frau Becker. After a few wrong turns, she found *Gartenstrasse* and leaned the bicycle against a tree of No. 34, then knocked on the door.

Shuffling feet approached. Frau Becker, even more rotund than the baroness remembered, wiped her hands on her apron. "Y-e-s?" The woman squinted, and then sucked in a breath. "Fräulein Marie-Louise? Is that you?"

"It's I, Frau Becker. *Guten Tag.*"

Frau Becker bustled out the door and opened her arms wide. With a little sob, but without hesitation, Marie-Louise hurried into Frau Becker's embrace and felt herself pressed against the woman's ample and soft bosom. Being held by the older woman felt so good, just like she remembered from her childhood years . . .

Finally, Frau Becker said, "I know I should keep my distance, but you're like one of my own. I'm so happy you're back where you belong, my dear. Come in, come in, and let me look at you. My, you have grown into a beautiful young woman—even prettier than your mother. How have you been all these years? And how is your mother? Are you finished with school?"

The baroness had to laugh. Frau Becker hadn't changed one bit, rattling off a thousand questions without waiting for an answer. But, oh, how she basked in the woman's warmth.

Frau Becker led her into the sitting room and invited her to sit on the sofa. "How's your aunt?"

"She's doing well, thank you for asking."

"You know, I've heard rumors."

"Rumors? What kind of rumors?"

"People say that she's acting strange."

"How so?"

Frau Becker lowered her voice to whisper. "It's rumored that she's into witchcraft."

Marie-Louise had to laugh. "That's ridiculous. Why do people think that my aunt is acting strange when they don't even see her?"

"But they do see her! Roaming the countryside with her dog and collecting all kinds of strange plants while reading her spell book and mumbling to herself."

Marie-Louise laughed again and explained, "My aunt collects herbs for medicinal purposes, for teas and ointments, but that has nothing to do with witchcraft."

Frau Becker looked dubious. "If you say so, Fräulein Marie-Louise, but it's strange behavior, nevertheless." Another thought seemed to strike her. "I've heard that she doesn't have any staff at the castle. Does that mean that your aunt does the housework, the laundry, the planting, weeding, and everything herself?"

"Yes, she does."

"I can't imagine that. Miss High and Mighty doing servants' jobs."

"She has developed into a gourmet cook."

With hands on her ample hips, Frau Becker made a disgusted sound. "Your aunt in *my* kitchen?"

Marie-Louise soothed, "Someone has to prepare our meals."

"Hmmm."

Then, as if she just now remembered her manners, Frau Becker hastened to apologize. "Please, forgive me. I'm rattling on and on and neglecting my guest. Can I get you anything? A glass of lemonade, a piece of cake?"

"No, thank you, Frau Becker. I actually came here to ask you where I might find Jakob."

"Poor Jakob," Frau Becker tsked. "He lives in a little shack in back of his sister's house. Doesn't like it much there, but has nowhere else to go."

"Do you know the address?"

"Yes. It's *Hubertusweg* 20. You need to go around to the backyard, but you'll have to talk loud because Jakob's a little hard of hearing in his old age."

Marie-Louise rose to her feet. "Thank you so much, Frau Becker. I'm sorry to have to leave, but I'll visit with you another time. *Auf Wiedersehen.*"

Jakob certainly was hard of hearing. Marie-Louise knocked on the door, but nothing happened. She knocked a second time, a little louder. Still nothing. Then she pounded the door with her fist until her knuckles hurt, and finally Jakob called, "Who's there?"

"It's Marie-Louise."

The door was flung open. There stood Jakob: bald, white whiskers on his chin, wearing blue overalls and bedroom slippers.

"Who d'ya say ye are?"

"Jakob, don't you recognize me? I'm Marie-Louise from the castle."

He squinted. "I'll be darned, little Marie-Louise! When did ya get back? Let me get me glasses to take a good look at ya."

He pulled his spectacles out of his pocket and carefully put them on. "Ya've grown so much, wouldn't have recognized ya, Fräulein Marie-Louise, if I'd met ya on the street. Sorry. Me eyes aren't what they used to be. It's a darn nuisance, the getting-older business, if ya ask me. Nobody cares what ya do. Nobody needs ya anymore. One day's as boring as the next, just waiting to die."

"I'm hoping that will change, Jakob."

The old man cupped his ear. "What d'ya say? Ya need to speak up, 'cause me hearing isn't the best anymore, either."

Marie-Louise had to suppress a smile. Yes, this was the Jakob she remembered, except that he'd gotten older, a little more bent with the years, but his manner of speech was still the same.

She reached for his hand. "I came to take you back to the castle, because I need you."

"What d'ya need me for?"

"I need you to help me restore Hohenstein, and I want you to move into your old quarters in the gatehouse. You'll have room and board, but . . ."

Marie-Louise hesitated. How could she tell him that she wouldn't be able to pay him much? Squaring her shoulders, she plunged on, ". . . there isn't much money, so I can only pay you a little stipend, and we can discuss the amount that is acceptable to you at . . ."

Before she could get any further, Jakob squeezed her hand. "D'ya mean it, Fräulein Marie-Louise? D'ya really mean it?"

Seeing the man's face light up almost brought tears to her eyes. "Yes, Jakob, I really, really mean it. How soon can you move up to the castle?"

A tear slipped out of Jakob's eye and rolled down his weathered cheek. "Just gimme a few days to straighten out me things, and I could be there next week if that's all right with ya."

"That would be perfect. You let me know, and I'll send a carriage to pick you up."

"Ya don't need to do that. I'll just walk up the hill."

"No, no, I'll send someone. You can't carry your belongings on your back and trudge up the hill."

Jakob took her soft hands in his calloused ones again and pumped them as if he'd never let go. "Thank ya," he said, teary-eyed, "thank ya so much. Ya don't know what it means to be needed again and wanted. You're the best Hohenstein yet!"

Satisfied with her day's work, Marie-Louise waved good-bye and skipped all the way to the bicycle.

On the way home, while pushing the bicycle uphill, she tried to think of all the repairs that needed to be made. With Jakob at the castle, they could spruce up the place in no time.

She furrowed her brow at the thought of the non-existent funds. Without money, they could only do so much. Having Jakob by her side would certainly make things easier, but materials would still need to be purchased. The little money she had left, plus her monthly allowance, wouldn't be nearly enough to cover all the expenses.

Her bank account showed only a low balance in her favor, and Ambrosia's finances didn't seem to be much better. If only her father hadn't put that blasted stipulation into the trust! Now she had to wait until she turned twenty-five, or get married before she had access to her inheritance. Her mother would only be too happy to marry her off to one of her wealthy acquaintances, but Marie-Louise didn't like the company she kept.

She sighed. Six more years seemed like an eternity, but with Jakob at the castle, she could at least get things started.

Chapter Five

Marie-Louise returned the bicycle to the carriage house and strolled across the yard to the main building. Upon entering the parlor, Ambrosia looked up from her book and scrutinized her niece over the rim of her reading glasses. "You look exuberant. What have you been up to?"

"I hired Jakob back."

Ambrosia put her book on the side table and looked at her niece. "You're not serious, are you?"

When the baroness nodded, Ambrosia asked, "How on earth will you pay him?"

"I offered him room and board and a small stipend, and he was more than happy to return to the castle."

"Well, I don't know how you convinced him, but he always had a soft spot for you. I hope it will work out and he'll be content with the *little* stipend you can afford to pay him."

Ambrosia's misgivings couldn't dampen Marie-Louise's exuberance. On the contrary. She went outside and whistled for Kaiser to accompany her on a little walk. Instead of taking her favorite route to the forest, however, today she chose a path via the vineyards that traversed most of the hillside that belonged to the estate.

She shielded her eyes against the sun and scanned the neat rows of grapevines that extended almost to the bottom of the slope. They stopped short of a cluster of residential homes at the lower part of the hill. Marie-Louise knew they hadn't been there when she left for boarding school, but felt sure they were built on Hohenstein land. She would have to ask her aunt about these homes and their owners. Perhaps she could sell some plots of land and obtain the necessary funds for the repairs that way. However—she frowned—the estate represented her inheritance, and she couldn't touch it yet.

Oh, fiddlesticks! She swiped at a bluebell by the side of the road and beheaded the dainty flower.

After checking Jakob's old rooms, Marie-Louise made a list of things for the cleaning woman to do, then she inspected the outside of the building. Hands on hips, she looked up at the eaves. Yes, they surely were in need of fresh paint, and she wondered if there was still some paint left in Jakob's old workshop. She'd take a look.

The workshop in the basement of the carriage house still looked the way she remembered it. Jakob had meticulously arranged his tools on boards fastened to the walls. There was a place for various screwdrivers, followed by a row of pliers. Hammers of all shapes and sizes were aligned on another wall, together with saw blades. Everything was neatly in place, and except for a rather thick covering of dust and plenty of cobwebs, the workshop looked pristine.

On a lower shelf, Marie-Louise discovered several cans of paint with a color dot on the lid of each for easy identification. She hoped to find some dark brown paint and scanned the dots. Sure enough, the exact color for the eaves had been kept. In a box labeled "Painting Tools," she found brushes, sponges, and stirring sticks.

Wonderful. She'd start on the painting tomorrow.

The next day dawned perfect and cloudless, ideal for painting. Marie-Louise positioned the ladder, looked up at the square two-story building, swallowed hard, looked up again, and closed her eyes. Several deep breaths steadied her nerves somewhat, and determined, she gritted her teeth and began the ascent. Paint bucket and brushes in one hand, she held on with her free hand and stepped on the first rung. Pause. She leaned forward and rested her forehead against the next rung. Another deep breath and she ascended to the third. Pause.

On the next rung up, the hem of her skirt caught under her foot. She pulled to get it free, but in the process almost lost her balance. A shriek. A gasp. The paint brushes dropped out of her hand. Marie-Louise looked down and let out her breath slowly. If she wanted to paint the eaves, she'd have to go after the brushes, no two ways about it.

Down on safe ground once more, she decided to make sure her skirt wouldn't hamper her again. She grabbed the fabric, pulled it between her legs, and tucked the hem into her waistband in the front, thus creating a form of trousers. *There. Now it won't bother me again.* She even had a pocket now to carry the paint brushes.

It still took a few deep breaths before Marie-Louise attempted the ascent again.

When she finally reached the top, she closed her eyes for a moment and again took a deep breath. Gingerly, so as not to lose her balance, she placed the bucket on the fold-out below the top platform of the ladder. Wobbling a little, she regained her balance and then resolutely dipped the bigger brush into the bucket. She began painting the exposed beams with dark brown paint. Whenever she found something to hold onto other than the ladder, she felt much safer and worked faster.

It took two coats of paint, as the old beams were extremely dry, and the sun had burned off the old paint almost completely. When she was done with one side, she leaned back and inspected her work. The square, tower-like gatehouse looked nice, but lacked something. She squinted, tilted her head this way and that—and then she knew what to do. With a smaller, tapered brush, she painted brown, scroll-type lines in each corner of the white wall where two beams met. It was delicate work, but something she enjoyed doing.

Engrossed in her work, Marie-Louise didn't notice the automobile that slid almost noiselessly past the gatehouse and into the cobbled yard, nor the tall figure of the young man with coppery hair who emerged from it.

"Good morning," he hailed.

Marie-Louise jerked at the sound of his voice. The paint brush fell out of her hand and left a brown smudge on her upper arm. She gave a little cry as the ladder swayed, and she grabbed hold of one of the beams of the fascia with one hand, the other keeping the paint bucket from following the brush. *Not him. Please not him.*

Painfully aware of her unusual get-up that showed not only her ankles but her calves also, she wished him anywhere but here. When she tried to position herself a little more inconspicuously, the ladder swayed to the other side and she shrieked.

"For goodness' sake, hold on!" he cried, and she heard his footsteps coming closer until she felt him steadying the ladder.

"Hand me the bucket," he commanded.

Eyes straight ahead, Marie-Louise bent at the knees. Grabbing the wire handle, she took the bucket off the fold-out stand and handed it down to him, stiffly, still looking straight ahead.

"Now, come down," he ordered.

Marie-Louise didn't heed his command, her body rigid.

After she didn't move, and he had waited a few seconds, she heard him climbing the ladder until he reached the rung below where she stood. She felt his arms encircling her waist, and she tensed and closed her eyes as if her action could make him disappear.

"Let's climb down together," he coaxed. "I'll hold on to you so you don't have to be afraid."

Marie-Louise didn't budge, but instead held on to the fascia even tighter until her knuckles showed white. Ulrich gave a little tug, but the baroness resisted.

"Let go of that beam and we'll be on safe ground in no time."

Instead of doing his bidding, she held on even tighter.

With one arm still around her waist, he stepped up one rung and straddled her exposed legs. She squeezed her eyes shut. How embarrassing. When he tried to reach the fascia to pry her fingers loose, she panicked. No sooner had he removed one hand, her other one shot up to clamp around another beam. The ladder swayed to the left and away from the gatehouse. She screamed, and Ulrich let go of his hold on her to grab the fascia himself in order to stabilize the ladder.

Marie-Louise clung to the beam for dear life, digging her fingernails into the ridges of the wood.

"Marie-Louise, let go. Slowly," he instructed.

Trembling, she finally released her hold.

"That's good. Now, put your hand on top of the ladder. Good."

Ulrich covered her hand with one of his, then coaxed, "Now let go the other hand and proceed in the same way."

Shaking her head, she stiffened, and no amount of coaxing would get her to take her hand off the fascia.

Several seconds passed when he whispered in her ear, "Tante Ambrosia is watching us with a very stern expression on her face."

While the baroness turned her head in the direction of the main building, Ulrich used that moment to pry her hand off the beam and hold her imprisoned with his arms. She struggled, but her efforts were weaker this time, and she finally slumped against him and gave up the fight.

He stepped down to the next rung and coached, "Now, let's walk down together, one step at a time, and I'll hold on to you until we reach safe ground." No matter what he said or how hard he pulled, she wouldn't budge.

"Trust me. I won't let you get hurt."

She still didn't move, but with a squawky voice said, "I think I'm going to be sick."

"Oh, no, you won't," he said in a stern voice as he tightened his grip around her waist. "Close your eyes and do as I tell you. Move one foot down until you feel the next rung."

When she wouldn't respond, he bent down and, one hand around her ankle, guided her foot until he placed it on the next lower rung.

Seeming to realize this was the only way she'd come down, he guided her feet down one rung at a time. "Keep your eyes closed and follow my lead."

Finally on safe ground, he led her to the bench outside the gate-house door. Watching her pale face for a moment, he commanded, "Take a couple of deep breaths before you open your eyes."

The baroness did as he ordered and leaned her head against the cool stucco behind her before she looked up at him.

"Feeling better?"

She shook her head. "Getting sick."

"Breathe." When she didn't comply, he shook her gently. "Come on, breathe."

She took a couple of deep breaths before she seemed to relax a little.

"Better?"

She nodded.

After several more deep breaths, she said, "I think I'm getting back to normal, although my stomach is still a bit queasy."

Harsher than intended, he scolded, "You don't have any business being on a ladder when you're afraid of heights."

"I did well enough until you came and startled me."

"I'm sorry, but you shouldn't be on a ladder anyway."

"There's work to be done around here. And remember, no money to hire help."

"No reason for someone of your rank to do menial work. It's—"

She pushed away from the wall, hands on hips, indignant. "Don't be so old-fashioned! You sound like my aunt. Why can't I be seen fixing up the place? Are we better than other people?"

"We have a reputation to uphold," he answered, "and I expect you to remember that."

Brows drawn together, she asked in a menacing tone, "Does that mean that you forbid me to restore Hohenstein?"

"No. You can do what you want as long as you do it discreetly."

"Meaning?"

"That you don't advertise that your family has fallen on dry ground by doing menial work in full sight of the public."

She shook her head in disbelief. "People can guess at our financial situation just by looking at the castle. It's deteriorating. See for yourself." She made a sweeping motion with her hand that encompassed all the buildings.

He put a hand on her arm. "Aren't there plenty of jobs inside that you could work on?"

"What's wrong with fixing up the first thing everybody will see when crossing the bridge?"

"Painting the gatehouse wasn't necessary. It could have waited. A broken window or a leaky faucet would warrant immediate attention, but not the exterior of a gatehouse that won't be used anyway."

"It will be used," she contradicted, and when he raised an eyebrow, she rushed on to explain, "Jakob, our old handyman, will move in next week."

The eyebrow lifted another fraction. "I thought there was no money for hired help?"

"Jakob agreed to work for us in exchange for room and board and a small allowance."

He relaxed. "It seems as if you've hammered out a nice deal with old Jakob. I'm impressed. What I don't understand is why you decided to beautify the place he'll be living in instead of your own residence."

"As I've told you, the gatehouse is the first thing everyone sees when visiting the castle. Besides, the job was small enough that I could do it in half a day and not get bogged down."

Trying to ease the mood of the conversation, he said with tongue in cheek, "I guess Jakob will be taking his meals with you and Ambrosia?"

"Of course not," she shot back. "Jakob would feel uncomfortable."

"How about Tante Ambrosia?"

Marie-Louise finally looked at him, and seeing his teasing expression, gave a gurgle of laughter. "She'd swoon. Can't you see her serving him chateaubriand on our Meissen porcelain?"

He laughed. "Still the little imp that I remembered, but the little girl from yesteryear has grown into a charming beauty."

"I spoke the truth." He fell silent.

Looking at him, she asked, "Why so pensive all of a sudden?"

Torn out of his reverie, he produced a smile. "I was just thinking how good a cold glass of juice would taste."

Jumping up, Marie-Louise apologized. "I'm sorry to have neglected my duties as hostess." She gave a mock curtsey and gestured toward the main building. "Won't you come in for some refreshments, Count?"

"How can I decline such a gracious invitation, Baroness?" he said with his hand over his heart and eyes twinkling. On a more serious note, he pointed to her skirt. "Perhaps you should let your skirt down before Tante Ambrosia sees you like that."

"Oops. Sorry. I forgot." She pulled the hem out of her waist band and smoothed the fabric.

Ulrich offered his arm and led her across the courtyard. What a hilarious sight they must present: he in his business suit, and Marie-Louise in a wrinkled skirt, her hair tied up on top of her head and held back with a lace scarf.

After a few steps, she stopped and turned to look at him. With a twinkle in her eyes, she asked, "By the way, what brought you to Hohenstein today? Did you find a way around the rigid trust after all?"

Seeing the flicker of hope in her eyes, he felt like a traitor, yet he couldn't budge.

"No, I can't change your father's will." He paused for a moment, trying to soften the blow with a smile. "I was in the area and decided to stop in and see how things are going."

"Oh."

The sound hung in the air, forlorn.

With a shrug of her shoulders and a sigh, she walked in silence the remainder of the way.

"Tante Ambrosia!" the baroness called as soon as they stepped into the vestibule, "We have a visitor."

By the time the young people reached the salon, Ambrosia had entered through another door, a welcoming smile on her wrinkle-free face. Gone was the apron used in polishing the *escritoire*. She looked as if she had just stepped out of her dressing room.

Hand extended, she greeted Ulrich. "Nice to see you, Count, and welcome to Hohenstein."

"Thank you. How do you do, Fräulein von Hohenstein?" Clicking his heels, correct to a T, he bent over her hand to barely touch his lips to it before stepping back again.

Like a drill sergeant and stiff as if he had swallowed a broom stick, Marie-Louise scoffed. Surely he didn't need to be this formal!

Judging by her aunt's graceful demeanor, though, the count's greeting was exactly what that lady had expected of him. Two slaves to the old traditions.

Although Marie-Louise laughed at his compliance with the antiquated codes of conduct, she had to grudgingly admit that Ulrich cut a superb figure adhering to these rules. She imagined him centuries earlier in Renaissance costume, at a time period when life revolved around social events, and courtly gallantries were the order of the day. He certainly would have been a nonpareil in those days—as he definitely was today.

Watching him entertain Tante Ambrosia with news from his family reminded Marie-Louise of the Knight's Code she had read that day at the bank. The stanza about chivalry requiring the performing of the most laborious and humble offices with cheerfulness and grace came to mind. Although talking to her aunt was neither laborious nor humble, she assumed that he'd rather be sailing or maybe flirting with a beautiful lady instead of conversing with two lonely women. Yet, he displayed a cheerfulness that seemed to come from the heart: a warmth that transformed Ambrosia from a stern disciplinarian to an amiable conversationalist.

While listening to the count and smiling pleasantly, Ambrosia seemed somewhat distracted as she tried to catch the baroness' attention. Puckering her lips in her severest fashion, her gaze resting on her niece's clothes, she motioned with the slightest of nods upstairs.

Marie-Louise knew her aunt wanted her to change into something more appropriate for such an important visitor as Count Ulrich, but she refused to heed the silent command. She didn't see any reason why she should don a dress when the count had already seen her wrinkled skirt. She had been working, for heaven's sake, and intended to continue after Ulrich's visit. Why change? Why the fuss about proper attire for an impromptu visit?

Finally, with a last effort to force the propriety issue, Ambrosia addressed her visitor directly. "Count, will you please excuse my niece for a moment? She will want to freshen up."

As he nodded, she turned to Marie-Louise. "Would you bring some refreshments on your way back, please?"

Marie-Louise turned on her heels and left the room, fuming. She felt manipulated, and worse—treated like a little child! She didn't mind serving refreshments, but had no intention of changing clothes. Just because Ulrich was the head of the Wolfburg family—a position that came to him by birth, not by any merit of his own—she refused to bow to the old title worship, whether her aunt liked it or not. This was the twentieth century, and things had changed.

After she washed her hands and smoothed her hair, she prepared some light refreshments and took them to the salon, wondering about her aunt's reaction to her open display of disrespect. Of course, she wouldn't lecture her in the presence of their noble visitor. That would come later. And although Marie-Louise was mistress of Hohenstein now, anticipating a scolding still sent cold shivers down her spine as in times past. The only difference between present and past was her open rebellion now, whereas her revolts as a little girl were executed in secret, which, unfortunately, didn't mean that Ambrosia never found out.

Chapter Six

Ignoring her aunt's disapproving look as she entered the salon, Marie-Louise pinned on her sweetest smile. "May I offer you one of these delicious *petit fours*, Count?" She looked at him, winked and curtsied, and he had a hard time keeping a straight face while Ambrosia's face flushed with indignation.

Ulrich tried to remain somber, but the corners of his mouth crinkled in suppressed laughter. "How nice of you, Baroness, to pay me such ardent respect. I'm glad that all those years at school have paid off, and I hope that your display of decorum is a sign of things to come."

"I wouldn't hold my breath," she countered with fluttering eyelids while offering him the refreshment tray. Out of the corner of her eye, she saw her aunt's bosom heave, and knew that a lecture was awaiting her as soon as their visitor was out of earshot, but Marie-Louise decided to stall as long as possible. For that reason, she accompanied the count out to his blue Mercedes with the red-spoked wheels as he prepared to leave.

She smoothed her hand over one shiny fender. "What a beautiful vehicle."

She imagined herself sitting at the wheel and coasting down the road with the wind whipping her hair around her face, and not a care in the world. *That would be heaven! Instead, I don't have any money, with a castle that's crumbling all around me, and no means to do anything about it.*

"How fast can you go in this beauty?"

"Between thirty-five and forty kilometers if the roads are in good condition."

She nodded. "That's amazing. Twice as fast as on horseback."

"Faster, because the automobile doesn't get tired like a horse."

With a last pat on the fender and a resigned sigh, Marie-Louise stepped back as Ulrich stood beside her. Before getting into the Mercedes, however, he smiled. "I'll teach you how to drive it someday."

"I already know how to drive a motorcar. I learned when I spent Christmas with Mama in Paris. So, why don't you let me drive it down the hill?"

He smiled. "These hairpin curves are a little difficult to maneuver without practice, but I promise that I'll teach you.

"Spoilsport."

He produced a lopsided grin and twisted one of her stray curls. "I'm sorry if I offended your sensibilities. I'll try to do better in the future."

Ready to pick up the banter, she narrowed her eyes back at him. "Count, you're making fun of me. And that's not nice after I've just fed you!"

"Baroness, if you think that a few *petit fours* and a glass of juice fill me up, I'll have to show you someday what it takes to really satisfy me."

She couldn't keep the laughter back any longer. "I never thought the estimable head of the House of Wolfburg could be so silly. Sir, you just ruined your reputation as a stern dictator and tyrant. From now on, I'll classify you among normal human beings."

"It would be interesting to know what class I was in before my fall to the normal level."

"You were on the same shelf with Zeus and Caesar, of course."

He threw his head back and laughed. Hugging her shortly, he pressed his lips to her forehead, still chuckling. Then he folded his virile length into his Daimler and was off before she had time to gather her wits.

She stood there, rooted to the spot, and looked after him even though he had disappeared over the wooden bridge and around the bend in the road quite a while ago.

"Ulrich," she mumbled. Drawing a deep breath, she shook her head as if to rid herself of all thoughts of him. He certainly didn't play by the rules of 'no touching' unless you were betrothed. Not that she minded . . .

Gingerly she touched the spot on her forehead that still burned from his brief kiss. Strange. It wasn't as if she hadn't been kissed before . . . but this innocently bestowed kiss confused her.

On the one hand, she resented him for being inflexible, although, to be fair, it was her father's trust that was inflexible and not the count. She resented him for his patronizing ways and for what he represented, but on the other hand, she felt comfortable in his presence and enjoyed his easy humor, enjoyed his . . . touch.

The man Ulrich didn't have much in common with the young lad she remembered from her childhood. She didn't think that she had ever seen him smile when he had visited Hohenstein in his youth. He had always seemed reserved, but with an aggravating air of superiority, though she had to admit that both times they had met within the last few days, she had detected neither of these faults. She had actually found him quite pleasant, even if he couldn't help her.

Sighing, she turned and strode back toward the stone steps. Time to endure one of her aunt's lectures on proper conduct. She pulled a face. *Might as well get it over with.*

"Marie-Louise, please join me in the parlor," Ambrosia called as soon as Marie-Louise opened the heavy oak door.

The baroness tipped two fingers to her temple in mock salute, clicked her heels—*Yes, ma'am*—and headed for the parlor.

Standing by the window, hands clasped in front of her, Ambrosia looked as forbidding as ever, and Marie-Louise felt the old familiar frisson of dread wash over her. *Ridiculous. I'm mistress of the castle. Why should I fear my aunt's scolding?* She straightened and jutted out her chin.

Her lips in a tight line, Ambrosia pointed to a chair. She rolled the edges of a handkerchief between her long, slender fingers before she addressed her niece.

"Marie-Louise, I assume you know why I need to speak to you." Penetrating the baroness with an icy stare, she probably anticipated a sign of admission, a nod, downcast eyes, or even a pleading look, but Marie-Louise refused to comply. Instead, she held her head high, an eyebrow raised in question.

Ambrosia smoothed her hands over her skirt. "I have never been more mortified about anything in my entire life as I have been about your conduct today. You behaved like a—like a commoner. No, a commoner would have paid the count more respect than you did. Whatever were you thinking of, treating him as if he were a farmer from down the hill? You didn't even have the decency to change into a suitable dress even after I urged you to do so—"

"I didn't see a need to change since he had seen me in my work clothes already."

"That's no excuse. I expected you to freshen up and present yourself in a way befitting the Baroness von Hohenstein. Your deplorable behavior not only cast a bad light on you, but on your family as well." Ambrosia wrung her hands. "What will he think of us?"

"He won't think any different of us than he did before, I assure you. Being the head of the House of Wolfburg doesn't mean that he has to be stuck up, does it?"

The older woman gasped. "Marie-Louise! Watch your language! That's no way to speak of the head of the House of Wolfburg. It's inappropriate." Shaking her head, she continued, "The count wouldn't expect just anyone to know the rules of conduct, but he certainly expects it from people of his own class."

Marie-Louise sighed. "Times have changed. Even Ulrich accepts that fact." *Well, that's not quite true, but no sense telling Ambrosia.*

Her aunt shook her head. "Times may have changed, but good manners will never become old-fashioned. The count even commented on the social polish you acquired while at school and expressed his satisfaction at the worthwhile investment."

The baroness gave a derisive laugh. "He meant it as a joke."

"He may have made light of the subject, but he certainly expects you to move within the traditional set of rules, believe me. I insist that you send him a note of apology."

Marie-Louise looked down so that her aunt wouldn't see her scowl.

After an indignant huff, Ambrosia smoothed her already immaculate coiffure and cleared her throat. "I felt humiliated by your conduct and wanted to sink into the ground."

Nettled, the baroness asked, "Why should my conduct humiliate you?"

Ambrosia looked down her chiseled nose. "It's a matter of family pride." Her chin tilting upward, she sniffed, "Something you may not understand."

"What are you implying?"

Ambrosia shrugged. "Your parents didn't display much family pride either, I'm afraid."

Her parents' wasteful lifestyle had always been a sore spot with her aunt, who blamed her father for the castle's present state of ill-repair and lack of funds. Still, she felt the need to defend her father. "When poor Papa returned to Hohenstein, he was too ill to devote much energy to the upkeep of the castle."

"He started to neglect the castle the minute he set eyes on your mother," Ambrosia countered through clenched teeth.

Marie-Louise lifted one eyebrow. "How so? He modernized some of the rooms."

Ambrosia sniffed and turned away from her niece, hands pressed to her chest, her breathing quick and shallow. Walking to the settee, she spoke after a moment or two, hesitantly at first, and then all her pent-up emotions surfaced as the story unfolded, gushing out like a waterfall that couldn't be stopped.

"She never loved Wolfram. She married him for his title and his money and because being his wife opened doors to her that otherwise were inaccessible. And while she still could, she made him sign his stocks and bonds over to her to ensure the lifestyle she craved. That left you with hardly anything to speak of, except a big headache."

Spent, Ambrosia leaned back against the cushions, her breath short and shallow. Regaining her composure, she went on, "When your mother came here as a young bride, she was only a little over eighteen. Your father met her at the ambassador's ball in Paris and fell head over heels in love with her, and when he brought her home, she took one look at Hohenstein and hated it.

"Wolfram thought that if he renovated the place and installed modern facilities, she wouldn't mind living here, but not Anique. She had other plans. And after you were born, the two of them took off on their pursuit of the sweet life, and only came for short visits once or twice a year to see you, usually for your birthday and Christmas."

Ambrosia fell silent. All her hatred seemed to have evaporated, leaving her staring into space with drooping shoulders and a bitter line around the mouth.

Marie-Louise was shocked. She had known that her parents spent a lot of time in Paris when she was growing up, but never knew the extent of their lavish lifestyle. She swayed between empathy for the older woman and anger. Empathy, because she understood how hard it must have been for Ambrosia to see her home fall apart around her and to be unable to stop the decay, and anger because of Ambrosia's resentment of Anique. Perhaps the animosity had been caused by jealousy. The jealousy of a spinster toward a young and beautiful bride.

Even though Anique had never been the doting mother, Marie-Louise still loved her and hated to hear anyone speak ill of her. Yet, at the same time, everything her aunt had said was true, and no matter how hard she tried, she couldn't come up with anything to say in her mother's defense other than, "Mama is so beautiful," but realized as soon as the words were spoken how childish they sounded.

Her aunt still sat motionless, looking into space. The baroness wondered what to do—if she should stay and say something, or if it would be better to simply leave. She didn't want to ruffle her aunt's feathers any more than they already had been, so after a moment's hesitation, she gave a soft cough.

"Tante Ambrosia, I'll go and take the ladder back to the workshop."

At her aunt's absent-minded nod, she hurried out of the parlor, glad to escape.

Before Jakob arrived, Marie-Louise needed to make a list of repairs that he could work on. Starting with the main house, she noticed that the oriental rugs showed bare spots, the walls could do with a new layer of silk wallpaper, and the drapes had worn thin and showed sun spots, especially on the south windows. But these were all things that could wait a little longer. There was more pressing work that needed attention first, so she only listed the most urgent repairs.

The parlor in the middle of the building that looked out over the park appeared fairly decent, except for the normal wear and tear on the rugs and upholstery.

Next, Marie-Louise entered the vestibule, where the stairs frame a landing for the hallways where the bedrooms were located. Two broad staircases on either side curved gracefully up to the second floor

She smoothed her hand over the ornate railing as she proceeded upstairs. There was a leaking faucet and discolored tiles in one bathroom, and also a water spot on the ceiling of the room next to Ambrosia's. These items were especially in need of attention. Other than these few problem areas and the broken window, the main building didn't need immediate work.

Marie-Louise tossed her head, left the castle, and proceeded toward the stables, notepad and pencil in hand. Once there, she added a sagging roof and another broken window to her list of repairs.

She sighed. She asked herself if she really wanted to tackle the work involved in restoring Hohenstein. Even with Jakob's help, it would be a huge undertaking.

When making his will, her father couldn't have foreseen the problems she faced now. Perhaps he wanted to protect Hohenstein from further mismanagement, perhaps even from her mother's clutches. Whatever reasons he had for putting the restraining clauses in his will, they surely made life difficult for her now.

Even the most minor repairs cost money. Money she didn't have.

Marie-Louise sat on the front steps with the pencil tipped against her forehead. How did other people get money for things like repairs, automobiles, et cetera? If they didn't have the money, they probably borrowed it from a bank.

She slapped her forehead with the palm of her hand. The Wolfburg Bank! Would the Wolfburg Bank grant her a loan? She was determined to at least give it a try. Tomorrow she'd speak with Ulrich.

Perhaps tomorrow would mark the turning point for Hohenstein.

The bright future, however, dimmed dramatically the next day when the postman delivered a registered letter from the county. Marie-Louise put the letter on the *escritoire,* intending to open it after she picked up Jakob and after her visit to the Wolfburg Bank, but Ambrosia urged her to read it right away.

"A registered letter must be something important."

The baroness shrugged, picked up the letter, tore it open, and started reading. The further she read, the more shocked she became. Her eyes widened, her hands trembled, and the color drained from her face.

"No, they can't do that," she whispered. The letter slipped out of her limp hands and fluttered to the floor.

Ambrosia rushed forward. "My goodness, Marie-Louise, what is it? You look ill."

The baroness pointed to the letter on the floor. "Read it," she whispered and sank onto the nearest chair.

Ambrosia picked up the letter and perused it. The color drained from her face, as well, and she grabbed the back of the settee to steady herself. "We're doomed," she said as she put the letter back on the *escritoire*. "What are we to do now?"

Marie-Louise shook her head. "I don't know."

"I don't understand. The stable roof caved in years ago, but has never posed any danger—at least, I don't think so. It doesn't even leak! Of course, it doesn't look nice, but if it doesn't bother us, why should it bother the county? Why do they demand a new roof?"

"And they graciously give us three weeks to comply with their request and threaten to have the building demolished at our expense if work on the roof hasn't started by that time." Marie-Louise gave a mirthless laugh. "If we don't have money to repair the roof, we certainly can't pay for a wrecker. What are they thinking?"

Ambrosia wrung her hands. The baroness brooded. "Have you ever seen anybody come to inspect the estate?"

"No, nobody ever came while I was around."

"Then how do they even know about our stable roof?"

"Exactly," said Ambrosia.

"What do you think I should do?" wailed Marie-Louise.

"You could write them a letter and explain your situation."

"I suppose that's the only action I can take at the moment."

Marie-Louise rose and paced the floor. Back and forth, back and forth. Whereas before, the money would have been nice to restore and beautify Hohenstein, now funding had become crucial with the county's threat hanging over their heads.

She sighed. A little while ago she had anticipated tomorrow's events, but now she sat with shoulders drooping, and dreaded the outcome of whatever tomorrow would bring.

Chapter Seven

The day's problems, however, were not over when Ambrosia remembered the message from the mayor's office.

"Marie-Louise, I almost forgot to tell you that an employee from the town hall came with a message. The mayor wants to meet with you and brief you on the upcoming ceremony at the hospital. If you are free tomorrow morning, he could meet with you in his office."

"That's just what I need right now! Why did I agree to be his show horse?"

Ambrosia reached over and patted her niece's hand. "Now, now. It's a good thing to be involved in the community. You'll probably enjoy getting out and talking to people other than myself. Besides, you can forget Hohenstein's problems for a time while you're involved with the ribbon cutting ceremony."

"You're right, of course, but this comes at a very inopportune moment. I have to deal with the county's request and need to concentrate on how to proceed. Oh, I wish I wasn't so blasted inexperienced. *Merde!*"

"Marie-Louise! Watch your language! Even if you're upset, you cannot debase yourself by using swear words. I'm shocked."

"I apologize. It slipped out."

Ambrosia huffed. "You shouldn't even know words like that."

Then how do you know what it means? I didn't know that French swear words were part of your *vocabulary.*

Marie-Louise avoided her aunt's stare. Just when she thought Ambrosia had mellowed a bit, she returned to her stern attitude. Of course, she had to admit that she should have more control over her emotions, but, for heaven's sake, couldn't a person be frustrated once in a while?

When the silence became oppressive, the baroness stood up. "Please excuse me."

Ambrosia nodded assent, her lips still in a tight line.

Alone in her room, Marie-Louise's thoughts turned to the upcoming event at the hospital. She hoped she would be able to fulfill her civic responsibilities to the satisfaction of the mayor. She knew that involvement in the affairs of the town was expected of the local nobility, and she was willing to do her part.

Now, she had to focus on two problems at the same time, but Hohenstein had precedence, and she knew she had to come up with a solution as soon as possible. Perhaps she should try to get a loan from the Commerce Bank. The people there would probably be only too happy to do business with her. Maybe she didn't even need Ulrich. Wouldn't he be surprised if she could secure funding elsewhere?

Whereas before she wanted to find funding to beautify and restore Hohenstein, her need for a loan had now become a necessity, the means of Hohenstein's survival.

Yet, her visit to the Commerce Bank met with another disappointment. Because Marie-Louise didn't own Hohenstein yet, and therefore couldn't use the castle as collateral, the bank director was unable to give her a loan. And because she didn't have enough of a regular income, she was too high a risk to be considered for a loan, especially in these turbulent times with talk of a possible armed conflict with France and her allies.

The bank director was being overly cautious, of course. Although the emperor Wilhelm II had been talking about war for some time now, it was just talk, and nobody gave it any heed. Waging a war under these circumstances would have been suicide. The bank director knew that, and he also knew that Marie-Louise wouldn't run away, and that the castle would be there for another hundred years, at least. So, what was the risk?

Marie-Louise groaned in frustration. If the Commerce Bank refused to give her a loan, she would have to get one from Ulrich.

Wandering from room to room and hoping for inspiration to her money problems, she couldn't come up with any other ideas. It was in the picture gallery when the thought first occurred to her to contact her mother. Anique certainly could afford to lend her the money, but would she? Marie-Louise hesitated to write the letter, wavering between getting out her stationery and forgetting the idea altogether. Finally, when she couldn't come up with any other solution to her financial problems, she decided to contact her mother.

The answer came by return mail.

Cherie,

What are you doing at Hohenstein, that awful place? I hope you won't stay long at that mausoleum. You should come and join us on the cruise. If you catch a train to Sicily, you can meet us there in a few days. There are so many droll people onboard, and some very handsome bachelors among them, as well. You'll love it.

As to your question about money, forget it. I'm not going to waste a single franc on that place. Was it Ambrosia's idea to keep you there and talk you into sprucing up the old relic?

Parbleu, Cherie, you need to be among people. And if the county *demanded the repair of the roof, let them fix it or tear it down. It's a lost cause, Cherie, and not worth the trouble. I'm sorry, but I won't butter any money into Hohenstein. And don't talk sentimental nonsense to me about your home. It's an ancient heap of rubble and should be condemned. If you want one of these new motorcars or a new wardrobe, you can have what you need, but nothing for Hohenstein, and that's my final word.*

Marie-Louise dropped the letter into her lap. She knew her mother didn't like Hohenstein, but had hoped against hope that she would help her only child. *So much for that.*

Her shoulders drooped. She was out of ideas and the load of her problems weighed her down. Her legs felt like lead as she walked into the library and dropped onto the settee. Too numb to feel anything, she wanted nothing but to be alone. She didn't want to talk to Ambrosia right now. She didn't even want to think.

After some time, she got up and went to the picture gallery and stood in front of her parents' picture. She studied her mother's lovely face. *Mama, don't you love me? Why can't you understand that Hohenstein is my home? I can't just turn my back on it.*

Turning to her father's picture, she held a one-way conversation with him also. *Papa, I know you loved me. Then why did you make it so hard for me to preserve Hohenstein? Why the clause in your will that ties my hands until I turn twenty-five or marry before that time? If you can hear my thoughts, will you please, please help me!*

The tears that had burned her eyelids now came to the surface. They weren't tears of frustration or even anger: they were tears of despondency, sadness, hopelessness. She sat on the floor in front of the paintings in their gilded frames, legs crossed, head down.

Tears spilled over and trickled down her cheeks, with an occasional sob breaking the stillness now and then. She had no idea how long she sat there, or how long she cried. When she finally closed her eyes and concentrated on her breathing, the tears stopped and her mind cleared.

Feeling sorry for yourself doesn't get you anywhere, she scolded herself.

She got up, and with a last glance at her parents' picture, went to the conservatory. The pianoforte caught her eye, and she opened the lid and touched a few keys. Pretty soon she picked out a melody, sat down, and positioned the piano bench so that her feet comfortably reached the pedals. After a few more tentative notes, the sad melody of Franz Lehar's song of the lonely Russian soldier standing guard at the Volga River filled the room. Although the song told of a young man's lonesome existence, the melody soothed her aching heart, and she soon forgot her own misery and, instead, commiserated with the young soldier. She felt his loneliness and tears.

Engrossed in the music Marie-Louise didn't hear her aunt enter the room. Ambrosia's hand on her shoulder startled her and, with a jarring discord, she turned around.

"I didn't mean to startle you," Ambrosia apologized. "When I heard this sad melody I came to inquire if you're feeling depressed."

Marie-Louise hung her head.

"You haven't come up with an idea where to get the funds for the roof?"

The baroness banged on the piano keys, and noticed that her aunt flinched but didn't say anything. With a huff, she explained, "The Commerce Bank won't give me a loan because I can't touch my inheritance yet and because I don't have enough income! And the bank director was also cautious because of the uncertain political situation in our country."

"There must be something that you can do to make the county extend their deadline. Can't you talk to them? Explain your situation?"

Marie-Louise produced a mirthless laugh. "I went to the county after I visited the Commerce Bank and spoke with the commissioner. I explained our situation, but he wouldn't budge." She sighed. "Jakob will move into the gatehouse tomorrow, but he can only do so much, and the roof is definitely out of his league. And even if he could repair it, there's no money for materials. Our hands are tied."

Ambrosia heaved a sigh. "It will be good to have Jakob back. At least he can work on some of the necessary repairs."

Marie-Louise nodded. "I don't even know what I'll do in the fall. I may go back to my studies, or I might even stay here, depending on how things develop."

"You also ought to think of your social life. You can't find a husband at Hohenstein."

Marie-Louise felt her cheeks burn. "That has time. I'm in no hurry."

"That may be so, but you don't want to end up like me."

The baroness didn't know what to say. Her aunt had never alluded to her single state, and hearing the bitterness in Ambrosia's voice made her uncomfortable. She studied the pattern in the Oriental rug when Ambrosia took up the conversation again.

"Count Wolfburg seems to be a charming young man and very handsome."

Marie-Louise agreed, "Yes, he is definitely good-looking."

"And he seems to like you. But you ought to show him more respect and act with more decorum, then he might consider you for a wife."

Marie-Louise shook her head and left the room. No sense telling her aunt that she wasn't interested in marrying someone from their own social circle.

It took two trips to haul all of Jakob's belongings up to the castle and to settle the old man in the gatehouse. As they approached the building, he pointed up. "Who was the artist there with the fancy paint work?"

"Do you like it?"

"It's all right."

The baroness laughed. "Thank you for the overwhelming praise. I only almost killed myself painting it."

Jakob looked at her. "Don't tell me ya climbed all the way up thar?"

"Yes, I did."

"You shouldn't have!" he said.

"Why not?"

"Ya know why. You're afraid of heights. I always had to help ya up the ladder to yer tree house, remember?"

"That was different. I was little then."

"You didn't get queasy?"

"A little," she hedged, and he nodded.

At that moment, Ambrosia approached to welcome Jakob, and the old man bowed low in greeting. *Hmmm, he never really bowed for me, and I'm the baroness. I guess Ambrosia's air demands subservience.*

"Welcome back to Hohenstein, Jakob. We're happy to have you back."

"Thank you, *Fräulein* von Hohenstein. I'm happy ter be back."

They led Jakob inside the gatehouse. The small sitting room with its sofa, chair, two-tiered shelf unit, and sideboard looked immaculate, and the adjoining kitchen, although small, was adequate for an old bachelor. A circular stairway led to the upstairs bedroom with a double bed, two nightstands with lamps, and an *armoire*. The light through the window bathed the room in a warm glow, and the view afforded a gorgeous vista of the town in the valley.

Jakob took a deep breath. "I'm happy ter be back. I missed me gatehouse."

Marie-Louise gave his arm a squeeze. "You're where you

belong."

Ambrosia interrupted this sentimental moment. "Jakob, there are sandwiches prepared at the castle. If you are hungry, you are welcome to get some. Your little pantry is also stocked with some essentials."

"Thank ya very much, *Fräulein* von Hohenstein. I'll gladly get some sandwiches. Moving all me things up here made me hungry."

"Then by all means, let's not waste another minute and get something to eat."

Marie-Louise couldn't wait to finish her meal because she wanted to show Jakob all the repairs that needed to be made, but she had to give the man time to eat and relax a little. She waited as long as she could before making her way outside.

As she approached the gatehouse, she saw Jakob on the bench by the front door, dozing. She thought about turning back and leaving him be, but her steps woke him, and he rose immediately.

"I want to take you on a tour of the estate to show you all the things that need attention."

"Right, *Fräulein* Marie-Louise. I already saw a few things I need to do."

They walked slowly while the baroness pointed to the weeds, the cracked stucco, and other minor repair projects. When Jakob saw the sagging stable roof, however, he scratched his bald head.

"That thar roof will cost a pretty penny, *Fräulein* Marie-Louise."

She sighed. "Yes, I'm afraid so, and the county gave us three weeks to fix it."

"Who'll repair it?"

"I don't know. I have to come up with the money first."

"Ya'd better get hopping before the time's up."

"I know. I'll go to the bank this afternoon."

Jakob scribbled something in his notepad before he addressed her again. "What d'ya want me to do first?"

"The leaky faucet needs to be dealt with, I think."

"*Jawohl, Fräulein* Marie-Louise. If ya don't mind, I wanna go to the workshop and see what tools and materials I can find to do the job."

The baroness smiled, "Your workshop looks exactly like it did when I was a little girl helping you. Not a thing out of place."

"That workshop was me pride and joy."

"Yes, I know."

It seemed as if a spirit of excitement had entered the castle with Jakob's return, albeit somewhat subdued. All afternoon long, the sound of a hammer or chisel or drill could be heard, and even Ambrosia seemed caught up in the general bustle of activity. If only the doom of the sagging roof wasn't hanging over them, things might be looking up.

At two o'clock Marie-Louise set out to visit the Wolfburg Bank—her heart heavy, her confidence shaky, her expectations low.

Chapter Eight

This time the baroness didn't have to wait long before Ulrich stepped into the little conference room.

He extended his hand. "Marie-Louise, how good to see you."

She produced a little smile but knew it didn't reach her eyes. Hohenstein's problems weighed too heavy on her mind, and Ulrich must have noticed.

"What happened? You look troubled."

She rummaged in her purse and produced the letter from the county, explaining the stipulated terms. "They give me only three weeks to comply. And I don't have the funds for a new roof. I need part of my inheritance."

Ulrich read the letter with raised eyebrows. He leaned back and surveyed her for the longest time. With his arms folded across his chest, he reminded her of a chess player, concentrating on his next move, taking into consideration every possible consequence. Finally, he spoke.

"Marie-Louise, your father's trust won't allow any flexibility. That means it can't be touched for any reason before your . . ."

"Yes, yes, I know. Before my twenty-fifth birthday or on my wedding day."

"My hands are tied. I'm sorry."

Lowering her head, she tried to hide her disappointment. She had been afraid that his answer would be negative, but she'd try anyway. "Can't you make an exception in this case?"

He shook his head. "I'm sorry. I can't change the trust."

"Can't I appeal it?" she cried.

He shook his head. "Sorry."

"Isn't there any money anywhere?"

He shook his head again.

"What will happen if I can't comply with the county's request? They'll come and tear down the building."

"So sorry," he mumbled.

She knew that Onkel Georg would have helped her somehow. If nothing else, he would have loaned her the money from his private funds, knowing that she'd pay him back as soon as she could. He would have found a way, but Ulrich didn't even try to offer his assistance, and she felt resentment toward the young count.

Smoothing a crease in her skirt, she tried hard to stifle this negative feeling and to regain her composure. Finally she asked the all-important question. "Couldn't you grant me a loan?"

When he didn't respond right away, Marie-Louise's hope vanished and she hung her head.

"Unfortunately, the bank has rules, and one of the rules is that we cannot lend money without collateral. As much as I would like to help you, I cannot go against these rules. I'm responsible to our shareholders." Ulrich shook his head. "I'm so sorry."

Now what? Ulrich had been her last hope. She buried her head in her hands—a gesture Ambrosia would find highly improper, but at the moment, Marie-Louise didn't care. Her world, her dreams, her ambitions had just received a death blow.

Ulrich spoke up, interrupting these morose thoughts. "Marie-Louise, look at me."

When she didn't respond, he squeezed her hand lightly as though to give more emphasis to his words. "Look at me."

She lifted her gaze to meet his.

"I'm sorry that I have to disappoint you. I wish I could help you, believe me."

She wanted to say, *You can,* but remained silent, and left him to wonder at her thoughts.

"You could get married." He concentrated on a speck of dust on the sleeve of his suit. With a calculated snip of the finger, it was gone. Still, he looked at the spot, hard, as if the wayward fleck was liable to come back.

She took a deep breath. "I may have to consider it if all else fails."

"If all else fails? What do you mean?"

Feathering a wisp of hair from her forehead, she restated his question. "Do I have any more ideas of how to procure funds for a new roof?" She wrinkled her brow. "Not yet, but since I apparently cannot tap into my inheritance, I'll need to come up with another way to find the funds I need. I don't know where, but I'll have to think of something."

"You could probably find a respectable position at an art gallery, or maybe at a . . . bank."

"I wouldn't earn enough money to pay for the roof," she pointed out.

"That's true, but you may be able to pay for the new roof in monthly installments."

"I hardly have enough to keep Hohenstein going *and* pay Jakob."

He nodded. "You could always spend time with your mother in France if the county agreed to wait six more years with their request."

The baroness shook her head. "I spent the last twelve summers with mother, and that's enough. I don't enjoy that sort of life."

He leaned forward. "You don't like *la dolce vita*?"

"No. It's shallow and meaningless."

After a small pause, he asked, "What about your social life? Won't you miss your friends?"

"Probably. But as I said before, I can find entertainment among common people."

He raised his brows. "Have you ever been to any public functions?"

"How could I? Remember, I was cooped up at boarding school for twelve years."

"The entertainment you're used to is quite unlike the one you so willingly want to embrace. You'll find a different set of rules, and a person of your rank may not fit in."

She chose to ignore his comment. Not in the mood to discuss the pros and cons of socializing with the townspeople, she was too disappointed at his rejection to make polite conversation. She tried hard to hide her feelings behind what she hoped was a pleasant expression.

He must have felt guilty at not being able to help her, because he said, "I'm sorry I had to disappoint you. The county may consent to wait six more years if you explain your situation. The roof has survived so far, and it will survive a little longer."

"But will the county see it that way?"

She had spoken with the commissioner already, and he wouldn't budge. Lifting her chin, she said, "I made up my mind. I'll get the money elsewhere."

After a moment's hesitation, Ulrich urged, "If you do, promise me one thing . . ." He paused, and when she looked up, continued on a serious note, ". . . to come to me before you make any major decisions. Although I cannot help you financially, I can still give you advice."

When she wouldn't commit herself, he pressed, "Don't forget!"

On the way home, Marie-Louise relived her conversation with Ulrich. Yes, she understood that his hands were tied when it came to her father's trust, but she thought that he could have helped her probably with a personal loan. He was director of the bank. Couldn't he have been more flexible? Or . . . she held her breath . . . did he not help her because he had a secret agenda? He may want to snatch up Hohenstein for himself for next to nothing.

No. She didn't think him to be devious. He couldn't, wouldn't be. Or would he? *Well, Count Wolfburg, you won't get Hohenstein. Just forget it!*

It didn't make sense. No, Ulrich wouldn't want another castle. Especially not one that needed extensive restoration work.

No need fantasizing about the count and his possible ulterior motives that were or weren't real. She needed to come up with a plan to find funding to repair the stable roof. If she didn't, she'd not only lose the building but also be charged with the demolition of it.

Life wasn't fair.

At least the situation with her tuition payment had been resolved. Mr. Roth, the solicitor, had finally written her a letter of apology. Apparently someone had made a mistake which had been corrected in the meantime, and the tuition had been paid.

Marie-Louise was glad that one problem was solved, but still harbored an uneasy feeling about it. Sure, mistakes could be made, but wouldn't the payments have been withdrawn from an account at a bank? She didn't know enough of banking systems or other business administration procedures to understand how a regular payment could get overlooked, and she wished again that she had taken classes in business and economics instead of art.

Marie-Louise remembered the upcoming briefing at the mayor's office and had an idea. Perhaps the mayor could pull some strings for her with the county. It was worth the attempt. She had tried everything else without success, and Ulrich's refusal hurt because he should have understood her situation and her loyalty to the ancestral home. She knew that he could have helped her, and the possibility of an ulterior motive stole back into her thoughts.

Marie-Louise wondered if he would still deny his help should the county enforce its demand and launch the demolition of the stable. Ulrich couldn't possibly want that to happen. But if she wasn't able to come up with the money for the cost of the demolition, the county might confiscate Hohenstein. Her father would turn in his grave should that happen, and she vowed to do anything to prevent such a fate. If that meant returning to Ulrich and begging for a loan on her knees, she'd do it. Do it for Hohenstein.

The thought of returning to the Wolfburg Bank was a bitter pill to swallow, especially since she had boasted that she would find funding elsewhere. At the time, she had felt certain that she could find a way to procure a loan. How silly and immature she had been! Ulrich must have had a good laugh after she left his office.

So much depended on her ability to secure funding for the roof repair. Not only was Hohenstein at stake, but Ambrosia's and Jakob's futures, as well. Both depended on her. Both were her responsibility.

Before she'd beg Ulrich, however, she'd talk with the mayor at the briefing. He had offered his help several times and he might be able to intervene in her behalf.

When the time for the briefing arrived, Marie-Louise entered the old half-timbered town hall and checked in with the receptionist. Apparently, the news of her arrival had spread like wildfire throughout the building because office doors opened, people walked the corridors to stare at her, and some peeked around corners to get a glimpse of her. She felt very much on display.

Before she even had time to knock on the mayor's door, he opened it himself.

"Welcome, welcome, Baroness. Please come in."

He ushered her to an adjacent conference room and motioned for her to have a seat in a comfortable chair. "Can I get you anything? A glass of *Saft* or something a little stronger?"

"Juice would be appreciated, thank you."

The mayor called into the outer office: "Barbara, *Saft* for the Baroness, please."

When the secretary arrived with the drink, she curtseyed before she placed the glass on the table in front of Marie-Louise. *I bet that gesture was rehearsed beforehand,* thought Marie-Louise and smiled at the young woman. "Thank you."

The mayor launched right into explaining the opening for the new hospital.

"The ceremony is scheduled to start at ten in the morning on Friday in the lobby of the hospital. Chairs will be set up theater-style, with a podium in front for the various speakers who will sit facing the audience. You, my dear Baroness, will also sit in front right next to me. An orchestra will be placed to the left of the podium, and after the speeches, they will play a march. You will step to the door where a ribbon will span the entryway, and with an oversized pair of scissors, cut the ribbon after the music stops. Make sure to turn toward the audience and smile, because a photographer will catch the moment on film."

"How long do you think the ceremony will last?"

"With all the speeches and the music, it shouldn't take longer than forty-five minutes. Following the ceremony, everybody is invited to tour the new hospital and attend a reception afterwards."

"Do you expect me to stay for the tour and the reception?"

"Of course I do. You will want to see the new hospital. Besides, you will be the main attraction, and we don't want to deprive the people of seeing you and getting acquainted with you. Not every town can boast to having its own homegrown baroness at arm's reach."

The mayor smiled at her. "I hope I didn't forget anything." He held up a finger. "Oh, yes, I'll send a personal invitation to Fräulein von Hohenstein. We would like to have her at the ceremony as well. I know she doesn't get out much, but she may attend to see her niece in action."

"Yes, it would be good for her to be among people other than Jakob and me."

She rose and the mayor followed suit. "Do you have any questions?"

"No, I think you covered it all. I'll be at the hospital shortly before ten on Friday."

"Great. You'll have your seat next to mine, and your aunt will have a reserved seat in the front row."

"Thank you, Herr Schmidt." She extended her hand in parting. "I'll see you on Friday then."

"*Auf Wiedersehen,* Baroness."

Marie-Louise left the office. Again, conspicuous activity in the hallway accompanied her on her way out of the town hall.

I guess I'm somewhat of an oddity in this town until they get used to seeing me around. Then I'll be an everyday occurrence, and nobody will even turn when I walk or drive by.

On the way up the hill she remembered that she'd forgotten to discuss the county's request with the mayor. She hit her forehead in disgust but decided to talk to him on Friday. She'd corner him after the ceremony and explain her situation then. Yes, she'd wait until she spoke with the mayor before she contacted the county again, and it might even prove unnecessary if the mayor could pull some strings.

Marie-Louise felt a glimmer of hope that the *Bürgermeister* would be able to intervene on her behalf and before long was so elated at the idea that she arrived at the castle, whistling a tune.

Better not let Ambrosia hear me whistle—ladies don't indulge in such bourgeois *behavior. Oh, well, I won't let her ruin my day. I'm confident that things will work out.*

Chapter Nine

As promised, the mayor's invitation arrived, and Ambrosia wrung her hands. She didn't feel comfortable mingling with so many commoners, and she generally shied away from all the publicity. However, supporting her niece at her first public appearance made the decision for her, and together the two Hohenstein women arrived at the hospital at exactly nine forty-five on the day of the ceremony.

The mayor was already there, bustling around, straightening a chair, talking to the members of the orchestra as they tuned their instruments, or greeting some guests. When he saw Ambrosia and Marie-Louise, he hurried to greet them and bent over their hands in a pompous fashion. The baroness looked at her aunt, but Ambrosia only smiled as the mayor led her to her seat on the front row. Then he accompanied Marie-Louise to her seat by the podium just as the music started.

More and more guests arrived, and a distinguished, graying gentleman took his seat next to Ambrosia. He seemed to be quite talkative and started up a conversation. At first, Ambrosia seemed reserved, but apparently warmed up to him and responded. Pretty soon, she seemed to be as animated as he was and was talking as much as he.

Marie-Louise couldn't believe her eyes: her aunt in deep conversation with a commoner. She wondered what they were talking about and what they had in common. She leaned over to the mayor. "Who is that man to the left of my aunt?"

"That's Dr. Paul Walter, our head surgeon."

Marie-Louise had never seen her aunt so animated. Miracles never ceased.

Her thoughts were interrupted when the mayor stepped to the podium, cleared his throat, and welcomed the guests. He outlined the day's itinerary and announced the first speaker.

One after another, the speakers praised the town's vision for the modern facility and the generosity of the donors. The director of the hospital spoke last, thanking the donors and the Town of Hohenstein and explaining the facility's latest technology, especially their modern x-ray apparatus. The mayor then rose and announced the cutting of the ribbon to signify the official opening of the hospital. He introduced Marie-Louise and handed her the scissors. The music started playing.

She looked at the audience and smiled, and with head held high, she majestically walked to the entrance and raised the scissors for all to see. The photographer stuck his head under the dark cloth covering his camera before he pushed the button to document the momentous event. After the ribbon was cut, Marie-Louise turned again to the audience, raised her hand, and smiled. The orchestra started up again, but the applause drowned out most of the sound.

She joined her aunt, and Ambrosia introduced Dr. Walter. "Your aunt told me about your ambition to preserve your ancestral castle. That's quite commendable."

"Thank you for your kind words, Dr. Walter."

"Ladies, I believe Dr. Hauser, the director of this fine facility, wants to start the tour. May I offer you my arms?"

The Hohenstein women smiled their assent and the doctor began guiding them down the corridor when a young man came up from behind and addressed Dr. Walter.

"I won't allow you to escort *two* pretty ladies on the tour. Let me offer my arm to the baroness."

"Ladies, excuse this young, impertinent doctor." Dr. Walter laughed good-naturedly, then consented, "All right, if the baroness doesn't mind spending time with you, Greenhorn, I'll entrust her to your custody." He turned to the ladies. "May I introduce Dr. Nikolas Neff? He has just finished his studies and has been hired to work with me as our doctor of internal medicine."

Dr. Neff offered Marie-Louise his arm, and together, they followed to catch up to the tour. He explained the various machines and their purposes, then showed Marie-Louise the x-ray room, the operating room, the exam rooms, and of course, the patient rooms, explaining things in simple layman terms without making her feel stupid.

At the reception area, she had a chance to look at him more closely. He was about her height with sandy hair, gray eyes, a warm smile, and comfortable manners, plus he was easy to converse with. She wouldn't call him handsome, but certainly not bad-looking; a little too serious perhaps, but that might be because he didn't know her well enough, and that certainly didn't detract from his likable personality.

Marie-Louise looked for her aunt and found her in deep conversation with Dr. Walter. Who would have thought that her aloof aunt wouldn't waste any time to latch on to a nice gentleman right away.

She saw the mayor standing by the beverage table all by himself and didn't want to waste her time, either, in taking this opportunity to talk to him about her problem.

"Would you excuse me for a minute, Dr. Neff? I need to discuss some business with the mayor."

Dr. Neff bowed, and she approached the mayor.

"Herr Schmidt, may I talk with you about a personal matter?"

"Of course, Baroness. Let's sit at the table over there in the corner where we can talk in private."

When they were seated, the mayor opened the conversation. "What's on your mind, Baroness, and how can I be of service?"

"I received a letter from the county requesting that our stable roof be replaced. I admit, the roof is sagging, and apparently has been sagging for a few years, but it doesn't leak, and is definitely no hazard to anyone. The county gave me three weeks to comply with this request, but I don't have the necessary funds at the moment. Do you have any suggestions on what I can do?"

The mayor turned red in the face and pounded his fist into his hand. "This is preposterous! Why would the county request a new roof when it is not necessary? I don't understand." He closed his eyes and put a finger to his temple, concentrating. "Baroness, let me speak to the commissioner and find out what's going on. Of course, I can't guarantee anything, but I'll do my best to convince him to table the request for the time being, and I'll let you know of the outcome."

Marie-Louise couldn't believe her good fortune. She put a hand over her heart. "I can't express how grateful I am to you for your assistance."

He bowed. "I'm glad to be of service, Baroness."

She rose and excused herself to go in search of Ambrosia, who held a glass of punch in her hand and was smiling at something Dr. Walter said.

As soon as Marie-Louise approached her aunt, Dr. Neff intercepted her. "Can I get you something to drink?"

"Thank you. I would appreciate a glass of lemonade."

Along with the drink, he also brought some tasty treats on a little glass plate with a napkin. "Do you want to sit down?"

"No, I think I want to join my aunt and Dr. Walter. Are you coming, too?"

"Certainly, if you wish."

She would have agreed to almost anything at the moment, she was so elated at the mayor's proffered help. She felt like singing and shouting and had a hard time concentrating on anything the young doctor said. All she could think of was her good fortune at having the mayor plead her cause with the county. She couldn't wait to tell Ambrosia, but unfortunately, it would have to wait until they were back at the castle.

"You did a good job with the ribbon-cutting, and I can't wait to see the pictures and article in tomorrow's paper," Ambrosia said. "I notice that you are happy today, especially since we returned from the hospital. What happened? I saw you talking with the mayor at the reception."

Marie-Louise couldn't contain herself any longer. She executed a little dance while Ambrosia looked on, bewildered.

"You won't believe it, but the mayor promised to intervene with the county on our behalf. He called their request preposterous and said that he would talk to the commissioner."

"That's generous of him."

"I was so excited that I had a hard time concentrating on Dr. Neff's conversation."

Ambrosia smiled. "He didn't seem to mind."

Talking about Dr. Neff reminded Marie-Louise that she wanted to know about her aunt's discussion with Dr. Walter.

"Tante Ambrosia, I saw you in deep conversation with Dr. Walter. Do you have interests in common?"

Ambrosia blushed and looked down to study her shoes before she answered. "We talked about medicine and natural healing. Dr. Walter agrees that there are old-time home remedies that definitely have merit, and he wants to see my collection of herbs."

"Really? That's wonderful. When is he coming?"

"We have not set a date. He'll let me know."

"And you don't mind interacting with a commoner?"

"It's just to exchange knowledge."

Marie-Louise looked at her aunt. The strict advocate for rank observance deviated from her own rules.

Seeming to guess her niece's thoughts, Ambrosia fidgeted with her collar. "You seemed to have quite a good time with the young doctor."

"He's nice."

"That's all?"

"Yes," Marie-Louise sighed, "that's all."

The next day brought a card from Dr. Neff. He thanked Marie-Louise for her enjoyable companionship at the hospital ceremony and wanted to know if she would like to accompany him to a concert on Saturday next.

She went to her aunt with the card in her hand. "Dr. Neff wants to take me to a concert next week."

Ambrosia looked a little annoyed. "He didn't lose any time securing your interest. Are you planning to go with him?"

"I don't know yet. I'm really not interested, but going out with him may break up the monotony."

Ambrosia sighed and nodded.

The mayor also sent a message. He had spoken with the commissioner and pleaded the baroness' cause, but no matter what he said, the commissioner wouldn't change the county's decision. The stable roof needed to be replaced within the three-week period. The best the mayor could do was to negotiate that the roof repair might have to start within three weeks, but did not necessarily have to be completed at the end of that time. He was sorry that he couldn't give her a more favorable report.

Marie-Louise sank onto a chair.

"Things didn't work out with the county?" Ambrosia asked.

"No, they won't change."

"What do we do now?"

Marie-Louise heaved a sigh. "I have no idea." After a pause, she stood up. "I need to go for a walk to clear my mind. I'll be back in a while."

"Take Kaiser with you."

Kaiser was excited to go for a walk. Oblivious to his companion's dark mood, he ran ahead, sniffed at every tree and shrub, chased a rabbit, and barked at a squirrel that clambered up a tree.

Addressing the dog, she asked, "What am I going to do, Kaiser? I tried everything I could think of. I visited the Commerce Bank and Ulrich and wrote to my mother. What more can I do? Why did my father make things so hard for me? I wish I could be as carefree as you are, chasing squirrels and sniffing out all kinds of good smells. Oh, well."

After she felt sorry for herself for about a minute, she pulled herself together. Self-pity wouldn't help. She had to come up with a solution to her problem, find the funds for the roof.

There had to be another bank, surely. Yes, she had seen the Hohenstein Savings Bank on the way to the hospital today. Perhaps they might be the solution to all her problems.

In the end, the Savings Bank couldn't give her a loan, either, for the very same reasons Ulrich had given her: she didn't have any collateral to secure a loan, and Hohenstein didn't belong to her yet. If she came back in six years as the legal owner of the castle, they would be more than willing to do business with her. In the meantime, they were sorry they couldn't be of help.

Almost two weeks had gone by since she received the county's letter, and she still hadn't come up with any funding. Now she'd have to go back to Ulrich and beg him for help.

Oh, she hated the thought of asking him again. What if he still declined? No, he couldn't possibly withhold his help. Her father certainly didn't want Hohenstein to fall prey to county bureaucracy.

She hated the idea of begging Ulrich for money, *her* money nonetheless, but she didn't see any other way out of her dilemma. She sighed.

Well now, let's see. It's Saturday afternoon, the bank will be closed until Monday. So, the earliest to see Ulrich would be on Monday. Very well, then, that is what I'll need to do.

"What happened?" he asked when she sat across from Ulrich the following Monday. "You look as if the world has come to an end."

"It has for me."

He raised an eyebrow. "That bad?"

"Worse."

"Tell me about it."

Her neatly formulated speech forgotten, she swallowed hard and then blurted out, "They persist with their demand for a new stable roof. The mayor negotiated that as long as work on the roof begins within the three-week period, we're in compliance. I only have a little more than a week left. You need to help me!"

She looked at him, searching for a sign that would give her hope in a hopeless situation, but didn't see one.

"Ulrich," she urged, leaning forward and penetrating him with her gaze. "Work needs to start immediately. And that's why I'm here. I need money."

He shook his head.

Desperate, Marie-Louise cried, "Surely in an emergency like this, I'm allowed to draw upon my inheritance!"

He shook his head again. "Sorry, but your father's will didn't provide for any eventualities."

"What about Hohenstein land? Couldn't I lease out the orchards and vineyards, or the forest?"

"That was done years ago to raise money for taxes. I'm sorry, Marie-Louise."

A lump formed in her throat as she tried one last venue. "I noticed a row of fairly new houses at the base of Hohenstein Mountain, and I know that those buildings sit on Hohenstein land. Couldn't I sell a plot of land to raise the money for the new roof?"

Again, he shook his head. "Your father sold the land years ago, but you won't be able to touch the estate until you legally own it, which is—"

"—on my twenty-fifth birthday or when I get married. Yes, yes, I know." She gave a sad little laugh and turned away from him to blink back the tears that threatened to spill over.

All these years she had lived sheltered and guided, and all of a sudden she faced a menacing world, alone in the battle against all manner of adversity. Everybody seemed to be out to bring her down. Even the count refused to help.

Gaining some control of her emotions, she faced Ulrich's worried frown. Reaching for her hand, he smoothed his thumb across her wrist with gentle, feathery strokes. "I'm sorry to see you so distressed. I wish I could spare you all these problems."

Marie-Louise wanted to tear her hand out of his as if burned, but instead only flashed him a sardonic look. *You may not be able to spare me these problems, but I'm sure you could help me if you wanted to. Your sympathy certainly won't help!*

Swallowing her frustration and pride, she asked, "How about a personal loan?"

At the ensuing silence, she glanced at him and guessed his response as she noticed the deepening of the lines around his mouth.

He closed his eyes for a moment and took a deep breath. "I wish I could give you a loan."

She hung her head.

Trying to sound positive, he asked, "Have you tried any other alternatives to your financial problem? You said you'd come up with something. Should you decide to stay with your mother until your inheritance is placed at your disposal, I'd contact the county to arrange for a deferment of their request until you return to Hohenstein. As long as you reside at the castle, though, I'm afraid the county will demand compliance with their request."

"I'm not running away from my responsibilities," she scoffed. "I'm not a coward."

He gave her a warm smile and nodded in understanding, with something like admiration in his eyes. "I know you're not a coward, and I admire your resilience. It would be a lot easier for you, however, if you stayed with your mother instead of facing the problems here."

Tucking a strand of hair behind her ear, she insisted, "I'm not going to spend the summer with my mother."

Even thinking of her mother brought a bitter taste to her mouth after her recent letter.

Ulrich's discreet cough brought her back to reality, back to his inquiring gaze. "I guess you haven't been too successful in securing funds, have you?"

Biting her lip, she shook her head. "No," she admitted bitterly. "The directors of the Commerce Bank and Savings Bank wouldn't risk their money, either."

"What were the reasons for their refusal?"

She lifted one eyebrow in the count's direction. "I don't have any collateral and not enough income, besides Germany's unstable economic situation makes them very cautious."

Remembering the scene at the Commerce Bank, Marie-Louise shuddered.

The count frowned. "Are you all right?"

"I'm fine. I just remembered the hideous man at the bank who bowed so much that I think he won't be able to straighten his back for an entire week—he was all obsequious benevolence. And if that wasn't enough, he had the nerve to take my hand and press a moist kiss on it. Yuck!"

Sparks appeared in Ulrich's eyes as he tried to suppress a smile. "I can envision it, and wish I'd been there to witness the spectacle—the young, innocent baroness in the claws of a wizened shark."

"You think it's funny, don't you?" she accused.

He burst out laughing. "It probably wasn't, but watching your facial expressions is quite amusing."

She looked at him, outraged, but finally softened so that she could see the comical side of the situation. "The man was so pompous but didn't even know that kissing a woman's hand doesn't have any room in the business world. I should have informed him that one doesn't quite touch the lady's hand with one's lips, but I couldn't afford to offend him since I wanted his money."

Ulrich's lips twitched. "Smart move," he approved, "but it didn't help you in the end, I presume."

"No, it didn't."

Covering her hand with his, he tried to comfort her. "Your problems may seem insurmountable at the present time but I'm sure you'll solve them eventually—"

"I need to solve my problems *now*—not *eventually*. I only have one more week for a new roof! Don't you understand? I need help *now*. Your help."

"All I can do is offer you a position at the Wolfburg Bank. At least you would have some extra income and could pay off the roofer's bill."

She shook her head.

"Why won't you accept my offer?"

"I need to be at Hohenstein to oversee the repairs. Besides, I agreed to volunteer for the town as special events representative."

"Ah yes, I saw your picture in the newspaper. You represent the town well, I'd say. A beautiful young woman with a title sounds grand."

"I thought it was my duty as Baroness von Hohenstein to get involved in the community."

"I see."

For some reason, she felt that Ulrich wasn't too impressed with her new role as special events representative for the town of Hohenstein, and she felt disappointed. Instead of being proud of her for accepting responsibility in the civic arena of Hohenstein, he looked skeptical, and she wondered why.

Clearing his throat, Ulrich said, "Involvement in the community is praiseworthy but it doesn't solve your financial problems. You ought to seriously consider marriage and leave all your troubles behind you."

She laughed. "There are always two people involved before a wedding can take place, or so I'm told."

He smiled. "Being sarcastic doesn't suit you, Baroness. But if you wish, I'll arrange a ball in your honor where you'll meet plenty of eligible young men."

"No need to go to all that trouble for me." Marie-Louise raised her chin defiantly. "I'm not going to marry an aristocrat."

Chapter Ten

Ulrich raised an eyebrow. "You're not? Any particular reason?"

She hesitated while he waited for an answer, his eyes never leaving her face. Finally, she lifted her shoulders. "I don't want to spend a life dictated by rules and regulations, every step measured and scrutinized, every move choreographed. I want to be free of this aristocratic straitjacket!"

Cheeks burning, she continued, "Even the choice of your marriage partner is prescribed. He has to be of noble birth, with no flaw marring his blue-blooded lineage, and no skeletons hidden in the closet. And if such a paragon is found, his rank may be below your own which, of course, would make him ineligible. You are not supposed to marry below your rank, after all—a lateral union would be acceptable, but an upward move definitely preferable."

She made a disgusted sound. "The whole system is so snobbish it makes me sick. Is anybody ever allowed to marry for love?"

He started to say something but she held up her hand to stop him. "My friend Elizabeth was in love with a young man and they made plans to get married when her parents whisked her away to meet a more eligible man and talked her into marrying him. Elizabeth was heart-broken."

The baroness continued, "Two of my friends had made plans to travel to America this summer, but Irene's parents found an older, eligible bachelor with the right kind of title and money and forced her to accompany them to his estate in Scotland.

"And look at my parents. My father needed a wife to produce an heir in order to continue the line of Hohenstein, but they didn't love each other . . ."

Ulrich, who had listened to this outburst with seeming concern, asked, "How do you know they didn't love each other?"

"Ha," she scoffed. "My mother would have stayed with my father during his illness had she loved him."

"They were probably very fond of each other when they married."

"Being fond of each other isn't the same as loving each other."

Bending forward, the count regarded her quizzically. "What do you know about love, Marie-Louise? How do you know when you're in love? What do you feel?"

She drew back, confused. She began to say something, but he held up his hand. "Don't answer."

Before she could guess at his intentions, before she had time to move, he sat next to her on the settee, taking her hand and turning it palm up.

"Do you feel shivers of pleasure running up your spine when I barely touch the base of your palm like this?"

He watched her while moving his thumb gently over the indicated spot and curved his lips in a satisfied little smile at her slight twitching reaction to his touch.

When she tried to pull her hand out of his, he tightened his hold slightly. "Don't pull back. We're not done yet."

Not knowing what to do or what to say, she lowered her head to hide the tell-tale heat that stole into her cheeks.

He released her hand but put his arm around her shoulders instead, drawing her closer to him.

She stiffened and tried to turn her head away from him, away from his persuasive voice. The fact that her body reacted in exactly the way he predicted filled her with confusion, and she stiffened even more. Never in her life had she felt so out of control. Her body seemed to have a mind of its own, responding to his merest touch, even to his voice.

At that moment, he stood up and pulled her with him. When she wouldn't look up, he put his index finger under her chin and gently coaxed her to lift her head.

Trance-like, she gazed into his crystal clear eyes, hypnotized by their depths.

Both hands on her shoulders, Ulrich gazed at her. "You're beautiful, Marie-Louise. Your eyes are like brown velvet, but I like them best when they shoot their golden sparks at me when you're angry. Right now, they're even darker than usual."

Dropping her gaze, she felt an embarrassing warmth creep into her cheeks and wished that he would stop torturing her. She wished herself far away at a place where she could feel safe, safe from him and these strange sensations and, above all, safe from her own feelings.

She tried to wriggle out of his hold, but he wouldn't let go. Instead, he gently brushed a wisp of hair from her cheek and tucked it behind her ear, his deep, sensual voice persisting, "How soft and shiny your hair is, the color of coffee—" he bent to touch his lips to the crown of her head, "—and when I kiss it, I smell apple blossoms."

She stood motionless, eyes closed. His masculine smell of tangy Irish moss tantalized her nose. She trembled inwardly. Part of her willed him to go on with his explorations, while her more rational self wanted to draw back. Yet, curiosity made her stay.

"You have the perfect height," he continued. "When I want to kiss your eyes, I just have to bend a little—like this . . . and your temples . . . Ah, you smell so good, and I'm certain you taste even better."

Barely touching, he eased his thumb across her lips, causing a quick intake of breath. Deliberately slow, he continued outlining her lips, over and over again, until her breath came out ragged and she shivered involuntarily. Still, he carried on, taking her almost to the limits of endurance, his eyes never leaving her face.

When she thought she couldn't stand another moment of this exquisite agony, she parted her lips, inviting the inevitable.

Ulrich eased his hold on her shoulders, wrapped his arms around her slender body, and drew her against him, all the while stroking her back with gentle rotating motions. When she didn't resist, he lowered his head, planted a kiss on the tip of her nose, and then claimed her mouth with his. She jerked back and he stopped, but when she didn't pull away, his tongue started teasing her still-swollen lips until they became pliable and responsive.

He trailed light kisses all the way to the corner of her mouth, very gently, immediately easing his ardor at the slightest tremor in her body.

With his hand mussing her hair, he softly drew her head back until their gazes locked. Again his lips touched hers, his teeth playfully nibbling, his tongue teasing until her breathing was shallow and her mouth followed his every move.

He paused a moment before he crushed her against him, holding her as if he'd never let her go, his mouth upon hers. Pressed against him, she could feel the pounding of his heart. Or was it hers?

Marie-Louise clung to him, her arms slipping about his neck, her body pressed into him as he continued the exploration of her mouth. Unable to control or understand the liquid fire that shot burning arrows through her body and made her legs go weak, she groaned his name, "Ullie . . .!" the name she had used when they were children.

"Patience, my love," his husky voice soothed before he claimed her mouth with his. This time, she didn't pull back, but responded somewhat hesitantly at first, becoming bolder and more inquisitive as the kiss deepened.

Marie-Louise clung to him and raked her fingers through his hair. She was lost to reality. What mattered was this moment of wonder, of sheer bliss, the rapid coursing of her blood, and the strong pounding of the count's heart against her own. Every heartbeat seemed to drum his name: Ullie, Ullie, Ullie.

She opened her eyes a fraction to see coppery hair, tousled now, swimming before her vision. Another moment and the picture became clearer: Ulrich. Count Wolfburg! A semblance of reality forced itself upon her mind as she stiffened.

The count immediately slackened his hold and with a deep sigh, released her. Stepping back, arms folded across his chest, legs apart, he watched her.

As if awakening from a deep sleep, shaking the cobwebs from her mind, she tossed her head, flinging her tousled hair back into place. Looking down, she pulled at her skirt that had slipped up a bit to expose her ankles. When she looked up again, her cheeks felt hot.

At last, she accused disdainfully, "That wasn't fair, Count."

An amused smile started at the back of his eyes as he agreed, "Maybe not fair, but very pleasurable. Don't you agree?"

The heat in her cheeks intensified. *How dare he mock her?* He had taken advantage of her innocence and now was laughing at her. *Well, not exactly laughing,* she corrected herself, but he certainly didn't feel any remorse for his actions. She should have pushed him away . . .

She wondered if he treated all the young ladies of his acquaintance in the same un-gentlemanly manner, or only the ones that proved to be a pain in the neck like the Baroness von Hohenstein.

He continued to watch her, but his expression had changed from slight amusement to something like guilt. Could it be that he felt sorry for his actions? She didn't care. All she wanted to do was get as far away from him as possible, and if she never saw him again, she'd be happy. He probably wouldn't dare show his face at Hohenstein again, anyway, so she would be safe. Good riddance!

"A penny for your thoughts?"

She glared at him. "You wouldn't want to know. They aren't too flattering."

"I could tell."

Darn him and his insolence!

"I advise you check your hair before returning to Hohenstein. Your aunt may become suspicious about your trips to Wolfburg."

The rat. Her anger flared at the laughter in his voice and she wanted to throw something at him, tell him exactly what she thought of him. Of course that would never do. Nobody in his right mind would ever act that disrespectfully toward Count Wolfburg!

He made an exaggerated bow and pointed to a door. "You'll find a mirror in there."

Marie-Louise, thankful for the privacy of the luxuriously equipped bathroom, collapsed onto the padded stool. With drooping shoulders, she sat motionless, seeing and yet not seeing. After a few minutes of staring into space, dry-eyed and utterly miserable, she turned toward the mirror to freshen her appearance. Her cheeks were flushed, her eyes wide, and her lips fuller than usual. Gingerly she outlined her mouth with her index finger as Ulrich had done a short while ago and noticed with irritation that her lips were still sensitive and responded to the merest touch, even her own.

What a treacherous body that seemed to have a will of its own! She should have never let him touch her, much less kiss her. She could have walked out. But no! She had stood there rooted to the spot, anticipating his next move. How stupid! Not only had she anticipated his kiss, she had encouraged it, participated in it, thrown herself at him. He must think her a totally wanton woman, lost to all decency!

His behavior couldn't be called *noble* either, taking advantage of her like that! As a matter of fact, as the head of the House of Wolfburg, he had acted inexcusably base.

Fury at his debauchery vied with anger over her own shameless behavior and left her red-faced and ready to sink into the ground. How could she ever face him again?

His kisses didn't mean anything. Marie-Louise realized that his pride hadn't allowed him to stand idly by when she had proclaimed that she wouldn't want to get involved with anyone from her own social circle. He had to at least show her what she was casting away. Or he may have hoped that she would fall in love with him so that he could give her the cold-shoulder treatment as punishment for her disloyalty toward the exalted state of nobility.

He had used her innocence to teach her a lesson. Wanting to avenge his tattered male ego in the most natural way, she had stepped right into his trap. She vowed to never again be found alone with him. If she ever had reason again to come to the Wolfburg Bank, she'd take Tante Ambrosia along.

Now that she had sorted out his behavior and understood, if not sanctioned, his actions, she tried to make sense of her own emotional involvement. The problem was that she couldn't put a name to the sensations she had experienced under his caresses other than that their body chemistries must be very compatible. Thinking of it, she felt heat creep into her cheeks again. Her heart pounded faster, and the liquid fire started coursing through her veins once more. "Silly," she said out loud and tossed her head.

After combing her hair and pinching her cheeks, she emerged from the bathroom and saw Ulrich sitting on the settee with his legs crossed, apparently absorbed in a list of columns. How could he get back to business as if nothing had happened? *Men!* He didn't seem to have a care in the world and looked as immaculate as ever. His tie hung perfectly straight, and his hair that she had ruffled now looked as if freshly groomed by his valet.

Marie-Louise stood a moment in indecision before she cleared her throat. "I'm leaving now."

Immediately, he was by her side. "I want to take you to lunch, Marie-Louise."

She gave him a sideways glance. *Probably a gesture of guilt.* Aloud she said, "Thank you for the invitation, but Tante Ambrosia is expecting me back by noon, so I'd better not keep her waiting."

He accompanied her as she walked toward the door, but before he opened it for her, he tapped her on the shoulder. "Don't forget that there is a job waiting for you at the bank whenever you need one."

She shook her head. *Not in a million years!*

"One other thing," he continued. "Don't forget what happened between us today."

Speechless, she stared at him. This was the last thing she expected him to say. Was he lost to all decency? Outraged at his audacity, she said in her most stilted way, head held high, "Count, the incident is already forgotten."

The corners of his mouth twitched. "Liar."

It was hard to give someone a condemning stare when you had to look up to do so, and of course, she failed miserably. Head still held high, she moved one step closer to the door.

"You're no gentleman, Count," she said and put as much disdain in her voice as she could muster before she darted past him and away from his disturbing presence.

Although she needed to feel the safety of the castle, she didn't go straight home. She couldn't face her aunt quite yet, not with her jumbled emotions. The problem with the county was pushed aside at the moment because her mind was too occupied with her encounter with Ulrich. Unable to stop herself, Marie-Louise lived and relived each and every sensuous moment.

She wondered if the memory haunted him as well, and if he found concentrating as hard as she did.

You're a silly goose if you think he so much as spares you another thought. It all seemed to be a big joke for him, his way of punishing a little girl who had strayed from the small and narrow way of traditional thinking.

Maybe she should accept Dr. Neff's invitation to accompany him to the concert hall. Getting away and seeing other people might help her forget Ulrich. Yes, she would go out with the doctor.

Having made up her mind to go to the concert with Dr. Neff, she forced Ulrich from her mind and, instead, wrestled with the problem of the roof and the non-existing funds again. Resolutely she took a small notepad and pencil and made a list of pros and cons associated with the new stable roof. She drew a line down the middle of the page and wrote PROS on one side and CONS on the other. Then she stared into space, unseeing, and chewed on the end of her pencil.

After a few moments of an absolute blank, she forced herself to concentrate on the problem again. Then she printed on the right-hand side of the paper in big, bold letters *NO FUNDS* and decorated the two words with fancy scrolls and calligraphic enhancements.

Well, that said it all, actually. She could elaborate and add *MATERIAL AND LABOR* while the left side of the page still stared at her empty. She would write down *GO TO WOLFBURG BANK FOR A LOAN* then draw a line through it. At least it would show that she'd acted, albeit in vain.

Marie-Louise wondered if she had any other alternatives. She could possibly take Ulrich's advice and talk the roofer into letting her pay in installments. With her pencil tipped to her forehead she considered the idea. It would be worth a try, and she added the option to the PRO column. When nothing else came to mind, she went in search of Jakob to find out if he knew a roofer in town.

Once the old man talked, he rambled on and on. "Yes, Fräulein Marie-Louise, I mean, Baroness, we've got a roofer in Hohenstein, and a good one at that. Heinrich Meissner's a young lad, diligent and willing. Good people. His folks started the business. Yeah, and now Heinrich's about to take himself a son-in-law to help with the work."

"But, Jakob, you said he was a young lad? How can he have a son-in-law?"

"Huh?" He scratched his balding head and grinned. "I guess the boy isn't quite as young as I remember him, seeing he has a girl to marry off. His only child, too."

"Will you accompany me to Mr. Meissner's office?"

Jakob seemed delighted if his wide grin was anything to go by. "Of course, Fräulein Baroness, I'd love to."

Over lunch, Marie-Louise's thoughts returned to Ulrich and the scene from that morning. Absentminded, she pushed her food around the plate without appreciating the delicious *Sauerbraten* and *Spätzle* her aunt had prepared.

"You look distressed. How did you fare at your audience with Count Wolfburg?"

"It was a complete disaster," she burst out, "and I hope I'll never have to deal with him again."

Ambrosia put knife and fork down and stared at her. "You weren't disrespectful, I hope!"

"No," she mumbled, "although he certainly hasn't earned my respect by any means."

Lips pressed into a tight line, Ambrosia stared at her. "What are you saying? Have you gone mad? That is no way to talk about the head of the House of Wolfburg."

How typical of her aunt to take the count's side without even knowing what had transpired. Marie-Louise wanted to make a hasty retort but decided to keep quiet lest her aunt suspect a scandal. That would never do. She clamped her mouth shut and stared at her plate to avoid her aunt's scrutinizing gaze.

Ambrosia probed, "Has Count Wolfburg refused to give you a loan?"

The baroness nodded without looking up.

"That's no cause to speak disrespectfully of him. He probably had his reasons for denying your request."

"Yes, I bet. He probably gets a thrill out of seeing me squirm. Maybe he's only waiting until he can snatch up Hohenstein for himself for next to nothing."

"Marie-Louise! That's blasphemy. The count would never do anything so dishonorable."

Well, he did something dishonorable this morning, but you wouldn't believe it even if I told you. You probably would find fault with my *behavior instead of his.*

Ambrosia pursed her lips. "I hope you haven't disgraced our family." Folding her hands in front of her, she looked heavenward in the sanctimonious gesture Marie-Louise detested.

After a few bites of Ambrosia's delicious stew, the baroness asked, "Do you know the count well?"

The older woman looked up. "Not really. I only saw him at some social functions, but didn't have the opportunity to chat with him much."

"Is he a womanizer?"

Ambrosia laid her spoon down. "Marie-Louise! I'm shocked." She puckered her lips and looked down her nose at her niece.

Although feeling uneasy about her inquiry, the baroness pressed on. “Is he a rogue?”

After a disgusted huff, Ambrosia said, “I wouldn’t know. I never read anything negative about him in any of the gossip columns. And why you should ask a question like that is beyond my comprehension, unless . . .” Ambrosia knitted her brows and looked at Marie-Louise, “. . . he acted unseemly. Did he?”

“No, of course not.” Marie-Louise lowered her head to hide her burning cheeks.

“I didn’t think so.” Ambrosia relaxed against her chair, but asked, “Why did you want to know if the count is a rogue?”

Fidgeting in her chair, she finally said, “He is very good looking and certainly old enough to be married.”

Ambrosia positioned her glasses. “Yes, he is an exceptionally good looking young man, and he will get married when he finds the perfect woman to be his countess.” She scrutinized her niece. “If you would show a little more decorum, he might even consider you.”

Marie-Louise gave a dry laugh which earned her a stern look from Ambrosia.

Short of making a biting remark, the baroness excused herself, went to her suite, and closed the door with more force than necessary. She pounded her fist into the cushion of the settee by the window. If her aunt only knew what had happened at the bank this morning, she wouldn’t think so highly of the count.

Marie-Louise closed her eyes. Reliving the incident, she could almost feel Ulrich’s gentle touch, hear his husky voice and experience those incredible sensations when his lips had educated hers. She could see his almost-violet eyes, feel his strong arms, his persuasive probing . . .

Stop, she told herself and pressed her hands against her burning cheeks. She breathed hard to gain control over her wayward emotions. *Having received your first real, earth-shattering kiss doesn't mean you have to swoon over the man.*

A thought occurred to her that made her sit up straight. What had happened to her image of the stiff Count Wolfburg? He might be stiff in his business dealings but certainly not when it came to pursuing women. She may have been correct in thinking that he might be a rogue.

Rogue or not, she needed to forget him and today's episode. Dwelling on the unfortunate incident didn't make it disappear, and neither did it make her feel any better about herself or about Ulrich. The best way to direct her thoughts into less dangerous channels was to prepare her negotiation with the roofer. She had asked Jakob to make an appointment with Herr Meissner right away, and anticipated the meeting with the roofer. She hoped that he would be amenable to her proposal of paying in installments.

When the day of the meeting dawned, it was with leaden skies and a light drizzle, and as the day wore on, the drizzle turned into a steady rain. Marie-Louise, with Jakob in tow, set out to talk with the roofer in the afternoon.

Things didn't turn out as planned, however. The baroness, familiar with the roofer's name plus half of his family history, was prepared to meet Herr Meissner. But instead of finding him, they were greeted by his wife and daughter. Both women offered a polite, if somewhat clumsy, curtsey.

"What an honor to have you in our home, Baroness. Hello, Jakob, good to see you. Heinrich's awfully sorry not to be here but the hospital in Endersbach had a leak in the roof, and they can't have these poor, sick people die of pneumonia because rain is dripping onto their faces."

Hard-pressed to quell a smile at the verbosity of the ruddy-faced woman, Marie-Louise tried to decide whether to leave and make another appointment or whether to have the roofer come up to the castle.

To make some small talk, she asked questions about the upcoming wedding as it must be foremost on the women's minds. And right she was.

"Jakob told me you're to be married soon, Fräulein Meissner?"

"Yes, in less than two months."

"I bet there's a lot to do, much to arrange, and plans to be made."

"Oh, you don't know the half of it, Baroness," said the mother. "We still haven't agreed on a location for the reception. Doris, here, wants a swanky place in Wolfburg, and Fritz, her betrothed, thinks Hohenstein would do just fine, and we as parents are in the middle. Since Doris is our only child, we want her wedding day to be the best this town has ever seen!"

"Veronika Hauser, my very best friend, had a dream wedding last year," Doris chimed in. "They celebrated in Wolfburg and the entire wedding party marched to the reception place procession-like with bows of flowers. Oh, that was absolutely grand! I guess nobody can outdo that!"

Among all this enthusiasm, an idea formed in Marie-Louise's head and snowballed into a concept of extraordinary proportions. Baffled by the impact of it, she could hardly contain her excitement.

Chapter Eleven

"Well," she said cautiously and with a certain dignified timbre in her voice, an eyebrow raised snobbishly, "I can see a wedding procession following a decorated open coach, drawn by two beautifully matched horses, bride and groom seated inside together with the flower girls and ring-bearer. They ride to the church, and afterwards have the reception and party in the crystal ballroom at the castle, all in high style."

She looked at her listeners to see if the picture she drew with her words had any effect on them. Mother and daughter stood there open-mouthed, and the baroness continued, "That, I would call *classy*."

Jakob stared at her, seemingly not quite following her train of thought. Doris, however, caught on immediately.

"Ooooh," she breathed, "that would be a wedding fit for a princess."

"Exactly," agreed Marie-Louise.

"But it's out of our reach."

Marie-Louise kept her voice purposefully mysterious. "Not necessarily, Frau Meissner."

"What can you possibly mean?"

"I have a proposition to make."

Both women looked at her wide-eyed.

"Hohenstein needs a new stable roof. That's the reason we came here today—to discuss it with your husband. When Doris spoke of a dream wedding, my mind started working. We have that beautiful crystal ballroom at the castle, and we also have a coach in our carriage house. So, why not strike a bargain?"

Mother and daughter still looked baffled.

"I put on the wedding. I decorate the coach, take care of the flowers, and provide a driver and the food in exchange for a new stable roof."

She looked at her audience. As her proposal sank in, their eyes lit up with excitement. Doris jumped up, clapped her hands, and exclaimed exuberantly, "That's too good to be true. I'll outdo them all! Oh, will they ever envy me!"

She ran up to the baroness, grabbed her hand, and shook it vigorously. "Thank you, oh, thank you so very, very much."

"Doris, dear, don't you think we ought to ask Father before we make a definite commitment?"

"He'll say yes, I know it. It's too good an offer to turn down."

Marie-Louise tried her best to suppress a smile. "If you take advantage of my offer, I need to know if you want to get married in our chapel at the castle or in the church here in town. You will probably be able to fit more people into the church than our chapel, but I didn't want to fail to mention this option."

"It would be nice to have the ceremony at the castle's chapel, but you're right; not everybody would fit in it. And I want everybody to see me."

"That's settled then, provided your father goes along with our little scheme. Just let me know and we can stick our heads together to work out further details . . ."

When she left the roofer's house, she felt exuberant, and knew that the Meissner women were equally elated. How fortunate that the roofer hadn't been there and she had an opportunity to talk to his wife and daughter. Once the women warmed to her idea, there was no chance in the world the roofer could back out! Marie-Louise rubbed her hands in glee.

"Baroness," Jakob said on the way back, "that thar was a very smart idea, but we don't have no horses to draw that carriage."

"We'll cross that bridge when we get to it."

Let his Nobleness, the Count, turn green with envy when he hears of this *business deal.* She knew he couldn't have done better himself, and she relished the idea of having bested him. If he didn't want to help her financially, fine! She didn't need his condescending help.

Oh, how good it felt to be free of at least one big burden, and she felt like singing all the way home.

The next hurdle to overcome would be Tante Ambrosia. Marie-Louise needed her help with the wedding preparations, but first she had to sell her aunt on the idea of serving commoners at the castle. Everything would fall through if Ambrosia wasn't willing to participate.

Marie-Louise decided to carefully formulate and rehearse the speech she would give her aunt, but when she saw her in the parlor upon her arrival, she couldn't contain herself and burst out, "We've done it!"

Ambrosia looked up from her magazine and pushed her glasses on top of her head. "What are you talking about? And why this hoydenish whooping?"

"The roof. We'll get a new roof."

Ambrosia wrinkled her brow. "Can you be a little more specific?"

"I bartered with the roofer—well, actually, with his wife and daughter. We put on a wedding, and they put on a new stable roof."

"You can't be serious!"

"It will work out perfectly." She paused, looking down at her shoes, before finally saying, "I need your assistance, though. Will you help me?"

Ambrosia sat speechless for a moment. Then she puckered her lips in her sternest fashion. "Commoners here at Hohenstein?"

Marie-Louise, who had been holding her breath, let it out slowly. "We'll have the wedding party for the roofer's daughter in the crystal ballroom. We decorate and provide dinner, refreshments, and the coach ride from the church to the castle."

"A coach ride, too?" Ambrosia drew the words out while raising her eyebrows. "What coach?"

"I'll find a suitable one in the carriage house."

"One of those old dilapidated vehicles? You can't be serious."

Marie-Louise bit her lip, but nodded.

"And did you mean to draw the carriage yourself?"

Anger surged at her aunt's sarcasm, but she swallowed a hasty reply. "I'll find a team of horses somewhere."

"Good luck," was Ambrosia's dry retort. "By the way, who will drive the team?"

"I will." Seeing Ambrosia was about to comment, Marie-Louise added, "Daddy taught me how to drive a team. I can do it."

"Absolutely not. You cannot debase yourself by driving a carriage. I will not allow it. You will have to find someone else to do it."

Marie-Louise twisted a ring around her finger. "Will you help me if I promise not to drive the team?"

"What did you want me to do?"

"Would you be in charge of the food?" Seeing her aunt's questioning look, she hastened to add, "Of course, we'll get Frau Becker and Jakob to help."

"Frau Becker will be needed, but definitely not Jakob. I don't want to see him in my kitchen."

After Ambrosia's consent had sunk in, Marie-Louise wanted to let out a whoop of relief but decided she better not jeopardize her aunt's cooperation with such an unladylike gesture. Instead, she grabbed her hand. "Thank you, thank you for agreeing to help."

Her aunt stiffened and Marie-Louise realized that her display of emotion was inappropriate in the older woman's estimation. Dropping her hand, she bent her head to await Ambrosia's lecture. It didn't come.

Surprised, she glanced at her aunt, who didn't look at all annoyed. Instead, she cleared her throat. "Shouldn't you get ready for your outing with Dr. Neff?"

"Oh, gracious! I forgot all about it. Please excuse me."

When Dr. Neff was ushered into the parlor, Marie-Louise descended the stairs leisurely to let him admire her in her black silk dress with the flounce in the back. She had fastened her hair on top of her head with a silver clasp that allowed her ringlets to cascade down in wild abandon. Silver heeled shoes and a silver handbag completed her outfit, and a strand of pearls around her neck was the only jewelry she wore.

Two pairs of eyes watched as she descended. Ambrosia nodded her satisfaction, and the young doctor smiled his pleasure. He bent over her hand, and even Ambrosia couldn't find any fault at his gesture.

He wore a dark suit and white shirt, his shoes shined to perfection, and his hair parted and slicked back. Not exactly handsome, he nevertheless looked quite elegant.

Marie-Louise gave him a smile as she took his arm, nodded to her aunt, and bade her farewell before she left the castle together with Dr. Neff.

He helped her into a black motorcar, not quite as nice as Ulrich's, closed her door, and took his seat behind the wheel.

"Is this your vehicle?"

"Oh, no. Dr. Walter insisted that I drive you in his automobile to the concert."

"How nice of him."

"Yes, he's a very nice man. And I want to thank you, Baroness, for accompanying me. It's an honor. By the way, you look stunning."

"Thank you, Dr. Neff."

After a few moments, she asked, "What's on the program tonight?"

He reached in his pocket and handed her a flyer.

"Aha, a medley of classical music. Mozart, Schubert, Bach, Beethoven, and Rimsky-Korsakov. Quite impressive. I'm looking forward to it."

"I hope it will be up to your standards."

"I'm sure it will be wonderful."

He maneuvered the motorcar around the last sharp curve before the road straightened. Turning to her with a smile, he said, "You have a wonderful castle, but I noticed variations in style. The drawbridge certainly dates back further than the castle itself, and I was wondering if there is a reason for the different styles?"

"Yes, a fire burned the castle and most of the outbuildings to the ground, I believe in the mid-1800s. Only the drawbridge, the gatehouse, and part of the stables remained. Baron Friedrich von Hohenstein rebuilt the castle in the Rococo style shortly thereafter, patterning the ballroom after the famous hall of mirrors at Versailles, only on a much smaller scale, of course. My father then renovated and modernized the castle when he married my mother, and that's the history in a nutshell."

"And do you live there with your parents now?"

Marie-Louise braced herself to speak the words delicately. "My mother lives in France now, and my father . . . passed away when I was seven."

Dr. Neff reached over and covered her hand with his. "Poor little baroness."

Marie-Louise swallowed. She didn't need him to feel sorry for her. The memory of her father didn't hurt anymore, and being pitied didn't help her frame of mind right now. No, she didn't need pity, she needed help—help he couldn't give.

Requiring two hands on the steering wheel to maneuver a sharp curve, Dr. Neff withdrew his hand. After a pause, he said, "I hope you like music."

"Very much, indeed."

"What's your favorite?"

"I prefer classical, instrumental, and romantic music, but it depends on my mood at the time."

"Do you play an instrument?"

"I play the piano. And you?"

Dr. Neff laughed. "Unfortunately, I don't have any musical talent. That all went to my younger siblings, Sabine and Markus."

Marie-Louise sighed with wistful envy. "It must have been wonderful growing up with siblings. I was never around other children when I was little. Only when the Count and Countess of Wolfburg came to visit and brought their two sons, was I able to play with other children. Actually, only with Peter. Ulrich was older and didn't join in our games."

"Poor little baroness. You missed out on a lot of fun."

"It wasn't all that bad. I had Jakob, our handyman, who let me tag along and who built a treehouse for me and made other toys. And then there was Frau Becker, the cook, who spoiled me with treats."

"What about your aunt?"

Marie-Louise took a deep breath. "She raised me after my mother left, and she was also my tutor."

"She seems to be of a serious nature."

"Yes, she is. She has lived a lonely life and was saddled with a rebellious child to raise."

"She did an excellent job of it."

Marie-Louise laughed. "I'm not so sure about that. She still corrects me every chance she gets."

"It must be tiresome to always have to live according to protocol."

She rolled her eyes. "You have no idea!"

Now, he had to laugh. "Most people would gladly change places with you."

"Yes," she agreed, "because they only see the glamour connected with nobility."

They drove a couple of kilometers in silence before Marie-Louise started the conversation again. "How did you become interested in medicine?"

The doctor considered the question for a few seconds. "I guess medicine runs in our family—that is, on my mother's side. My grandfather has his own medical practice which he inherited from his father, and I probably will take over once he retires."

"What does your father do for a living?"

"He invests in businesses—big projects, such as hotels and resorts, department stores, et cetera. Now, if you'd ever consider turning Hohenstein into a resort, he'd be interested, and I would certainly point him your way."

Marie-Louise shook her head. *Never in a million years.*

At last they reached the concert hall. After Dr. Neff showed the tickets to the usher, they were directed to their seats in time to hear the musicians tune their instruments.

Dr. Neff turned to the baroness. "Are you comfortable?"

"Yes, thank you."

The first bell rang, reminding the audience to take their seats. They had to stand up to let people pass by on their way down the row. The shuffling of feet and rustling of paper soon stopped when the second bell rang, followed shortly thereafter by the third and final bell before the lights dimmed and the conductor stepped up to the podium. He turned to the audience, bowed, turned to the musicians and bowed again, before the lights went out and the first notes started.

Marie-Louise closed her eyes to let the music wash over her, trying to be in tune with the composer's mood, feeling his agony or joy or happiness and love.

During intermission, Dr. Neff directed her to the foyer where he purchased some refreshments. "Are you tired?"

"No. Why do you ask?"

"I thought you fell asleep during the concert."

She smiled. "I always close my eyes when I listen to music. I want to concentrate on every note, every nuance and feeling."

He looked at her as if he didn't quite understand what she meant. "You must really enjoy music."

"Yes, I do."

As they walked toward a settee, a photographer raised his camera and snapped a picture of them, and Marie-Louise wrinkled her brow.

Dr. Neff looked after him. "Do you want me to go after him and demand that he destroy that picture?"

"No. Don't bother. Making a big fuss would only increase his interest."

"I guess you're right."

The incident had put a damper on her enjoyment, and Marie-Louise was glad when they could return to their seats. The soft strains of Mozart's *Kleine Nachtmusik* filled the concert hall and helped her forget everything around her. She was again one with the music.

When they left the concert, they saw more cameras flashing in their direction and hurried to get away.

"These photographers can be quite annoying. Do they always follow you wherever you go?"

"Actually, this is my first encounter with any of them. It's a new experience for me and I don't like it." *All the more reason to avoid the oh-so-glamorous life of nobility!*

In a somber mood, they arrived at the castle, where the doctor helped Marie-Louise out of the vehicle and led her up the steps to the front entrance. He let go of her arm but held her hands instead. "Baroness, thank you for your company. I enjoyed this evening tremendously."

"Even with the boldness of the photographer?" Marie-Louise couldn't help but ask.

He smiled. "Even with the photographers."

He was a gentleman and quite attentive—but a little dull. But what did she expect on a first rendez-vous? He might change when they got to know each other better, if he'd ever ask her out again. At least being with him had saved her from an even duller evening with Tante Ambrosia.

"Baroness, may I call on you again?" he asked.

"Certainly. Goodnight, Dr. Neff." She turned to go inside, but he held on to her hand.

"May I kiss you goodnight?"

Marie-Louise tried to hide her astonishment at his request but leaned toward him and offered him her cheek. He gave her a small peck, squeezed her hand, and opened the door for her. "*Gute Nacht*, Baroness."

Inside, she leaned against the door. *Well, Dr. Neff is a nice man but not very exciting. We'll see what happens next. At least I'm getting to know eligible men outside the distinguished realm of aristocracy!*

She walked up the stairs to her suite and fell asleep almost as soon as she climbed into her canopied bed, the idea of having bested Ulrich her last triumphant thought.

When Marie-Louise joined her aunt for breakfast the next morning, she noticed Ambrosia's stern expression.

"*Guten Morgen,* Tante Ambrosia."

"Good morning."

The baroness couldn't figure out why her aunt looked so stern. "Are you upset about something?"

Ambrosia pressed her lips together and pointed to the newspaper on the table. Marie-Louise picked it up and froze. There, on the front page, she saw herself smiling up at the doctor, with the heading YOUNG BARONESS IN LOVE.

"How ridiculous," Marie-Louise exclaimed. "At the moment the picture was taken I was thanking the doctor for bringing me some refreshments. Nothing more. And how the photographer came to the conclusion that I was in love with the man is beyond me."

Ambrosia took a deep breath and then exhaled before she said, "I believe you."

The baroness looked at her aunt in astonishment. Never before had Ambrosia sided with her. "Thank you, Tante Ambrosia."

"Marie-Louise, you have to understand that these reporters and photographers make their living by exploiting the lives of noteworthy people. The more outlandish, scandalous, and outrageous their pictures and stories are, the better the readers like them. You have to be very careful in your actions, and if you can avoid public places, so much the better."

"I didn't know I was considered a noteworthy person."

"You're a novelty around here right now, and people want to know everything about you—what you do, who you associate with, who you fall in love with, and so on."

"That sounds horrible." Marie-Louise put both elbows on the

table and rested her chin on her hands, which earned her a stern look from Ambrosia.

"Please, don't slouch."

There she goes again. Criticizing everything I do. Can't I be myself for a change? Especially in my own home?

"You are a celebrity around here if you like it or not, and as such, you will be on display as soon as you leave the property."

"I'd rather not be a public figure."

"You can't choose because you were born to this life. Just be extra careful."

Marie-Louise wiped a hand across her forehead. "Ugh." She buttered a roll and spread black currant jam on top when her aunt cleared her throat.

"By the way, Dr. Walter will visit at four this afternoon to look at the garden and at my collection of herbs, and I would appreciate if you would be here. I plan on inviting him to dine with us."

"That's a wonderful idea, Tante Ambrosia. Of course I'll be here. He seems to be a very nice man. Does he have family?"

Ambrosia blushed. "He has grown children who have families of their own, but his wife passed away a few years ago after a bout with consumption."

"Poor man."

Ambrosia nodded, still flushed.

Jakob's knock on the door interrupted the conversation. The old man pointed to the stable. "Fräulein Baroness, the roofer's outside and wants to talk to ya."

"Thank you, Jakob, I'll be right out." Turning to Ambrosia, she worried, "Do you think he'll tell me that he won't agree to the barter?"

"I don't know. You'll just have to go and find out."

Chapter Twelve

Marie-Louise steeled herself, shoulders straight, and with a smile on her face addressed the roofer. "Herr Meissner, I'm happy to meet you at last. Your daughter told me all about her wedding plans."

"Yes, she is very excited about your offer. I came here today to look at the roof and what it will take to fix it."

"That's wonderful, Herr Meissner. As you can see, the roof is sagging in the middle; however, there are no leaks as far as we can tell."

"I'd guess that some of the beams were weak or cracked and gave way under years of snow and ice in the winter."

Marie-Louise frowned up at them. "Could it be that the fire in the mid-1800s weakened the beams?"

"That's quite possible, but I need to inspect them more closely to tell for certain."

The roofer took a notebook and pencil from his pocket and made a sketch of the roof before he went inside the stable to check the rafters. Marie-Louise and Jakob followed him. Finally, he turned to Marie-Louise. "Baroness, I will order the materials first thing tomorrow morning, and I hope that work can begin by the end of the week, if that's convenient for you."

"Absolutely. I'm delighted that you can fit this repair into your work schedule so quickly."

He winked. "My women are pressuring me."

She laughed. “I understand.”

The roofer stowed his notebook back into his pocket and walked to his truck. “My crew will probably be here Wednesday morning. I’ll let you know if there’s a delay in the delivery of the materials, but I don’t expect so. *Auf Wiedersehen,* Baroness.” He then turned to Jakob. “See you around, Jakob.”

The handyman watched him leave while he rubbed his hands, “Didn’t I tell ya, Fräulein Marie-Louise, that Heinrich’s a good lad?”

She agreed. “You were right. Herr Meissner seems to be a nice man.”

“And you’re a very smart young lady to come up with a trade for the roof. You’re doing the Hohensteins proud.”

Although she didn’t want to brag, she had to admit that the idea of the barter was quite ingenious. Let the high and mighty Count refuse his help. She, Baroness von Hohenstein, could manage without him. She didn’t need him.

At the thought of Ulrich, however, the scene in his office flashed before her mind’s eye and she felt heat steal into her cheeks. *I’d better concentrate on planning a wedding and the work that needs to be done before that event. No time to waste on thoughts of Ullie. Oh, heavens, now I even think of him in familiar terms. Blast the man!*

Back at the castle, Ambrosia was busy preparing for Dr. Walter’s visit while Marie-Louise planned the wedding. She chose appropriate music, possible decorations, the setup of the tables and the dance floor. She also had to find a photographer, or would the groom take care of that? No, she had promised that she would put on the wedding with all the bells and whistles and she was determined to keep her end of the bargain.

"Marie-Louise.” Ambrosia stood by her niece. “Dr. Walter asked if he could bring Dr. Neff along, and I told him that it would be our pleasure to have the young doctor join us. I hope you won't mind."

"Of course I don't mind."

"Good. They'll be here at four."

Marie-Louise nodded and turned back to her notes. She couldn't say that she was excited at the thought of Dr. Neff's visit. It didn't matter one way or the other. It was true that he wasn't as charming as . . . *oh, don't go there! Thinking of him puts you on dangerous ground.* However, she couldn't help herself imagining little laugh lines surrounding blue eyes and the gentle smile that was so endearing—

Stop, stop, STOP! Marie-Louise put her hands over her ears as if to shut out the memory of his laughter. *All right, that's it.* She put pencil and paper aside. *I need to go for a walk.*

She jumped up and walked out of the castle, whistling for Kaiser to accompany her. A good, brisk stroll never failed to clear her mind, and as usual it worked like a charm, until she reached the old treehouse. Immediately, her dream with the rescuing prince popped into her mind and she sat down with her head resting in her hands.

It's no use. I can't get him out of my mind. I'm glad Dr. Neff is coming this afternoon— maybe if I could get interested in him, I could erase Ulrich's memory . . . but the good doctor is a bit boring. Maybe if I tried harder to feel more for him than—

She stopped herself, laughing ruefully. *Feel more for him than what? I sound confused even to myself. I might as well let things develop naturally. Who can dictate one's heart, anyway? It's simply preposterous, and I'm crazy to think that I can force something that doesn't exist. That wouldn't be any different than forcing a noble marriage alliance.*

Life had become complicated. Not only did she have the problem of a decaying castle, but also the problem with—Ulrich.

She wished she hadn't gone to him in the first place. It would have saved her a lot of trouble.

She took a deep breath. It was time to go back. Since she couldn't solve most of her problems right that minute, she might as well concentrate on Dr. Neff's visit.

Whistling for Kaiser, she directed her steps back toward the castle, where she freshened up and then offered to set the table.

The two men arrived at four o'clock sharp, a fact that Ambrosia noted with a satisfied nod. Both men presented the ladies with bouquets of flowers and thanked them for the invitations. They conversed for a while in the parlor before Ambrosia asked them to follow her into the dining room, where the table was laid with the Meissen porcelain, heavy and ornately decorated silver, and crystal stemware, with the white damask tablecloth and floral arrangement adding to the elegant setting. Ambrosia's *chateaubriand* with *béarnaise* sauce was cooked to perfection and was very much appreciated by the guests, judging by their hearty appetite.

Dr. Walter entertained the ladies with anecdotes from his work and his life as a student, and even Dr. Neff contributed to the light conversation with a few stories of his own. After the meal, Ambrosia led the group back to the parlor and closed the dining room door, apparently to prohibit the guests from noticing the absence of staff and to guess that their hostesses were the ones to have to clear the table and wash the dishes afterwards.

Ambrosia wanted to show Dr. Walter her garden while Marie-Louise took Dr. Neff on a walk around the premises to explain the history of each building. He was especially impressed with the old carriages and climbed into them to inspect them more closely. At last, Marie-Louise gave him a tour of the castle proper with the main rooms and especially the grand ballroom.

"What a gem you have here, Baroness!" he said as he looked around.

"It needs a lot of work to bring it back to its original glory."

"Yes, but it would be fun to work on it a little at a time."

Surprised, she asked, "You really think it would be fun?"

"Yes, it would be an interesting challenge. Don't you think?"

"It would be if I had the necessary capital. Restoring Hohenstein requires a lot of money."

He agreed. "I guess so, but it would be worth it. You could start a resort or even a sanatorium—that would bring in a good profit."

"Yes, but I want the castle to be my home. And if I ever have children I want them to be raised right here at Hohenstein."

Dr. Neff nodded and smiled, seemingly pleased by her answer. "I understand."

Marie-Louise glanced over her shoulder when she heard footsteps behind them. "Oh, look, here comes Dr. Walter with my aunt. They seem to be getting on quite well with each other. I've never seen my aunt so animated."

The doctor nodded. "Dr. Walter is a very charming man, and I think he fancies your aunt."

"It looks like it, but she is very rank-conscious."

"Really?" he said.

"Yes, she's from the old order, very strict and proper."

They waited for the older couple to catch up and walked together to the conservatory.

Dr. Walter moved to the piano and smoothed his long, slender fingers over the lid. "What a beautiful instrument. Who's the musician?"

Ambrosia stood beside the doctor. "We both play. Marie-Louise is quite proficient."

Marie-Louise shook her head. "Don't let my aunt mislead you. She's an excellent musician, and also plays the flute."

Dr. Walter smiled. "And I play the violin—we should have a concert sometime. What instrument do you play, Dr. Neff?"

"Unfortunately none, but I like to listen to music."

Turning to Ambrosia, the older man asked, "What do you say, shall we have a concert someday?"

Ambrosia blushed. "That would be lovely. What type of music do you prefer to play, Dr. Walter?"

"You decide and I'll follow."

Looking from her aunt to the doctor, the baroness smiled. There surely seemed to be more than just polite interaction between those two, and she found it charming. She was drawn out of her musings, however, when Ambrosia asked, "Marie-Louise, what shall we perform? Should we have a theme?"

"How about we each pick one or two of our favorite pieces so that we can practice and then perform them?"

"That sounds like a good plan. Do you agree, Fräulein von Hohenstein?" asked the doctor.

"I'll go along with that arrangement," said Ambrosia. "Why don't we think about what we want to play, and then let the others know and start practicing? If you feel comfortable we can have our very own concert next Sunday or two Sundays from today, whichever is convenient for you."

Dr. Walter clapped his hands. "Excellent. I'll send you a note with my selection in a few days, and you can let me know what you ladies decided on."

"And I'll bring my camera and take a picture or two as my contribution to the event," said Dr. Neff.

Giving him a calculating look, Marie-Louise asked, "Are you a good photographer?"

"I'm fairly good, I think."

"What kind of pictures do you take?"

"Mostly of things that I see during my travels—nature, scenery or buildings."

She stepped closer to him. He might just be the person she

needed for the upcoming wedding. It would solve the problem of the photographer, but she had to be sure that he was up to the job. "Do you also take pictures of people and events?"

"Yes, sometimes I do."

"Have you ever taken wedding pictures?"

"No, never, but then I never had an occasion to do that."

"Would you mind trying your hand at wedding pictures?"

He scratched his head. "Whose wedding do you have in mind?"

"We're going to put on a wedding here at the castle, and I'm looking for a photographer. Would you be interested?"

"If you tell me exactly how you want the pictures to look and where you want them taken, I suppose I could do it."

Marie-Louise clapped her hands. "Wonderful. You're hired then."

He laughed. "You're a natural businesswoman, Baroness. It suits you."

His praise warmed her heart and created a feeling of friendship for him.

After the men left, Marie-Louise helped her aunt clear the table and wash the delicate dishes and stemware, all the while humming a little melody.

"You seem happy. Do you like the young doctor?"

"He is a nice man."

"He seems to be, and Dr. Walter is very fond of him."

"What about Dr. Walter? Do you like him?"

Ambrosia blushed a little. "He is a nice man," she parroted Marie-Louise and smiled.

"That's all?"

"That's all for now."

My, my, I think Ambrosia has a tendre for the good doctor. She winked at her aunt and bid her good night.

Sleep didn't come quickly because her mind was working overtime on all the events of the coming week: the new roof, the task of finding team horses for the coach ride, inspecting the coaches to find a suitable one for the wedding, and her day at the town hall. Yet, as always, the last thoughts before drifting off to sleep strayed to Ulrich. Too tired to push the memories to the back of her mind, she relived the day she had visited him in the office and found herself in his arms. Even too tired to separate reality from fantasy, she imagined him in love with her or at least having a *tendre* for her as Ambrosia assumed, and in her drowsy state this scenario didn't seem distasteful at all. She remembered his heartbeat, his lips on hers, his seductive voice . . .

A few days later, Marie-Louise heard his voice, but this time it didn't sound seductive at all. It sounded more like a command.

The grass in the moat hadn't been cut in quite some time and Jakob was replacing one of the tiles on the carriage house roof, so she decided to get the scythe and mow the grass herself. She wanted the premises to look good for the wedding, after all. The day was hot and the job harder than she had imagined. Jakob had to teach her how to use the scythe, and it took some practice before she felt comfortable with the tool.

Leaning on the handle of the scythe, she wiped perspiration off her brow when she saw Ulrich's blue Mercedes drive by. He must have seen her because the vehicle screeched to a halt, and the count reversed until he was even with her.

How dare he show his face here after what happened in his office! Doesn't he have any decency? Marie-Louise watched as he unfolded from his motorcar but felt too weary and exhausted to care how she might look or what he might think of her. Closing her eyes for a moment, she steeled herself for his reprimand and was surprised when it didn't come. Instead, he took one step closer to the moat and reached out his hand to help her up.

She ignored his gesture.

"Marie-Louise, please let me help you up."

Not sure if she wanted to leave her almost finished work and accompany him to the castle, she swung the scythe and mowed another half circle of grass. However, etiquette dictated that she welcome the Count into her home and play hostess. Hesitantly, she laid down the scythe and reached for his proffered hand. He clasped her fingers in a strong grip that sent shivers up her arm.

"Thank you," she breathed as she reached level ground, unable to say any more at the moment.

Standing on the shady side of the vehicle, she untied the silk scarf she had twisted around her head and dabbed at her temples. Perspiration trickled down her spine, and she felt hot and sticky and not at all in the mood to entertain a visitor, especially not him. Dizzy and afraid that her legs would buckle under her at any moment, she leaned against the Mercedes for support.

"Aren't you overdoing it a bit? This is no work for a dainty woman like you."

Although his voice sounded concerned, she still noticed a touch of annoyance in it and quickly glanced up to gauge his mood.

Grudgingly, she admitted, "I'm not used to hard labor, especially not in the blistering sun. From now on, I'll come out here early in the morning and again in the evening when it's not so hot."

"Why can't your handyman, what's his name, do that kind of work?"

"Because he's up on a ladder at the carriage house at the moment—and his name is Jakob."

"I see, but couldn't this job here," he motioned with his chin in the direction of the moat, "wait until your man was free to do it?"

"No," she said harsher than intended. "We have too many things to do and no time to waste any manpower—or womanpower for that matter."

He looked as if he wanted to lecture her on the unsuitability of one of her rank to be seen doing menial work, but probably thought better of it when he noticed the determined jut of her chin.

"Stubborn woman," he mumbled instead, but it sounded more like an endearment than a censure. Opening the door to help her in, he said, "We'd better get you out of this heat and give you something to drink."

"I need to finish my job first."

"Oh, no, you don't."

"It's only a little more—"

"It can wait. Just get in," he said, "I don't want you to collapse out here."

As soon as the Mercedes rumbled over the wooden bridge, he saw the new roof gleaming in the late afternoon sun and came to an abrupt stop. Hands still on the steering wheel, he stared at the unfamiliar sight for a few moments before he turned to Marie-Louise.

"I see you have a new stable roof. How did you manage that?"

Eyes closed, head resting against the firm cushion of the seat, she mumbled, "A wedding."

She heard his quick intake of breath, but he didn't say anything. Maybe he didn't deem her to be in a fit state at the moment to elaborate on the subject, and decided to wait until later for details.

Ambrosia, upon seeing her niece plopping exhaustedly into the nearest chair, wrung her hands.

"She'll be all right," Ulrich soothed, "but she needs to drink lots of water."

"Yes, of course, I'll go and get some. I always told her not to—"

Ulrich never found out what Ambrosia always told her niece, because she rushed out of the room to get the water, talking all the while. When she returned, she still carried on ". . . the reporters would have a heyday if they saw her working like a servant, looking like a bedraggled waif. We have an image to uphold. It's expected of us. Can't you talk some sense into her, Count?"

"I'm afraid not. The baroness won't listen to me, either."

"When I was young," Ambrosia lamented, "we obeyed our elders . . . we wouldn't have dared to go against their counsel."

To end Ambrosia's uncharacteristic rambling, Ulrich took the empty glass from Marie-Louise, helped her out of the chair, and shoved her gently toward the stairs. Ambrosia called after her, "Hurry and freshen up. I'll have some treats waiting."

It didn't take long before the baroness descended the curved staircase in a summery dress. She looked refreshed and very young with her hair still damp and her dark ringlets framing her face.

The count gave her an admiring look. "Your aunt told me about your successful barter with the roofer. How did you manage that?"

"Actually, I bartered with his wife and daughter. I don't think he had a chance to back out once his women were convinced."

"What a clever and resourceful woman you've turned out to be! I'm impressed."

Despite her resolve to show him the cold shoulder, she was pleased at his compliment.

His eyes, more than his words, conveyed his praise, and Marie-Louise looked away quickly to shut out the additional message she read in their azure depths. It was a message of shared intimacy, a message that brought warmth—and no doubt color—to her cheeks. He shouldn't remind her of something she wanted to forget.

To bridge the gap in conversation, she asked, "What brought you to Hohenstein today?"

"I was on my way back from a business meeting and took the scenic route when I saw someone mowing the grass by the road.

And when I looked closer, I couldn't believe what I saw: the beautiful baroness herself doing a man's job."

Marie-Louise squared her shoulders. "The job had to be done, and we don't have the means to hire help."

Ulrich leaned forward and covered her hands with his. "I appreciate your determination to restore and beautify your home and surroundings, but I'm worried that you'll do too much and jeopardize your health."

When she wanted to withdraw her hands, he squeezed them and looked deep into her eyes. "I know that it must be frustrating to see the decay and not be able to stop it for the lack of funds, and I'm sorry that I couldn't grant you a loan. One day you'll understand and hopefully forgive me."

What's there to understand? He refused to help.

Apparently reading her thoughts, he said, "My hands are tied, but if you ever need a paying job, please come to me. People with your determination and resourcefulness are invaluable in business."

She looked at him as if questioning his sanity, then replied stiffly, "Thank you for your offer, Count. I may have to take you up on it someday."

"I wish you would."

Under no circumstances would she want to work at his bank. Seeing him every day and being reminded of their intimacy every time she saw him would be pure misery. No, working for him was out of the question.

She shook her head.

When Ulrich steered the conversation toward a safer subject, she breathed a sigh of relief, but her relief was short-lived.

"How was your rendez-vous with the doctor?"

"How did you know?"

"I read the paper."

"The article was in the Wolfburg paper, too?"

Ulrich nodded. "Did you enjoy yourself?"

"Very much. The doctor is a real gentleman."

"Oh, how boring."

She glared at him and wanted to tell him that not every man was as brash as he, when she saw the twinkle in his eyes. *Drat!* He had laid a trap and she had unfailingly stepped into it, had made it clear that the doctor hadn't awakened any deeper feelings in her. It was downright annoying that he could read her like an open book.

His next question, fortunately, led back to a safer topic. "How do you like your work at the town hall? Did you have any duties to perform besides cutting the ribbon at the opening of the new hospital?"

"I'll meet with the mayor on Friday—that's the day I'm going to be at the town hall. There are a few events coming up, such as the dedication of a new school, a tour of the water treatment facility, and the opening ceremony of the annual town pageant." She waved her hand. "The mayor will explain everything when I get there. I'll even have my own office."

"Will you have a lot of contact with him?"

"I don't know," she said with a shrug, "I suppose I'll find out."

He nodded. "Naturally." A pause. "The mayor knows that he got the very best person for the job."

She scanned his features for any sign of cynicism, but his praise seemed sincere. She wagged her finger. "You're flattering me, Count."

His lips twitched. "Why so formal today, Marie-Louise? Usually you call me Ulrich . . . and at our more intimate moments, it's even Ullie."

He reached over and tucked a wayward curl behind her ear, stroking her cheek in the process. "You're lovely, Snow White, especially when your eyes shoot daggers at me." He gave her a gentle smile that warmed her heart, and she berated herself for basking in that smile.

She quickly averted her gaze and interlocked her fingers. Never knowing how to take his compliments, whether he was serious or teasing, she was more confused than ever. If he were a gentleman, he wouldn't remind her of an episode that should be as distasteful to him as it was to her. He thought he did her and the entire lot of nobility a great service by his ardent demonstration, his show of virility. It didn't prove anything to her except that the estimable Count Wolfburg didn't live by the code of conduct displayed in his office. *Ha*, she scoffed while she suppressed the softening of her own wayward heart.

Knowing how inexperienced in love-matters she was, he had counted on her total surrender. She gnawed on her lower lip. No, he didn't expect her total surrender. Of course not. He didn't want her to become infatuated with him since he had no intention of burdening himself with her, as his refusal for the loan showed.

She didn't understand him. Yes, he had wanted to show her that the men of her own rank were made of flesh and blood . . . and passion, and she wondered if his caresses had been a show of passion or just—skill? They certainly didn't have anything to do with love, and that thought hurt deep down for some reason.

She tossed her head and tried to rid herself of the all too vivid memory of the incident, but this proved hard with him sitting across from her. She drew a shaky breath, all the while aware of his scrutiny.

When Ambrosia entered the room, she looked from one to the other and pursed her lips but didn't say anything.

Shortly thereafter, the count departed and left Marie-Louise in a confusion of irrational emotions. She wished he wouldn't come visiting, knowing full well how uncomfortable his presence made her feel. If they could go back to the way they had been, she would have looked forward to these visits as welcome interruptions to her otherwise dull life. But, of course, their relationship could never be the same again. He had destroyed her trust.

She sighed. Things weren't as clear-cut as she wished them to be. To be honest, she had to admit that she had participated in his kisses, maybe not willingly at first, but certainly driven by curiosity. That meant that she had participated of her own free will and carried at least part of the blame.

And now she reaped the consequences of her actions. Whenever he looked at her with that half-smile, her heart performed somersaults while a treacherous heat flooded her cheeks. It felt as if her body welcomed him whenever he was near, and she questioned if her body would ever stop reacting to him in that way. She had played with fire and got burned.

Plagued by self-accusations, she stormed outside and immersed herself in hard, physical labor. Working until she felt drained seemed to be the only way to forget the count and to still her treacherous emotions. Bone weary, she'd fall asleep after an exhausting day as soon as her head hit the pillow, eliminating the unwelcome thoughts. Even her bad dreams wouldn't haunt her then.

Chapter Thirteen

The time had come to decide which carriage to choose for the wedding procession, so Jakob maneuvered the three coaches out of the carriage house and into the courtyard.

Marie-Louise tried the door to the *coupe*, and it opened with a squeak. Nothing that a few drops of oil wouldn't cure. Next, she pulled on the leather strap before she eased the window down between the door and its panel. The strap showed holes like a belt that could be slipped over a brass notch to secure the window at various stages. A brass handle accommodated easy opening and closing.

The interior, although somewhat faded, didn't give cause for alarm. The *coupe* was a charming vehicle and would have to do if the others proved irreparable.

The other two coaches were bigger and could seat the flower girls and ring-bearer as well as the bride and groom, and would most ideally fit Marie-Louise's vision when she had made the barter.

The *landau*, a good-looking carriage, was her favorite. It was heavy and sported two calash tops that locked together in the center and could be let down in pleasant weather. It seated six to eight passengers and would do very well in nice as well as inclement weather, but when she tried to pull the two folding tops up, she saw cracks in the black leather material. It would be acceptable if the weather promised to be beautiful, but who could tell for sure beforehand? The upholstery, plush burgundy velvet, was covered with dust but looked perfect otherwise.

The last coach she inspected was a *berlin*, heavier built than the *landau* with its roof forming an integral part of the body, and the interior spacious enough to seat six to eight passengers. The upholstery, threadbare and shiny on the seat, was passable. Maybe she could throw a nice blanket over it.

Marie-Louise stood back, hands on hips, head tilted to one side as she assessed the carriage. Not too bad. If the brass hardware was polished to a shine, the windows sparkling clean, and the *crème*-colored paint touched up here and there, it would look quite magnificent. The family crest with the howling wolf on a mountain peak needed a little revitalizing, but she felt she could do that easily enough. As a matter of fact, she looked forward to the task.

The work, however, proved more difficult than she had imagined. She couldn't get the exact shade of paint—it was close enough but not perfect. The touch-up spots appeared dull against the highly lacquered finish of the vehicle, and not even the shellac she used afterwards could compete with the glow of the old paint.

With a deep breath and raised eyebrows, Marie-Louise acknowledged defeat. She walked several paces away and looked at her work from a distance. Then she moved her head from side to side to consider the effect. Well, the flaws couldn't be seen from where she stood, but knowing it wasn't perfect bothered her.

Squinting, she envisioned the coach with the proposed floral decorations. If she draped a garland of fir boughs studded with flowers from the front in swags to the sides and over the door, she would be able to conceal most of the patches. Yes, that should do. She clapped her hands.

Now, she needed Jakob to look over the harnesses to see if they were in good order. The leather may have become brittle over the years and torn in places, but the old man could treat it with the saddle soap she had discovered in the stable the other day. He would also polish the silver ornamentation on the harnesses. Oh, she could see it all in her mind's eye: a proud equipage in the old tradition.

The task of finding a team to draw the coach, however, proved a little more difficult. She had sent Jakob to some of the teamsters in town to see if anybody would lend them some horses. Because the wedding was scheduled for a Saturday, which was the busiest day of the week for the teamsters, he could only come up with two horses, both from different owners.

When Marie-Louise saw the animals, her heart sank. The horses were not exactly pure-breds, and together they looked anything but a team. The first horse stood tall and lean with a barrel chest, and the second one was short, stout, and heavy.

Jakob scratched his head. "Fräulein Marie-Louise, d'ya think we ought to use them ugly horses?"

"What other options do we have?" She hung her head. It wasn't what she had envisioned, and not what the roofer's family would expect.

"I hope ya know how hideous these beasts will look drawing a coach."

She nodded. "Yes, I'm well aware of it, and I dread the day when we try them out."

The dreaded day arrived when Jakob hitched the horses to the coach. The old man looked at Marie-Louise, and she at him, and they both burst out laughing. It was too funny a sight.

"Well, we'd better bring them together and find out how they'll do," Marie-Louise said finally.

The animals were quite docile and moved to the side or backwards as Jakob coaxed them to do, but the moment they stood side by side, their eyes took on a wild look and they both balked, one pulling to one side and the other in the opposite direction.

"Whoa, whoa!" Jakob grabbed the reins close to the horses' heads to keep them under control, but it was still hard to slip the bit into their mouths and the leather gear over their heads, and it required more patience than Marie-Louise thought she could muster. To top it all off, Kaiser sprang around the group with loud, excited barks which confused the beasts even more, and it wasn't until Marie-Louise locked him in the stable that they managed to complete the task.

The horses still looked wildly around as if seeking an escape, and Jakob had to hold them at bay while Marie-Louise climbed onto the driver's seat and took the reins. Her heart gave a dull thud and a feeling close to fear overcame her. *What if . . . ? Nonsense.* Although it had been quite some years since she had driven a team, she hadn't forgotten how to do it. She only needed to concentrate. Like riding a horse, one never forgot how to drive a team once learned.

Her father had taught her the art of driving when she was about six years old. They would take off on a Saturday, usually in the *coupe*, and explore the countryside. One time, her father had taken her to a driver's competition. That had been a fun event. The obstacle course led through muddy areas, over rough terrain, around sharp corners, through dense forests, swamps, and over sandy stretches. All kinds of vehicles were allowed in the competition, not only coaches but also hay wagons and other farm transports drawn by horses.

"Aren't you going to try it, Fräulein Marie-Louise?"

Blinking, she pushed the memories to the back of her mind and focused once more on the task at hand. With a click of her tongue and a slight touch with the reins on the horses' backs, she willed them to move. Both animals lurched forward but not at the same time, which resulted only in a momentary wobbling of the coach and then—nothing. The horses, probably shocked at the result, stood motionless.

Marie-Louise repeated the procedure. Again the same result. She was sure both reins had touched the animals at the exact same moment. What was wrong? Again. This time the language of the reins was a bit more pronounced. Yet, the same outcome.

"Jakob, please fetch the riding crop from the peg by the stable door. Maybe that'll do the trick."

Marie-Louise took the crop. Apparently the beasts were used to the whip because they hardly flicked their ears when touched.

Maybe a little bribery was in order. Jakob hung a sack of oats around each horse's neck, and immediately they dug in and munched away as if they had no worry in the world.

Marie-Louise climbed down from her lofty seat, gave the horses a sideways glance, and muttered under her breath, "Stupid creatures."

After the horses had their fill and also some water, she tried again. They were willing, but somehow, the outcome was still the same.

With her elbows propped on her knees, her chin resting on her hands, Marie-Louise felt helpless. She had tried all the tricks she knew. What more could she possibly do?

She sat motionless for a moment until she felt a tremor ripple down her spine. Somebody was watching her. Heaven knew she didn't need an audience! Reluctantly, she turned to look over her shoulder and sucked in her breath. Not twenty meters away, she saw Ulrich, who leaned against the stable wall, arms crossed over his chest, and was obviously enjoying the situation, judging by the amused twitch of his mouth.

The riding crop slipped out of her hand. Why did he have to come to Hohenstein today of all days? Too occupied with the horses, she hadn't heard him drive up.

Marie-Louise wished the ground would open up and swallow her—coach, horses, and all. The situation was embarrassing enough without an audience, especially one that seemed to derive such great diversion from the spectacle and caused every nerve in her body to tingle.

Blast the man! His frequent visits to Hohenstein puzzled her, and she wished him anywhere but there. Perhaps he delighted in seeing her restoration projects fail. No, she corrected herself. Whatever his faults might be, spite wasn't one of them.

His visits were more likely designed to remind her of their potent body chemistries. *Ha!* Never in a million years would she fall in love with him. Love had not been on his mind when he had kissed her, and neither had it been on hers. She promised herself that love would be the only motivation that would cause her to one day walk down the aisle to share her life with the man of her dreams—but that man certainly wasn't going to be Ulrich!

She watched as he detached himself from the wall and strolled toward her, hands in his pockets, a quirk at the corner of his mouth.

That's just what I need, she thought as she dragged her mind away from her own personal feelings and back to the problem at hand, *someone to make fun of this nerve-racking horse business.*

Steeling herself for the certain mockery, she tossed her head and would try one more time to get the horses moving. And this time, she would succeed!

Closing her eyes, she sent a prayer heavenward. *Please, make it work while he looks on.* With a quick flick of her wrists, she touched the reins to the horses' backs. Both animals moved at the exact same time, but the result still remained the same. Exasperated, she wiped a hand across her brow and dropped the reins. She felt like screaming, but instead, clenched her fists until her knuckles showed white.

Suddenly, she heard the sound of muffled laughter and sat bolt upright. The offending noise didn't come from the count's direction as expected, nor was it a masculine sound. Deliberately slow, Marie-Louise turned and couldn't believe what she saw. Ambrosia stood at the top of the stairs with a handkerchief pressed to her mouth to stifle the laughter.

Perplexed more about her aunt's unusual show of merriment than at her audacity to laugh, Marie-Louise glared at the older woman, which only resulted in another bout of laughter.

Incensed, she looked from her aunt to the count, who tried to suppress his own mirth.

After she gained some semblance of normalcy, Ambrosia approached the group and, patting one horse's flank, said, "Poor animals."

"What do you mean, *poor animals*?" Marie-Louise bristled. She felt *she,* and not the animals ought to be pitied.

"They look hilarious," Ambrosia choked, "one tall and barrel-chested, and the other small and stocky." Sobering, she said, "You're not serious about using them."

When Marie-Louise gave a curt nod, Ambrosia drew a sharp breath. She looked in the count's direction, but he had walked around the carriage to inspect the wheels.

"You'll make us the laughing stock of the entire county," Ambrosia said. "Look at them! What a mismatch!"

"What would you have me do?" snapped Marie-Louise, "Pull the coach myself? I promised the bride a coach ride, and a coach ride she'll get."

Immediately, she regretted her waspish retort when she saw her aunt's sad eyes. *Tante Ambrosia must be getting sentimental in her old age*, she thought. She had never seen her being anything but stern and felt at a loss with this new development. Dealing with a strict aunt—one, Marie-Louise thought, devoid of any emotion except maybe hurt pride—had become almost second nature to her. She knew exactly what to expect when dealing with her, and how to handle her, but a sad Ambrosia made her feel guilty.

"I'm sorry," she mumbled and turned her attention to the count, who tested the harnesses, and bent to check the shaft. He didn't have to examine everything so closely; she knew how to ready a coach.

"Here's the problem," he said and stepped back to stand beside the driver's seat. "Although the animals move at the same time, they don't hit the shaft at the same time because the big one is barrel-chested and hits the shaft before the small one does. Come and see for yourself."

She ignored his outstretched hand, swung one leg over the side of the coach, and started to clamber down with her back toward him, uncomfortably aware of his eyes on her every move. She gritted her teeth and tried to descend as gracefully as the high steps would allow, when all of a sudden she felt his hands spanning her waist. Her heart skipped a beat at the touch before it pounded with accelerated force against her ribs and generated an overabundance of heat she could feel rising to her cheeks.

Before she had time to consider whether or not she should refuse his help, he lifted her up in the air and set her down on level ground where he propelled her toward the horses' heads. Pointing to the shaft he said, "It won't work. You might as well give up."

Give up? Never!

She pressed her lips together and gave him a sideways glance. Of all people, why did he have to be here to witness such an embarrassing moment in her life and then suggest she give up the promised coach ride? She closed her eyes for a moment and wished she could wake up to find out that the entire episode had been a bad dream.

Trying to hide her frustration, she asked in a tight voice, "What do you suggest?"

"You need to get rid of the horses."

"Get rid of the horses?" she almost shouted, "Are you—?" but stopped short before the word *mad* slipped out. Calling the count mad wouldn't do at all. Her aunt would swoon for sure at her audacity, although Ulrich's suggestion was nothing but pure insanity.

"Do you have any idea how to make these horses work together, Jakob?" she asked, glad to be able to turn her attention away from the count.

"Yes, I think I got the solution . . ." he stroked his stubbled chin, ". . . if we bring the small horse forward a little, like so . . ."

He fidgeted with the leather straps and moved the horses until he positioned them to his satisfaction. "Now try it again," he encouraged.

With a triumphant look in the count's direction, Marie-Louise swung up onto the seat, tucked a strand of hair behind her ear, and took the reins. A flick of her wrists set the horses in motion. The coach rocked from side to side, gave a lurch, and then wobbled forward unsteadily.

Frustrated, Marie-Louise shook her head, halted the equipage, and climbed down. "So much for that," she muttered and glared at the horses as if to blame them for the rocky ride.

After an ominous silence, Ambrosia suggested, "Maybe the bride and groom could use the coach as a backdrop for a photograph."

"No."

"Will you give up the idea with the coach altogether, then?"

"No."

Ambrosia wrung her hands. "What are you going to do? You can't use these horses. They look utterly ridiculous."

"They're the only ones I've got," Marie-Louise mumbled under her breath.

"Think of—"

Unable to bear her aunt's tirades another moment, Marie-Louise handed Jakob the whip, nodded a curt apology in Ulrich's direction, and headed for the castle. She realized how inexcusable her behavior must appear to the count, almost running away, but right now she needed a few minutes to calm herself. If she'd ever felt like throwing something, it was now.

As soon as she closed the door behind her, she let out an angry growl and rushed with long strides toward the piano. Opening the lid, she hammered at some keys, loud and wild. Pretty soon, the notes crescendoed into a tune of Wagnerian proportions, an outcry of her frustration.

Spent, she finally dropped her hands into her lap and closed her eyes. She knew she ought to go outside and apologize for her behavior, but what could she say? She had not only behaved in an inappropriate manner by walking away from the head of the House of Wolfburg, but had probably cut her aunt to the core with her harsh words. She hung her head.

She didn't know how long she sat there on the piano bench when she felt a hand on her shoulder and another one stroking her hair. She hadn't heard anybody approaching but had probably been too annoyed to listen for any sounds anyway.

She held her breath for a moment as the caress continued. It couldn't possibly be him! He wouldn't dare! No. She would have sensed his presence.

She turned, and what she saw shocked her more than the thought of Ulrich. Instead of a pair of pant legs, she saw Ambrosia' skirt. She felt a lump forming in her throat and tears stinging her eyes.

What was wrong with her aunt today? She was acting completely out of character, and Marie-Louise didn't know how to deal with this new Ambrosia. She had never seen her laugh as heartily as she had out in the courtyard. Even stranger than her merriment was her attempt now to give comfort—another first. Instead of the expected lecture, her aunt was showing her kindness.

"I-I'm sorry I behaved so badly," she choked.

"You were upset."

"Yes, but I should have controlled my temper."

"The Count will understand."

Marie-Louise jumped up. "Oh, heavens!" she groaned. "I forgot all about him. We'll have to offer him some refreshments."

She started to rush out of the room, but Ambrosia detained her. "He's gone."

"Gone?"

"Yes."

"Was he very upset?"

"I don't think so. He had a good laugh."

And so did you, Marie-Louise remembered, but kept it to herself. After a moment, another thought struck her. "Why did Ulrich come to Hohenstein, anyway? Certainly not to witness the fiasco with the horses?"

"No, of course not. He dropped off a health insurance plan for your signature."

When Marie-Louise raised a questioning eyebrow, Ambrosia hastened to explain, "He added you to the Wolfburg plan."

"Do I need health insurance? I'm hardly ever sick."

Ambrosia walked to the settee. "You never know what will happen in the future—you may fall off a ladder and break a leg with all the work you're doing around here. You need to be insured, believe me—"

"But I don't have the money for the premiums."

Ambrosia held up her hand. "You don't have to worry about that. The Count pays that from the family fund for all the Wolfburg clan. As a matter of fact, I believe the Wolfburgs own the insurance company, or at least have a large stake in it."

Why am I not surprised? If Ulrich could afford to pay health insurance for all the members of the family, he surely could have lent her some money. It wasn't as if she would have run off with it—unless he had plans for Hohenstein . . .

At the moment, she wasn't interested in health insurance or Ulrich's secret agenda because she had weightier matters to consider. First and foremost, she had to make the horses walk in unison or else the idea of the coach ride would have to be abandoned, a move she desperately wanted to avoid. Maybe Jakob could start training the animals right away . . .

" . . . The insurance even covers a stay at a sanatorium after a severe illness."

Marie-Louise had been so engrossed in the problem with the animals that she hadn't been listening to Tante Ambrosia's elucidations. In order to cover her lack of concentration, she said, "The policy sounds very good, indeed, and I'm glad that the Count is so generous toward the members of his family." She frowned. "I still can't understand why he went out of his way to bring me the insurance forms instead of mailing them?"

Ambrosia produced one of her rare smiles. "Have you ever considered that he might have a *tendre* for you?"

"Of course not!" Marie-Louise said quickly—too quickly, and lowered her head so that her aunt wouldn't see the color she felt rising to her cheeks.

Not noticing her niece's unwillingness to dwell on the subject, Ambrosia continued, "The Count has visited Hohenstein several times since you arrived, but has never visited *me*."

"That's because I had asked him for a loan to repair the stable roof, and he wanted to see for himself if the buildings were in as bad a shape as I had described them."

"You asked him for money? Marie-Louise, you can't be serious!"

"I only asked him for an advance of my inheritance, and when he said he couldn't do that, I suggested that he grant me a loan, that's all."

Ambrosia wrung her hands. "That's a total outrage, and I wish you had confided in me before you rushed headlong into such an embarrassing scenario."

Well, it turned out to be an embarrassing scenario, but not the way you imagine it. Aloud she said, "Well, that's water under the bridge because he refused the loan, but I guess he still wanted to see the decay for himself."

"I didn't see him inspect any of the buildings, but I saw him paying ardent attention to you."

Marie-Louise's cheeks grew hotter and she turned away from her aunt, pretending to pluck the wilted leaves off a potted plant. She didn't want Ambrosia to suspect any more than she already did, and wished that her aunt would drop the subject.

No such luck. Ambrosia evidently felt a need to steer her in the right direction. "You couldn't wish for a better match than Count Wolfburg. Of course, you'll have to encourage him a little, and above all, don't act so disrespectfully toward him. He needs a wife of impeccable breeding."

"I'm not interested in marriage." *And especially not marriage with him.*

"Don't waste your time daydreaming. A catch like the count comes along only once in a lifetime."

"I can't marry anybody I don't love."

"Love is a very overrated emotion in my estimation. Respect lasts a lot longer. Besides, love may come with courtship. Give it a chance."

I don't want to give it a chance—and I never will!

Chapter Fourteen

Wanting to steer her aunt's thoughts away from her matchmaking scheme, Marie-Louise asked, "Why did you never marry?"

As soon as she saw her aunt's lips tighten she realized how inappropriate her question had been. Ambrosia would turn into the stern disciplinarian again with a lecture on how a lady of her breeding should or should not behave, and Marie-Louise looked heavenward to steel herself for the unavoidable.

It didn't come. After what seemed an eternity, her aunt spoke in a dry, matter-of-fact voice, "I was engaged to be married to the most handsome officer in Kaiser Wilhelm's army, Friedrich von Hardt, but a few months before the wedding, he was wounded in a routine drill. A few weeks later, he died of complications."

Silence. Ambrosia rested her hands in her lap but didn't look up.

Finally, Marie-Louise whispered, "Oh, Tante Ambrosia, I'm so sorry."

"I'm fine. The memory doesn't hurt anymore." Hands folded in her lap, the older woman didn't look up.

Not knowing how to comfort her aunt, Marie-Louise finally said, "You were so young then. Didn't you find another man you wanted to marry?"

"No. I wanted to be loyal to Friedrich."

"Be loyal to Friedrich? Do you think he would have wanted you to spend the rest of your life alone?"

"I don't know. All I know is that I loved him, and I wanted to preserve this love. As the years went by, however, the memory dimmed, and now my love is so far in the past that I have a hard time even remembering it. Isn't that sad?"

The baroness dabbed at her eyes. "I think it's natural. If you have a love in your heart and nobody to give it to or to share it with, it shrivels and dies."

"Yes, that's what happened." As if to herself, Ambrosia added, "If it wasn't for his picture on my nightstand I'd have trouble even remembering him."

Marie-Louise could only nod. The lump in her throat wouldn't go away. Poor Tante Ambrosia. She was such a good-looking woman and had wasted her best years at Hohenstein caring for her niece.

Ambrosia got up and smoothed her skirt. "I'd better get started on dinner, and you ought to make a decision about those sorry horses. They're really a discredit to Hohenstein and would in no way serve the image you want to present. Think about it. If you want to turn castle weddings into a profitable business, you cannot use these rough-looking farm horses."

After her aunt left the room, Marie-Louise lowered herself onto the settee. Elbows on her knees, head buried in her hands, she considered what Ambrosia had said. Of course, she was right. The horses looked ridiculous, but she had promised the bride a coach ride and she would not renege.

Perhaps she could take her aunt's suggestion and use the coach in the wedding picture with the castle as backdrop. It wouldn't be a coach ride, but might be the best she could offer.

She sighed. She'd have to go to the roofer's family and explain her predicament, hoping that they'd understand the situation and go along with her suggestion.

She wiped a hand across her brow. All her energy seemed to have dissipated, and she felt old and weighed down with the burden of her inherent responsibilities. Perhaps she could tackle the problem tomorrow. Yes, tomorrow she'd think about it. She didn't want to face another setback today.

The next day dawned, a day that she would never forget as long as she lived.

They had just sat down to breakfast when Jakob pounded on the door. "Baroness! Baroness!"

Marie-Louise jumped up, alarmed, envisioning all kinds of mishaps. What could have gone wrong now? Did the horses escape? She rushed into the vestibule, followed by Ambrosia.

There stood the old handyman, grinning from ear to ear, eyes flashing, face flushed. He pointed to the door. "Ya have to come and see!"

"What, Jakob? What is it? The horses?"

He nodded—too exuberant to speak.

"You got them to move as a team?"

He shook his head.

"No?"

"Come and see."

At first, she only saw a big contraption parked in the middle of the courtyard. Not comprehending, she looked from Jakob to Tante Ambrosia, and back to Jakob.

"Come," he said again and motioned for the two women to follow him.

As soon as she saw the horse trailer hitched to the contraption, she stopped and reached for Ambrosia's hand. Off to the side whinnied a pair of perfectly matched horses, their glossy, rust-colored coats gleamed in the morning sun. As in a trance, she walked over to them and gently stroked their necks. What a difference from the burly horses they had stabled!

Marie-Louise knew who had sent them without having to look for the Wolfburg coat-of-arms on the side of the trailer.

"Some prime horseflesh, them two," commented Jakob, and Ambrosia nodded.

A discreet shuffling of feet drew Marie-Louise's attention to a man waiting at the trailer whom she hadn't noticed before. He stepped forward, bowed, and handed her a letter.

"Count Wolfburg sends his regards. He would've come himself but had a previous engagement. I'm Fritz, the groom, and I'm to hitch the horses to the coach and take 'em for a spin to see if they perform to your high expectations."

No sooner had the man uttered the last two words than Marie-Louise fell into a coughing spasm. One look at her aunt with a handkerchief pressed to her mouth sent her fleeing to the sanctity of the stable where she laughed until her sides hurt.

Wiping the tears from her eyes, she plopped onto the nearest bale of hay and wondered if Ulrich had actually instructed the groom to mention her *high expectations*, or if Fritz had inadvertently used this phrase. High expectations, indeed! That was the overstatement of the century. After being prepared to make do with two misfit farm horses, Ulrich knew that her expectations were lower than low.

She sobered. It was mighty generous of him to let her use this beautiful pair for the wedding so that she didn't have to renege on her promise and could drive the bride and groom in style to the church. Ambrosia had been right—the farm horses would have made her the laughing stock of the county—and Ulrich knew that, too. Still, he didn't have to send his team unless he feared that showing up with the heavy work horses would reflect negatively upon his family or the whole lot of the nobility as well.

Right now she didn't want to think negative thoughts. Things were looking up! Had Ulrich been here, she'd probably have embraced him, despite her resentment of him and his previous actions.

Reading Ulrich's letter, she rejoiced at his suggestion to keep the horses at Hohenstein for the time being and was more than willing to exercise them every day. Fritz would be available to drive them for the wedding.

At that moment, her aunt entered the stable to look for her. "I think it's very generous of the count to send his team."

"He's even letting us keep the horses here at Hohenstein for some time," beamed Marie-Louise.

"That's very noble of him. Maybe he thinks that you'll have more weddings in the future."

Marie-Louise read the letter one more time and wrinkled her brow. "He won't let me drive the team, though, except for my own pleasure."

"Very sensible of him."

"I'm a good driver," Marie-Louise argued, then amended, "at least, I used to be."

"That doesn't have anything to do with it. The reason he doesn't want you to drive the coach is simply that he wants to protect you from gossip and scandal mongers."

"Gossip? Scandal mongers?" Marie-Louise wrinkled her brow.

"What do you think would happen if the newspaper people found out that the Baroness von Hohenstein is driving a coach to earn money? They'd cling to you like vines, exploiting every facet of your life to satisfy their readers' curiosity and cater to their never ending thirst for scandal."

The baroness hung her head. "I guess you're right. I hadn't thought of that."

"We're always in the limelight and have to be very careful what we do and how it will come across. People look up to us. They put us on pedestals and want us to stay there and act our part. If we don't, their fairytale is shattered, and they don't take kindly to that."

When Marie-Louise didn't respond, Ambrosia turned to leave the stable. On a livelier note, she said, "Let's go and see if Fritz has harnessed the horses yet."

They stepped out into the sunlight as the groom tightened the last strap, and Marie-Louise agreed to accompany him on a test run. One click of his tongue and the beautiful pair moved in unison. Slow at first, they circled the cobbled yard before they headed for the open road where Fritz constantly instructed her on how to handle a right curve, a sharp left one, or how to *change the tempo* without any bumpy interludes.

When they had almost reached town, Fritz handed her the reins. A little shaky at first, she rapidly gained confidence and handled the horses quite well, which earned her Fritz' praise. Despite her prowess, however, she felt relieved to know that he would come to Hohenstein to drive the bride and groom on their wedding day.

Marie-Louise was so elated about the favorable turn of events that she could sing and dance all day long. Every time she looked across the courtyard, she had to pinch herself to make sure the new stable roof was real and not a dream, and that the horses in the stable were there to be hitched to the coach that would take the bride and groom to their wedding ceremony.

In these same high spirits, the baroness reported for work at the town hall Friday morning, where the mayor was already waiting to welcome her. Shaking her hand vigorously, he said with a smile, "*Guten Morgen,* Baroness. I'm so happy to welcome you on your first regular day of work for the Town of Hohenstein."

"Thank you, Herr Bürgermeister. I'm eager to learn my job."

"First of all, I want to introduce you to our staff. If you would, please follow me."

They went from office to office, where Marie-Louise shook hands and exchanged a few pleasantries with each person—or, not so much exchanged as gave, since she was the only one talking because the others were too awed to utter coherent sentences.

The introductions over, the mayor showed her to her office which was across the hall from his own and where she made herself at home. He brought her a list of upcoming events together with the appropriate files containing the information relative to each occasion, and pointed out certain issues that needed particular attention.

"If you have any questions, please feel free to ask me or my secretary. We'll be more than happy to help you in any way we can."

The mayor stepped closer and lowered his voice. "Baroness, I am concerned about the problem with your stable roof. I have been lying awake at night thinking of how to help you, but nothing came to mind. Were you able to come up with a solution?"

"Thank you for your concern, Herr Bürgermeister," she smiled. "Yes, thank goodness, we already have a new stable roof. I was able to make a deal with the roofer."

"Bravo, Baroness, my compliments! You're a formidable business woman, and the town of Hohenstein is lucky to have you as its patroness."

"Thank you, Herr Bürgermeister. I can't tell you how relieved I am that this problem is solved."

"I can imagine, and I'm happy for you."

She smiled, and the mayor left the office.

Later that afternoon on her way home, she wondered how Ulrich spent his time away from the bank. Would he invite ladies to the theater or to a ball, and what kind of women did he prefer, and did he kiss them the way he had kissed her? At that thought she gingerly feathered a finger across her lips and immediately felt a treacherous quiver ripple down her spine. *Stop it! Stop it right now! Remember, you loathe him for his ungentlemanly behavior!*

Well, no, I don't loathe him, I loathe his behavior. He *would be all right.*

All thoughts of the count were put aside when, upon her arrival at the castle, Tante Ambrosia reminded her that they had to practice their music for Sunday's concert. She showed her niece a list of the music Dr. Walter had suggested.

"Did Dr. Walter come up with this selection all by himself?"

Ambrosia's cheeks took on a rosy glow, "Actually, we worked on it together."

Marie-Louise raised an eyebrow, "Did he come here to discuss the concert?"

Her aunt looked down at her shoes before she faced the baroness and confessed, "Dr. Walter invited me to lunch, and that's where we decided what pieces were fun and not too time-consuming to practice, because they're so well known."

"Aha, I see. Now, then, let's look at the list. Johann Pachelbel's *Canon in D.*" Marie-Louise thought for a moment, and then agreed that it was a good choice because all three instruments could participate. She glanced at the list again and smiled, "I like the next two selections, Rimsky-Korsakov's *Flight of the Bumblebee* and Chopin's *Minute Waltz*, but do you think that the good doctor is up to these two fast-paced pieces?"

"It's my understanding that he's quite the virtuoso on his instrument. As a matter of fact, he wanted to study music when he was young, but his parents decided that he should study something that would pay the bills instead of becoming a poor musician. And that's why he studied medicine."

"You seem to know quite a bit about the doctor. It must have been an interesting lunch meeting."

Ambrosia blushed again. "He's a very entertaining conversationalist," and when she thought that her niece might misunderstand, she explained, ". . . that doesn't mean that he only speaks of himself. He's also a good listener." After a short pause and with some trepidation, she wanted to know, "Do you think it's wrong of me to enjoy his company, the company of a commoner?"

"No, I don't think it's wrong at all. I'm glad that you're happy when you're with him."

Ambrosia nodded and smiled. "It's very generous of you to say so, especially when I have always been so adamant that you should not mingle with commoners, and now I find myself doing what I have condemned before. I have to say, however, that my case is still somewhat different than yours. Titled nobility should not associate with commoners, at least not to the point of getting seriously involved. I, on the other hand, don't hold a title and therefore am not interesting enough for the general public. I enjoy a little more freedom and know that I won't be pursued by the reporters, nor will my actions be discussed in the local paper, unless, of course, I make a spectacle of myself."

Marie-Louise asked, "Why haven't I heard you say anything about my friendship with Dr. Neff, then?"

"A friendship can be tolerated, but beware that you don't develop any romantic feelings."

"How can you say that when you told me not too long ago that love comes with courtship if given a chance? Aren't you worried that I might develop romantic feelings toward Dr. Neff?"

Ambrosia looked at her niece and smiled. "I think your feelings are already attached elsewhere."

Marie-Louise stared at her aunt. "What do you mean, attached elsewhere?"

Ambrosia smiled but didn't elaborate, and the baroness fumed. *She probably thinks of Ulrich, her favorite subject.* Aloud, she said, "I think you'll be disappointed on that score."

"We'll see," Ambrosia said and smiled.

After dinner, the two women practiced their music, and every time they had a spare moment. Ambrosia was satisfied with their progress and voiced one of her rare compliments, "We sound good, and I think Dr. Walter will be pleased. You have developed into quite a good pianist, Marie-Louise."

"Thank you, Tante Ambrosia. It's fun to make music together."

"Yes, it also gives me great pleasure. I had to play by myself for so many years, and it feels good to finally have accompaniment."

The two women prepared the conservatory for the concert, propped open the lid of the pianoforte, arranged the music stands so that all the musicians could see each other, and moved a comfortable settee to conceal a bare spot in the carpet. A vase with fresh flowers on a side table put the finishing touch to the setting.

They were ready for the guests when they heard Dr. Walter's motorcar pull up to the front steps, and shortly thereafter, both doctors entered the castle. The older man set his violin case down, took out his instrument, and placed it on top of the pianoforte.

After a period of light conversation, the musicians settled down to business. Dr. Walter tuned his instrument and Marie-Louise positioned the piano bench while Ambrosia fingered her flute, ran her tongue over her lips, and tried the mouthpiece. Then she nodded and the music started.

Dr. Walter impressed both women with his proficiency with the violin, and proved that he had no problem whatsoever keeping up with his hostesses.

Poor Dr. Neff, on the other hand, had a hard time staying awake. Every so often his chin would drop to his chest and he would wake up with a start and open his eyes wide, but after a few moments the process would repeat itself.

The first piece over, Dr. Walter explained, "Dr. Neff was on call last night. Usually not much happens at night and the doctors can sleep in the doctors' lounge, but there was an emergency and he had to perform an appendectomy, which robbed him of several hours of sleep. On top of that, he was on duty today and now he can't keep his eyes open. I suggested that he stay home and go to bed, but he insisted on coming."

"Should we let him sleep in one of our guest rooms?" asked Ambrosia.

Dr. Walter shook his head, "As long as he doesn't disturb us by snoring, he should be all right here on the settee."

Marie-Louise looked over her shoulder at Dr. Neff. *I suppose the life of a doctor isn't all glamour and prestige. Working twenty-four hours without sleep can't be easy. I wonder how often they have to work long hours like that.*

The concert over, Ambrosia served refreshments, and Dr. Neff woke up. "What did I miss?"

"Just about the entire concert," answered his superior with a smile, and the young doctor looked embarrassed.

"Forgive me," he apologized, "I had a rough night last night and a busy day today."

"Yes, Dr. Walter told us about the emergency surgery. We understand," soothed Ambrosia, and Marie-Louise nodded and offered him the tray.

She wanted so much to feel something, anything, for the young man but couldn't even feel the slightest tingling of her skin or fluttering of the heart. If Ulrich would have sat on the settee, she probably wouldn't have been able to concentrate on the music at all because he would have made every fiber in her body respond to his nearness. She closed her eyes for a second and imagined his golden eyelashes, his gentle smile and twinkling eyes, then scolded herself. *Stop daydreaming and get back to reality.*

She produced a smile for Dr. Neff, "Please have some refreshments. They'll keep you awake until you get home."

"I feel so bad that I dozed off. I was so looking forward to the concert, and now I missed almost all of it."

"There'll be others," she promised, "when you don't come here after a twenty-four hour call of duty."

"That would be nice and much appreciated."

At that moment, Dr. Walter turned to him. "We had better get home now before I have to carry you out to my vehicle."

The two gentlemen said their good-byes. Dr. Neff held Marie-Louise's hands for a bit longer than necessary, and thanked her for a wonderful evening. Before he left the castle, Dr. Walter reiterated the promise to have another concert soon.

Alone, Ambrosia and Marie-Louise looked at each other. "It was a successful evening, Tante Ambrosia. Everything worked out perfectly—the music, the guests and the refreshments. And you were right. Dr. Walter is a superb violinist, and it was a joy to listen to him."

"Yes, he is good, isn't he? I was very pleased."

"Maybe we can turn castle concerts into a side business. What do you think?"

"It's a possibility. Right now I'm too tired to give this thought my full attention, but we could discuss it further tomorrow. Let's go to bed."

For Marie-Louise, however, sleep didn't come quickly. Her mind worked overtime on her latest business idea of castle concerts. They could invite local musicians to participate, and she already envisioned hundreds of visitors lining up. This positive thought kept her awake until the early morning hours when sleep finally overtook her.

Chapter Fifteen

With the concert out of the way, Marie-Louise turned her full attention to the wedding preparations. Many hours of planning, organizing, agonizing, and hard work promised the success of her first business venture, and the day couldn't have been better. A clear blue sky spanned the horizon, and a balmy breeze turned an otherwise hot day into a pleasant one.

Marie-Louise had been up and working for several hours before Ulrich's groom arrived to brush the horses down and to inspect the harnesses and coach. With the floral decorations in place, the upholstery cleaned and the brass hardware polished to a shine, the carriage looked as if it had been taken right out of a fairytale book. No blemish marred its stately appearance.

Frau Becker had been hired for the occasion, and she had enlisted the help of several women from the town to assist with baking cakes, tortes, and cookies. For days, the women had been busy preparing and were already hard at work chopping vegetables, stewing meat, and making sauces for the big meal.

Tante Ambrosia, in charge of the crystal ballroom, put the last touches to the table decorations. A sea of fresh flowers, together with cut young birch branches, created the natural setting she wanted to achieve, and the open French doors let the sun stream into the room to intensify every color to a brilliance beyond description.

Marie-Louise stood transfixed at the double doors. Dozens of mirrors reflected the splendor of the room to make it appear endless, while shards of rainbow colors from the chandeliers' prisms flitted through the air like butterflies.

"How beautiful," she exclaimed. "This will be a dream wedding."

"With many more to follow, I hope." Ambrosia seemed pleased at her niece's praise.

"I'm sure."

"At least castle weddings will give us some additional income to put aside for necessary repairs."

Marie-Louise nodded. "I'm only sorry that you have to work so hard."

Ambrosia tilted her chin in a determined way. "The stable roof and our peace of mind are worth it."

"That's true," agreed Marie-Louise and hurried off to give Fritz last-minute instructions for the coach ride.

On her way, she detoured through the family picture gallery and stopped for a moment to look up at her ancestors in their heavy gilded frames. "It's going to turn out well," she whispered. "It may take me some time to restore Hohenstein, but I promise I won't let you down. You'll see."

As the time of the wedding party's arrival drew near, Marie-Louise walked to the gatehouse and listened for the rumbling of a coach. Shielding her eyes against the sun, she saw no movement on the road leading up to Castle Hohenstein.

Back at the castle, she stuck her head into the kitchen. "Everything under control, Frau Becker?"

"We're just waiting for the guests, Fräulein Marie-Louise."

Where's Dr. Neff with his camera? I hope he won't be late. I need him here when the coach draws up! She ruffled her hair in frustration. *Oh, thank goodness. Here he comes!*

Marie-Louise rushed to greet him.

"Nervous?" he asked, grinning.

"I want everything to be perfect, and there are so many

people who depend on me to tell them what to do and when to do it."

"Like me, for instance."

She laughed. "Yes, like you. I need you to be here when the coach arrives. Photograph the coach, the bride and groom. I really appreciate you doing that for me. How can I ever thank you enough?"

He took her hand. "Just let me be your friend."

"Deal."

He paused before shaking hands. "If we're to be friends you can't call me Dr. Neff. You need to call me Nick."

"Okay, Nick it is, but then you need to call me Marie-Louise."

"Deal," he confirmed.

She rushed off to the ballroom where everything looked perfect; no place setting needed her corrective touch, no knife a last-minute polish. She drew a deep breath and wandered into the parlor where she found her aunt.

Strolling to the window, she craned her neck but still couldn't see the wedding party. Hands behind her back, she walked back and forth between window and fireplace. Back and forth, back and forth. Every time she approached the window, she checked the courtyard. Still no sign of the guests. She drummed a staccato on the windowsill.

"Marie-Louise," she heard her aunt's stern voice, "sit down. You make me nervous."

"I can't sit still. I'm too tense."

"Try to relax. We've done everything possible to ensure a successful wedding. All we can do now is wait for the guests."

Marie-Louise stopped her pacing and leaned against the wall. "Everything depends on this day," she mused. "If the wedding proves a success, we may get a business started and—"

Suddenly she pushed away from the wall, head cocked. "Listen! Can you hear something?" She rushed to the window. "They're here!"

From that moment on, Hohenstein resembled more a beehive than a castle. People milled about, servers balanced platters of food above their heads, and the kitchen staff clambered with pots and pans. Out in the courtyard, Fritz positioned the coach for the best possible photograph, and Dr. Neff moved from side to side to find the best position.

Marie-Louise tried to be in several places at the same time and heaved a sigh of relief as the guests moved into the crystal room, but as they filed into the ballroom she felt as if on display, continually being ogled like a rare bird.

The meal was excellent and the servers had their hands full trying to comply with the guests' requests for seconds. With dinner over, the band took their seats at the stage on one end of the room and tuned their instruments. Before the first country dance was announced, a hush fell over the guests and all heads turned toward the entrance. Marie-Louise glanced to see what caused the sudden lull in conversation, and then almost dropped the goblet she was holding in her hand.

There in the doorway stood Ulrich in his gala uniform, tall and straight. Dead silence. Only whispers here and there could be heard until they finally became audible: "*Count Wolfburg.*"

The guests were clearly impressed. Marie-Louise expected any minute to see the ladies curtsey and the men bow. Of course, nothing like that happened, even if the awe-inspired silence prevailed.

After surveying the room in his usual haughty manner, he saw her and inclined his head a fraction in acknowledgment. Making his way toward the bride's table, he bowed military-style and conversed with the couple for a while, probably wishing them well on their future together.

To Marie-Louise's astonishment, however, she saw the bride rise, take the count's proffered arm, and be led onto the dance floor.

He's executing the old traditional right as lord over the land to have the first dance with the bride. How antiquated! This privilege would actually be hers were she a man, because the barons of Hohenstein used to be the lords over the village. Was this action his only reason for coming here today, she wondered.

Even if she considered the tradition outdated, she had to admit that it was a hit with the bride, judging by her exuberant smile. This dance with Count Wolfburg would always be remembered as the highlight of her wedding day, and although she stumbled a few times over her own feet, she never stopped smiling.

Ulrich seemed to listen intently to his partner, looking into her eyes as she spoke. *A gentleman of the first water*, thought Marie-Louise. *Most of the time, anyway.*

The guests had all risen and surrounded the dance floor, not wanting to miss this extraordinary moment.

Nobility's condescension, scoffed Marie-Louise inwardly, the thought irritating her. Not so much the fact that Ulrich had arrived and stolen the show, but the reaction of the people to him—and to her, for that matter. Maybe Tante Ambrosia was right when she said that it was the commoners who kept nobility atop their pedestals and not the aristocrats themselves.

At the end of the waltz, Ulrich bowed to the bride, and the guests applauded enthusiastically.

After returning the bride to her new husband, Ulrich crossed the room to meet Marie-Louise. On the way, he nodded in greeting in all directions with a pleasant, debonair expression.

"What a theatrical performance, Count," she commented as he stood by her side.

"What an unusual greeting, Baroness," he countered. Inclining his head, he whispered with a twinkle in his eye. "You'd better be civil to me today. The world is watching."

She rolled her eyes. "Don't I know it! I feel as if I've been sitting on a silver platter ever since the guests arrived."

He laughed. "These are the joys of nobility. You grin and bear them." As if to demonstrate, he lifted his hand in a salute and smiled at the crowd.

"What are you doing here, anyway?" Marie-Louise asked.

"Contributing to the success of the event," he returned in a matter-of-fact voice. "If you promised a wedding fit for a princess, you need a prince. And if you don't have one, I figured a count would do."

She looked at him sideways and laughed. "Well, it will be a wedding to be remembered, that's for certain."

"I thought that was the purpose." After a few moments he asked, "How did the team work out?"

"The bride and groom didn't have enough good things to say about their coach ride. They loved it, and every young woman of marriageable age envied the couple." She laughed. "I guess your horses will be quite busy in the near future, if you don't mind."

"As long as Fritz or Jakob sit on the driver's seat and not the Baroness von Hohenstein."

"Yes, I read your instructions."

"I'm glad we understand each other." After a few moments, he gave one of his crooked smiles. "I saw that you took advantage of the doctor and his photography skills."

"I asked him and he agreed to take the pictures."

"Are you paying him?"

"N-no."

"Is he expecting payment of any sort?"

She looked at him, anger tinting her voice. "What are you insinuating?"

"Nothing—just asking."

A sign from the bride and groom at this moment invited everybody to join the couple on the dance floor and prevented Marie-Louise from voicing a cynical retort.

Ulrich reached out and took her hand, his fingers barely touching her skin. When she tried to pull her hand away, he closed his fingers around it and steadied not only her hand but the liquid in the goblet as well.

"Careful," he drawled in his deepest voice and looked at her from under half-closed lids, while the corner of his mouth twitched. Gently he took the goblet out of her hand and set it on the podium, then bowed. "May I have the pleasure of this dance, Baroness?"

She wanted to say something, anything to break the spell he wove about her, but her mouth felt dry and her pulse sounded in her ear like the surf on a rocky beach. She could only nod.

He guided her through the mass of dancers to the lesser crowded sidelines.

"You look lovely," he mumbled so close to her ear that she could feel the warmth of his lips feathering her skin. She promptly missed a step and would have stumbled had he not tightened his hold around her waist.

"Steady," he admonished with a low chuckle. "Concentrate on the music and follow my lead."

I'd love to concentrate on the music if only you'd let me, she wanted to shout and tried hard to block him from her mind. She closed her eyes to shut out his knowing smile and instead focused on the dance steps.

Despite his disturbing nearness it felt good to glide over the parquet as if on air, secure in his arms. Once her body became one with the music, Ulrich added figures to the steps and she followed his lead with ease. Oh, that the dance would never end!

He must have felt the same way because he said, "We ought to do that more often."

She took a deep breath. "I'd like that."

Marie-Louise hadn't realized until now how much she missed social events. The past few weeks had held nothing but hard work and problems, in addition to her duties at the town hall.

"A penny for your thoughts," he said and smiled.

She sighed. "I was thinking about Hohenstein."

"I figured as much. Hohenstein is never far from your mind, is it?" He didn't wait for an answer but continued, "Today's success should make you happy, and although you won't experience any financial gain from the wedding, the new stable roof will remind you of its material benefit every time you see it. There'll be other weddings and functions that'll bring you the needed cash. You've worked hard and should be proud of your achievements."

Marie-Louise lowered her gaze to hide the joy she felt at his praise but couldn't keep from smiling.

"You look relaxed today," he said with a smile in his voice. "Your smile is as sweet as a sleeping baby's, and except for the moments when you harbor cynical thoughts, you present the picture of propriety."

"Wouldn't Tante Ambrosia like to hear you say that!"

"What? The part with the cynical thoughts?" He laughed a deep, melodious sound.

Annoyed at his teasing, she pouted. "You know what I mean."

"Where's your aunt today? I haven't seen her."

"She's probably in the kitchen overseeing the work there."

"Didn't she want to be where the guests are?"

"Not Tante Ambrosia. She doesn't believe in mingling with commoners."

Sobering, he drew her closer, and with concern in his voice he asked, "You still don't see eye-to-eye with your aunt, do you?"

"She's very old-fashioned and strict in her views."

"I seemed to feel a mellowing last time I visited, or was that my imagination?"

Marie-Louise shook her head. "I'm not sure. That day, she acted so out of character that I didn't know what to think." Remembering how he had witnessed the drama with the farm horses and her embarrassment, she chuckled.

"I guess that laughter broke the spell of the unbending disciplinarian. Am I right?"

"Probably," she said and pondered the possibility. "Later that day, she told me about her fiancé."

Ulrich raised an eyebrow. "She is engaged to be married?"

"She was—many years ago. Her betrothed died."

"I didn't know."

"Neither did I, until that day."

They made a turn to the left and he lowered his head to whisper in her ear. "Look around you inconspicuously."

She did and almost missed a step. "They're all watching us." Everyone had left the dance floor to watch them.

"You'd better not trip over my feet," he said with a twinkle in his eye.

"I'm only following your lead," she countered. "You'd better do a good job."

"I'm trying my best." He smiled.

As the strains of the music ebbed away, Ulrich led her back to her place by the podium. "It was a pleasure, Baroness." He bent to touch his lips lightly to the back of her hand.

She looked up. "You're not leaving, are you?"

The lines at the corner of his eyes crinkled. "So fond of my presence?"

She bit her lip. "It's a shame to deprive the wedding guests of the main attraction."

He laughed. "It's about time they focused their attention on the bride and groom, don't you think?"

With an empty feeling, she watched as he disappeared through the crowd. *As if someone had turned off the lights*, she thought, and wondered at this strange emotion. *I thought I hated him, but I don't. What happened?*

Right now, she didn't have time to analyze her feelings. Seeing that the beverage supply was running low, she needed to find Jakob and send him down to the cellar for more.

She saw Nick every so often as he took another photograph. On one occasion, when their paths crossed, he wanted to know who her dashing dance partner was.

"That was Count Wolfburg."

"A relative?"

"Yes—so-to-speak."

"What's a so-to-speak relative?"

"Going back several centuries when two feuding families finally wised up and intermarried."

He laughed, but it didn't sound quite as amused as it should have—as a matter of fact, Marie-Louise thought she detected a little jealousy in it, but she didn't have time to think about it right now. She was busy every minute until the last guests left the castle in the early morning hours.

She went in search of her aunt and found her in the parlor looking as exhausted as she, herself, felt. The baroness dropped into a chair and took in a heavy breath. "It was a success! Thank you for your hard work."

Her aunt smiled. "You worked as hard, if not harder, than anyone else, and I'm proud of you."

Tears of gratitude stung Marie-Louise's eyes at the unexpected compliment. She felt like hugging Ambrosia but shied away from displaying her emotions because her aunt wouldn't like that. Instead, she got up. "I can hardly keep my eyes open. Let's go to bed."

Bone-weary, she knew that her dreams would be pleasant. Things were looking up for her and Hohenstein. Today she'd proved to herself and to Ulrich that she could turn the fate of Hohenstein around, even without his money. Today she felt good, and she smiled as she climbed the stairs to the upper floor.

Chapter Sixteen

Marie-Louise rounded the corner on her way home from a walk with Kaiser when she saw a tall, good-looking young man about to climb the steps to the main entrance. She squinted against the sun to try and see who the stranger might be. When he saw her, he turned around and came toward her, arms outstretched, but it took a moment before she recognized him.

With a squeal of delight, she ran into his arms and hugged him while he laughed and lifted her off her feet. Kaiser ran circles around them, barking.

She was the first one to find her speech. "Peter, is it really you? How wonderful to see you after all these years. Let me look at you."

Taking a step back, she cocked her head to one side. "You're taller and even more handsome than I remembered, but the smile is still the same rascally smile."

"And you, my little adorable friend, are not so little anymore either, but certainly ravishingly beautiful. And Ullie told me that you have developed into a veritable radical."

Marie-Louise stopped walking. "He said that?"

Peter nodded.

"I'm not a radical."

He grinned. "You're probably one of these suffragettes, marching for a five-day work week for laborers."

She put her hands over her ears. "Stop. Stop. You're making all this up to tease me."

He pinched her cheek. "You're cute. And I bet you have a whole slew of admirers at your feet."

She laughed. "How can I have admirers when I was cooped up for years at school?"

"You weren't there during summer holidays," he pointed out.

"True." She linked arms with him, and together they approached the main entrance.

He squeezed her arm. "I bet you came to Hohenstein to escape your admirers."

Marie-Louise stopped walking and turned to him. "Don't be silly."

He laughed. "You look charming when you pout. Did Ullie ever tell you that?"

Her heart skipped a beat before it pounded with renewed vigor against her ribs, and she felt heat rise to her cheeks. Not wanting Peter to notice her discomfiture, she asked in a flippant voice, "What does Ullie have to do with anything?"

He shrugged. "I thought you were sweet on him."

"What?" She glared at him, hands on hips. "You're mad! I'm not sweet on him."

He held up his hand, "All right, all right. Don't take my head off."

"Don't say things like that. They aren't true, and they make me furious."

"Calm down," he said. "I'll only tell Ullie that he has made a conquest."

"Don't you dare," she cried, "or I'll hunt you down and . . ."

". . . and what?"

". . . and punch you in the nose!"

He laughed out loud. "That would prove to be quite interesting."

Before they arrived at the door, he said, "By the way, Ullie told me that you have our team horses here."

"Yes, he loaned them to us."

He chuckled. "I heard that you had problems with some old farm horses."

She looked at him. "Did Ullie tell you what happened that day when we tried to hitch the horses to the carriage?"

"Yes, he told me about the fiasco, and how you got mad and stormed off." He laughed. "Why didn't you ask Ullie for our horses in the first place?"

"I couldn't."

"Why couldn't you?"

That was a hard question to answer. She couldn't possibly tell Peter the reason why she didn't want to ask help from his brother, that he had refused to help her in the past. Or that she just couldn't bring herself to approach him for reasons she didn't even want to explore.

"Marie-Louise," he said and put an arm around her shoulder, "why are you blushing?"

Rascal. A gentleman should never notice a lady's embarrassment, and especially not mention it, even if they were childhood playmates. She tilted her chin and said, "I'm a little hot after my walk. Let's go inside and get some refreshments."

His eyes twinkled, but he dropped the subject and guided the discussion to a safer topic. "How's your aunt? Still impeccable and strict?"

Glad to be on neutral ground again, she said, "Well, I think she has mellowed some, but she still slaps my hand when I do or say something inappropriate in her view."

"She slaps your hand?"

"Figuratively speaking."

He grinned. "Still the old disciplinarian, I see. We sure gave her a hard time when we used to skip out into the woods."

"Poor Tante Ambrosia—but we sure had fun! Remember, Ullie never joined us. He probably felt that our games were beneath him."

"I bet he would've loved to have joined us but didn't have it in him to disobey orders. I don't think he ever did anything that was against the *rules* set up for him as future head of the House of Wolfburg."

Marie-Louise looked at Peter as if to say, *if you only knew.*

Peter raised an eyebrow. "You don't agree?"

Now they were on dangerous ground again, and Marie-Louise needed to steer the conversation away from Ulrich and her own wayward feelings. Thank goodness Tante Ambrosia entered the parlor at that time, and Peter went to greet her.

"Welcome to Hohenstein, Herr von Wolfburg. It has been quite a few years since I saw you here as a young lad."

He smiled and bent over her hand. "I believe I often was the cause of your displeasure when I enticed Marie-Louise to escape to the woods."

Now it was Ambrosia's turn to smile. "I think that my niece didn't need much prodding to go traipsing through those woods with you."

"I still have very fond memories of our explorations and our games of hide and seek, or knight in shining armor rescuing the damsel in distress who was trapped in a tall tower. Jakob's treehouse afforded us hours and hours of adventures."

Marie-Louise reminisced, "I remember one afternoon when we played Rapunzel and I had to let my hair down, but it got caught on a branch and I couldn't get it untangled. You climbed up to the treehouse and tried to help, but it only got worse. Finally, I sent you to get Tante Ambrosia and a pair of scissors, all the while anticipating a good scolding. When she saw she was so horrified that she didn't even say a word. She just handed the scissors to you and you cut me loose."

"You two children were like two peas in a pod. What one didn't come up with, the other would, and you were always into scrapes." Ambrosia wagged her finger.

"It was a glorious time." Marie-Louise smiled before she left the room to get the promised refreshments. When she returned with a tray of puff pastries and tall glasses of juice, Ambrosia excused herself and left the two young people to visit with each other.

Marie-Louise joined Peter on the settee. "What are you doing for fun during your semester break?"

"Mostly spending time with friends. That is, I go sailing when Ullie lends me the yacht." He turned to her. "You ought to come with us sometime."

She put her hands in her lap and imagined sitting on deck of a yacht with the wind whipping her hair in her face and the spray of the water on her skin. "That would be wonderful, but I'm not sure I'll have time with everything going on around here."

"What is it you do for fun, then?"

"Nothing much, really. I went to a concert with a friend, had a house concert here at the castle, but that's about all."

"I'll have to speak with Ullie about that. He needs to get you out once in a while."

The baroness quickly put a hand on his arm. "No, don't. I'm fine. Don't worry about me."

"If you say so." He didn't seem convinced but dropped the subject.

To break the ensuing silence, Marie-Louise asked a question that had plagued her for some time, and one that Peter could possibly answer. "Does Ullie have a sweetheart?"

As soon as the question was asked, she felt heat flooding her cheeks and looked quickly away to avoid Peter's curious gaze.

He suppressed a smirk. "Haven't you ever asked him?"

"Of course not," she snapped. "That would be highly inappropriate."

He grinned. "To tell you the truth, I don't know how serious he is with any of the women of his acquaintance. He has to be very careful and not show undue favoritism unless he is absolutely sure that he's going to propose to that particular woman. So far, I haven't heard any rumors, so I can only guess. Does that answer satisfy your curiosity?"

"I'm not curious. I'm trying to make conversation."

"Sure you are. Tell me then, why you are blushing again?"

She pressed her hands to her cheeks. "I'm not blushing, it's a little hot in here, don't you think?"

"I think I was right, and you do have a *tendre* for my brother."

She turned on him. "How dare you say something like that? I certainly don't have feelings for Ullie, and don't you even think it." If only the heat in her cheeks would go away.

"Sorry, I didn't mean to upset you. I was just teasing."

She breathed a sigh of relief. "Don't tease me about . . ." she wanted to say *Ullie*, but caught herself in time, and instead said, ". . . something like that."

He nodded and stood up. "I'd better get going. I just wanted to see you and say hello. Please, give my regards to your aunt."

Marie-Louise walked with him to the door and gave him a hug. "Thank you for coming, and please come again soon."

"If not before, then I'll see you at the ball at Castle Wolfburg."

"Is Ullie planning a ball?"

"The usual end-of-summer event," he said. With a twinkle in his eye, he added, "I think he'll announce his engagement at that ball."

"Engagement?" croaked Marie-Louise. "You said that you hadn't heard any rumors about an attachment."

He patted her cheek. "You'll see." He sprinted down the steps to his automobile.

Marie-Louise waved and waited until he disappeared over the drawbridge before she went inside where she leaned against the heavy wooden door.

Engagement? Her heart seemed to squeeze into a tight ball. *Ullie engaged?* Who was the woman? Had she fallen in love with his smile, his crinkling eyes, his golden eyelashes, his coppery hair? Had he kissed her like he had Marie-Louise?

She stood motionless while tears welled up in her eyes and trickled down her cheeks. Did he tease his future wife like he did her?

A sob escaped her and she hurried up to her room. She certainly didn't want Ambrosia to find her crying over the count.

She flung herself onto her bed, buried her head in her pillow and let the tears wet the satin fabric. *Oh, Ullie, I miss you already.*

Life went on despite Marie-Louise's misery and despite repeatedly telling herself that the count's upcoming engagement shouldn't affect her in any way. She wasn't interested in him and especially not as a possible marriage partner. The only reason why she felt bereft was that she feared losing him as a distraction whose visits were a welcome change to her otherwise boring life at Hohenstein.

No matter how hard she tried to forget him, thoughts of him and longing for him crept up at the most inopportune moments, and only hard work kept those feelings somewhat at bay.

She didn't notice Ambrosia's worried look or Jakob's frown until finally the handyman came right out and asked, "Fräulein Marie-Louise, what's the matter with ya? Ya don't smile anymore and ya work like the dickens. Are you all right?"

"I'm fine, Jakob, thank you for asking."

He scratched his head, looked at her askance, and went back to his work.

It proved a little harder to shake off Tante Ambrosia when her aunt stopped her after lunch one day.

"Marie-Louise, I'm worried about you. You don't have much of an appetite and you walk around as if the world is coming to an end. Your step has lost its spring and you don't smile any more. Are you feeling unwell?"

"I'm fine, Tante Ambrosia." Perhaps she should explain her apathy because her aunt didn't seem convinced. "Maybe I worry too much."

Ambrosia nodded. "What are you worried about? Things are looking up with two more weddings booked and hopefully more to come. That should make you happy."

"You're right, and I'm happy that we have some success with the weddings, at least." She had to be more careful in the future and show a more cheerful face.

"Have you heard from Dr. Neff lately?" asked Ambrosia.

"Yes, he sent me a note a couple of days ago and invited me to go to the ballet with him in Stuttgart."

"And—are you going with him?"

"I don't know. I haven't given him an answer yet."

"You should accept his invitation—at least it will get you away from here for a while and may help you back to your normal, happy self."

Her aunt must really be worried about her if she was sanctioning an overnight outing with the doctor. Thinking about the diversion the ballet would bring, Marie-Louise agreed. "You're right, I should go with him. I'm a little hesitant, though, because he wants to introduce me to his family, and I'm not certain if I'm ready for that."

"I suppose it can't be avoided if they live in Stuttgart. You're not planning on spending the night at his parents' home, I hope."

"No, of course not. I'll check into some hotel."

"Yes, that would be appropriate."

With more enthusiasm than she felt, she said, "I'm actually looking forward to seeing *Swan Lake* but I don't want to give him false hopes."

"That's perfectly understandable. On the other hand, I can see the family's desire to meet a real baroness since it's probably the only time in their lives that they'll have this opportunity."

Marie-Louise laughed. "That makes me feel like a show horse all over again."

"Just be yourself and keep your distance."

"What do you mean by *keeping my distance*?"

"Impeccable demeanor, courteous, and . . ." with a rare attempt at making a joke, Ambrosia continued, ". . . smiling down from your pedestal."

The baroness had to laugh again. "I think that's the first time I've heard you make a joke."

Ambrosia squared her shoulders and smiled one of her rare smiles. "It's good to hear you laugh again. Maybe I'll have to come up with more jokes in the future to lighten your mood."

"I'll try not to let the situation at Hohenstein get the better of me. After all, life goes on."

"That's right."

Tante Ambrosia had certainly mellowed in the last few weeks, and Marie-Louise liked the new and improved aunt. Life around here would be almost perfect if she only could get Ulrich out of her mind and heart. Resolute, she told her aunt, "I suppose I'll accept Nick's invitation."

"You're on a first-name basis?"

"People are not as formal these days as they used to be. Are you still calling Dr. Walter by his title and family name?"

Ambrosia stammered a little. "O-of course. We haven't had occasion to become familiar with each other yet."

"Any word from the good doctor lately?"

Ambrosia's cheeks took on a rosy hue. "He invited me to an organ concert at the cathedral in Freiburg."

"That's wonderful. It looks as if he doesn't waste any time, either . . ."

As she left, Marie-Louise brooded on the situation. *Filling my time with Nick will let me forget Ullie. I don't want to sit at home moping and envisioning the count conversing with and smiling at another woman. And maybe, just maybe, I can fall in love with Nick.*

They left on Saturday morning and arrived at the Stuttgart train station late afternoon. Dr. Neff's family lived in an old mansion in a prosperous part of the city surrounded by other wealthy homes and vast park-like yards overlooking vineyards and the city below.

Nick's parents answered the door.

"Mama, Papa, may I introduce Marie-Louise, Baroness von Hohenstein? Marie-Louise, these are my parents."

Marie-Louise extended her hand. "It's a pleasure to meet you. Nick has spoken very fondly of his family."

"It's an honor to have you in our home, Baroness. Please come in."

Nick hugged and kissed his mother and patted his father on the shoulder after Marie-Louise took the flowers from him, unwrapped them, and offered them, together with an elaborate box of Swiss chocolates, to Nick's mother.

"What lovely flowers, Baroness. Thank you very much. And how did you know that these chocolates are my favorites?"

The baroness smiled up at Nick, and Frau Neff wagged a finger at her son.

"Please, come and meet the rest of the family. Sabine, Markus, come and meet Baroness von Hohenstein."

Sabine, an attractive blonde, and Markus, a lanky young man in his first semester at Stuttgart, appeared in the hallway and greeted Marie-Louise.

"Let's go into the parlor while I finish dinner. Sabine, would you please come and help me?"

Marie-Louise was led into the spacious room with heavy leather couches and sturdy furnishings.

Markus was the first to ask a question. "You're a real baroness?"

"Yes, I am."

"And you live in a castle?"

"Yes."

Nick's father entered the discussion. "Nick tells me you've been attempting to restore the castle. Have you ever considered a venture of a larger scale?"

Marie-Louise leaned forward. "Nick mentioned that you're investing in resorts and other big projects. Is that what you have in mind?"

"Of course, not having seen the castle, I can hardly venture a guess at what can be done." Smiling at her, he continued, "I'd like to someday see it, if I may be so bold as to ask your permission. Funding wouldn't be a problem if a project like that could materialize."

She had to dampen his enthusiasm without hurting his feelings, but there was no way she would see her home turned into a resort. "Your idea has merit, but I'm not so sure that I would like to have strangers roaming the castle. It's my home and I hope to one day raise a family there."

He reached over to cover her hand with his. "Turning your castle into a holiday resort wouldn't necessarily mean that you would have to leave, but like I said, I would have to see it to know what could be done and how it could be arranged."

"Thank you for your interest, Herr Neff. The time may come when I need your services."

He smiled. "You can count on me, Baroness."

At that moment, Sabine announced, "Dinner is ready," and invited everyone to move to the dining room.

Because of the round table there was no specific place of honor, and Marie-Louise was seated between Nick and his brother.

Before they started serving, Herr Neff asked Nick to say grace.

Everybody joined hands while Nick said a short and simple prayer. Curious to see what everyone was doing, Marie-Louise risked a peek out of one eye to see heads bowed, eyes closed. They all seemed to be familiar with this ritual. The prayer over, hands were squeezed and everybody wished *Guten Appetit* before the food was served.

The beef medallions were excellent, and the vegetables cooked crisp-tender were tasty.

Herr Neff put his arm around his wife's shoulders. "Thank you for a delicious meal, dear."

"I'm glad you liked it."

Marie-Louise followed suit. "*Danke* for this wonderful meal, Frau Neff. Beef medallions are among my favorites."

"Then I'm happy to have hit on a favorite," smiled Nick's mother.

Nick interrupted. "I'm sorry to cut the conversation short, but we'd better get going or we'll be late."

Marie-Louise rose immediately. "Thank you so much for the meal, Frau Neff, and thank you all for letting me be part of your family today. I hope to see you again soon, maybe at Hohenstein."

"That would be wonderful," exclaimed Markus.

"Auf Wiedersehen."

"Nice to have met you, Baroness."

She waved and followed Nick out the door.

On the way to the opera house, she turned to him, "I envy you."

"Why do you envy me?"

"You have such a wonderful family."

He laughed, "You mean they're a pain in the neck. I have to apologize for my father's interest in Hohenstein. He's always the businessman, always looking for projects."

"You don't have to apologize. Your family is what I always envisioned a family to be, eating together, discussing things together, bantering and joking and loving each other. You know, I never experienced family life, and a family like yours is exactly what I wish for."

A lump formed in her throat. He didn't know how lucky he was.

They walked through the *Schlossgarten* to the theater. The ponds in front of the opera house reflected the lights of the gas lamps, adding to the glamour of the open theater doors. The evening air with its balmy breeze feathered the skin and ruffled Marie-Louise's hair. Free of the burden and stress of Hohenstein, she felt like walking on air.

Nick squeezed her hand. "You seem happy tonight."

"I am. It's so nice not to have to worry about the castle and the needed repairs for a while and just be able to enjoy the evening."

"I'm glad you're enjoying it with me." He smiled, and she nodded.

They ascended the steps to the theater and were ushered to their seats shortly before the first bell rang. The lights dimmed and the musicians took their places in the orchestra, some tuning their instruments. The second and third bells rang in short succession, the lights went out, and the curtain opened as the music began.

Marie-Louise relaxed against her seat while Nick put his arm around her shoulders. She had to resist the urge to shake him off. Why couldn't she just enjoy the contact? He was a nice and eligible young man and had everything she wanted in a husband: a respectable job, a lovely family, and last but not least, he was a commoner. She liked him just fine. Unfortunately, he wasn't as handsome as someone she'd rather not think about—and there was just no body chemistry.

It would be so simple if she could only fall in love with him! They could get married and she would have access to her inheritance and could finally restore Hohenstein. She simply needed to try harder.

She turned and gave him a sweet smile, putting her hand on his knee. He squeezed her shoulder in response. *Well, that's a beginning.* When she closed her eyes, however, she envisioned someone's smile, glacier blue eyes, and ever-so-soft caresses, and a shiver ran down her spine.

"Are you cold?" Nick pulled her closer to him.

"No, I'm fine."

She forced herself to concentrate on the music and the action on stage and soon was drawn into the story of *Swan Lake,* identifying with the unfortunate princess. "Fabulous," she whispered.

"Are you enjoying the ballet?" asked Nick at the intermission.

"I love it," she enthused, and sighed. "I wish I could dance like that."

Smiling, he asked, "Did you ever take ballet lessons?"

"Yes, we had ballet lessons at school, but I didn't have the patience it takes to become really proficient. I much preferred the tennis court."

He put his arm around her shoulders. "Then we have to play tennis together sometime, not that I'm very good at it, but it would be fun."

"Yes, I would like that." Playing tennis would break up the monotony of her days and hopefully help her forget Ulrich and his imminent betrothal.

The bells called them back to their seats for the second part of the ballet, and Marie-Louise wished it could go on forever. "Beautiful," she breathed as the curtain finally fell and the audience rose in applause. Afterward, they made their way out of the theater and stood for a while at the pond in silence.

At last Nick said, "I'd better get you to your hotel. You must be tired."

"Thank you so much for a very enjoyable evening, Nick. Everything was perfect—your family, the ballet, the stars overhead, this beautiful park, you being so kind . . ."

"I enjoyed the evening, as well, and especially your company." He put an arm around her waist and led her along the path to the *Hotel am Schlossgarten.* Stopping under an overhanging tree, he turned her to face him. With both hands on her shoulders, he looked deep into her eyes. "You're so beautiful and you visit me in my dreams at night, did you know that? I'm the luckiest man to be your friend."

He drew her to him and lowered his head to kiss her cheek, her nose, and finally, his lips found hers.

Chapter Seventeen

She invited his kiss, anticipating the sensations she'd felt when Ulrich had kissed her, but there were no fireworks, no tingling of her skin or shivers down her spine, no heat coursing through her body. *Concentrate!*

She moved closer, her hands seeking his, but still no sensations. *Concentrate!* His kiss deepened, still nothing. *Maybe if I imagine him to be Ullie . . . no, I can't do that—that wouldn't be fair.*

She massaged the back of his neck, and he moaned his pleasure. *At least one of us is enjoying it.*

At last, Nick broke contact and breathed deeply. "You're wonderful, sensational."

I wish I could say the same about you. She didn't say anything, though, but smiled up at him.

"Come, let me take you to your hotel before you totally bewitch me, my little baroness." With his arm around her he guided her toward the hotel. "I'll see you tomorrow at nine for breakfast at the hotel before we head south to Hohenstein."

He gave her a little kiss in the lobby. "Sleep well, my pretty baroness."

"*Gute Nacht,* Nick. Please give my regards to your family."

Walking away, he turned and waved. "Thank you. I will do that. Sweet dreams."

She watched him leave the lobby before she handed her valise to the porter and followed him to the third floor.

Her dreams that night were haunted by a wicked sorcerer who tried to keep her away from her true love by turning her into a beautiful swan, and her true love with his blue eyes and coppery hair reached for her in vain. The lake was too deep, and they were too far apart.

Several times during the night she awoke with a start and grieved.

Nick had a surprise for her the next day. They took the train to a small town in the Black Forest, and from there, he hired a chaise and chose the scenic route through the woods. They veered off the main roads and drove through the beautiful countryside, through darkly forested areas and along lush pastures with gurgling brooks.

"The scenery is breathtaking," exclaimed Marie-Louise. "Oh, and look at all the wildflowers on the meadows. This pasture here looks as smooth as a carpet and practically invites you to frolic down its slope."

"Do you want me to stop the carriage so you can get out and pick some flowers?"

"No, I'll enjoy seeing them as we drive by. The world certainly is beautiful, isn't it?"

"Yes," he agreed, searching her eyes and smiling, "especially this part of the world."

Nick was such a gentleman, and Marie-Louise wished she could feel more for him than friendship. She hung her head.

When they entered a quaint village, he stopped the carriage in front of a little *Gasthaus*. "I think we'd better have an early dinner here before we go on, what do you think?"

"That sounds good to me. I'm hungry."

They found a table by a window and were presented with the menu from which Marie-Louise chose Black Forest trout with *sauce almondine*, and Nick opted for *Schnitzel* with *pommes frites*. Having placed their orders, they were both startled by a voice behind them.

"Baroness von Hohenstein! I didn't expect to see you here."

Marie-Louise turned and was equally astonished to see the mayor of Hohenstein standing behind her. "Herr Bürgermeister, what a coincidence! You remember Dr. Neff from the ribbon cutting ceremony at the hospital, don't you? And, Nick, this is Bürgermeister Schmidt."

Nick rose and the men shook hands as a woman joined the mayor, who introduced her as his wife.

"Pleased to meet you, Frau Schmidt."

"The pleasure is all mine, Baroness, Dr. Neff." She turned to Marie-Louise. "My husband's told me a lot about you and is very impressed with your resourcefulness, Baroness."

Marie-Louise smiled. "He's probably greatly exaggerating."

"Not at all," countered the mayor. "You have good business sense and determination, two characteristics that will eventually bring you the success you seek."

The mayor's praise warmed her heart and she made an inviting gesture toward their table. "Won't you join us?"

"Thank you, but we're just leaving. Are you staying here for a few days?"

"No. We're on our way home from Stuttgart, and Dr. Neff was so kind to choose the scenic route to show me the beauty of the Black Forest. Are you on holiday here?"

"No, we're spending an extended weekend in our cabin, not far from the village."

"How lucky you are to be able to escape to such a beautiful spot!"

"Yes, we really like the area," said Frau Schmidt. "You ought to take a walk after your meal. The scenery is breathtaking."

"That would be nice," Dr. Neff returned, "but we better go straight home."

The waitress approached their table with the food tray, and the mayor took a step back to give her room.

"There's your food, and we'll let you two enjoy it. I'll see you at the office on Friday, Baroness." He nodded toward Dr. Neff and everybody shook hands before the Schmidts left the *Gasthaus*.

After a delicious meal, Nick asked, "Did you see all the curious stares from the guests at the restaurant after the mayor greeted you with your title?"

"No, I didn't realize that people even heard what was going on at our table."

"I wouldn't be at all surprised if your picture appeared in the village paper tomorrow."

"Well," she quipped, "you seem to be as prominent these days as I am, so your picture could be in the paper as well."

"I'm happy with that," he smiled and reached for her hand, "as long as you're in the picture with me."

She felt like a traitor. She knew his feelings were genuine but knew hers left much to be desired. *Remember what Tante Ambrosia said: love will come with courtship. I certainly hope she's right. So far I haven't noticed any change in myself. I wonder what Ullie is doing at this moment, maybe kissing his soon-to-be-betrothed? Stop. Stop. STOP. Forget him!*

She channeled her thoughts back to Nick, smiling at him and squeezing his hand. "Thank you for a wonderful weekend, Nick. Everything was perfect."

"I'm glad you enjoyed it," he said simply and returned the squeeze.

"What time do you start your shift tomorrow?"

He laughed. "My shift actually starts at nine o'clock tonight, so we'd better get going to catch the train back to Hohenstein."

Marie-Louise put her hands to her face. “Oh, my. Now I feel bad for taking up so much of your time. You should be sleeping right now to be fit for duty.”

“Don’t worry about me; I prefer being with you much more than sleeping. If everything goes well tonight, I might even get a good night’s rest.”

“I certainly hope so.”

They pulled into the courtyard just as Ambrosia was accompanying Dr. Walter out to his black automobile.

“There you are,” boomed Dr. Walter, “we almost posted a lost person call to the police. Did you have trouble with the transportation?”

“No. We just took the scenic route home.”

He winked at the young couple and turned to Ambrosia. “Thank you for a lovely meal, Fräulein von Hohenstein. I’ll stay in touch.”

Ambrosia’s cheeks flushed when Dr. Walter gave her a peck on the nose, and her blush deepened even more when he whispered something in her ear, but she smiled nonetheless and whispered something back.

He nodded his satisfaction and folded his length into his motorcar. Before he waved and drove off, he admonished Nick, “Don’t be late for work, Greenhorn.”

Nick shook his head and laughed. “He must be in love. He is always jovial, but now he is downright exuberant.”

“Yes, I think so, too,” said Marie-Louise.

They both turned to look at Ambrosia to see if she had overheard them, but she’d already ascended the stairs. Probably feeling their stares, she turned and wagged her finger. “What are you two conspiring about? You look suspicious, just like Marie-Louise did as a little girl before she embarked on one of her escapades.”

“We were commenting on Dr. Walter’s exuberant mood,” said Marie-Louise. “You wouldn’t have anything to do with it, would you?”

Ambrosia's finger wagged again, but she didn't answer and turned away, probably to hide her flushed face. Marie-Louise and Nick looked at each other and nodded. "They're both in love."

The baroness sighed. "I don't know what my aunt will do about it, though. Will she follow her heart or deny her feelings in the interest of the old rules and regulations?"

Nick looked at her, surprised. "How can she deny her feelings? If she was against Dr. Walter's advances she wouldn't have allowed him to kiss her, even if it was only a kiss on the nose."

His words stirred the guilt in her. She had allowed Nick to kiss her passionately and even participated without loving him. What would he think of her if he found out? And he would need to find out sooner or later, unless she could manage to fall in love with him after all. But she couldn't dictate her heart.

Nick touched her shoulder and startled her out of her depressing thoughts. "You're daydreaming, my sweet baroness. Have you even heard what I said?"

She nodded, then sighed again. "I hope my aunt follows her heart. She has been alone for too many years, and she deserves some happiness."

Putting an arm around her shoulders, he said, "You need to encourage her. Dr. Walter is a wonderful man and a great doctor, and he, too, deserves happiness again."

"I'll do what I can."

"I know." He smiled at her. "I love you."

There. He'd said the three dreaded words she didn't want to hear from him—yet. She wasn't ready and she felt bad because she couldn't reciprocate his feelings. Of course, she could tell him that she loved him, too, but that would be a lie. She liked him—a lot—as a friend, but nothing more at the moment. She felt miserable and berated herself for leading him on.

Because he was obviously waiting for a response, she patted his cheek and pressed a kiss on it. "You're wonderful, and I want to thank you again for a lovely weekend. Won't you come in?"

He looked a little sad but still produced a lopsided smile. "I'd better get going to prepare for my shift. Let me carry your bag inside for you and then I'll be off."

He carried her bag to the front door for her, bent down, and kissed her lightly on the lips. "See you soon, my pretty baroness."

"*Auf Wiedersehen,* Nick. I hope you'll have an uneventful night at the hospital."

He blew her a kiss and ran down the stairs, taking two steps at a time. She watched him, waving, and then entered the castle.

Ambrosia looked up as she entered the room. "Why the frown, Marie-Louise?"

"Oh, Tante Ambrosia, I feel so wretched." She slumped down onto the settee. "I don't love Nick but he loves me, and I feel like a traitor."

Her aunt moved to sit beside her. "Don't berate yourself for being unable to force feelings that are not there. You respect him as a friend and that should be enough."

"But you said that love comes with courtship, remember?"

"Yes, I remember, but there are always exceptions to the rule. You may not be meant for each other, or your heart is already engaged elsewhere."

Oh, please don't mention the word engaged *because it reminds me of Ulrich, and I can't bear to think of him with another woman. And if you still think that Ullie might choose me for a wife, you're mistaken because he's already spoken for.*

Marie-Louise sighed. "Life's not easy, is it?"

Ambrosia shook her head. "It wasn't meant to be."

"Things certainly seem easy with Dr. Walter."

The older woman put both hands to her cheeks. "Yes. But they are progressing too fast for me."

"You seem to be very fond of him, though."

"I am. He's wonderful and a gentleman, and entertaining, and . . ."

Marie-Louise put her hand on her aunt's shoulder. "Then follow your heart."

Ambrosia sighed. "That's easier said than done."

"Yes, I know." Marie-Louise took a deep breath. *At least you love someone who doesn't have ties to someone else.* Sighing, she excused herself to go to her room and freshen up. She had returned from a nice weekend and should be happy and thankful, but her thoughts kept dwelling on Ulrich and how he had spent the weekend. And, more importantly, who spent it with him.

Resolutely she shook her head. *Enough. I refuse to think about him and will go on with my life.* She squared her shoulders and smiled at her image in the mirror before she left her room to join Ambrosia in the parlor.

Had she known of the bombshell that awaited her a few days later, however, the smile would have frozen on her lips.

The official-looking letter arrived on Thursday while Marie-Louise prepared a speech for the opening ceremony of the new primary school in the area the following day. She turned the envelope over. *From the county office. Maybe they want me to be present at the ribbon cutting ceremony for the new highway.*

Putting the envelope on the table next to her note pad, she returned to her speech. At an impasse in her writing, she opened the letter and scanned the page.

Her eyes widened as she read on. Her brow furrowed and her temper rose. "For heaven's sake! That's ridiculous," she exclaimed and slammed the letter onto the table when Ambrosia walked by.

"What's the matter?"

"Read this." Marie-Louise pushed the letter toward her aunt. "Another bogus request from the county." She rose and paced the room. "Why should I have to pay for railing along Hohenstein Road where it runs along our moat? Isn't that the town's or the county's responsibility? The moat has been here for hundreds of years and it never bothered anybody. There's never been any accident as far as I know."

After reading the message, Ambrosia agreed, "You're right. Why on earth should *you* have to pay for the railing? That's not your business."

"Exactly." Marie-Louise brushed a hand across her forehead. "It seems as if someone's trying to make life hard for us. Why? They say this stretch of road is Hohenstein property and with more and more motorcars on the road, it is our obligation to secure the moat. Without asking they'll put up the railing next week and charge us for material and labor." She produced a sarcastic laugh. "Whenever I think things have quieted down, I'm faced with yet another hurdle. Where will we come up with that kind of money? The few weddings didn't bring in nearly enough."

She sat down with her head buried in her hands.

"Oh dear, oh dear," wailed Ambrosia, "I wish I knew what to do. If we only had some source of income other than our allowances, things like that wouldn't trouble us as much."

"I'm trying to come up with ideas for a business, but each one I consider requires starting capital which we don't have, and nobody is willing to give us a loan."

"Maybe Count Wolfb—"

"No," interrupted Marie-Louise sharply, "he would be the first one to deny his help."

Ambrosia looked down her nose. "I beg your pardon?"

"It's true enough." Marie-Louise tilted her chin up. "Every time I ask him for a loan or even an advancement of my inheritance, he denies it."

"He may have his reasons."

"Certainly," scoffed Marie-Louise. "And it would be very interesting to know these reasons."

Ambrosia fixed her with a disapproving stare. "You're not implying that his reasons are dishonorable, are you?"

"I wonder sometimes . . ."

"Marie-Louise!" exclaimed her aunt in horror. "Watch what you're saying."

The baroness only tilted her chin a notch higher, but fell silent.

"You're distraught. After all the nice things the count has done for us, you shouldn't suspect him of foul play. He didn't have to send us his team horses, nor did he have to put in an appearance at the wedding. He did it for you, to help you make the wedding a success."

Marie-Louise lowered her head. "You're right."

Appeased somewhat, Ambrosia nodded. "I think you read too much into both requests from the county for improvements in the interest of public safety."

Marie-Louise shook her head. "I don't believe in coincidence, and can't get rid of the feeling that I'm being bombarded from all sides."

Shoulders hunched, her hands mussing her hair, she stared into space. "How can I come up with that kind of money . . . ?"

She glanced at the letter on the nearby table and wished that she could discuss it with Ulrich. Even though he had never offered the help she wanted, he had always pricked her pride, had provoked her into fighting the odds so that she came up with alternative solutions to her problems.

She needed him now, but visiting him at the bank was out of the question after her experience there last time, and especially after Peter's disclosure of Ulrich's upcoming engagement. If she saw him, it had to be here at the castle, but she would not, could not, contact him. She didn't want to give the impression that she needed him or wanted to see him. In fact, she would be better off not seeing him ever again. At that thought, however, her heart constricted and she felt as if the sun had ceased to shine. *I can't stand the thought of him with another woman.*

She sat down and closed her eyes while visualizing deep blue eyes and full lips that came closer, ever closer . . . *NO,* her mind screamed as she jerked upright. She wanted to forget the episode in Ulrich's office, wipe it from her memory, but her body reacted at the merest thought of him. She could almost feel his gentle touch, hear his husky voice, imagine the texture of his hair . . .

Tossing her head, Marie-Louise wiped these pictures from her mind, scolding herself for being a fool. *I'd better get back to my speech,* she thought, but had a hard time focusing even without Ulrich. The county's request haunted her thoughts. How on earth could she come up with the money for the railing?

When Marie-Louise packed her handbag for her workday at the town hall the next day, she tucked the envelope with the county's notice in, too. Maybe she would have a chance to talk to the mayor and get his advice on the situation.

She didn't have to wait too long before the mayor visited her in her office. *"Guten Tag,* Baroness. How are you doing?"

"Life would be wonderful if I wouldn't get these unpleasant notices from the county."

She handed the letter to the mayor, who read it and handed it back. "The county is responsible for the safety of our roadways and feels that some railing would prevent possible accidents. I understand that payment poses a hardship for you, but perhaps we can come up with a solution to that problem."

Scratching his chin, he plopped down on a nearby chair. "Now, let me think. There has to be something we can do." He put his finger to his temple and closed his eyes while the baroness watched him, half hoping that he might come up with a solution, half doubting. Finally, he held up his finger.

"I've got it, and the solution is so simple that I can't believe I haven't thought of it before!" His eyes lit up as he sat back and smiled, obviously pleased with himself.

Impatient, Marie-Louise wanted to shake him to get him to hurry up, but he took his time savoring every moment of her anxious anticipation. "What would you think if I offered you a personal loan?" he asked finally.

She jumped up. "You would really do that for me? Even if I can't offer you anything as collateral?"

"We can word the contract so that Hohenstein can be the collateral."

"But you know that I don't own Hohenstein until I turn twenty-five."

He smiled. "Yes, you told me, but it doesn't matter. We can project into the future, can't we?" Seeing her confusion, he elaborated. "I offer you a personal loan called a promissory note on demand. This is a loan that needs to be paid back when I demand the money. The only problem would arise if my construction business fails, which is highly unlikely. Then of course, I would need the money right away, within a week's time. My business, however, is doing quite well and is expected to keep doing so in the future." He paused and asked, "How much money do you think you'll need?"

Marie-Louise couldn't believe her good fortune. She wanted to jump up and down for joy but refrained from doing so. "I'll need to pay for the railing and I also would like to start a business."

The mayor raised an eyebrow. "What kind of business?"

"I thought of opening a café and souvenir shop at the castle, and I'm certain that it would be quite profitable."

The mayor nodded. "I have all the confidence in your business sense. I'm sure it will be successful. How much money do you need?"

Marie-Louise was speechless. This would help her establish a business that would support her and Tante Ambrosia, and even give her a chance to put money aside for the necessary repairs and restoration projects.

Never having imagined that her dreams would materialize, she didn't have a clear idea of how much money she would need. Besides, she'd need her aunt's cooperation, and she hadn't even once mentioned her plans to her. Everything was happening so fast, making her head spin.

The mayor was still waiting for an answer. Not wanting him to think that she was undecided, she said, "I need to go home and look over my notes and then I'll get back with you, if that's all right with you."

"That's fine, Baroness."

She reached for his hand. "Thank you so much for your generosity. You don't know what it means to me to finally be able to establish a business that will support my aunt and me. You won't regret it."

At home, Marie-Louise sat down and made a list of things she would need: furniture, a kitchen stove and other necessities, materials, and possible wages she would have to pay. Next, she needed to find out the cost for the items on her list. Once she had all the numbers, she visited the mayor.

He looked over the list and whistled through his teeth. "That much?"

She wanted to sink into the ground but held firm. *I won't let him intimidate me. I think the amount is very conservative.* Chin raised, she admitted, "Yes, I tried to be frugal and know that this amount will only cover the bare minimum without any extras."

The mayor smiled. "Baroness, I trust you, and you shall get the desired amount."

She wanted to hug him, but refrained, and instead shook his hand. "Thank you, thank you so very much, Herr Schmidt. You're a life-saver, and I really appreciate your trust. I won't disappoint you."

"I know that you'll succeed. Before I have my attorney draw up the contract, however, I need to know if you want to think the deal over or discuss it with your aunt?"

She shook her head. "That's not necessary. If you can draw up the contract, I'm willing to sign it."

"All right then, I'll have my attorney prepare the paperwork, and we can sign it before the day's over."

With her hand over her pounding heart, she said, "Herr Bürgermeister, I can't thank you enough. I can finally start a business that will provide an income for my aunt and me, and I can't wait to get started."

He smiled. "And *I* can't wait to see the finished product. I know the café will be a gold mine, and with you as the driving force, it can't fail."

"Thank you, Herr Bürgermeister."

"If you need help in finding an architect or builder, please let me know and I can put you in touch with the right people."

She squeezed his hand. "You are so good to me. Thank you, thank you."

"It's my pleasure to help, Baroness."

She could only nod, not trusting her voice, as a lump formed in her throat and tears of gratitude started to blur her vision. Waiting several more hours before she could tell Tante Ambrosia the good news was hard to bear. She wanted to shout for joy, to sing and dance, but she had to wait until she was back at the castle.

Chapter Eighteen

"My goodness, Marie-Louise, are you hurt? What's all that hollering about?"

Marie-Louise waved the check in front of her aunt, who took a step back. "What's this?"

"This is the ticket to our financial freedom." She waved it again. "A business loan."

Ambrosia took the check from Marie-Louise and perused it. "A business loan? Are you out of your mind? What kind of business, and who gave you a loan?"

She stared at her niece over the rim of her glasses, and although Marie-Louise hadn't expected her to whoop for joy, she had certainly hoped for some kind of relief that their unstable financial situation would finally come to an end, maybe even admiration.

A little less enthusiastic now, she explained, "The mayor gave me a personal loan to finally start a café and souvenir shop."

"You must be joking. Serving the public here on a regular basis? Organizing weddings and concerts at the castle are one thing, but a café?"

Leave it to Tante Ambrosia to sour someone's joy. "Why are you so worried? It shouldn't be that much different than putting on weddings."

I'm trying to create an income for us, for goodness' sake! If she wasn't so stuck up, she'd have come up with ideas for supplementing her income years ago. She could have taught piano or flute lessons. But no, Miss High and Mighty would rather live like a pauper than expose herself to the public.

For the first time, Marie-Louise questioned her aunt's fatalistic attitude. What was wrong with Ambrosia? Why did she sit back and let life pass her by? Watch Hohenstein fall into disrepair? Even now, when presented with a plan for their financial independence, she was hesitant. She should jump at the opportunity to work for an additional income. Why the reluctance?

After what seemed an eternity, Ambrosia said, "You don't have any experience running a business. You're jumping headlong into a venture you don't know anything about."

Marie-Louise wouldn't let her aunt's worry diminish her excitement, not when she was so close to the fulfillment of her vision. "The café will be a gold mine, you'll see."

Her dreams that night were filled with tables and chairs and work men, and once in a while there was also a tall young man with coppery hair and laughing eyes, but he disappeared quickly. No place for him at the construction site.

Notepad and measuring tape in hand, a pencil tipped to her forehead, Marie-Louise leaned against an empty stall. If she wanted to situate a souvenir shop in one end of the stable, she'd have to put up a wall between the shop and the horses' stalls.

At the sound of Ulrich's voice, Marie-Louise jumped and her heart skipped a beat before it constricted. She had been so engrossed in her calculations that she hadn't heard him enter the building. How could she possibly forget him when he kept showing up here all the time?

Ulrich pointed to her notepad. "I thought it was the servants' quarters you're turning into a café and not the stables." He looked at her with one raised eyebrow and wrinkled his nose. "I'm sorry to tell you, but I think the smell won't blend too well with the pastries."

She couldn't help laughing. "Of course the café will be in the servants' quarters. This will be a souvenir shop."

"What are you planning to sell?"

"Post cards, of course, and candy for the children, Black forest dolls, maybe even cuckoo clocks, and other souvenirs."

Ulrich looked impressed. "Good idea. What you'll need is a counter and some wall space to showcase your wares. You also need floor space for a display stand. So figure the length of the counter and some space for the clerk to get behind it." He stretched out both arms. "That's probably enough for the counter and the walk space, and the display stand could be placed along this wall here. That should do, don't you think?"

She couldn't believe how quickly he could turn a problem into a solution. "Thank you, yes, I think you're right. So, the wall would have to come here, and we would only lose three stalls."

As she scribbled some more ideas on her notepad, Ulrich asked, "All these renovations will cost money. Have you come into an unexpected inheritance?"

"Of course not. Mayor Schmidt gave me a personal loan."

He whistled—a long drawn-out sound starting at a high pitch and descending lower and lower until he ran out of breath. "Interesting. Very, very interesting." He fell silent.

She looked at him. "Aren't you going to congratulate me for having found a way out of my dilemma?"

"I'm impressed," was all he said, and she experienced a definite feeling of let-down. She didn't know exactly what she had expected him to say or do, but he could have been a little more enthusiastic about her good fortune . . . unless he didn't want her to succeed. She had expected at least some praise.

She gave him a sideways glance but couldn't detect any emotion behind his guarded expression. He stared into space, apparently deep in thought. "What kind of loan did you say the mayor offered you?"

"A personal one."

"Yes. You mentioned that." He smiled, but it seemed thin. "I wanted to know what the terms are and how you are going to pay the money back."

"I have two years to pay it back with fourteen percent interest. And by then, I hope the business will be so well established that I won't have any difficulties procuring a loan from the bank if necessary."

"No other clauses?"

She tried to remember. "Well, the mayor said if his business ever was in trouble—which was highly unlikely—then I would have to pay the money back within a week."

"A promissory note on demand, then."

"Yes, I believe that's what he called it."

Ulrich leaned against the wall. "That's what I thought," he mumbled more to himself than to her.

Worried by his morose mood, she asked, "Is a promissory note on demand something bad?"

"No, not as long as you can pay up when the time comes."

She heaved a sigh of relief. It felt good to talk with somebody who understood the money business better than she or Tante Ambrosia. She had to admit that she had been more than a little concerned about the deal, especially since her aunt seemed so worried about the success of her business venture. If Ulrich knew about these kinds of loans and thought them appropriate, she didn't need to be troubled.

Perhaps his somber mood stemmed from the fact that she had ignored his advice to come to him before making a major decision like accepting a loan from the mayor. Would he have sanctioned the deal had she discussed it with him? He pushed away from the wall. "By the way, the workers need you in the servants' quarters."

"What for?"

"Something about a wall to be taken out."

She raked her fingers through her hair. "They have the blueprints."

"Maybe there's a problem."

Having him around and being able to ask his opinion or to just talk to him made her feel more at ease with the situation at hand, although his proximity also made her heart flutter. Never having been involved with a construction crew, she felt more than a little overwhelmed and, although enthusiastic about her new venture, she sometimes felt unsure of her own judgment. With Ulrich by her side to share the responsibility, she felt confident.

As they crossed the cobbled yard, he asked, "Are you all right?"

"Of course. Why do you ask?"

"You're not as chipper as you normally are, and you haven't once bitten my head off today. Is something bothering you?"

"No. Just tense, that's all."

"That's understandable with all the activity going on around here. By the way, how does your aunt feel about your plans?"

Marie-Louise glanced around before answering in a low voice, "She hasn't said much, but I know she's worried because she walks around wringing her hands and mumbling to herself. I think that the concept of us running a café and waiting upon commoners in a truly serving capacity goes against her set of values. The old stuffiness, you see."

"Have you told her of your plans?"

"Of course I have."

"Do your plans involve her?"

She looked at him as if she doubted his mental faculties. "Certainly. I can't do it alone."

"What do you expect her to do?"

"I want her to oversee the kitchen once the café is open for business. That way she wouldn't have to deal with the guests directly but will still be the one in charge, giving the orders to the kitchen staff."

"Good thinking." He stopped and put a hand on her shoulder and looked into her eyes. "Don't you think it's about time you involved her in the planning stage? Instead of just asking for her help when the café is set up. She needs to feel a part of all this. Let her help with the planning, make a list of things that need to be purchased, and ask her opinion." He squeezed her shoulder. "Promise to talk to her?"

"I-I'll try."

He released his hold on her and instead caught one of the stray tendrils of hair, wrapping it around his finger and tracing little circles on her cheek near her ear. Even this light touch sent shivers down her spine until she pulled away.

His lips twitched. "What are you afraid of?"

You, she wanted to shout but instead squared her shoulders. "I'm not afraid of anything or anybody," she said in her most haughty tone.

His eyes darkened with suppressed laughter. "Of course not. Why should you be?"

They walked in silence toward the servants' quarters. Was she afraid of him? No, not of him, but of herself and her reaction to him. Since the encounter in his office, he had never again given her cause for complaint, although he had neither forgotten the incident nor allowed her to forget it. And had she not found out from Peter that he was to be engaged soon, she would still enjoy his visits and . . . his touch, but things had changed. She still liked his visits, liked him and his smile that always started in his eyes, but knowing that he belonged to someone else caused her heart to break.

He had turned out to be quite pleasant, and she had looked forward to his visits, had enjoyed his warm sense of humor and the way they had often laughed at the same things. She liked the way she could talk with him and use him as a sounding board, and she wished she still could feel this light-hearted familiarity, but alas . . . things could never be the same again.

If she could only deal with him in a cool, detached manner . . . She heaved a sigh.

"Problems?" he asked.

If you only knew! She shook her head. "Nothing that I can't handle."

"That's good to know." His lips curled into his familiar slow smile.

She looked at him with suspicion. Oftentimes, she felt that his words carried a hidden meaning, something she didn't quite understand, and it was this unknown factor that made her so wary.

As they arrived at the servants' quarters, Ulrich paused. "Good luck with your plans."

She felt as if somebody had doused her with ice cold water. "You're not leaving me now, are you?"

"Do I detect sorrow at my parting?"

Regret's more like it. Out loud she said, "Of course not. I just thought you might come along to help me with a possible problem."

"Sorry," he apologized, "duty calls."

Marie-Louise put a hand on his sleeve as if to hold him back. She didn't know anything about construction and didn't know if she could answer the questions the workers might have. If Ulrich came with her, she'd feel much better. She looked up into smiling eyes.

He consulted his watch. "Sorry," he said again. "I have an appointment to keep."

She released her hold. *Maybe he's meeting his chosen one.*

"You look cute when you pout," he said with a chuckle in his voice, "but it won't help you one bit." He performed an exaggerated bow and turned to leave.

"I wasn't pouting," she called as he walked away.

Without slowing his pace, he looked over his shoulder and winked at her.

Self-possessed creature. He could have easily come with her, Marie-Louise thought. Ten minutes wouldn't have caused him to be late, surely? Knowing Ulrich, she felt certain he would never arrive late to any appointment. He lived by the principle she had heard her aunt recite often enough: "Punctuality is the courtesy of kings."

Disgruntled, she turned and entered the servants' quarters.

Later that day Marie-Louise followed Ulrich's advice and sought out Ambrosia. All afternoon she had mulled over in her mind how best to approach her aunt without alienating her, and whenever she had come up with an introduction, she found a flaw in the wording and discarded it.

Her childhood days came to mind. She remembered the anguish she had suffered before gathering enough courage to approach her aunt and confess that she had done something wrong. She had always tried to use the right kind of words so her aunt wouldn't be too upset, and after all these years she still tried to hone her skills. She didn't want to sound overbearing but neither did she want to appear as if begging for mercy—after all, her business venture was designed to help both of them.

It was about time her aunt came down from her lofty pedestal because she wasn't any better than anybody else, and if the Baroness von Hohenstein could do menial work, so could

Ambrosia. To think that one person was better than another solely on account of one's birth into a certain family was antiquated and wrong. Yes, she herself had basked in the luxury of her social status not too long ago, but since returning to Hohenstein, she had come to realize the validity of the proclamation in the constitution of the United States of America that *all men are created equal.* And if she heard Ambrosia say one more time that they owed this or that to their status, she'd say something she might regret later.

After they had cleared away the supper dishes, Ambrosia retired to the parlor with some newspapers and Marie-Louise joined her there with a list of items she needed to take care of.

Not able to concentrate on the list, she watched her aunt. Ambrosia seemed engrossed in her paper and didn't look up. Marie-Louise cleared her throat. Nothing.

Frustrated, she began drawing little circles. The circles grew bigger, but Ambrosia paid no attention.

Drumming her fingers on the armrest of her chair, she glanced at her aunt and knew that she should say something, but nothing came to mind. Tante Ambrosia probably didn't want to be disturbed in her reading, so perhaps she could try to talk to her in the morning . . .

No. She had to talk to her today. She had promised Ulrich.

She cleared her throat again. This time, Ambrosia looked up, pushing her reading glasses down to the tip of her nose and regarding her niece over the rim of the glasses. "Marie-Louise, what is it? You have been fidgeting in your chair for the last five minutes."

Marie-Louise almost dropped her pencil. She had assumed her aunt was too preoccupied to notice her foolish attempts to attract her attention. She felt like a child caught snatching a cookie from the kitchen.

"Well?" probed her aunt. Putting her magazine down and taking her glasses off, Ambrosia waited.

"It's about the café," Marie-Louise said finally, rolling the pencil between her fingers.

"Y-e-s?" prodded her aunt.

"I would like for your input in planning."

Ambrosia didn't say anything. Determined, Marie-Louise pushed on, "I thought you might be able to help me pick out the furniture and the necessary things for the kitchen."

She paused to give her aunt the opportunity to consider the request, but Ambrosia didn't say anything.

She's making it hard for me on purpose. For goodness sake, I want to let her be part of the planning process, something she should be pleased about.

Gathering the remains of her courage, Marie-Louise said, "I need your help, Tante Ambrosia."

After what seemed an eternity, the older woman leaned forward. "I already agreed to oversee the staff in the kitchen and the inventory and supplies, and I thought that you had already ordered the necessary furniture, appliances, and dishes."

"I want you to help make the final decision."

Her aunt let out a deep breath and relaxed against the back of her chair. "Have you hired any kitchen staff yet?"

"No. I want to leave the hiring up to you also. Frau Becker would be good to have, and she knows women in town who wouldn't mind making some extra money."

"Good old Frau Becker! She always had a soft spot in her heart for you," said Ambrosia with a far-away look in her eyes. "I can't count the times she took the blame when you got into mischief."

Marie-Louise's breath caught in her throat. "You knew?"

"Of course I knew."

"And you never mentioned that you caught on to our plots?"

Ambrosia smiled. "Well, it just so happened that I had a soft spot for you, too."

Silence.

Marie-Louise sat frozen. Had she heard correctly? Was it possible? No. Ambrosia never showed any signs that she even liked her niece, and Marie-Louise always thought that raising her had been a distasteful duty for her aunt.

She thought back to her childhood. She had sought love from Frau Becker and Jakob, but never from her aunt. And Ambrosia certainly never offered it.

Finally, Marie-Louise choked, "Why didn't you ever show me?" She searched her aunt's face. "You were always so strict that I didn't think you cared for me."

Ambrosia sighed. "You looked so very much like your mother, and I didn't want you to become like her. I thought I could drum loyalty and responsibility into you by strict rules."

Head bent, Ambrosia murmured, "I was too strict, and I can see that now. Frau Becker was the opposite. She showered you with love and indulgence, and I envied her ability to show that love, but couldn't find a way out of my role as disciplinarian."

Her aunt dabbed at her eyes with a handkerchief. "I ended up in a corner with my scheme for your rigid upbringing, and I didn't know how to back out gracefully. There I was, loving you like I think a mother must love her child, but you were afraid of me and ran to Frau Becker when you scraped your knee or had a problem."

"I had no idea," whispered Marie-Louise, hands pressed to her heart.

"It's my fault," lamented Ambrosia. "First, I thought that every emotion had died inside me with Friedrich's death. I had forgotten how to laugh, and I had no clue how to make a little girl happy. Oftentimes I wanted to take you into my arms and hold you, but the propensity of my feelings frightened me, and I suppressed the urge."

Ambrosia fell silent and covered her face with her hands. Her shoulders shook.

With a choked sound, Marie-Louise rushed to kneel by her aunt's chair and put an arm around her. She had never seen her aunt like this, and she didn't know what to do. All her resentment seemed to wash away on a wave of empathy for the older woman who had spent a life devoid of love.

Marie-Louise thought of the many lonely hours both she and her aunt had endured when they could have enjoyed each other's company. Tears stung her eyes as she whispered, "I wish you hadn't hidden your feelings. Life would have been so much easier and more enjoyable, and I might have turned out a better person."

"Oh, dear, no," cried her aunt on a sob, "you're everything I could wish for. You came here, and despite the odds, you stayed and worked hard to bring life and beauty back to Hohenstein. Your ancestors would be proud of you, and so am I."

Marie-Louise sniffed.

"When you arrived at the castle, I didn't think you would last very long, but you have proven that you have backbone and a strong sense of family pride." Shyly, Ambrosia touched her niece's bent head. "It's so good to have you home."

Marie-Louise looked up, unbelieving. When she saw the warm glow in her aunt's eyes, although shimmering with unshed tears, she leaned her cheek against Ambrosia's and reached for her hand. "Thank you," she said simply.

"Will you forgive me for my hard-heartedness?"

Marie-Louise smiled and blinked away a tear. "It's never too late to make a fresh start."

A little anxious, Ambrosia asked, "Will you help me?"

Marie-Louise nodded. "We'll help each other."

As they embraced, they heard a knock on the door.

Chapter Nineteen

With an impatient murmur, Marie-Louise went to open the door.

"Ulrich?"

He smiled at her with a warm and gentle smile. "Have you spoken with your aunt?"

Marie-Louise laughed. "As a matter of fact, I have."

"And?"

Before answering, she craned her neck to see through the half-closed door into the parlor where her aunt still sat in her chair. Although Ambrosia couldn't possibly hear her, Marie-Louise still lowered her voice and said in hushed tones, "We had a good woman-to-woman talk and cleared the air."

"No ruffled feathers?"

"None."

"That must have been quite some talk! I'm impressed." He sounded sincere and she could see the warmth in his eyes to match that of his voice. "See, it wasn't so hard to approach her."

Emphatically she countered, "You don't know Tante Ambrosia and how she can give you that look that makes you shrivel into nothingness. I almost lost courage."

"I'm glad you didn't. What made you prevail?"

You, she wanted to say, but caught herself in time. No use boosting his already inflated ego. After a moment's hesitation she answered, "I didn't want to be a coward."

"Good girl," he chuckled. "I knew you could do it."

For a moment she basked in the warmth of his voice. She couldn't imagine that she had ever thought him rigid and dull. His position required him to adhere to a strict set of rules, but in private he was a warm individual with a good sense of humor—*and a sad lack of scruples when it came to taking advantage of innocent females.*

"Daydreaming?" he asked, interrupting her thoughts.

"Of course not," she snapped. "I was thinking of all the things I have to do to get ready for our grand opening."

"That's too bad," he teased. "You looked as if your thoughts dwelled on more pleasurable things than business matters."

And you shouldn't be saying things like that to me when you're almost engaged. "Business is all that's on my mind," she lied.

"Maybe we ought to do something about that, don't you think?"

"Of course not!"

He laughed. What nerve he possessed to taunt her like that! She would like to know if he treated his betrothed the same way. Of course, she couldn't ask him that. Lowering her head, she hid her burning cheeks. If he saw her blush, his ego would skyrocket. He knew very well how uncomfortable his gibes made her feel, and yet, he persisted in reminding her of an incident she tried to forget.

His voice interrupted her thoughts. "Still thinking about the event?"

"Don't flatter yourself, Count."

"Whatever do you mean?" he asked in mock innocence. "I was talking about the grand opening."

She could have bit her tongue. Nothing came to mind to cover up her *faux pas*, and she seethed inwardly at the injustice of it all. Where was her wit when she needed it? He knew where her thoughts had dwelled and had set a trap she neatly fell into.

She opted to ignore his question and instead gestured him into the parlor, where he greeted Ambrosia with a bow. "Marie-Louise told me of her business plans, and I'm impressed."

"Yes, we were talking about ordering furniture, dishes, and everything else necessary, and also how much staff we'll have to hire."

Marie-Louise entered the conversation. "The workers said that in another week they would be ready to install the stove and sink, and then we can have the tables and chairs delivered the following week."

"That's fantastic."

After some small talk, Ulrich stood up and said that he had to leave and had only stopped in because he was in the vicinity.

Marie-Louise accompanied him to the door. "Will you come to the grand opening?"

"When will that be?"

"Saturday, in two weeks."

Ulrich thought it over. "Hmm. This is short notice, but I'll see what I can do."

She couldn't repress a grin. "I certainly hope so. Having you there is good business, as you well know."

He laughed. "How mercenary of you, Baroness!"

When she returned to the parlor, Ambrosia commented, "You seem to have warmed up to the Count."

"Don't get too excited, Tante Ambrosia. I'm only a diversion for him."

The idea seemed to scandalize her aunt. "Marie-Louise! I don't think that Count Wolfburg pays you his attentions without a good reason. He is honorable."

Well, I don't understand him or his reasons, but I know he certainly doesn't see me as anything more than a member of his family empire and someone he can laugh with and taunt. And when it comes to being honorable, I don't know if that word can be applied to him one hundred percent, at least not where I'm involved. No sense in telling Ambrosia that, however.

Ambrosia had invited the two doctors for dinner and a card game afterwards, and when Marie-Louise found out, she called Nick and asked him to bring his camera. She'd love to have photographs of the castle at the souvenir shop, and she'd ask Nick if he wouldn't mind taking a few pictures.

While Dr. Walter helped Ambrosia with dinner, Marie-Louise accompanied the young doctor in his search for appropriate locations for his photographs. The old drawbridge with the gatehouse and armory caught his eye first. Next on his list was the outside of the castle with the curving stone stairs.

"Why don't I take a picture with you standing on the steps?"

Marie-Louise shook her head. "Oh, no, I don't want to be in any of the postcards."

"Then let me take a photograph of you just for fun."

"Fine," she conceded.

When all the outside photographs were taken, Nick suggested he take one or two inside the castle. The great ballroom, the vestibule, and the picture gallery would be ideal to show off, but it took him some time before he convinced Marie-Louise to let him go ahead with his plan. If she wanted to promote castle weddings, then she needed to show off not only the premises but also inside the walls.

Another of his ideas was to bring one of the coaches out to the cobbled yard and hitch the horses to it with Jakob in his livery, and she had to agree that this was excellent advertisement.

Because dinner was ready, they decided to continue the next day.

"Too bad that the construction is still under way, or else we could add some photographs of the café and souvenir shop," Nick mused. "When will the café be open to the public?"

"Two Saturdays from now, and I hope that you can come to the grand opening." She remembered suddenly that she had also invited Ulrich, and she definitely didn't want to have to entertain both men at the same time. How to avoid a possibly uncomfortable encounter?

"What date is that?" he asked.

"The twenty-second."

"Drat! I'll be on duty starting at two in the afternoon."

Thank goodness for his work schedule. Not wanting to sound too relieved, she said, "You could come in the morning before the crowds arrive."

He stroked her cheek with his finger and smiled into her eyes. "Great idea. I really want to be there with you on this important day as moral support, so to speak."

"Thank you, Nick. It would mean a great deal to me to have you there."

He put his arm around her shoulder and kissed her on the cheek.

Feeling guilty for still not experiencing any pleasure from his touch, she forced a smile. "I also want to invite your family, but they probably want to come on a day that's not so busy so I can show them the castle myself."

"Let me find out when they're all free to come to Hohenstein, and I'll let you know. It'll be fun to have them here when you have time to give them the grand tour."

Marie-Louise warmed up to the idea of having Nick's family visit Hohenstein. "I could give them a carriage ride and show them the grounds connected with the castle."

"Excellent idea," said Nick, "They'd really love that."

"It's a deal, then." She smiled and led the way back to the castle, where they joined Ambrosia and Dr. Walter for dinner.

Marie-Louise couldn't keep from smiling when she caught the older couple exchanging covert glances, and she even saw Dr. Walter brush Ambrosia's hand when reaching for the salt shaker. She looked at Nick to see if he had noticed this exchange also. He had, and suppressed a smile.

"What's the grinning about, you young folks? Haven't you ever seen anybody flirt before?"

Marie-Louise stared at him, not sure that she had heard correctly. Never in her wildest dreams had she thought that he would be so open with his feelings for her aunt. She looked at Ambrosia to see if her aunt objected to the doctor's declaration, but she only looked down on her plate with flushed cheeks, obviously uneasy about the doctor's frankness but not displeased.

My goodness, I can't imagine my aunt in the arms of a man. She was always only Tante Ambrosia, a spinster.

She wondered what the doctor had done to awaken Ambrosia's romantic side after all these years, then speculated if the two of them were on the path to marriage. Marie-Louise would be left in the castle alone then, unless she also married. *Not very likely!* She was actually envious of Tante Ambrosia, she realized. Not that she resented her happiness, but she wanted it, too.

Looking at Nick, she knew with a sinking heart that he wasn't the one that could fill the void in her heart, yet the one who could was beyond her reach.

The thought of Ulrich as a marriage partner startled her. Where was her resolve to never marry someone from her own rank? Just because the count had chosen another young lady to become his countess didn't mean that Marie-Louise would have married him had he chosen her as his future wife. She could admit that she had an infatuation for him, and, yes, perhaps even more than just an infatuation, much more, but would that have been enough to throw all her resolves to the wind?

She had seen Nick's family and wanted the same kind of relationship for her own future family, but knew that this would be impossible if she married within her circle. Under no circumstances did she want her children to grow up the way she had, left to be raised by an aunt and cared for by servants. That did not constitute a happy childhood or a normal family life.

Nick's touch brought her back to reality and she smiled at him as she squeezed his hand.

"You had a faraway look, but I'm glad you're back with us again."

"The café is never far from my mind these days." Thank goodness he couldn't guess where her thoughts had dwelled. She'd do better to push them to the back of her mind and concentrate on her guests.

With dinner over, the men helped clear the table, and Ambrosia stacked the dishes to be washed later while Marie-Louise set up the card game.

They played as teams, and Nick and Marie-Louise won every hand, probably not because they were luckier, had better cards, or were the better card players, but because Ambrosia and Dr. Walter were busy exchanging glances—Dr. Walter openly, and Ambrosia covertly.

At the end of the evening, Dr. Walter complained, "You young kids beat us badly." Whereupon Nick countered, "You didn't concentrate enough. Your thoughts were clearly elsewhere."

Dr. Walter laughed his hearty laugh while Ambrosia's blush deepened. "The young folks nowadays don't show any respect to their elders." With a twinkle in his eye, he continued, "I wouldn't have dared to point out the distractions that kept my superiors from performing at their best."

Nick burst out laughing and even Ambrosia had to chuckle. Leave it to Dr. Walter to diffuse an embarrassing moment! Marie-Louise liked the old doctor very much and hoped that her aunt would overcome her scruples and marry this charming commoner.

The last weekend in July saw throngs of people flocking to Hohenstein Castle to attend the grand opening of Marie-Louise's business venture. Advertisements all around town announced the event and brought the populace out to hopefully catch a glimpse of the young and beautiful baroness.

She flitted from the café to the souvenir shop and back again, making sure everything ran smoothly—visiting with the guests, exchanging friendly greetings, and helping wherever it was needed most.

Nick showed up around eleven o'clock and stayed until he had to leave to start his shift at the hospital. He took a few photographs of the interior and the display case with all the cakes and pastries.

In the afternoon the reporters arrived, interviewed Marie-Louise, and took pictures for the next day's paper.

Mayor Schmidt visited with his wife and walked sedately around the premises, admiring the improvements that had been made.

Despite her light summer dress, Marie-Louise felt hot and rested for a moment in the shade of a tree. Her feet felt like lead and her head ached, yet she couldn't be happier with the success of this first day in business.

After she had roughly calculated the proceeds of the day and realized the substantial profit they would make, Marie-Louise felt almost dizzy with joy. She calculated again with the same result. She couldn't wait to tell Ulrich. How surprised he would be! In the meantime she would share the good news with her aunt.

She would have skipped all the way to the kitchen had she not been concerned for her image. *I'm becoming like my aunt*, she thought ruefully.

Entering the kitchen, she saw Ambrosia giving orders, looking as stately as ever. Not a hair was out of place, and her dress was as fresh and neatly pressed as if it had just come out of the closet and not been worn for several hours in a hot kitchen. Too bad her aunt wouldn't go out to the café—the guests would be greatly impressed.

Marie-Louise looked around. The women were busy filling orders, brewing coffee, cutting cake, and washing dishes, and everything seemed to run like clockwork. Thank goodness for Frau Becker and her crew, and thank goodness for Tante Ambrosia.

With a friendly smile, Marie-Louise nodded to the women as she walked to stand by her aunt.

Ambrosia gave her a questioning look, laced with hope, and Marie-Louise squeezed her arm and nodded without words. "I'm proud of you," her aunt said and put an arm around her niece's shoulders.

Later that day, when Ambrosia left to get more supplies from the castle, Frau Becker took Marie-Louise aside. "How are things going with your aunt?"

The baroness smiled. "We finally came to terms."

"Do you mean to tell me the woman has a heart?"

"Of course she does, but she has a hard time showing her emotions."

"Pooh!" Frau Becker shrugged. "A little late to show her feelings now."

"Better late than never."

On her way out of the kitchen, Marie-Louise glanced out the window. No blue Mercedes parked in front of the café. She leaned her forehead against the cool glass and sighed. He hadn't come. The sun was already slipping past the tree tops, and the café would close in less than an hour. The probability of Ulrich visiting became slimmer with every passing minute. She wanted him to witness her success, share in her happiness . . .

What if he came and brought his future wife with him? *I think I'd faint on the spot!*

Without the prospect of his visit, her joy seemed to diminish somehow. *He said he'd try to come. Oh, well, he probably had more important things to do than attend the opening of a café and mingle with commoners. He's probably flirting with his sweetheart.*

Marie-Louise turned away from the window, feeling let down.

The mayor hailed her from one of the tables, and she joined him and his wife for a little chat. At one point in the conversation, she noticed the mayor look up. When she turned to see what had caught the man's attention, she almost choked on her breath. There in the doorway stood Ulrich—tall, broad-shouldered, authoritative. Her heart stopped a beat before it thundered against her ribs. He had come after all!

Marie-Louise felt as if someone had turned a light on inside of her, and she wanted to jump up and run to him. Instead, she forced herself to remain in her seat but smiled at him in greeting and continued her conversation with the mayor's wife until the couple excused themselves to leave for the evening.

Heart hammering in her chest, she made her way to Ulrich's table. "You decided to grace Hohenstein with your presence, Count. I'm overwhelmed and flattered."

He gave her a lopsided smile. "I said I'd try to come."

"It got so late that I feared you'd never show up."

"Missed me, didn't you?" He smiled.

"Purely business reasons."

"Yes, I know. All these people came here today to catch a glimpse of a real-life count."

"Exactly."

He laughed. "Liar. I saw the admiring looks that follow you everywhere you go. The people came to see *you*, and they were greatly rewarded. Greeted by a real-life baroness with shining eyes and a contagious smile."

Although she knew he was bantering, his compliments still made her heart flutter. "Flatterer," she said, fluttering her eyelids.

He seemed crushed. "Baroness, you're doing me an injustice. I spoke the truth." His voice grew serious as he reached across the table to cover her hand with his. "May I congratulate you on your success? You've done a marvelous job."

"You really think so?" she beamed.

"Yes, I do."

The waitress came to take Ulrich's order.

He turned to Marie-Louise. "What do you recommend?"

"Definitely Tante Ambrosia's *Schwarzwälder Kirschtorte*, the best Black Forest cake you'll ever taste."

Smiling up at the waitress, he said, "Please bring me the *Schwarzwälder Kirschtorte.*" The waitress curtseyed, and Marie-Louise whispered that the count's order was free of charge.

He looked over to her. "Aren't you eating anything?"

Marie-Louise shook her head. "No, I'm not hungry. Besides, I couldn't eat even if I wanted to. I'm too nervous today."

"You've had a big day, but you still should eat something."

"I will after all the guests leave. Then I can sit down in peace and quiet and enjoy a meal, if Tante Ambrosia isn't too exhausted to prepare something. In that case, a slice of bread with butter and jam will have to do."

The waitress brought his order, curtseyed again, and left.

Ulrich dug into the cake with relish. "Mmm, you were right, this cake is excellent." Putting his hand over hers, he looked at her and winked.

Her heart leaped at his touch and she felt the familiar heat creep into her cheeks as she pulled her hand from under his.

"Marie-Louise, what's wrong? You've been acting strange lately. I realize that you're under a lot of pressure, but I'm concerned about you. You make conversation and you smile and even laugh sometimes, but you look as if you barely hold back the tears. What's going on? Can I help?"

She clamped her mouth shut to stifle the sob that had risen to her throat. Oh, how she wished she could bury her face in his chest and let the tears come, but that was impossible. She could never tell him of her feelings, not when he was to be married to someone else in the near future.

Probably to avoid the curious stares from the guests, he said, "Would you mind showing me the souvenir shop?"

She immediately rose and he followed her out of the café. Alone and hidden from prying eyes, he stopped her. "Now, tell me what's bothering you."

Shaking her head, she didn't look up until he lifted her chin with his finger and forced her to face him. "What is it?"

Good grief, are my feelings so obvious? That will never do. I have to get over my feelings for him, and I will, even if it kills me! She'd been moping around for long enough, and from now on, she would think of him only as Count Wolfburg, head of the House of Wolfburg, and nothing more. *Although he is the handsomest man I have ever seen . . . Oh, stop this nonsense!*

"It's nothing really," she hastened to explain. "The last two weeks were so hectic with all the commotion around here—the workmen with their never-ending questions, the decisions that had to be made and the constant running around—that

I'm plain worn out, but nothing that a good night's rest won't cure."

Although her reasons sounded good to her own ears, he didn't seem to believe her. "Are you sure that's all that's wrong?" He put an arm around her shoulders to draw her a little closer. "I'm worried about you."

"There's no need to worry." She produced a little smile and tried to wriggle out of his hold, but of course, he only drew her closer. He buried his face in her hair, and she felt the all too familiar shivers run down her spine and heat rise into her cheeks.

"Will you promise me that you'll come to me if you run into any problems?"

Sure, just like you helped me before when I came to you with problems.

"I know what you think, that coming to me for help hasn't been too productive in the past, but I still want to help you if I can."

She shook her head. "Now that I have the capital to run my business, I should be set."

"Nevertheless, problems may arise and I want you to come to me if you need help."

She finally nodded half-heartedly because she wanted him to drop the subject and channel the conversation to less dangerous topics. "You mentioned that you wanted to see the souvenir shop," she reminded him, and with a motion of her head indicated for him to follow her.

When they entered the stable building where the souvenir shop was located, Marie-Louise asked the clerk, "How was your day, Hans, and how are you holding up?"

"Thanks for asking, Baroness. I'm doing all right as long as I can sit down once in a while."

"Ullie, this is Hans Falke. Hans, this is Ulrich, Count Wolfburg."

To her astonishment Ulrich shook hands with Hans, who beamed up at the count. "How was business today, Herr Falke?"

"We had a steady stream of customers, and the children seemed to be drawn to the store." Turning to Marie-Louise he said, "I think sugared nuts would be popular. At least, *my* children always ask for them when we go to the county fair."

"Thank you for the suggestion, I'll check into it."

When they were outside again, Ulrich wanted to know, "Where did you find this man?"

"I didn't find him. He was practically put into my lap."

"How did that happen?"

"On my very first day at the town hall, one of the employees asked me if I had a job for her husband at the castle. Of course, at the time we didn't need anybody, but as soon as I had the money to start the business, I remembered Ingrid telling me that her husband had been injured and was an invalid staying at home with the children while she worked and brought home a paycheck."

"That was very kind of you." Ulrich put both hands on her shoulders to turn her to face him. "You're a warm-hearted and generous person, Baroness von Hohenstein. Your ancestors would be proud of you." He bent his head and feathered a kiss at the corner of her mouth, barely touching her lips with his but enough to draw an involuntary moan from her.

He chuckled. "Just wanted to make sure that we still speak the same language."

Before she could think what she was doing, she punched him in the side for his impudence. As soon as her fist made contact with him, however, she was shocked at her own audacity. He, however, chuckled and looked as smug as if he had just won first prize in a horse race. *Men!*

When he bent down again, she took a cautious step back. "Don't worry, I won't kiss you again. I only wanted to whisper in your ear that you're not only a warm-hearted person but also a passionate woman. Now, stop glowering at me and paste a smile on your face because the reporters have discovered us and are descending upon us. Turn around and look."

Was that a ploy to distract her? No, out of the corner of her eye she saw them with cameras at the ready. "Heavens, that's all I need!"

"Stay calm and follow my lead."

She wanted to give him a piece of her mind about his behavior but only said, "I don't understand men."

He laughed out loud. "You have a lifetime ahead of you to study them."

She made a dismissive gesture with her hand. "Even a lifetime isn't long enough." When the photographers had almost reached them, he reminded her, "Stay calm, don't be nervous or angry, act professional."

"*Guten Tag,* Baroness von Hohenstein, we're glad to have found you. Would you please . . . Count Wolfburg?"

Ulrich inclined his head and smiled.

"Did you attend the grand opening to witness the baroness's success?"

"Yes, indeed, and I am very impressed with the undertaking and predict a successful season."

"Baroness, what was the reason for opening a café and shop at the castle?"

Because I was desperate, poorer than a church mouse—but Tante Ambrosia would murder me in my sleep if I said that. "I wanted to make this beautiful castle and the surroundings available to the public, and the best way to do that was to establish a place where families could come on the weekend and enjoy the scenery together and sit down to coffee and cake and visit with friends."

Ulrich added, "Don't forget the philanthropic aspect of this enterprise, Baroness." Turning to the reporter he explained, "The baroness employs men and women from the town of Hohenstein who need additional income. Take the shopkeeper, for instance. Herr Falke was injured at his previous job and was an invalid with no income. The Baroness offered him a job that not only gets him out of the house but also provides additional income for him and his family. You ought to interview him—it would make for a good story."

The man looked at the count as if he wasn't sure whether he was dismissed or whether he should stay and ask more questions but decided to take one more photograph and leave to find Herr Falke at the shop.

Marie-Louise turned to the count after the reporters had left. "I'm amazed at how elegantly you shooed them away without offending them."

He laughed. "It takes practice."

"I hope they don't make up a story about us together."

"They won't dare fabricate a story."

She raised an eyebrow. "Are you so sure? They made up a love story about Dr. Neff and me that wasn't true."

"True, but they won't do that where I'm concerned."

She laughed. "You think you're above their gossip?"

"Yes."

Hands on hips, she looked at him. "My goodness, you're presumptuous!"

He stopped walking and turned to her. "My dear Baroness, I have stock in most of the newspapers around here. They wouldn't dare offend me."

"Why am I not surprised?"

His eyes crinkled, and she heard the mirth in his voice. "It's good business practice to have as many eggs in as many baskets as possible."

Is he talking only about business, or also about women? She sighed.

"Tired?" he asked.

"Yes, very."

"Well, the day is almost over."

She sighed again. "Not for me. After we close up, I have to do the bookkeeping."

"Can't you save that for tomorrow?"

"I guess I could, but I really want to know how much money we took in today. I need to see the fruits of our labors."

"I think that you will be pleasantly surprised."

"I certainly hope so."

On their way back to the café they saw several of the guests leaving the premises. A look at her watch confirmed that it was almost six o'clock and time to close the café. She walked Ulrich to his motorcar.

"Thank you for coming. It meant a lot to me."

"I wouldn't have missed your special day for the world. Now go and relax."

He waved and smiled, backed up his Mercedes, and revved the engine before he headed for the drawbridge. Marie-Louise watched him round the bend before she turned toward the café.

She was really grateful that Ulrich had come to the grand opening. Had he kept his distance, everything would have been fine. Just when she was sure she had her feelings for him under control and would be able to treat him like a friend, he knowingly and deliberately awakened her passion again. Being almost engaged, he shouldn't even look at another woman, much less flirt with her. Getting over her feelings wasn't going to be easy, and what should have been the happiest day of her life was marred by her weakness in responding to his touch.

I'm like a puppet that moves at the will of the puppeteer, or like a figure in a chess game that can be moved to whatever position the player determines. Will I ever manage to get him out of my system? I wish I could talk with Tante Ambrosia and get advice from her, but she would faint if she knew what was going on under her very nose . . .

Chapter Twenty

Business was going well. They didn't have the same crowds that had milled the castle at the grand opening, but a steady stream of visitors continued to visit. When she wasn't helping bake cakes and pastries or preparing other refreshments for the café, Marie-Louise was sitting over the books and entering every expense and income. It took more work to run a business than she had thought possible.

Planning and shopping and advertising needed to be done, not to mention the extra work when they had a concert or wedding scheduled. Frau Becker proved invaluable with her never-ending string of friends who would come to help almost at the drop of a hat.

Besides running a business, Marie-Louise had to attend public functions in her capacity as the town's special events representative and spent every Friday in her office at the town hall. That didn't leave much time for leisure, and she often felt too exhausted in the evenings to even sit down with a book or listen to a phonograph, had there been one. Come nine o'clock, she went straight to bed, and as soon as her head hit the pillow, she fell asleep.

She had added one more feature to her weekend business: carriage rides leaving the castle every hour on the hour, with Jakob as designated coachman. People liked to feel like nobility in a classy carriage drawn by pure-bred, matched horses, and a coachman dressed in a green livery with gold tresses and buttons. And judging by Jakob's wide smile, he enjoyed this activity as well.

The public, and especially the children, embraced this new venture, and there wasn't a ride that wasn't booked to the limit.

Marie-Louise would have liked to act as coachman once in a while but remembered her promise to Ulrich that she wouldn't set herself up for adverse publicity. If she went against his wishes he might take his team away, and they'd lose the income from the rides.

She was happy, therefore, when Nick's family came for a visit and she could show them the castle grounds and surrounding areas in the *landau*.

It was a very pleasant time. Markus and Sabine were so excited about the carriage ride, while Mr. Neff's interest centered solely on the castle's possibilities as a holiday resort.

After the Neffs left, Ambrosia commented, "What a delightful family! They were very pleasant and well-spoken."

Marie-Louise sat with her chin in the palm of her hand. "Yes, they are nice people, aren't they? I envy them for their loving relationship."

Ambrosia sounded concerned. "You sound depressed. Is everything going all right?"

"No . . . that is, I don't know what's wrong with me. I had a wonderful day with Nick's family and I like them very much, but I feel guilty."

"Why?"

"Because they probably assume that I'm in love with Nick, and I'm not." Marie-Louise mussed her hair.

Ambrosia put her arm around her niece's shoulder. "Yes, I know that you're not in love with him, but can't he be your friend?"

"That would be wonderful, but I think he expects more."

"Then you'll have to tell him the truth. The sooner the better, before his feelings get too involved."

Marie-Louise looked up. "I'm afraid to tell him because he may not want to be around me anymore, and I need him."

"You *need* him?"

How could she tell her aunt that she was, in fact, using Nick to forget Ullie. She felt so selfish and ashamed for playing with the doctor's feelings but knew that she didn't want to lose him, not yet anyway.

In answer to her aunt's question, she hedged, "Well, it's nice to have someone to go out with once in a while and to do things with."

"And to use as photographer when the need arises," Ambrosia finished.

Marie-Louise hung her head. "Yes. I'm such an awful person, and I hate myself."

"You never told him that you loved him, did you?"

"No, I didn't."

They both fell silent, but after a few moments Marie-Louise said, "To make matters worse, we met a newspaper photographer in town, and I'm afraid to see the kind of story he will make up."

Ambrosia gasped. "How did they know that you were out for a ride today?"

"I have no idea, but someone must have seen us and alerted them."

Pressing her lips into a fine line, the older woman said, "Well, we'll find out tomorrow morning when we read the paper."

The article in the paper the next morning showed a picture of Marie-Louise on the front page, sitting on the box driving the team. Next to her sat the doctor with his arm around her. The headline read, BARONESS WITH FUTURE IN-LAWS.

Marie-Louise hung her head. "I'm ruined! How can they get away with these lies? They waited for an embarrassing moment and took a picture."

"Yes, that's what they get paid for." Ambrosia shook her head. "What I don't understand is that you let yourself get caught in an embarrassing situation like that. You shouldn't have let the doctor put his arm around you in public."

"I didn't encourage it, you know," she defended herself. "But I'll talk to him when I see him next."

"Yes, do, because your reputation is at stake."

Marie-Louise moaned, burying her face in her hands. "Oh, I hope Ullie doesn't see this paper."

"You mean *Count Wolfburg*."

That was missing the point entirely, but Marie-Louise thought better than telling her that. "Yes—oh, how can I ever face him again?"

"I'm sure he'll understand because he knows how these reporters are."

The baroness moaned. "Yes, he knows, and that's the problem. He told me that nobility has to be especially discreet, and now he'll see that I didn't heed his advice. Oh, how could I have been so careless?"

Ambrosia stroked her niece's bent head. "Now, now, don't berate yourself; what's done is done. Don't waste any more energy in feeling sorry for yourself. Instead, think in terms of limiting the damage."

"Yes, but how?" Marie-Louise snorted. "Short of announcing my engagement to Nick, which I somehow think might give him the wrong impression."

"You'll come up with something."

Nobody in her circle would touch her with a ten-foot-pole after the newspaper article came out, and although she didn't intend to ever marry someone from her own rank, the fact that she wouldn't be considered eligible any more still rankled. Even Ulrich would stay away from her now, as his silence all too clearly demonstrated. He could devote all his time to his future wife from now on, but the thought was anything but comforting.

She knew that he would be angry about the article in the paper and about her indiscretion. However, he didn't have the right to point a finger when he, who would soon announce his engagement, was still flirting with her—against her will, nevertheless! The only difference between the two scenarios was that he was discreet about his clandestine flirting, while she, innocent though it might be, had committed the unpardonable sin of showing affection in public—affection she didn't even feel.

She had worked herself into a nice anger and was ready to give the count a piece of her mind should he come calling. But he didn't.

Nick called instead. "Did you see the newspaper article?" he wanted to know.

"Of course I saw it, and I'm furious."

He laughed. "Come on, it wasn't that bad."

"Not that bad!" she almost shouted. "My reputation is ruined because of this article. We're not engaged, and your parents are not my future in-laws. At least not yet."

"Calm down. It's not worth getting all worked up over. People will soon forget the story and go on to something else."

"It isn't as easy as that," she snapped. "In our snobbish circles these kinds of *faux pas* are not readily forgiven."

"You don't want to marry any of the blue-blooded aristocrats anyway."

"That's true, but I still have to interact with them."

Nick snorted. "I don't understand you. If you don't want to be allied with them, you should just forget about them."

"It's not that easy to turn my back on my heritage, Nick."

"Listen to yourself! I don't think you know what you want because you're contradicting yourself constantly. You want to sit on the fence and enjoy both sides, and that won't work. You have to make up your mind and choose your own destiny."

For a moment, she was speechless. He had never spoken sharply to her before, and her feelings were hurt. She needed his understanding and not a lecture, though she understood he probably felt as frustrated as she did, but for a different reason. He must know that her feelings for him did not run as deep. It was a terrible thing to put him through.

"I'm sorry, Nick, for venting my frustration on you. I hope that you're right and that the episode will be forgotten soon enough."

"There," he soothed, "that sounds much better. Now, to take your mind off this unpleasantness, I want to take you to the theater tonight. Can I pick you up around six-thirty?"

"I don't know if I dare go out in public."

"You have to. Otherwise, you'll give people even more food for gossip."

Marie-Louise sighed. "All right, but please no show of affection in public anymore."

"A good thing that it will be dark during the show," he teased.

"I'm serious, Nick."

"You're probably right. I'll see you tonight."

Although Marie-Louise didn't feel like going anywhere at the moment, she realized that getting away from Hohenstein for a while would do her good and take her mind off her problems.

Nick picked her up in Dr. Walter's black motorcar at the appointed time, and she turned to look over her shoulder to see if anybody was following them.

"What are you looking for?" he wanted to know.

"I'm making sure that we're not being followed."

"No need to be paranoid. Tell you what. I'll check every so often and let you know immediately if I see someone trailing us."

"Good," she said with a sigh and relaxed against the seat cushion.

She sat still for a few moments but couldn't help turning around again when she saw a vehicle. "Someone's behind us."

"Of course. It's a public road."

The automobile behind them caught up but didn't pass them and adjusted its speed to theirs.

"Do you think they're reporters?"

"No."

She settled down again, but a flash followed by Nick's outcry a short time later startled her.

"*Donnerwetter*, the passenger just took a picture of us. They're reporters."

Marie-Louise immediately lowered her head. "Can't you drive faster and get away from them?"

"I won't do any such thing," he said. "Don't let them intimidate you. We're proceeding as planned."

"Are you sure?"

"Yes. They can follow us to the theater but what can they report? That we have seen such and such a show? Their readers won't be interested in a dull story like that."

Sighing, Marie-Louise reluctantly settled back. "I guess you're right."

Nick's prediction proved to be correct. The reporters followed them to the theater, took some more pictures, but left them in peace after that.

"Thank goodness," breathed Marie-Louise. "They're gone. Now I'll be able to enjoy the show." *And forget my problems for a while.*

Nick placed his hand under her elbow and guided her into the theater and to their seats. Because the lighting was dim, not too many people recognized the baroness, especially since she kept her head down.

She wiggled into a comfortable position, relaxed her shoulders, and was ready to be entertained. It felt good to leave her problems behind for a few hours and watch someone else's on the stage, instead. Even Nick's arm around her felt soothing in the dark, and his shoulder provided a comfortable head rest. His hold around her tightened as he pulled her closer and rested his chin on her head.

"Hmm, I could sit here like this all night," he mumbled into her hair.

This is actually not unpleasant—perhaps I could fall in love with him after all. That would solve all my problems. I could get access to my inheritance and be able to restore Hohenstein and, in addition, wouldn't be bogged down with the restrictions of my rank any more. Just when she'd arrived at that thought, a picture of laughing eyes, coppery hair, and a quirking mouth came to mind. She imagined Ulrich's lips teasing hers, and his fingers gently touching her cheek, and immediately her body responded with a wave of heat that started somewhere in the vicinity of her heart and rose quickly to her cheeks. *Traitor*, she scolded herself. *How can I ever forget what happened when my body overrules my mind?*

They didn't run into any more reporters on the way back to the castle, which gave Nick the opportunity to take his time to accompany Marie-Louise to the front entrance. He turned her to him and gently kissed her eyes, her nose, her cheeks, and her neck until he finally captured her lips with his. She held her breath and willed herself to feel the sensations she knew she should, but although the kiss wasn't unpleasant, it didn't involve her whole body, her feelings, and all of her senses—no fireworks at all. She responded to his kiss, but it left her unfulfilled.

He pulled away but held her gaze. "I love you, Marie-Louise. I love you with all my heart and want to be together with you forever."

"Oh, Nick," was all she could say and leaned her head on his chest. She had dreaded the time when he would declare his love, because she knew that he would want her to respond with a declaration of her own, but she couldn't lie, even if the lie would make him happy for the moment. Now it had happened for the second time, and she wasn't sure if this would mark the beginning of the end when no declaration from her was forthcoming.

She had been content with the *status quo* and was sad that it would have to come to an end, but not tonight, not this moment. Hadn't Nick said that she was afraid to make a decision and that she couldn't have it both ways? He was right, of course, and she guessed that he sensed that her heart was somewhat divided. *Poor Nick.*

"You're tired. Let me unlock the door for you so that you can get your beauty rest." He opened the door and gave her a little pat on the back. "Sweet dreams, my lovely baroness."

"*Gute Nacht*, Nick, and thank you for a nice evening."

"Sleep tight."

It would be so easy to say *I love you*, but it wouldn't be honest, and she couldn't lie to him. Eventually, his feelings would get hurt, but she didn't want him to remember her as a liar.

She didn't go straight to her room but detoured via the picture gallery, where she stood in front of her father's portrait again. *Papa, what am I to do? I feel like a traitor. What should I do?*

She looked up into his smiling face, and it was as if he was talking to her heart. She nodded. *You're right, I have to face the music and tell him the truth. I don't want to be a coward or live a lie because of selfish reasons. I'm a Hohenstein, and Hohensteins are known for their valor and integrity.*

With this resolve, she went to bed and fell into a dreamless sleep.

Chapter Twenty-one

The next morning, Marie-Louise received a message from Ulrich. Her heart plummeted to her stomach when she read that he would come to see her as soon as his schedule would allow, but it would definitely be that day. That sounded business-like, but didn't give her any clue as to whether he was upset with her or not.

She waited all morning, but he didn't come. No matter how often she walked to the window to look for his blue Mercedes, she always returned to the parlor more deflated than before. Not that she looked forward to the encounter. No. She wanted to get it over with as soon as possible. The longer she had to wait, the more miserable she felt.

Finally, she sat at the pianoforte and picked at some keys, but soon closed the lid and moved to the window again. While there, she plucked at a plant before she fluffed the pillows on the settee. Next, she smoothed a wrinkle in the drapes and walked to the little side table to straighten the doily and center the vase.

"Marie-Louise," said Ambrosia in her sternest voice, "you're making me nervous with all your fiddling. Sit down and collect yourself for the count's visit. He won't bite your head off."

"Oh, Tante Ambrosia, I'm afraid of what he'll say."

Softer than before, her aunt admonished, "Don't get all upset. Things have a tendency to work out well eventually."

Marie-Louise twisted her hands. "I wish I could believe that. Oh, there he is!"

"Go and open the door and remember to be demure but confident."

Easier said than done. She squared her shoulders, smoothed her hair back, and went to greet their visitor.

"*Guten Tag,* Count Wolfburg. Won't you come in, please?" She smiled and gestured for him to enter.

"Good to see you in such good spirits, Baroness von Hohenstein," he returned, but the smile didn't reach his eyes, and her already low confidence dropped a few more degrees.

Ulrich bowed and touched his lips to Ambrosia's outstretched hand. "You look younger every time I see you, Fräulein von Hohenstein."

Ambrosia smiled. "Having my niece around keeps me young."

My blunders keep her on her toes, more like.

He turned back to Marie-Louise. "How is the business coming along?"

Glad to be on safe ground for the time being, she replied with more enthusiasm than she felt. "We're quite pleased with the steady flow of customers on the weekends, and have been very fortunate to have had such beautiful weather for the last few weeks."

Addressing Ambrosia, he asked, "Fräulein von Hohenstein, the work at the café isn't too strenuous for you?"

"No, not at all. We have Frau Becker and some other women from town to help with the baking and kitchen duties, and I have to say that I enjoy the activity."

"You're an important part of this business undertaking, I assume."

Marie-Louise agreed, "I couldn't do it without my aunt."

What is he waiting for? He's making small talk but without his usual tongue-in-cheek humor. He must be angrier than I thought.

Turning to the baroness, he said, "A few weeks ago I promised to let you drive my automobile, remember?"

She looked at him askance. *What is he up to?* Nodding, she returned, "Yes, I remember."

"Well, then, let's do it."

"Right now?"

"Why not? Or do you have any other obligations at the moment?"

"No, of course not."

"Then let's go." Turning to Ambrosia, he politely inquired, "Fräulein von Hohenstein, can you spare your niece for a couple of hours?"

Marie-Louise feared she was in for a severe lecture if he wanted to talk to her for a couple of hours. Apprehension washed over her and she sent her aunt a worried glance, but Ambrosia only nodded reassuringly.

"Coming?" asked Ulrich over his shoulder.

Marie-Louise rose and joined the count, feeling like a lamb going to the slaughter. Putting a hand on the small of her back, Ulrich bowed to Ambrosia, and then led the baroness out to his blue Mercedes.

He opened the door for her and pointed to the ignition. "The key's already there." Walking around the front, he folded his length into the passenger seat.

Marie-Louise sat with her hands on the steering wheel but didn't turn the key.

"What are you waiting for?"

She took a deep breath and turned to him. "You're upset with me and I understand why, but it makes me feel very uncomfortable."

He produced a short laugh that wasn't like his usual warm chuckle. "Let's go to a place where we can talk unobserved. Start the engine and I'll direct you to our destination."

"That sounds as if you're telling me to dig my own grave."

"Being melodramatic?"

"I'm not going anywhere with you if you can't be civil," she retorted.

"I'm trying very hard to be civil, so start the engine!"

"No."

A little softer, he entreated, "Marie-Louise, please start the engine."

"No, not until you . . ." She wanted to say *love me*, but stopped herself in time.

He immediately pounced on her unfinished sentence. "Not until I do what?"

At least now he was looking at her, which was an improvement over his detached demeanor from a moment ago. She had to come up with an answer to his question, though, and thought quickly. "Not until you give me one of your smiles that starts in your eyes."

He sighed but smiled, and this time his eyes smiled also. "How can I remain angry with you when you look so cute with that puckered kissable mouth of yours?"

She glared at him. "You shouldn't say things like that."

"Like what?"

"What you just said."

Ulrich lifted an eyebrow. "Why not?"

"Because . . ." she fidgeted in her seat, ". . . because things like that should be reserved for your future wife."

"I appreciate your concern for my future wife, and I will try to remember your sentiments."

She thought she detected a grin in his voice, but simply nodded.

"Now that you voiced your opinion, you could go ahead and start the engine."

She gave him a sideways glance, depressed the gas pedal and made the wheels spin. Too quickly, she took her foot off the brake, and the Mercedes lurched forward. *How embarrassing. First I make a fool of myself telling him what to say or not to say, and then I show him how inexperienced I really am when it comes to driving an motorcar.*

"Easy on the gas, and let out the clutch slowly," he admonished.

How can I concentrate on driving when you make me nervous?

"Take the back road around town and head toward Wolfburg."

To show him that she was a good driver, she eased off the gas before a curve, then again depressed the pedal hard until the next bend in the road came into view.

"Whoa, easy now on these curves. We don't want to tumble into town on a shortcut!"

"Wouldn't the reporters have a heyday if that happened?" *Oh, wrong thing to say.*

"Why do you think I asked you to take the back road?" he asked. "Should someone from the newspaper see you with two different lovers in the same week, your reputation would be irreparable."

"But you're not my lover," she scoffed.

"And the doctor is?"

"Don't be silly, of course not." When she realized that she had just called the head of the House of Wolfburg silly, she clapped a hand over her mouth. "Sorry."

Now he laughed in earnest. "Something tells me you meant exactly what you said."

"Well, yes, I meant what I said, although I should have kept my opinion to myself."

"Thank you for your honesty. At least I'm not left in the dark regarding your sentiments on every score."

She looked at him to see if he was teasing and, judging by the laugh lines fanning the corners of his eyes, he was.

"Watch out!" he exclaimed as they veered off the road and onto the banking. He reached over and grabbed the wheel and steered the Mercedes back onto its course. "Keep your eyes on the road if you don't want to send us both into the hereafter."

Obediently, she eased the Mercedes to his prescribed speed and looked straight ahead.

"Turn left at the next intersection, and after you pass the fire station you can step on the gas and see what this vehicle can really do."

She followed his instructions and pushed the gas pedal all the way to the floor. The automobile shot forward and reached 30, 40, and 45 kilometers per hour in no time at all. "We're flying!" she shouted in delight.

"Now, take your foot off the gas pedal because there's a sharp curve coming up, and right after the curve we'll turn right and park."

She did as she was told until the Mercedes came to a complete stop. Ulrich walked around to her side to open the door to help her out.

They walked a few paces, when they noticed two little boys about three years old playing in the gravel. Pretty soon, the play became rough, and it didn't take long before one of them tripped and fell. He seemed to try very hard not to cry, but when he looked at his knee and saw blood oozing out of a scrape, he couldn't hold the tears back any longer.

Ulrich rushed over to the little chap, and Marie-Louise wondered what he was going to do. Without concern for his business suit, he knelt down and inspected the wound. When the child didn't stop crying, he picked up the dirty little fellow, cradled him in his arms, and spoke soothingly to him. He pointed to the wound, took his handkerchief out of his pocket, and dabbed at the scuffed knee.

She watched the count in amazement as he administered to the child, marveling at his gentleness. *He'll make a good papa,* she thought, and had to stifle a sob. *Oh, I envy his future wife—does she even know how wonderful he is with children? I don't think I like the woman, even though I don't even know her.*

She shook her head to clear her mind and watched Ulrich's interaction with the child.

"There now," he said, "the scratch doesn't look so bad anymore, does it? And if we ask Marie-Louise to kiss it and make it all better, would you like that?"

The little boy scrutinized the baroness, sniffed twice, then nodded, and Ulrich turned to her. "All right, Marie-Louise, come and work your magic."

She took a few steps forward and looked into the child's face. His lower lip trembled and his eyes were wide. Marie-Louise tilted her head to the side and smiled at him. "Where does it hurt most?" she wanted to know.

He wrinkled his brow in concentration before he pointed to the middle of his knee cap. "There," he said with a sniff.

"All right, I'll kiss it right there and you tell me if it feels better."

The boy nodded, and Marie-Louise planted a soft kiss on the injured knee. "All better now?"

Two more sniffs and a nod.

Ulrich tousled the boy's hair and smiled. "I have some medical supplies in the glove box, and if Marie-Louise would be so kind to get them, we might find a bandage to put on your knee. Would that help?"

A vigorous nod signified the child's approval, and the baroness went to retrieve the requested items and returning with a nice-size bandage that she placed on the boy's knee. He looked at it with pride and wiggled out of Ulrich's hold, ready to resume his play.

Ulrich chuckled, "What an adorable little fellow. I wouldn't mind having a castle full of children one day."

She looked at him, startled. "Does your future wife know about your plans for a large family?"

"Of course not."

"And don't you think you ought to let her know?"

He smiled. "All in good time."

"Hmm."

Raising his eyebrow, he asked, "What does that mean?"

"I think that you should discuss this subject with her as soon as possible." Marie-Louise turned her head because she didn't want him to see the fluid in her eyes.

"I'll try to remember that," he promised. "What about you? Do you want to have children someday?"

"Of course I do, but I want to be able to raise them myself, and not leave them for others to watch them grow."

"Is that the reason you don't want to marry someone from your own rank—because you're afraid that you wouldn't have a normal family life?"

She concentrated on how to answer. "Yes, I suppose that's one of the reasons."

"You know," he said, his voice gentle, "your parents' marriage wasn't the norm." He took one of her wayward tendrils of hair and wrapped it around his finger. "Take my family, for instance. Although sometimes my father had to be away on business, we usually were together for family meals and spent a good amount of quality time as a family."

"You were very lucky. Did you have a governess?"

"No, we had a nanny and tutors until we were old enough to go to boarding school."

Marie-Louise looked at him in surprise. "You were cooped up at boarding school, too?"

He laughed. "I wouldn't call it *cooped up,* exactly. We came home almost every weekend."

"I envy you."

Ulrich put an arm around her shoulder and drew her close. "Poor little baroness. I didn't mean to make you feel sad. I'm sorry. I shouldn't have bragged about my wonderful childhood and family life. Come. Let's go for a walk to dispel the morose mood."

Immediately her pulse accelerated. The time had come for the confrontation. Stalling, she asked, "Do you come here often?"

"Not too often. No."

She rolled her eyes. "Only when you need to scold one of the wayward members of your family empire?"

A frown appeared on his features. "I'm not going to scold you, Marie-Louise, although I was quite frustrated about the newspaper article and your indiscretion, but we will discuss what to do to avoid further publicity of that kind."

They walked in silence for a few seconds before he asked, "Did you hear from anybody at the town hall about the article?"

"Unfortunately, yes. The mayor asked if congratulations were in order."

"How did you respond?"

"I told him that I had no inclination of getting married in the near future."

He nodded. "Good answer." After a few seconds, he asked, "How serious are the doctor's intentions, or should I ask how serious are you with him?"

She bit her lip and tried to come up with her best non-committal answer. "Which question do you want me to answer first?"

"I see that you want to stall, so let me rephrase my question. Has the doctor declared his feelings for you?"

She hedged, "Do you mean, has he . . . ?"

"Yes," he said with a hint of impatience, "has he told you that he loved you?"

"Y-yes."

"And?"

"That was all."

"Marie-Louise." Frustration put an edge to his voice. "How did you respond?"

She rolled her eyes. "Goodness, I can't remember."

He stopped walking and stepped in front of her. "Don't make this harder than it has to be. Just answer my questions. I'm here to undo the damage that the article has caused, but I need to know where you stand with the doctor. Did you also tell him of your feelings for him?"

"No, I didn't."

He nodded. "I didn't think so. You're honest and wouldn't tell him a lie."

Her breath caught in her throat. The nerve he had to assess her feelings for Nick! They were definitely none of his business. "What makes you think that I'm not in love with him?"

He laughed and stroked her cheek lightly with his finger, sending tremors down her spine that made her shiver involuntarily. "You can't possibly be in love with him when you react to my merest touch the way you do."

"Body chemistry," she mumbled.

"What did you say?"

"Body chemistry," she almost shouted.

Again he chuckled. "If you say so."

He became serious again, combing his hand through his hair and ruffling it. "Well, let's see if we can get you out of his predicament."

She lashed at him, "Now wait a minute, I didn't do anything wrong. It was the reporter who spread the lies about me and Nick."

"I told you to be discreet and what did you do? You paraded around town with your lover and his family, and if that wasn't enough, you allowed him to put his arm around you in full view of the public. That, my dear, is a fact that's hard to defuse."

She bit her lip.

"How are you going to resolve the situation with the doctor?" he continued.

"What do you mean?"

"We came to the understanding that you don't love him, but how will you break it to him, and how do we break it to the public?"

She scowled at him but remained silent. *That's none of your business.*

"I can see that I'm not going to get an answer, but you'll have to agree that we need to discuss the least harmful way to resolve both problems. Of course, it would help if one or both parties could disappear for a while until the rumor has died down, but that won't happen. He has his job at the hospital, and you're needed at Hohenstein."

She scowled and finally grumbled, "I thought I'd talk with him."

"Good," he said. "And this discussion should take place sooner rather than later. You don't want to keep leading the poor man on."

"I never told him that I loved him."

"But you let him kiss you!"

She rounded on him. "You kissed me, too!"

"And if you don't stop looking at me with that adorable pout, I'm going to kiss you again."

"You wouldn't dare!"

"Want to bet?"

His head came closer as his eyes darkened and his mouth quirked. Alarmed, Marie-Louise scooted a little farther away from him, and he laughed. "What are you afraid of?"

When he straightened again, she couldn't suppress a feeling of letdown, her body still on the alert.

He looked at her and grinned. "I'm sorry I disappointed you."

"You're way too cocky for you own good, Count."

"Now, Baroness, didn't your aunt teach you to treat your elders with respect?"

She produced a derisive laugh. "If I told Tante Ambrosia what has been going on, she would swoon—actually, she would simply not believe it."

"Isn't that fortunate?" he said with a twinkle in his eye.

She couldn't believe his nerve. "Is that why you can do what you want because you're discreet about it?"

"You're almost right, but don't forget that we're bound by honor and integrity."

She looked at him with one raised eyebrow. *What part do honesty and integrity play when you're almost engaged and still flirt with me on the side?*

"What's that skeptical look all about?"

"Oh, nothing, nothing."

"Little liar." He chuckled and took her face in both his hands and looked deep into her eyes before he lowered his head and feathered gentle little kisses on her eyes, her temples, her nose, the edge of her mouth and her chin. His thumb caressed her lips until they fevered for his kiss, but it didn't come. With one last peck onto the tip of her nose and a deep chuckle, he released her.

Bewildered, she looked up at his smiling eyes while her nerves still tingled with anticipation, and her whole being ached for his embrace. She gingerly outlined the contour of her lips with her finger. They felt dry and cracked, and she moistened them with the tip of her tongue while Ulrich never took his eyes off her face.

Perhaps he'd been thinking of his future wife and stopped himself before he betrayed the woman's trust any further. She determined for the second time that day that she didn't like her, whoever she was.

He put an arm around her shoulders. "Sorry, Marie-Louise, I shouldn't have come here with you where we're alone." He sighed and continued. "We still haven't decided what to do about your reputation."

How can he switch from passion to business at the drop of a hat? I'll never understand men! When she had calmed her nerves somewhat, she said, "Can't I lie low until the episode is forgotten?"

"Yes, I certainly think that's the best solution. And you'll need to speak to the doctor as soon as possible."

She hung her head. "He may not want to have anything more to do with me after I tell him that I don't love him."

"Don't underestimate yourself and the pull of nobility." He smiled. "It's good publicity for him, too. You can still attend events, as friends. But discretion is of the essence."

"The aristocratic straight jacket again," she observed.

"It's not as bad as you make it sound. Use common sense, that's all." He took her hand. "Come, let's go back if we don't want Tante Ambrosia to get suspicious."

Back at the castle, he helped her out of the Mercedes and accompanied her to the door. "Take care, little Baroness."

"Auf Wiedersehen."

She waited until he disappeared over the bridge before she went inside. Thank goodness, she didn't see Ambrosia and was able to run up to her room and close the door. She sat by the window looking into space, not seeing anything. She berated herself because she had been absolutely determined to ward Ullie off should he try to kiss her. And despite telling him not to flirt with her, she enjoyed his touch, had anticipated it just like the first time, except this time she knew beforehand what to expect. She knew how she reacted to him and yet, she had fevered for his touch as if she was the chosen one and not the other woman.

Where was this elusive woman anyway? She had never seen her with him or read anything in the gossip columns about her. Maybe she lived in a foreign country, and Ullie had visited her this past week. She should have asked him where he had been. In fact, he seemed to be out of town quite a bit lately.

What she couldn't understand was his behavior. How could he flirt with her and act as if he loved her when he was promised to another? That went so against his character.

Then there was the matter of Nick. She had promised to be honest with him, and she would have to keep her word.

Chapter Twenty-two

One morning, they had just sat down to breakfast when Ambrosia got up from her chair, hand on her abdomen, and walked out of the parlor, almost doubling over. Marie-Louise shot up and ran after her, bewildered. "Tante Ambrosia, what is it? Are you ill? Can I help?"

Face contorted, her aunt shook her head. "I'll be all right in a little while. Go and eat your breakfast."

"Are you sure?"

"Yes, yes."

Ambrosia held on to the railing with one hand, the other still on her abdomen, and took step after slow step upstairs to her room.

Dazed for a moment, Marie-Louise shook her head as if to rid herself of a bad dream. Perhaps Ambrosia came down with a touch of a stomach infection. Come to think of it, she had been acting strange for the last few days—not much of an appetite, and staying in bed later than normal. Maybe she was seriously ill . . .

Quickly, Marie-Louise went in search of her aunt. She ran up the stairs and stopped on the landing, listening. No sound.

"Tante Ambrosia!"

No answer. She turned down the hallway toward her aunt's suite. The door stood wide open, but she couldn't see Ambrosia anywhere. Undecided, Marie-Louise paused inside the door for several moments, biting her lip. She had never been in Ambrosia's rooms. With purposeful strides, she crossed the room to stand in front of the bathroom door, raising her hand to knock.

"Tante Ambrosia! Are you in there?"

"Yes," came the weak reply.

"What's wrong? Do you need my help?"

"No. Go back to your breakfast. I'll be down as soon as I can."

"For goodness sake, tell me what's wrong. I'm worried. Are you sick? Do you need a doctor?"

"No. No doctor. I'll be fine in a little while."

Marie-Louise wrung her hands and looked at the door. Her worries not at all alleviated, she turned and descended the stairs. She'd have to wait until her aunt came down and join her.

Almost an hour went by before Ambrosia descended the stairs, slow and pale, and still bent over with pain.

Marie-Louise jumped up to pull the chair out for her. "Tell me what happened," she begged.

"The pain won't go away . . . my right side . . ." Ambrosia had to stop as a wave of nausea swept over her. "I'm afraid . . ." she doubled over again, "appendicitis . . . ?"

Marie-Louise led Ambrosia to the settee. "Sit here while I get Jakob to rig up the horses."

When they arrived at the hospital, Marie-Louise jumped out of the carriage and ran into the building to find Nick, quickly explaining to him what had happened.

Nick didn't wait, but stormed outside and motioned for an orderly to bring a stretcher. They lifted Ambrosia onto it and wheeled her immediately in.

Marie-Louise followed. "Will Dr. Walter be there also?"

"No, he's gone to visit his daughter for a few days. I'll perform the tests. Now, go to the waiting room. I have an examination and possibly a surgery to perform."

Marie-Louise had never seen him so stern and business-like, but appreciated his concern.

Before she went to the waiting room, Marie-Louise told Jakob to go to the Wolfburg Bank and tell the Count what had happened.

Although there were newspapers available for reading, her nerves were too frazzled to concentrate on anything. She paced the floor, the handkerchief in her hands ripped to shreds already. How long would a surgery last? What if . . . ?

It seemed like Marie-Louise waited forever alone. The minutes ticked by and she couldn't imagine what Tante Ambrosia was going through. Suddenly, the nurse ushered Ulrich into the waiting room, Marie-Louise rushed toward him with a little cry. "I'm so glad you're here!"

He enfolded her in his arms, and she leaned her head against his chest. For a few moments, neither of them spoke. Ulrich held her until she felt she could face him without going all to pieces.

As she stirred in his arms, he led her to the only sofa in the room and sat next to her, holding her hand in his. Gently he asked about Ambrosia's condition.

She shrugged her shoulders in a helpless gesture. "Appendicitis, maybe. She's been acting strange for a few days, not eating much, and looking unwell. I don't know what's going on in there." She blinked away a tear when all of a sudden her anxiety and penned-up emotions burst forth.

"Ullie, please hold me." When he enfolded her again, she buried her head in his chest and breathed in his scent, aftershave coupled with fresh air. She snuggled even closer before she started telling him what had happened.

"Tante Ambrosia looked as white as our tablecloth, and I was so scared. I feared the worst."

Stroking her back, Ulrich soothed, "Everything will be all right."

"How do you know?" she asked on a sob.

"I'm sure the good doctor will discover the problem. Besides, an appendectomy is a pretty routine surgery these days, as I understand."

She lowered her head. "I hope you're right. I don't want to lose her." As an afterthought, she added, "Not because of the café, but because . . . I need her."

"You love her, don't you?" he asked and brushed his finger across her cheek.

"Yes, I suppose I do."

"Have you ever told her that you loved her?"

"No."

"I think she would like to hear it."

She looked up at him. "We're talking about my aunt. She isn't one for expressing feelings freely."

"People change."

She sighed. "I know. Lots of things have changed since I returned home."

They sat in silence for a while before the door opened and Nick, in his white coat and a cap, stepped into the room and saw the baroness in Ulrich's arms.

Both Marie-Louise and Ulrich rose.

"How's my aunt?" asked Marie-Louise, stepping forward to stand by the doctor.

"She was right. Her appendix was infected. The surgery went well, and it was fortunate that you brought her to the hospital immediately."

"Will she be all right?"

Nick nodded. "Of course. She'll stay in the hospital for a few days before she can go home, but needs to take it easy. I would even suggest a stay at a sanatorium for a few weeks. Then she'll be as good as new."

Just now remembering to introduce the two men, Marie-Louise said, "Ullie, this is Dr. Nicolas Neff. Nick, please meet Count Wolfburg."

The two men shook hands. "Pleased to meet you, Doctor."

"A pleasure to meet you, too, Count Wolfburg." The words were spoken politely enough, but Nick's eyes shot daggers at Ulrich.

The count inclined his head, and Nick left the waiting room.

Marie-Louise sighed. "What am I going to do?"

Apparently misinterpreting her expression, Ulrich tried to comfort her. "Don't worry about the cost. Both you and Ambrosia are covered under Wolfburg's health plan, which also provides additional benefits, such as recuperation after severe illnesses or, in your aunt's case, surgery."

"This time I *did* mean the café," she admitted. "How will I manage with Tante Ambrosia gone for so many weeks?" She sighed. "I may have to give up my assignment at the town hall."

"You can't do that," he said quickly.

"I'll have to. There's no other way I can fill Ambrosia's shoes and do my work for the town."

"The town can't do without you, either. Perhaps the woman you're so fond of, I forgot her name, could take on more responsibility."

Ulrich seemed to be eager to keep her at the town hall, but she didn't remember him having been overly enthusiastic when she'd accepted the position. She couldn't figure out why he had changed his mind.

Hands behind his back, he walked to the window and looked out. Shifting his weight from his heels to his toes, he rocked back and forth and looked like a man wrestling with a decision. After what seemed like an eternity, he turned around to face her.

"I'll send you Frau Zimmer."

Confused, she stared at him. "I don't follow."

He reached for her hand and guided her to the sofa where they sat down. "It's simple. I'll send you my housekeeper to take over Ambrosia's duties, and you don't have to quit your job at the town hall."

She thought it over for a minute. "No," she said with finality, "I can't accept that."

"Why not?"

How best to tell him that she didn't want to be any more beholden to him than she already was? He had stabled his horses at Hohenstein for her to use, and now he offered his own housekeeper to work at the café. She couldn't accept that. Ambrosia wouldn't want to inconvenience him, either.

She wondered if Frau Becker could take on Ambrosia's job for a few weeks, but discarded the thought. The woman was competent in the kitchen and overseeing the personnel, but wouldn't be able to work as independently as her aunt. The only alternative open to Marie-Louise was to quit her job at the town hall.

Glancing up, she noticed Ulrich's exuberance at his own plan. He looked like a little boy who had just brought his mother a dandelion, proud of himself and sure that his gift would be well received. This glimpse into his soul made her want to reach out, touch him, tousle his rusty hair, kiss those blue eyes, and brush her cheek against his.

Her gaze traveled to his mouth when the corners curved upward and his eyes took on a darker hue.

"Daydreaming?" he teased.

"No," she snapped and looked at his striped tie instead. "Considering the reasons why I can't accept your housekeeper's services."

"And? Have you come up with some good ones?"

"I certainly have." She paused to organize her thoughts. "First, I cannot take your housekeeper away from you. How would you fare?" She held up her hand to keep him from interrupting. "Second, even if I accepted her services, I don't even know if she would be willing to do such menial work."

"Don't worry on her account. I pay her well, but I expect her to do the work I assign her to do." It was his turn to hold up his hand to silence her outraged retort. "I know, I know, you think me a hard taskmaster for deploying her at Hohenstein, but as I said, I pay her very well, and she knows it, too. As to your first concern about my well-being without a housekeeper, rest assured, I won't be inconvenienced."

I didn't think you would.

"I'll borrow a housekeeper from one of my other estates."

Marie-Louise shook her head. "I still can't accept."

His brows drew together. "Actually," he mumbled, "it's not your decision to make."

"You can't force your help on me!"

He rolled his eyes. "Heaven forbid." Leaning forward, he asked, "How do you plan to convince your aunt to go to the sanatorium if she's worrying about the business?"

Marie-Louise frowned. She hadn't thought of that.

"Well?" he prompted.

"I still can't accept, I—"

"There's no other solution."

Marie-Louise folded her hands in her lap and stared into space. He was right. His housekeeper would solve all her problems, although accepting another one of Ulrich's hand-outs would be hard to swallow. No matter how hard she tried to come up with an alternative scheme, nothing came to mind, and asking her aunt not to go to the sanatorium was out of the question. She'd have to accept—for Ambrosia's sake.

Her mind made up, she looked at Ulrich and nodded slightly. His eyes lit up and he extended his hand, which she clasped in hesitant agreement.

"Good girl," he praised, "I'm glad you saw the light."

Although Frau Zimmer proved to be everything the count had promised, things didn't always go as smoothly as Marie-Louise had hoped. One particular Sunday tried her patience to the limits. It started when the machine that toasted and glazed the nuts broke down in the middle of a fresh batch.

A goodly number of people had already visited the souvenir shop when they ran out of candy. Due to the influx of guests, Frau Becker went over to the castle to retrieve several cakes from the cool basement and to decorate them, while Frau Zimmer went to her room for an aspirin.

Marie-Louise took charge of the kitchen while the two women were away.

"Baroness, we're running out of sugar. What shall I do?"

With one hand on her aching head, her eyes shut in exasperation, Marie-Louise plopped onto a stool. What would come next?

"Baroness, are you all right?" the kitchen help asked. "Do you need an aspirin, too?"

"I'm exhausted," she said and got up. "If we don't have any more sugar at the cafe, you'll just have to get it at the castle from Frau Becker. Thank you."

Alone, she tried to focus on the task at hand. The dishes needed to be washed, and the countertop could do with a scrubbing. Like an automaton, she started on the chores, when the waitress appeared at the window to place an order.

Looking at the clock, she sighed. *Will this day never end?* She wished nothing more than to shut herself in her room, put her feet up, and relax. If only Ulrich would come. She hadn't seen him these past few days, and she missed him, missed his teasing, and above all, the way he could make her laugh despite her problems.

She couldn't deny that she needed him today more than ever, and her need caused her almost physical pain. Imagining leaning her head on his shoulder, feeling his strong arms around her, and inhaling his clean masculine scent created a longing within her that she ascribed to her loneliness. Her mind told her that she didn't have a right to his embrace, the comfort of his nearness, but her heart refused to believe it.

At that moment, the kitchen help came in the door and interrupted Marie-Louise's morose thoughts. She placed the bag of sugar on the counter. "Here's the sugar. What do you want me to do with it?"

"You can fill the bowls on the tables and stick a teaspoon into each one." Was there no end to these questions? Why couldn't the woman figure out for herself what needed to be done?

"How do we know when a bowl is empty and needs refilling?" asked the help.

Almost at the end of her patience, she said, "The waitress will have to tell us."

"Then I'll fill another one and give it to her?"

"That's correct."

"Or should I go out to the café and replace the sugar bowls?"

Marie-Louise realized that she had to make a definite decision before she could go on with her work. "The waitress will be responsible for the sugar bowls," she said and turned to stack the clean dishes before putting them away.

How could her aunt stand this constant questioning? It drove her out of her mind.

After two-thirty in the afternoon they experienced the usual influx of visitors, but with both Frau Becker and Frau Zimmer back at the café, Marie-Louise decided to finally take a break and eat a late lunch.

She had prepared a sandwich and just sat down to enjoy it when someone rang the doorbell loud and long. Reluctantly and with a sideways glance at her food, she got up and opened the door.

Oh, no! The kitchen help again. Seeing the woman's horror-stricken look, Marie-Louise steeled herself for the worst.

"Baroness," she panted, "come quickly."

"What happened?"

The woman had to catch her breath before she could explain, "The waitress fell and hurt her wrist. Please, hurry."

Marie-Louise reached for her key, slammed the door shut, and followed the woman to the café. She found the waitress sitting on a chair, her face distorted with pain, Frau Becker and Frau Zimmer hovering over her. The guests stood around in a circle, giving advice and relating stories of similar accidents.

The general noise died down eventually and all eyes turned to the baroness, waiting for her pronouncement. She looked at the injured wrist, swelling nicely now.

Frau Zimmer hastened to explain, "It seems broken, Baroness. Here, you can feel the bone."

Addressing the girl, Marie-Louise wanted to know, "How did the accident happen?"

"I had just cleared a table and was carrying the stuff to the kitchen when I tripped over a chair and fell."

Seeing the girl's pallor, Marie-Louise said, "I'm sorry you're in so much pain. I'll have Jakob take you to the hospital in the carriage. The children will just have to forego their coach rides this afternoon."

She helped the girl up and led her out of the café.

When the baroness returned, Frau Zimmer threw her hands up. "Thank goodness you're back, Baroness, we've got our hands full."

Marie-Louise looked around and suppressed a shudder. The kitchen help, filling in for the waitress, did so good-naturedly but clumsily.

"What do you need me to do, Frau Zimmer?"

"Would you mind taking over as waitress?" She gestured toward the café. "The good woman is not cut out for the job, and we need her in the kitchen." After a moment's hesitation, she added, "Or would you rather be in the kitchen?"

"I'll wait on the tables, thank you."

Marie-Louise tied the flat black leather pouch that contained coins, a note pad, and pencil around her waist and covered it with the tiny apron of starched white eyelet material. She had never done this kind of job before but felt sure she could manage. After the first few mishaps, mainly forgetting which guests had ordered what, things went smoothly. It wasn't every day that the visitors were served by the local nobility.

Marie-Louise smiled until she thought that the smile would be permanently frozen onto her features. Her feet ached, her legs felt like lead, and her arms grew stiffer with every order she carried. Would the day never end? She longed for the peace and quiet of her home, and a decent meal.

That peace and quiet would have to wait, she learned, when she found out that Herr Falke, who manned the souvenir shop, had taken ill and had gone home. Upon hearing the bad news, Marie-Louise plopped onto a stool in the kitchen and wanted to cry. Nothing was going right today.

She looked at her faithful helpers. They were needed here. Besides, none of these women knew anything about the shop, the prices, the cash register, or the wares. She took a deep breath. Closing the shop seemed to be the only solution.

"Baroness, why don't you go and attend to the shop while we run the café," suggested Frau Zimmer.

Marie-Louise looked at the housekeeper and then at the kitchen help, and back at the housekeeper again.

Frau Zimmer assured her, "I'll wait on the tables."

"You'll be short one person, though. Do you think you'll be able to manage?"

"We'll try."

Marie-Louise closed up the shop early and hurried back to the café. Upon opening the door, she stopped and stood rooted to the spot. She stared at the tall apparition in shirt sleeves and coppery hair who was balancing a tray of pastries above his head. She blinked. It couldn't be. Not him. She must be seeing things. Ulrich performing a menial task? Serving commoners? What had gotten into him?

She didn't think that Frau Zimmer had persuaded him to help. No, she wouldn't have dared to take him off his pedestal!

Looking at him now, one would never guess at his reluctance to mingle with common folk. He had told her on more than one occasion that he avoided public places, that he kept his distance.

He wasn't keeping his distance today. As a matter of fact, he was as much on display as the pastries he balanced on the tray above his head. If he was aware of the stares that followed his every move, he didn't show it. And no matter how unperturbed and casual he tried to appear, he couldn't hide his status. Nobody would call to him, '*Hey, waiter, over here,*' even if the guests didn't know who he was. They would patiently wait until he noticed their empty glasses or their desire to have the tab presented, and then accept his services with the deepest gratitude.

Marie-Louise had to smile at her noble waiter as her heart went out to him in gratitude. How could she have thought of Ulrich as a snob?

Her eyes followed him as he approached another table. Even with partially rolled-up shirt sleeves he still looked as immaculate as ever—and as handsome. At that moment, he looked up and saw her standing at the door. Her heart gave a little lurch as she felt embraced by his warm smile that seemed to illuminate his eyes.

He gestured to a corner table and told her in passing that he would be right with her.

Chapter Twenty-three

From the kitchen came the muffled sounds of the general clean-up prior to closing, and Marie-Louise relaxed for the first time in hours—though she felt a little guilty for doing so, knowing how much work there was to be done in the kitchen.

She tried to get up and help, but Ulrich looked at her and shook his head. *Stay*, he mouthed, and thankfully she settled back in her chair. It felt good to have someone else make the decisions and shoulder the burden of responsibility for a change, even if only for a little while.

She watched Ulrich clear the tables after the last of the guests left the café and marveled at his apparent ease, and wondered where he had learned his domestic skills—he who had always been surrounded by servants.

Not only did he perform his task with ease, but also with the precision of a chess player. He stacked the dishes onto the tray in perfect order, the glasses on one side, the cups on the other, and the plates in the middle. No helter-skelter work where he was concerned!

She watched his smooth movements and especially his beautiful hands as they picked up the china cups. The show of muscles in his arms as he lifted the heavy tray brought back memories of times when she had felt the strength of those arms around her.

Oftentimes, before she fell asleep at night, she relived those moments, tried to recapture the sensation of his lips on hers, his gentle touch . . . She sighed. It couldn't only be their very compatible body chemistries that made her long for him the way she did, but rather the infatuation of a besotted girl . . . or could it even be more than that? She only wished that she held the same power over him as he did over her.

Marie-Louise watched him carry another load to the kitchen while a last golden ray of sunshine slanted across the room and made his hair glisten like rich, dark amber. Oh, how her fingers itched to run themselves through it—

Stop it, she told herself, and tried to steer her thoughts onto less dangerous ground when she felt his hand on her shoulder.

"What lovely rosy cheeks," he commented with a twinkle.

Rascal. A gentleman would overlook a lady's embarrassment, but not Ulrich.

As innocently as possible she said, "It's a little warm in here, don't you agree?"

His lips curled. "I find the temperature quite comfortable."

But I don't. She pointed to a chair. "Won't you have a seat? You must be exhausted after all the waiting on tables. You were great, and I really appreciate your help."

He bowed with a flourish. "My pleasure, Baroness." After a moment he asked,

"Are you ready?"

"Ready for what?"

"When was the last time you had anything to eat?"

She wrinkled her brow. "I had just made myself a sandwich when the waitress broke her wrist, and I had to take charge. So, I guess, my last meal was breakfast."

He frowned. "All right. That settles it. I'm going to take you out. How soon can you be ready?"

"I'm too tired to go out. I'll have a bowl of soup and—"

"That won't do. You need a decent meal. I'll give you fifteen minutes."

"That's impossible. I can't get ready in fifteen minutes. My hair is a mess, I feel disgusting, and I'd much rather go to bed."

"Fifteen minutes," he insisted.

"I can't leave now before everything is cleaned up."

"Of course you can. Remember, your staff is getting paid for the job."

She looked toward the kitchen, then back into Ulrich's determined face, and got up.

"Good girl," he praised.

The meal over, Ulrich pushed his chair back and relaxed. With a twinkle in his eye he said, "Now that you're not famished anymore, you can tell me about your day."

Marie-Louise folded her hands in her lap and looked heavenward. "It's been a nuisance of a day. Everything went wrong! We ran out of candy, the waitress broke her wrist, and the kitchen help got on my nerves."

"I'm sorry you had such a bad day. Do you want me to send you an assistant to Frau Zimmer?"

"Thanks, but that won't be necessary." She laughed. "I don't anticipate another day like this one ever again. Besides, if I ever need a waiter again I know where to find an excellent one. You definitely were a hit with my guests. With you at the café, business would double."

He fell in with her bantering. "Sure, why don't you put me in a glass case on display?"

"Good idea, but you'd have to step down from your pedestal."

"What do you mean, pedestal?"

"You'd have to come down from your lofty, aristocratic heights."

His eyes crinkled. "Ever since you stepped into my life several weeks ago, you've done nothing but hammer away at that pedestal.

I have no height left, whatsoever. Soon I won't be able to attract any more guests because I'll be as common as the next man."

She glanced at him. Never in a million years would he look common, not with his air of superiority. His size and good looks also set him apart from most of his species, and even without his title, he commanded attention.

He interrupted her thoughts with a question about her aunt. "How's she doing health-wise?"

"She'll be in the hospital until Wednesday, come home for a few days, and leave for the sanatorium the following Monday."

"I bet you miss her."

"Yes," Marie-Louise agreed, "I wish she could be here to witness our success. She's worked so hard, and would be proud to see the fruits of her labors. In her quiet way, she's contributed to its success."

"Not every weekend will be as successful as this one," he cautioned.

"I realize that. There will be rainy days, cold days, and overcast days. I'll have to make the best of the business when the circumstances are right. I even thought of expanding."

He leaned in toward her. "What do you have in mind?"

She gnawed on her lower lip and gathered her thoughts. "I may purchase a few ponies and offer pony rides for the children, and I could also add light snacks and a limited number of entrees to the menu which would draw even more people. Hikers could stop at the castle for lunch, and fathers could take their families out to dinner."

He nodded. "Sounds good, but you would need to invest more money."

"I could use some of the profit I've made."

Holding up his hand, he warned, "Go easy on your money. You never know when the county will strike again."

She almost choked and eyed him with apprehension. "What do you know about their schemes?"

"Only what I found out from talking to you."

"But you anticipate another request from that corner?"

"It's possible."

She pondered his answer for a moment. "It looks as if someone is out to make life hard for me, but I can't figure out why. Maybe I imagine things." Tilting her head to one side, her eyes held his. "You wouldn't have anything to do with it, would you?"

He flinched before he lowered his gaze. After a few moments, however, he looked calm and collected again, even a little arrogant. "Don't be silly. Why would I be interested in destroying you? I'm the head of the House of Wolfburg, remember? And as such, I'm responsible for the welfare of its members."

"I'm sorry," she apologized, ashamed of her suspicion. He had never given her reason to suspect him of foul play, and denying her a loan didn't mean that he was in any way connected with the other incidents.

She gave him a covert look. A hard line around his mouth bespoke his annoyance at her accusation, and he sat straight and rigid in his chair as his former relaxed mood had given way to one of . . . determination. Determination to do what? she puzzled. She must be seeing things.

Uncomfortable with the atmosphere her hasty words had created, Marie-Louise laid her hand on his arm and waited until he looked at her.

"Ulrich, I'm sorry," she said again. "I didn't actually mean to accuse you. But there seems to be a red line connecting all these negative incidents, from you denying me funding, and the local banks' refusals to grant me a loan to the county's various requests."

He gave her a little smile, but it didn't reach his eyes. "I told you, my hands are tied in your case, and my refusal to give you a loan didn't have anything to do with the other events. They were purely incidental as far as I'm concerned." Covering her hand with his, he continued, "Believe me, if I could've spared you all these problems, I would've done so." After a small pause he added in a low voice, "It wasn't possible."

He looked so glum that she wanted to cheer him up. "Don't worry about me. Things are looking up. The business is doing well and I'm on my way to financial independence. Should the county send another unreasonable request, I'll just have to come up with a new scheme."

Leaning forward, he placed both arms on the table and reached for her hand. Feathery strokes on her wrist sent delicate shivers up her arm. "You're a remarkable person, Marie-Louise," he said in a husky voice.

Pulling her hand back she whispered, "Please, Ullie. Don't."

"Don't what?"

Touch me the way you do and talk to me in that low voice that makes me want to be close to you. Of course she couldn't tell him that. She couldn't tell him the effect he had on her, couldn't let him know how she longed to feel his arms around her. The warmth that flooded her cheeks would reveal her longing, but she bent her head to hide the evidence from him, aided by the muted light in the room.

Suddenly he placed his index finger under her chin and gently guided her to look at him. "Don't what?" he urged.

Mesmerized and caught in the spell of the moment, she nevertheless managed to prevaricate, "Don't give me such lavish praise." With a little smile, she added, "It may go to my head."

He shook his head. "I doubt it."

The waiter chose that moment to bring the dessert and thereby broke the spell.

Marie-Louise tried to stifle a yawn, which earned her a concerned look from Ulrich. "You're tired. I'd better take you home."

"It has been a hard day, and I'm exhausted."

"You've been working too much the past few weeks and need a holiday."

She laughed. "That's exactly what the mayor said when he visited the café today. He offered me his cabin in the Black Forest again. Of course, I can't accept his generosity; he has done so much for me already."

"Has he?"

"You know he has."

Ulrich nodded. "He certainly was around when the going was tough."

Her eyes moistened. "He's like a father to me."

He raised an eyebrow but didn't comment. Instead he rose to his feet and offered her his hand. "It's getting late and you need your beauty rest."

When they approached the castle, Marie-Louise saw its stark outline silhouetted against the night sky, and a feeling of pride permeated her whole being. Right now, she felt at one with her ancestors, felt a part of a long line of Hohensteins, accepted into their midst because she, too, had contributed to the legacy of the castle. She had a right to be here, had proved herself worthy to carry the name . . . and the title.

Goodness, she interrupted her self-important thoughts, she had become a traditionalist like Tante Ambrosia. She hoped not. She was proud of her accomplishments, that was all.

The niggling thought of having become a traditionalist, however, could not be silenced. Could it be that she had started to erect a pedestal for herself? She gnawed on her lower lip and pondered the question as Ulrich gave her a sideways glance.

"Aren't you a little apprehensive of staying at the castle with only Frau Zimmer around?"

"I've never given it any thought," she replied. "I'm not scared, if that's what you mean. I've never encountered a ghost nor heard the floorboards creak or chains rattle at night, so I feel perfectly safe."

"I'd feel better if you had safety locks on the doors."

"Don't tell me you're worried," she said, surprised.

He didn't reply immediately as he maneuvered the Mercedes over the bridge and into the courtyard. After he turned off the ignition and headlights, he relaxed against the back of his seat and turned to face her.

"Yes, I worry about you," he said at last.

"Why?" Marie-Louise held her breath. She didn't know what she wanted to hear, but all of a sudden his answer was very important to her. Not trusting herself to look at him, her gaze focused on a moonbeam that painted his hair a pale silver. He was so close yet seemed miles away in his thoughts. Had he even heard her question?

Finally he returned to reality. "I worry about you because I'm responsible for you."

"What an unromantic answer," she pouted.

He cradled her face in his hands and smiled into her eyes. "What did you expect?"

"Anything but what you said. I don't want you to feel responsible for me. That sounds an awful lot like being a burden, and I don't want to be a burden to anyone."

"Relax," he soothed, "you're anything but a burden."

When she wouldn't stop pouting, he threatened with a twinkle in his eye, "Don't look at me like that, or I'll have to . . ." his hand sneaked around to the back of her neck, ". . . use methods . . ." his fingers found a sensitive spot, ". . . to help you . . ." and with feather-light strokes coaxed her body to respond, ". . . warm up to me."

Despite her initial rigidity, her body responded with a leap of her heart that set her pulse racing. The familiar warmth spread through her body and left her with only one thought in mind, being close to him.

"That's better," he acknowledged with a low chuckle and pulled her head against his shoulder.

They stayed in this position for a short while until he muttered under his breath, "These automobiles are good for driving only, but nothing else."

Disgruntled, he climbed out, walked around to the passenger side, opened the door, and proffered his hand to help Marie-Louise out. Holding on to her hand, he immediately pulled her into his arms as if this was the natural thing to do.

"Mmmm. Perfect," he mumbled as she pressed against him, her arms around his neck. With one finger he tilted her chin up, lowered his head and feathered little kisses with his eyelashes on her eyes, her cheeks, and her nose.

She trembled, and every nerve in her body vibrated with heightened sensitivity until she wanted to melt into him. Her lips parted, hungry for his touch, inviting him to explore, and she shivered in anticipation.

Ulrich stopped and drew back a fraction to look at her. *Don't stop*, she wanted to beg, but held her breath and waited for his next move.

With a low, guttural sound he pressed her against him and slowly lowered his head. His lips sought hers, teasing and tasting. A satisfied little sound escaped her as she marveled at the exquisite sensations his touch could bring to life.

At last, with a deep sigh, he lifted his head a little, his lips still hesitant to leave hers. Light, feathery touches were the lingering adieus before they broke apart. For a few heartbeats, they stared at each other before a smile lit his features. "You're a natural," he said, and she didn't know whether that was good or bad. At the moment, however, she didn't want to find out. She didn't want to face reality quite yet, but instead hug the magic of the moment as long as possible. Tomorrow she'd analyze his words. Tomorrow she'd sort out her feelings and the implication of her actions. Tomorrow . . .

With his arm around her shoulders, Ulrich urged her gently forward toward the curving stone steps and up to the front door.

They paused, and he held out his hand for the long and ornately crafted key with the intricate beard. "After you lock the door, put the deadbolt into place," he instructed. "I'll send the locksmith tomorrow to install safety locks."

She didn't think this measure necessary, but knew better than to argue the point.

"In the meantime," he continued, "you should take the dog into the house with you at night. At least he can warn you of any possible danger."

She laughed. "Who would want to break into the castle and disturb us?"

"Better safe than sorry," was his dry rejoinder.

Inside, he examined the heavy beam latch. "Do you think you can manage this contraption?"

"I think so." She grabbed the ancient lever with both hands, but it wouldn't budge until she put her entire weight behind the effort.

"I'll wait outside until I hear the beam slide into position and know you're safe."

Before he turned to leave, he caught a lock of her hair and drew her toward him. Kissing her ear, he whispered, "Sweet dreams," then turned on his heel and motioned for her to lock the door.

Marie-Louise leaned against the door, her hands pressed to her hot cheeks. Her blood drummed in her ears and her nerve endings still tingled in remembrance of Ulrich's touch, the magic that had carried them both beyond the bounds of reason.

Now that he had left, her brain started functioning again, sluggish at first, but gaining momentum with every heartbeat. And every heartbeat brought her closer to the realization that she had to stop her amorous entanglement with Ulrich. In fact, she deplored her own weakness of falling into his arms whenever he beckoned. Why couldn't she stay cool and detached and give him a sophisticated brush-off? And why did he play with her emotions when he was to be engaged to his chosen one in the very near future?

If she responded to him the way she did, he might assume that she felt more for him than friendship which, of course, she did, but didn't want him to know. There was no real danger of him developing a *tendre* for her with his impending engagement.

Were he not promised to another woman and were to pursue her in earnest, and had she given him reason to believe his suit to be acceptable, she would be expected to accept his official courtship which would inevitably end in marriage.

To be honest, she *had* enjoyed this evening without giving any thought to anything but the moment at hand. Ulrich, too, had shown a lamentable disregard for the traditional code of conduct. Come to think of it, his attentions had surpassed the limits of propriety a long time ago, she was sure of it.

Marie-Louise pushed away from the door and squared her shoulders. She had to put an end to their intimacies even if it meant confronting him on the subject. Under no circumstances did she want to get hurt more than she already was. She had to keep him at arm's length. *Easier said than done,* she reminded herself, *especially when it felt so good to be in his arms.*

She sighed. Yes, she liked to be with him—and not just for the body chemistry. She liked the way his eyes danced when he teased her, the way his lips curled with suppressed laughter. She closed her eyes to conjure his image in her mind. How easy it was to talk to him, how attentively he listened to her problems, and if it weren't for their entanglement, she couldn't wish for a better friend.

Yes, he had always been pleasant when he had come to her rescue no matter what the circumstances, and except for his refusal to grant her a loan, she couldn't find any fault with him.

She wished her aunt was here. She needed somebody to talk to, somebody who could sort through her tangled emotions. Then the thought hit her that she couldn't possibly tell Ambrosia the reason for her confusion. Her aunt would swoon if she knew of Marie-Louise's wanton behavior, not to mention the count's dishonorable conduct. No, she vowed, Tante Ambrosia would never find out about her involvement with Ulrich.

Her entanglement had gone far enough. She had to put a stop to it. Now. Heaven help her should she fall in love with him, an unrequited love at that.

When a preposterous thought entered her mind, she stopped as if hit by lightning. What if the count decided not to get engaged to the other woman but to offer for her hand in marriage instead? Rejecting an offer from the head of the family clan was unthinkable, but marriage to him would mean that she'd not only acquire a husband, but also a complete new set of rules stricter than she had known before. She shuddered. If she'd ever marry at all, she'd choose a commoner. This resolve, however, appeared a little lame in light of her feelings for Ulrich.

Chapter Twenty-four

Equipped with a bouquet of flowers from Ambrosia's garden, and a sizeable piece of her favorite *Schwarzwälder Kirschtorte,* prepared by Frau Becker, Marie-Louise entered her aunt's hospital room to find Dr. Walter sitting on the edge of the bed, holding Ambrosia's hand.

The baroness stopped. "Am I interrupting?"

Her aunt looked up. "Oh no, dear, please come in. I'm so glad to see you."

Marie-Louise stepped to the other side of the bed and bent down to kiss her aunt's cheek before she acknowledged the doctor.

"Dr. Walter, what a pleasure to see you." With a wink she observed, "It looks as if things between you two have progressed quite favorably."

He smiled and nodded while Ambrosia's cheeks flushed a nice rose color.

Turning to Ambrosia, Marie-Louise held out the bouquet. "I brought you some flowers from your own garden and some of your favorite Black Forest cake from Frau Becker."

Dr. Walter wagged his finger. "No cake for Ambrosia yet."

"I'm so sorry. I shouldn't have brought it to tempt you, Tante Ambrosia."

"It's all right. It's the thought that counts, and I'm sure that Paul will be only too happy to eat it."

Marie-Louise looked from one to the other. "Oh, it's Paul, is it?"

The doctor nodded and laughed, "And pretty soon it will be Onkel Paul for you."

"My, my, Dr. Walter, you're a fast mover!"

"No sense wasting precious time—we're not getting any younger, you know."

"When did you propose?"

"Yesterday evening as soon as I returned to the hospital."

Ambrosia pointed to a vase with at least two dozen beautiful red roses. "Paul even got down on one knee, very *apropos.*"

They all laughed, and Marie-Louise hugged and kissed her aunt and walked around the bed to embrace the doctor. "I'm glad that you'll be a part of our family soon."

"And I'm happy to add you to my family, Baroness. As soon as Ambrosia is up and about again we'll have a party and accept each other formally into our families."

"That sounds like a wonderful idea."

Ambrosia, who had listened to that exchange with a happy smile, now spoke up. "Marie-Louise, do you think Paul should talk to Count Wolfburg before we announce our engagement to the world?"

The baroness thought about that for a while before she nodded. "That may not be a bad idea. Not that he would have any objections, but it would be nice to keep him informed."

Dr. Walter turned to Ambrosia. "*Liebling,* do you think I should write to him?"

"Yes, please do. Marie-Louise probably has his address."

After a few more moments, Dr. Walter sighed. "Well, I think I should go and see my other patients before they complain that I neglect them."

He bent over Ambrosia and planted a gentle kiss on her lips before he rose, gave Marie-Louise a quick hug, and left the room.

The baroness turned to her aunt. "Do you love him, Tante Ambrosia?"

Ambrosia nodded. "Yes, I do. My feelings are not what they were when I was young and expected fireworks, but that's all right. I appreciate and respect him, and I like the way he treats me. I want to be with him, and when he's away I can't wait to see him again. If that isn't love, it's pretty close to it."

"I'm happy for you, Tante Ambrosia."

After a little pause, Ambrosia asked, "How are things developing between you and Count Wolfburg?"

"Count Wolfburg?" she asked and felt the tell-tale heat infuse her cheeks.

"Yes, dear, Count Wolfburg."

"But-but I'm courting Dr. Neff."

"I know, but that's not where your heart is."

Marie-Louise hung her head. "I'm so confused, Tante Ambrosia."

"Yes, I can imagine that you are, but I'm sure that everything will work out all right in the end."

Marie-Louise sighed. "I don't think so."

Ambrosia patted her niece's cheek, "Give it some time."

At that moment, the nurse entered the room with a tray full of vials, clearly intending to draw blood.

Marie-Louise rose to her feet. "I'd better leave, but I'll be back tomorrow. Is there anything you want me to bring you?"

"Yes, if you could bring me the book I was reading before I went to the hospital. I think I left it in the parlor on one of the little side tables."

"I'll bring it with me tomorrow." She bent down to kiss her aunt's forehead before she left.

In the corridor, she bumped into Nick.

"Oh, hello, Dr. Neff." She curtsied.

"Marie-Louise, I came to find you. Dr. Walter said that you were here. Do you have time to get a little snack?"

"Of course, lead the way."

He put a hand under her elbow and walked down the hall to the doctors' lounge where he found a small table away from a group of other doctors.

"What can I get you?"

"A tall glass of lemonade would be lovely."

"I'll be right back."

He returned with the lemonade for her and mineral water for himself, and two sandwiches.

After a few sips of lemonade, she asked, "Did you know that Dr. Walter has proposed to my aunt?"

"Yes, he told me this morning."

"I'm happy for them."

"Yes, they seem to be a perfect match."

She looked at him, "You're not very talkative today. Is anything bothering you?"

"As a matter of fact, yes." He cleared his throat before he explained, "When I saw you on the day of the surgery, you seemed to be on extremely familiar terms with your *so-to-speak* relative."

She dropped her gaze. This conversation entered dangerous ground and she wasn't ready yet to discuss this delicate subject. Careful to phrase her answer in as objective a way as possible, she said, "I was distraught and he comforted me. Besides, we have known each other since we were children."

"I understand, but I don't know if you realize that the man is in love with you."

She gasped. "How do you figure that?"

"The way he looks at you, the way he touches you, his smile, everything shows his love. And don't forget that I saw you two dancing together at the wedding."

"Dancing together doesn't mean anything."

"You're mistaken. At first I only noticed him and his feelings for you, but after I worked on the photographs, I saw much more. I saw you and your love for him."

"But I don't love him."

"You can deny it all you want, but it's there nevertheless. I know that you don't want to get involved with someone from your own rank, and I was handy as a welcome diversion."

She wanted to protest, but he held up his hand. "I was hoping to win your love, but I know now that your heart lies elsewhere."

She reached to cover his hand. "Oh, Nick, you don't know how much I want to love you. I love your family and would like to be a part of it. I admire you and think the world of you. Besides, I consider you my best friend."

"Friend!" He gave a short laugh, more like a bark than a laugh, that tore at her heart. After a moment he wanted to know, "Are you going to marry him?"

"Marry Ulrich? No."

"Why not, when you're both in love with each other?"

"For one thing, I don't want to marry an aristocrat, and for the other," she twisted her hands in her lap, "he's going to announce his engagement to someone else at the annual summer ball."

He drew his brows together. "You're jesting."

"No, it's the truth," she whispered.

"That's despicable." His voice was hard and censorious. "How can he marry another woman when he's in love with you?"

Marie-Louise put her hand on his arm and looked at him. "Nick, I don't think that he's really in love with me. You may have that all wrong."

"No, Sweetheart," he said harsher than she had ever heard him speak, "it doesn't take a psychologist to see that he loves you."

She sighed, "Can't we just forget him and go on with life?"

Leaning back in his chair, he sighed. "It's not that easy. My feelings are hurt, and you're hurting. What are we to do?"

"I don't know. I wish I was far away from here."

"You can always visit your mother," he suggested.

"No thank you," she said defiantly. "I'm staying right here. I have a business to run. I'm stuck."

"We're both stuck, but I have a suggestion. I bought tickets to the Festival of Lights in Liebenzell this Saturday evening. If your women can manage the café without you for a few hours, we can go there and I promise you it'll be well worth your time."

She looked at him, "You still want to go with me?"

"You said we're friends."

She leaned over and touched his cheek. "You're sweet."

He looked at the clock. "Oh dear, I need to get back to work. I'll see you tomorrow when you visit your aunt."

"Sure." She gave him a quick hug and left the hospital. *Poor Nick. I feel like a beast, and he is so nice and still wants to spend time with me. Actually, I don't know if he really wants to go with me or if he didn't want to waste the extra ticket to the Festival of Lights. Oh, now, Marie-Louise, don't think negative thoughts. He doesn't deserve that.*

Oh, why did life have to become so complicated when you grew up?

Her aunt returned from the hospital the following week, but only to pack her clothes and books and other necessary items for her three-week stay at a sanatorium in Schömberg. Dr. Walter arrived at the castle early on the morning of her departure and carried all her suitcases to his black motorcar. Marie-Louise and Ambrosia embraced as he entered the parlor.

"*Liebling*, it's time to go," he said and took Ambrosia's

arm, but she wasn't quite ready to leave yet. She turned to the baroness.

"Marie-Louise, are you sure you can handle the café and shop without me for such a long time?"

"I'll miss you, but Frau Zimmer and Frau Becker are both quite competent, and I'm confident that I'll manage. And maybe the weather will be so bad that no one will come up to the castle."

"Oh, I hope not."

"Relax and enjoy your stay in Schömberg. I'm sure that Dr. Walter will visit you, and I will also try to see you there."

"That would be lovely."

Dr. Walter stepped in. "Ladies, it's time to say your goodbyes."

Ambrosia hugged her niece and gave her a peck on the cheek. "Take good care of yourself."

"I will. Have a good trip. I'll miss you."

"I'll miss you, too, Marie-Louise."

Dr. Walter put his arm around Ambrosia's shoulder and turned her toward the door. "Time to go, my love."

Marie-Louise walked with them out to the stone balustrade where she watched the doctor cradle Ambrosia's face and plant a kiss on her lips before he helped her into the motorcar. He then turned to look at the baroness, winked at her and climbed into the driver's seat. He waved and guided the vehicle out of the courtyard.

Lucky for Tante Ambrosia to have found such a charming man in her older years. Who would have thought that her prim and proper aunt would be seen kissing a man for all the world to see! She was happy for her, but also a little jealous, because she, too, would like to have what her aunt so richly deserved.

Life went on as usual: ordering supplies, going over the books, giving instructions, going out with Nick once in a while, and going to the town hall on Fridays. The mayor had offered his cabin for her use again and pointed out that she worked too hard. She actually didn't work any harder than she had been these past weeks, but her days were pretty nondescript, especially because she hadn't seen Ulrich for a week or so. She wondered if he was courting his betrothed and making wedding plans. Thinking about him, however, was not conducive to a pleasant mood. And today was no different.

The day had started out hot and muggy. Shortly after eight, Frau Zimmer had shut all the windows and drawn the curtains to keep the heat out of the building. Jakob had announced that he would busy himself in his workshop below ground where it was cool, and Marie-Louise had left for her day at the medieval town hall. Her office on the top floor with the two casement windows would be hot and stuffy, and she envied those who could stay at Hohenstein.

She felt sluggish and didn't accomplish as much as she had set out to do. She listened to hear the chatter and sounds of the usual office activities, but the building seemed deserted. Even the public stayed home today. No sound could be heard except the buzzing of a couple of flies that bumped against the window pane now and then.

Marie-Louise got up and walked to the window. The town square below looked deserted except for a motley gang of boys who were playing soccer on the village green. She wondered if Ulrich was spending the day in his office.

Did Ulrich think of her? *Nonsense*, she scolded herself. She hadn't heard from him for some time, and this fact rankled. She had expected him to visit and inquire how she was doing, but he hadn't come. He had sent his locksmith as promised to install safety locks on all outside doors as well as on all ground floor windows—a total waste of money in her estimation. She sighed. He hadn't even come to inspect the work!

Heavens, the heat must be making her cross and miserable!

As the afternoon wore on, several puffy white clouds appeared on the horizon, and Marie-Louise watched them move closer. Their shapes changed from powder puffs to sheep and later to elephants. It used to be one of her favorite pastimes as a child to lie on her back in the soft grass and watch the clouds go by. On their wings, she would ride into all kinds of grotesque adventures and create her own fairytales as she sailed along.

Today, the fairytales gave way to reality, and the reality was closely linked to Ulrich.

By the time Marie-Louise left the office, most of the blue sky had disappeared and the once snowy clouds had taken on a grayish hue. The sun, completely obscured by now, only painted silver linings around the puffy formations. Nature waited for the much needed rain, but it took several more hours before the deluge came.

Marie-Louise and Frau Zimmer made sure that all the windows were closed and the tub beneath the leak in the roof was in place. Candles and matches in strategic places were held in readiness for an eventual power outage.

Thus prepared, the women sat in the library awaiting the storm. Nature itself seemed to hold its breath before the big spectacle. Everything was quiet. Not a leaf quivered on the trees, not even the song of a bird could be heard, and the stillness carried an eerie quality with it.

Finally the elements broke loose. A gust of wind whipped through the trees, ripped leaves off the branches, whirled them in the air and eventually dropped them like forgotten toys. Another gust of wind rattled the shutters and whistled around the corners of the building. It gripped small objects in its path, tossed them high in the air before slamming them against the wall.

Among the howling of the wind, Marie-Louise heard a loud bang on the roof. Something heavy thumped its way down the tiles until it crashed on the ground. Again. The same sound. And then nothing. She wondered what it could have been.

As soon as the wind abated somewhat, heavy raindrops fell, as big as coins. The rain fell slowly at first but intensified rapidly until the clouds burst and the rain came down with full force.

A sigh of relief. The spell was broken.

Marie-Louise rose. "We'd better check on the leak. The tub might be overflowing."

The sight that greeted the two women as they entered the attic surpassed their worst nightmares. Water everywhere! The tub was already full, spilling its contents onto the floor—and the rain still came down in sheets.

Sheets? Marie-Louise looked up. "Good grief," she groaned. Through a big gap in the roof she saw the dark mass of sky looming above and the rain pouring in. Now she knew what it was that she had heard earlier; roof tiles shattering on the ground. Something had to be done, and fast.

"Frau Zimmer, hurry! Get Jakob and round up some buckets on your way back."

Marie-Louise ran down the stairs, opened the front door and made a mad dash for the stables where she picked up an armload full of left-over tiles from the new roof. On her way back, she passed Jakob.

"Go get more tiles. We'll need them."

Drenched, she lugged the heavy tiles up the stairs, leaving little puddles of water behind with every step.

Chapter Twenty-five

Back in the attic, Frau Zimmer scooped out buckets full of water from the big galvanized tub, and dumped them out the casement window. She worked frantically while the rain came down with undiminished force.

Marie-Louise set the tiles on the floor and watched the procedure. "This isn't going to work." She looked around for some boards or big pieces of fabric to temporarily cover the hole until Jakob would arrive. A piece of canvas caught her eye. She picked it up and felt its rough texture, and then surveyed the area around the hole.

She could fastened the canvas to the roof somehow and stop the rain from coming into the attic. It might work. She had to try. Dragging an old trunk to below the hole, she stepped onto it and tucked one side of the canvas between a rafter and the tiles, and repeated the procedure for the other side. Tilting her head to one side, she tried to figure out how to secure the other ends with no rafters nearby. If she had the right kind of tools, she might nail the cloth to the horizontal slats that held the tiles in place, and she hoped that Jakob would bring his tool box.

While she waited for the old man, she helped the housekeeper dump more water out over the roof.

Finally, she heard the old man shuffling up the stairs. He indeed carried his heavy metal box with the tools in addition to the tiles. After he had caught his breath, he surveyed the damage.

"Seven tiles a'missing," he announced. He then pointed to the canvas. "What's that?"

"If we nail the ends of the canvas to the slats, the problem might be solved."

Hands on hips, he looked at the contraption. "It's no good, Fräulein Marie-Louise. If the canvas would be stiff, it might work, but it'll give under the weight of the water and form a dip. If it's not taut, it'll leak. And when it can't hold any more water, it'll either be so heavy that the weight will pull out the nails, or the water'll spill over and ya have the same mess again."

Marie-Louise closed her eyes for a moment and visualized the picture Jakob had drawn with his words. She massaged her temples and sighed. "I see that you're right. It won't work."

She yanked the cloth out from under the rafters and turned to Jakob. "Do you think we can replace the tiles from the inside?"

He looked up and scratched his bald head. "Nope."

"I was afraid of that," she mumbled.

She gave the roof another glance, and with a sigh, turned to the task of dumping water out the window. Jakob followed suit.

To conserve their own strengths they formed a line with Frau Zimmer filling the buckets, handing them to Jakob who, in turn, handed them to Marie-Louise to be dumped out.

This activity went on for about half an hour when Marie-Louise stretched and massaged her aching back. Looking out the window she could see neither moon nor stars, and figured that the rain might last for many more hours. She shuddered to think that they might have to spend the night in the attic.

She surveyed the hole again. If they couldn't place the tiles on the roof from the inside, they would have to do it from the outside, but how were they going to accomplish this? There were only two openings that led out onto the roof, the hole itself, and the casement window. The latter provided a bigger opening than the hole and, in addition, offered more security with its frame to hold onto. The gutter below the window would also be a welcome aid. She'd have to try.

"Frau Zimmer, please fetch the lantern from the kitchen. I'm going out onto the roof."

"Baroness, no! You can't do that. You'll kill yourself."

"Go and get me that lantern."

Marie-Louise paced the floor, hands clasped behind her back. Every now and then, she grabbed a bucket full of water and dumped it out on her way.

Jakob watched her pacing. "Fräulein Marie-Louise, the housekeeper's right. Ya can't go out thar. It's too dangerous for a little thing like yourself. Let me go instead."

Marie-Louise stopped. She looked at him, not really seeing the old man. For a moment, she envisioned his slight form disappearing through the window, and she herself handing him the tiles through the opening in the roof. Simple and safe. For her, anyway.

Immediately following this picture, another one settled before her mind's eye. The old man struggling to climb the steep roof, his foot slipping on the wet tiles, his fingers groping for some hold and, getting his footing back, trying again with the same result. Except this time, his arthritic fingers didn't find a ledge to hang onto. He slipped and slipped lower and lower until a hollow thud announced his contact with the cobbles below.

She raised her head high with chin jutted out, and pronounced in her most authoritative voice, "No, you're not going out on that roof. I need you to hand me the tiles while Frau Zimmer holds the lantern." She looked toward the door and wondered what took the woman so long.

At that moment, she heard the housekeeper puffing up the stairs. When Frau Zimmer stepped into the attic, she pressed her hands to her heaving bosom and took a few deep breaths. Finally she managed to say, "I couldn't find the lantern. Where exactly in the kitchen is it? I looked through all the cupboards."

Marie-Louise tried to suppress her irritation. "It's in the pantry on the bottom shelf, toward the back."

"I'll go look again," she said and hurried down the stairs while Marie-Louise and Jakob busied themselves emptying the oval tub.

I wish Frau *Zimmer would hurry with that dreaded lantern before I lose my courage.*

After a few minutes, the housekeeper appeared. "Baroness, I'm very sorry, but the lantern isn't in the pantry."

Half turning to run downstairs and look for it herself, she thought better of it and turned to Jakob with an exasperated sigh. "Would you please get me a light from the workshop?"

Immediately, the old man set down the bucket and scuttled down the stairs, but not before he exchanged glances with the housekeeper.

"Hurry," Marie-Louise called after him.

When Jakob came back with the light, and the rain still pelted the roof, Marie-Louise took a deep breath. She clenched her fists and walked with purposeful strides toward the window, steeling herself for the ordeal.

Frau Zimmer wrung her hands and pleaded, "Baroness, please reconsider. Wait for another half hour. The rain might stop."

"She's right, ya know," said Jakob. "Let's wait a wee bit longer."

Without turning to look at her helpers, Marie-Louise said, "If you'd give me a hand while I climb out, I'd appreciate it."

Resigned, Jakob gave her a hand-up as she pulled herself onto the windowsill. Twisting sideways, she stuck one leg out, then the other and held on to the frame while turning onto her stomach. She grabbed the windowsill with both hands and lowered her body until she felt the edge of the gutter beneath her feet. It creaked under her weight, and she held her breath and waited. Several seconds passed. Nothing happened. Time had come for her to move on.

As long as she could, she held on to the dormer, while the light from Jacob's lamp showed her the direction she had to go. It looked like a long way up to the hole, and she faltered. She ought to start climbing now, but without a decent hold of any kind, it was an almost impossible task.

Before she let go of the dormer, she pressed herself flat against the tiles, still standing on the gutter. *What on earth am I doing out here? Maybe Frau Zimmer was right, and the rain will stop soon.* She closed her eyes. *Oh, dear, I don't want to do this!*

The light beckoned and she saw row upon row of wet tiles glistening in its silvery beam. It was a long way up, and her courage faded. She felt cold and miserable as the rain pelted her, matting her hair to her scalp, and running in little rivulets down her forehead and into her eyes. If she'd thought she was drenched before from running across the yard, she felt as wet as a rag now, her movements hampered by the added weight of her wet clothes.

She guessed the distance between her present location and her destination, and felt her mouth go dry. She looked back at the open window, and then up again toward the gaping hole.

Still holding on with one hand to the dormer, she groped with the other to find a hold. Her fingers found a small ledge where one row of tiles overlapped the previous row. Though minute, she curled her fingers around the ledge and pulled herself up one centimeter at a time.

Scared but secure for the moment, she considered her next move. She had to bring one foot up a ways to push herself higher, but her foot slipped again and again before the sole of her shoe hugged the tile securely. She gave a sigh of relief. After a few moments, the time had come to pull away from the gutter—and from safety. One false move and she could slip to her death.

Jaw clenched, she inched her way higher and higher until at last her hand came in contact with something soft and warm—the housekeeper's hand.

Relieved, she clung to that hand and breathed deeply to steady herself for her next ordeal, the fitting of the tiles, while rain streamed down her face and mingled with her tears. She clenched her teeth, and took the tile that Jakob handed her.

The tiles were shaped so that the ridge on the back of the tiles fitted perfectly over the horizontal wooden slats of the roof, while the lip on the top hugged the tile of the previous row. The job would have been fairly easy could she have used both hands, but she had to hold on with one hand and balance the heavy tile into place with the other.

With the last tile in place, Marie-Louise rested her head against the roof. She needed to climb back now. Only supported by her hands, she clung to the small ledge. She looked down and shuddered at the thought, that while holding on with one hand to the ledge, the other hand needed to grope for the ledge below. What if she missed?

She rested her forehead against the wet tile and waited. *I have to get off this roof. I can't stay here. Come on, girl, get moving!* She heaved a sigh and loosened her grip, her fingers stiff from cold and fear.

As soon as her hand left the safety of the ledge, her body slid down a fraction, and she screamed. Panic-stricken, her hand shot up to find the ledge again, but couldn't. Frantically, she clawed at the wet tiles. Where was the ledge? Sobbing, she continued her search until she felt it again. With a sigh, her heart still thudding in her throat, she rested her forehead against the wet roof again, and wished nothing more than to fall asleep and wake up in the morning in her comfortable bed.

"Fräulein Marie-Louise, what is it? Why don't ya move?" Jacob's anxious voice sounded above the downpour. When she didn't answer, he sounded frantic, "Come on, ya can do it! It's not far. Start moving. Come on!"

Still pressed against the roof, tears of fear and frustration mingled with the rain on her face. She was chilled to the bone. *I have to get off this blasted roof.* She reached for the ledge below, and in so doing, almost lost her hold on the upper one.

"Slow," Jakob coaxed. "Ya'll make it. Get yer courage up and try again."

It took her a few moments to collect enough fortitude to go on. Her movements were even more unsure and timid than before, and her first attempt failed. Spread-eagled and hanging on for dear life, she shook her head in frustration.

"Up and at 'em! Come on. Try again. Ya'll make it!"

Jakob's voice, muffled by the rain, penetrated her mind, and she lifted her torso slightly off the tiles, slid her right hand down one row, until her fingers felt the ledge and held on. Then the right side of her body sagged lower. She repeated the procedure with her left hand.

Suddenly, her foot slipped. With a shriek of terror, her fingers lost their hold; she slid down, slow at first, then a little faster. Wildly groping, she tried to grab hold of something—anything.

"Merciful heavens! Leave yer hands on the roof. Calm down. Quick."

At last! The ledge! She clamped her fingers around it, panted, exhausted, and more frightened than ever. Pressed to the roof, she shivered with cold, her teeth chattered, and her will to fight ceased.

From far away, she heard someone calling. "Fräulein Marie-Louise, ya've rested long enough. Get moving."

She only shook her head. She couldn't.

She hung there for what seemed an eternity, when she heard some commotion below. Yelling and scraping, and more yelling. She didn't dare turn her head to look. She heard the housekeeper's "Thank goodness," and Jakob's command to stay put and hang on.

"He'll have ya down in no time."

She didn't know who *he* was, but didn't care. Nothing mattered at the moment. She felt cold and numb, and all she wanted was to close her eyes and go to sleep.

A scraping on the tiles below her caught her attention before she heard a familiar voice.

Marie-Louise shook her head. She must be delirious.

There was the voice again. Closer this time.

"Marie-Louise. I'm here to help you down. Relax and do what I say."

It wasn't a dream. Those were Ulrich's words when he had coaxed her down the ladder. She must be dreaming. She lifted her head a fraction and turned to see if he was real or not. When she saw his head above the rain gutter, she felt such relief that she released her hold on the ledge and immediately slithered further down the roof.

"For goodness sake, don't let go yet." He reached up, but couldn't quite get a hold of her. The ladder wasn't tall enough.

"Marie-Louise, can you move down just a little bit more so that I can reach you?"

The baroness shook her head, teeth chattering.

When she wouldn't move, she heard Ulrich's voice again. "Frau Zimmer. The rope, please. Toss one end to the baroness."

"Marie-Louise, Frau Zimmer is throwing a rope to you. Please grab it, if you can, with one hand, and hold on to it. Can you do that?"

She nodded with chattering teeth.

The first attempt failed. The rope fell short of the spot where Marie-Louise hung on. Reeling it back, Frau Zimmer tried again. This time, it fell within easy reach, but the baroness didn't dare ease her grip on the tile.

"Marie-Louise," coaxed Ulrich, "try to grab the rope. Now."

"Can't," she chattered.

"Unless you want to spend the night on this roof, you need to hold on to the rope. Come on. You can do it."

She turned her head to see where the rope was.

"Now, grab it," came the command from the ladder.

Marie-Louise hesitated, but finally inched one hand toward the rope. A shriek. She slipped. Fumbling to find another hold, her tears flowed and mingled with the rain on her face. She trembled and pressed her body hard against the tiles.

"Marie-Louise, you have to try again. Don't give up now."

She looked sideways at the rope, and this time, she moved her body toward it, millimeter by millimeter. Finally, her body rested next to the rope. She could feel it beside her, but didn't dare loosen her grip.

"Take the rope, Marie-Louise. Please."

Shaking, she eased one hand toward the rope, but quickly reached for the ledge again.

"You almost had it. Try again," coaxed Ulrich.

Holding onto the ledge became more and more difficult as her fingers were stiff from cold and wet. And holding on with only one hand seemed an impossible task.

"Let go of the ledge with your right hand."

"Jakob and Frau Zimmer, are you ready to pull when the baroness grips the rope? I'll let you know exactly when to pull. All right?"

The two people in the attic answered in the affirmative.

"Marie-Louise, NOW."

She closed her eyes, sent a prayer heavenward, looked at the rope again, and let go with both of her hands to reach for it. Of course, in the process, she slithered down a few centimeters, and screamed.

A gasp from the ladder.

At the last moment, Marie-Louise grabbed the rope with both hands.

"Pull. Slow and steady."

Marie-Louise held on for dear life, although her hands were ice cold and hurting. Gradually, her body was pulled, first to the side to be positioned under the casement window, and then upward toward the window.

Once the windowsill was in easy reach, Marie-Louise let go with one hand and grabbed it. Immediately, Frau Zimmer took her cold hand and pulled her into the attic.

"Thank goodness, Baroness, you gave me such a fright."

Marie-Louise collapsed onto the attic floor, unable to say anything.

A few minutes later, Ulrich hurried up to the attic. He rushed to kneel beside her and took her into his arms to warm her and to calm her shivering.

"Frau Zimmer, what the baroness needs now is a warm bed and some hot peppermint tea. Could you also please heat up some water for a hot canteen? I'll lead her downstairs."

He turned to Jakob. "You can clean up this mess tomorrow. Frau Zimmer can also make you some hot tea. And hurry to get out of those wet clothes."

"Thank you, Count Wolfburg."

Ulrich led Marie-Louise downstairs where he handed her over to Frau Zimmer. "While you take care of the baroness, I need to dry off, too."

"There's a closet full of men's clothes in the late baron's room. I don't think the baroness would mind if you borrowed some of her father's clothes."

"Great. Thank you."

Ulrich visited Hohenstein the following day. "How do you feel after yesterday's ordeal?"

"Still a little shaken up, but otherwise fine, except for—" she sneezed, "—a little cold."

"I'm glad to see you still in one piece. You gave me such a fright when I saw you hanging on that roof."

Marie-Louise looked at him sideways. "By the way, how did you know that I was on the roof and needed your help?"

"I didn't."

"Then why did you come?"

"I was on my way home from a business meeting when the rain started and I got drenched. Automobiles are great, and I like my Mercedes, but it's open to the elements, and I get wet when it rains."

"So, why did you come here?"

"I was in the vicinity and thought to find shelter at Hohenstein. When I drove into the courtyard and saw you splayed out on that roof, I thought my heart would stop. What on earth were you thinking climbing out of that window and onto the roof?"

Glaring at him, she said, "Something had to be done to stop the rain from flooding our attic."

"It was already flooded. You could've waited until today."

"Not likely. I couldn't stand by and watch my home be ruined by water."

He shook his head. "Stubborn woman! Someone who's afraid of heights shouldn't venture to climb up on a steep roof—and a wet one at that. I don't even want to think of what could have happened had I not stopped by."

Marie-Louise pouted. "Don't scold me. I'm glad you came and rescued me."

"Once again."

She smiled. "Yes, once again."

"How's your aunt?"

"She seems to be doing quite well, and Dr. Walter is visiting her on weekends when he's free."

"By the way, have you told her that you love her?"

"I have."

"And?"

"It felt good."

"Great, I'm proud of you." After a moment, he added, "How about that talk with your beau? Did you straighten things out with him?"

"He's not my beau," she snapped. "Just a good friend, and yes, I have spoken with him."

"All right, all right. Calm down. When did you speak with him?"

"In the hospital, when I visited my Tante Ambrosia."

"How did he react?"

This was none of his business. Who did he think he was, interrogating her like that?

Ulrich pushed on. "Was he upset?"

"He was sad, but not too surprised."

"Smart man. I think I'm starting to like him."

She almost responded that Nick probably wouldn't like the count, but caught herself in time. Had she said *that*, Ullie would have probed for the reason, and she definitely didn't want him to find out that she loved him, Count Wolfburg, the High and Mighty. Loved him? Did the thought of loving him really come from her? Her mind must be befuddled after her ordeal, because she definitely didn't love him. No, no, at best, she had a crush on him that was all. The thought of loving him was very disturbing, and she had to purge it immediately.

Ulrich looked at her, brows raised. "What's the matter? You look as if you have seen a ghost."

She shook her head and quickly came up with a little white lie. "I just relived the ordeal on the roof."

He patted her hand. "Poor little baroness."

"Now you're making fun of me," she pouted.

"Absolutely not. I almost died when I saw you on that roof and watched you slither down those wet tiles. Please, never do anything like that again."

She shuddered. "I think I can promise that I will never climb onto a wet roof again as long as I live."

"I'm glad to hear that."

Probably to guide her thoughts in a different direction, he asked, "How are things going at the town hall and with the mayor?"

"Oh, he generously offered me his cabin in the Black Forest again for a week or so, because he said that I looked exhausted."

"Did you accept?"

"Of course not. I can't get away from here, especially now that my aunt is gone."

He nodded. "The mayor is very generous."

"Yes, he's a very nice man."

"Obviously."

A few days after her escapade on the roof, she received a letter with the Wolfburg coat-of-arms embossed in the upper left-hand corner, and Marie-Louise wondered what Ulrich had to write to her about. He didn't have to be so formal. He could easily come over and tell her what he wanted her to know. Perhaps it was an invitation to the dreaded ball where he would announce his engagement. In that case, she wondered if she could fake an illness, so that she wouldn't have to attend.

She turned the envelope over, still puzzled. Then she quickly opened it in her usual manner, with her finger creating bizarre peaks along the opening. The envelope was lined with crisp, royal blue tissue paper and smelled faintly of lilies of the valley.

Strange. He wouldn't use perfumed stationery unless—her breath caught in her throat—his future wife had mailed the invitations. Her hand trembled as she took out the single sheet of paper, folded three times.

Chapter Twenty-six

The letter, hand-written in a wonderfully even, yet assertive handwriting, definitely showed a woman's hand.

Dearest Marie-Louise:

They say news travel fast, but it takes a little longer to reach Falkenberg, for I only found out recently that you have returned to Hohenstein. I would like to come and see you and welcome you back. Alas, this is impossible at the moment as I am a little under the weather. For that reason, I request the pleasure of your visit here at Falkenberg on Saturday, July 17. Please, be prepared to spend a week with me.

Affectionately,
Sybilla Countess von Wolfburg

Marie-Louise stared at the letter for a few seconds. She was summoned to Falkenberg. What about her business here? With Tante Ambrosia at the sanatorium, and she herself at Falkenberg, who would run the café and souvenir shop? She couldn't possibly leave everything to strangers, although the housekeeper and Frau Becker were very competent.

She could write to Sybilla that she wouldn't be able to visit her that particular week. Impossible. Nobody declined summons from the Countess Wolfburg, not unless you lay on your deathbed, or something similarly drastic.

She'd have to plan ahead, plan for unexpected eventualities for the two weekends she would be gone, and order enough supplies to last for the duration of her absence. She sighed. This invitation came at a very inopportune time.

She wondered if Ulrich would be at Falkenberg also. The countess hadn't mentioned him at all.

Marie-Louise read the letter again. No. It sounded as if she would be the only visitor there, and she didn't know whether to be glad about that or not.

She'd have to inform the mayor of her proposed absence, and hoped that he wouldn't take umbrage at her accepting the countess' invitation when she had declined his various offers of recovering at his cabin in the Black Forest. He'd understand when she told him that summons from Falkenberg simply could not be declined.

The mayor did indeed understand. In fact, he stressed again that she needed a break, and that he was glad that she took some time off. He even offered his assistance should anything unforeseen happen at the castle during her absence.

With comparative peace of mind, therefore, Marie-Louise set out for Falkenberg to visit the countess. On the train there, she wondered for the umpteenth time why Sybilla had invited her. Was it Ulrich's doing? And if so, what could be his motive?

Thoughts of the count flooded her mind, with the events of the stormy night still fresh in her memory. She had stopped a long time ago to see him as the rigid dictator of the family clan, but instead, a man dedicated to serve those under his jurisdiction. No, not only those under his jurisdiction, she corrected herself. He would help anyone in need as he proved with the little boy who had scraped his knee. Then why hadn't he helped her when she needed a loan? It just didn't add up.

She knew now that he didn't mean her any harm, but felt that there was something he hadn't told her, something he held back, something to do with his refusal to grant her a loan, and she couldn't imagine what his reasons might be. Didn't he know he could trust her? *Men!*

Falkenberg, a castle built in the latter part of the eighteenth century, overlooked the scenic *Iller* valley, and the mountain range of the *Sattelhorn* with its snow-capped peaks, formed the majestic backdrop. From afar off, the graceful structure beckoned the traveler to come closer and admire its beauty.

At first, the castle could only be seen as a small white dot against the dark purple of the mountains. As the train neared the town of Falkenberg, the white spot took on shape, and Marie-Louise could recognize the dome-shaped middle section with its two annexes on either side. A few more kilometers brought the terrace and stairs, curving from two sides up to the terrace, into view. The rest remained hidden behind the trees.

The driver with the Wolfburg chaise waited at the train station and loaded her cases into the hold. On the way out of the little town of Falkenberg, she admired the quaint half-timbered houses, most of which had murals painted on the front walls.

Outside the town boundaries began the steep climb up the hillside to the castle, where the road snaked through pasture land, lush and green. The bells around the cows' necks chimed with the animals' every move, big bells, medium-size ones, and small ones, produced the tranquil, soothing sound she liked.

Before the last and steepest incline, the road entered a forested area, and the castle disappeared from view. But what a magnificent sight when they left the forest, and the road leading through the tree-lined avenue leading to the castle! The Wolfburg flag, hoisted atop the cupola, indicated that the countess was in residence. The flag was divided in half horizontally, with the upper half being bright yellow, and the lower half black. The middle, on a white background, showed the Wolfburg coat-of-arms, a wolf's head overlooking a pinnacled fortress.

When the coach stopped in front of the stairs, a liveried footman rushed to her side, opened the door and helped her out. A second servant took her luggage and carried it upstairs.

Marie-Louise turned to face a statue-like man in black, apparently the butler, who greeted and escorted her to the terrace. Both wings of the French doors were open, and upon the threshold waited the countess.

Marie-Louise's heart stopped, but only for a moment after which warmth filled her whole being, and joy welled up in her that spilled out of her eyes. It felt like coming home all over again. With a little cry, she ran into the countess' outstretched arms.

"Welcome to Falkenberg, child. I'm so happy to see you." She held Marie-Louise at arm's length. "Let me look at you! Oh my, how beautiful you are. Even more beautiful than your mother," she exclaimed, and led her into the parlor.

The days at Falkenberg were low-key and relaxing. The two women went for long walks, went out riding, played cards or made music together, Marie-Louise accompanying the countess' violin playing on the piano. Neither of them mentioned Ulrich at all.

One day, she helped Sybilla sort through photographs which gave her a glimpse into the family's history.

She saw Ulrich's and Peter's baby pictures and followed the two boys through their toddler years into early adolescence. A picture of Ulrich as a lanky teenager reminded her of her childhood days, when he had come to Hohenstein with his parents for a visit, and when he had deemed himself too mature to join in Peter's and Marie-Louise's adventures.

Then there were photographs of Ulrich on horseback, Ulrich in gala uniform, Ulrich at his graduation from university, and Ulrich playing sports. One photograph showed him at the rim of the swimming pool after a polo game. Water droplets glistened on his muscular torso while he laughed and held up his arms in triumph.

Studying the picture, she smiled and wondered if he still found time to do the things he enjoyed, because he always seemed so busy, even when he visited Hohenstein. He either was on his way to some meeting, or on his way back. *Well, not always,* she conceded, and remembered the day he had taken her out to dinner. He had seemed relaxed, with no thoughts of business at the time, and had been the perfect escort, listening to her gripes, and soothing her frazzled nerves.

Her mind wandered further to the moment when he had taken her into his arms without so much as a struggle from her. She had fallen into his hands like a ripe apple, and although her mind professed that she didn't care for him, her body spoke a different language.

She closed her eyes and felt a rush of heat in her face. At first, she had tried to ascribe her wayward behavior to their magnetic body chemistries, but had finally come to the realization that it was more than that. Even the admittance, that her *tendre* for him was fading rapidly to make room for a much more potent emotion. But what was the use of accepting the fact that she had fallen in love with him when she knew he was promised to another woman?

If he were a commoner, a lawyer or a doctor, or even an engineer or merchant, she wouldn't have hesitated to accept his advances, but she didn't want to allow herself to be shackled to a life of rules and conventions. Traditions she could live with, but not the strict dictates imposed by the ancient stalwarts of nobility. In the meantime, however, this resolution had weakened because she had discovered that even commoners were bound by rules and regulations. Take the farmers, for instance. They couldn't just up and leave and go on holiday. Their animals needed to be fed every day, the cows needed to be milked twice a day, and the fields needed to be tended.

Doctors, also, were bound by their profession. Nick had to be on duty at all hours of the day and night, and in case of an emergency, he had to be available.

She also remembered Ingrid from the town hall who had become the sole breadwinner for the family after her husband's injury, and who sacrificed without complaint.

Then why did *she* rebel against the sacrifices imposed by her rank?

If she had known a few weeks ago what she knew now, would she have encouraged Ulrich? Well, of course not, when she knew that he was promised to another woman. She could never be so selfish as to destroy the happiness of someone else. And did Ullie even love her, Marie-Louise? He never said so, and how could he when he had someone waiting for him. She had a hard time understanding how he could flirt with her, and kiss her the way he did, when he knew that he was to be married soon to someone else.

Marie-Louise looked at Ulrich's photograph again. No, she admitted, he had never revealed his feelings for her—if he had any at all. *That's just as well.*

With her hands in her lap she stared into space. If it was just as well, why did she feel so miserable at the thought? Perhaps his flirting and his kisses were an indication of his feelings for her. Or perhaps they were only the triumph of the hunter.

She studied the photograph again. Was there a triumphant sign for his victory over her, also?

She remembered his gentle touch, his laughing eyes, his strong arms, and her heart skipped a beat. It couldn't all have been a game. Maybe it was at first, when he wanted to teach her a lesson—a lesson she had refused to learn.

Looking up, she noticed the countess' watchful eye. Hopefully Sybilla hadn't seen her dreaming over Ulrich's photograph, and she quickly put it back in the box and closed the lid. She'd work on the pictures of the count and countess, instead.

Half-hearted at first, she sorted them by topic: business, social, personal. There were photographs of their wedding, their honeymoon on board their yacht, and the birth of their two sons. Photographs of holidays, their twenty-fifth wedding anniversary, and finally, pictures of the couple at Falkenberg, the count sitting in his wheelchair with Sybilla standing behind him, her hand on his shoulder, and smiling down into his upturned face.

Awed, Marie Louise said, "You and Onkel Georg were very much in love, weren't you?"

Sybilla smiled and, after a moment of silence, patted the seat next to her on the settee. "Come here, dear. Sit down."

Seated next to each other, the older woman took one of Marie-Louise's hands between both of hers, and looked dreamily out the window.

"Yes, we loved each other very, very much. It's a miracle to me, how our love had grown over the years, and I feel fortunate to have been blessed with such a fine husband."

"Was it love at first sight?"

"Oh, no." The countess chuckled in remembrance. "No such thing. Georg's proposal came unexpected and quite unromantic. I didn't even love him at the time."

"How come you married him anyway?"

"That's a long story. Remind me to tell you sometime. Right now, it suffices to say that, tradition-bound, I accepted, but not without a fight."

"Oh, please, Tante Sybilla, tell me your story. It sounds intriguing."

The countess took a deep breath before she started. "Oh, very well, here it is. One day, my family received an invitation to attend a ball at Castle Wolfburg. This wouldn't be of any interest, except that this ball was given for the young count to choose a wife from among the eligible young ladies."

Marie-Louise drew back. "Are you saying that all the young ladies were invited for the sole purpose of being inspected like cattle, to see if they would be good enough as a wife for the count?"

"Something like that, yes."

"That's preposterous!"

"That's exactly what I thought, and I didn't like the idea one bit, but felt quite certain that I wouldn't be chosen, being more of a tomboy than a proper lady."

"Couldn't you refuse to attend the ball?" asked Marie-Louise.

"No, that wasn't an option."

The baroness pondered this scenario for a moment. "Is that tradition still practiced today?"

"No, we did away with it."

"Thank goodness. The young ladies must have felt like slaves, sold to the highest bidder."

The countess smiled, "I can see that you're as rebellious as I was."

"What happened at the ball? Obviously you *were* the chosen one."

"When Georg announced that I was to be his countess, I was too stunned to even run away, and I can't remember how I even survived the following weeks before the wedding. I didn't participate in any of the preparations; all I wanted to do was die."

"Somehow you must have fallen in love with him, though."

"I was a very stubborn young woman, and decided that I would be his wife on paper only."

"And he went along with your wishes?"

"Georg was the perfect gentleman. He never pressured me or forced me to do anything against my will. We each had our own bedrooms and saw each other only at mealtimes. Other than that, he didn't even seem to notice me, which actually bothered me. So, I tried all kinds of escapades to make him pay attention to me."

Marie-Louise looked at Sybilla. "What kind of escapades?"

"There was a young lady that I had met at the ball who befriended me and who took me to all kinds of different places—dance halls, shows, you name it. One evening, she took me to another dance hall. During the evening, an argument broke out in one corner of the hall. The shouting escalated, and pretty soon it evolved into a full-blown brawl with fist fights and punches. I was scared and looked for my friend, but couldn't see her anywhere. When the door opened, and several policemen entered the establishment, they grabbed the troublemakers and everybody else close by, me included."

Marie-Louise had listened with interest. "How awful that must have been for you."

"Yes, it was. We were transported to the police station, and you can imagine how frightened I was. I told the officers that I was the Countess of Wolfburg, but they didn't believe me. When I insisted, they sent an officer to the castle."

"Did they let you go free then?"

"Not yet. My brother-in-law Wolfgang had listened to the officer and wanted to rescue me and spare Georg the embarrassment, but Georg wouldn't let his brother do the dirty work, and came to the police station himself to free me. When I saw him walk through the door, I thought I would die of humiliation. His face was as if chiseled in marble, and I knew that I was in deep trouble, but at least he noticed me. However, I was afraid that this evening would mark the end of our marriage, and I realized then that I didn't want it to end, that I had developed tender feelings for him."

Sybilla twisted her hands in her lap. "Georg found out who had taken me to that awful place, and explained that not everyone who professed to be my friend had my best interest at heart, especially not my lady friend. Apparently, she'd had hopes of becoming countess, and when Georg didn't choose her, she decided to destroy our marriage and become countess after the divorce."

"That's despicable."

"Yes, it was devious," said Sybilla.

"How did things develop after this experience?"

"My love for Georg grew, and we became a very happy couple."

Hands in her lap, Marie-Louise asked, "What made him choose you in the first place?"

"We had actually met the winter before the ball at a ski lodge, although I didn't know who he was at the time, but he apparently liked me from the start."

"Did you recognize him when you saw him at the ball?"

"Yes, I did, but I still didn't think that he would choose me."

"What an interesting story, Tante Sybilla. I didn't know you were a rebel."

Sybilla's eyes crinkled like Ulrich's, and little imps danced in their depths. "I was a rebel, all right. And quite stupid."

"I doubt that."

"Unfortunately, it's true. And through my selfish actions, I almost lost a jewel of a husband. I had fallen in love with him gradually, but fought my feelings with an obstinate determination, and had to learn a hard lesson."

Marie-Louise chewed on her lower lip. Perhaps she had more in common with Ulrich's mother than she had thought possible.

After a while, the countess continued, "I didn't want to live a regimented life. I wanted to be free."

"You, too?" Marie-Louise asked, perplexed.

Sybilla smiled. "Yes. Me, too."

"How did you cope?"

"It wasn't always easy. Oftentimes, the family had to take second place behind social obligations, and sometimes *etiquette* dictated a course of action contrary to my wishes."

"How could you live such a restricted life?"

"I loved my husband, and that made all the difference in the world. Whenever we spent time together, he made sure it was quality time."

"I bet you miss him terribly."

"Yes, I do. I'm glad we moved to Falkenberg after his stroke, where I had Georg all to myself." She closed her eyes and smiled. "It was a glorious time, like a second honeymoon."

"Marrying Onkel Georg was obviously right for you."

Sybilla nodded and dabbed at her eyes.

"How can one be sure to make the right decision?"

"Follow your heart."

That night, sleep was long in coming. How could she follow her heart when the way was barred by that other woman? She had fallen in love with Ulrich after she had fought so hard to suppress her feelings, only to find out that he was out of reach. Probably the punishment for rebellion.

Oh, well. Ullie would get married, and she would be at university in the fall. She had decided to pursue a degree in Business instead of Art—and that would take her mind off of Ulrich.

Sybilla never mentioned Ulrich, and Marie-Louise was glad, because she didn't want Sybilla to get suspicious.

The two women had a wonderful time together, but the baroness couldn't wait to get back to Hohenstein and look after the café.

Had she known what awaited her upon her return to Hohenstein after her one-week holiday, Marie-Louise wouldn't have been so anxious to get back.

Chapter Twenty-seven

Frau Zimmer handed her a registered letter from a contracting firm, and Marie-Louise looked at it with suspicion. Most of her obstacles had come by mail, and she hesitated to open it. She turned the envelope over, and wondered why a contractor would send her anything, much less by registered mail. With apprehension, she finally slid her finger into the flap and tore it open. Upon reading the letter, her eyes widened in disbelief, and her hand trembled. She read it a second time, but the message remained the same.

"That's impossible," she whispered. "It can't be true. He said it was highly unlikely."

The single sheet of paper slipped out of her lifeless fingers.

The housekeeper rushed forward and picked it up. "Baroness, what is it? What's wrong? You look ill."

Marie-Louise steadied herself by holding on to the back of a chair, and murmured, "I'm ruined."

After a pause, she continued, "All our efforts were in vain—and we tried so hard."

"I don't understand, Baroness."

Marie-Louise took two deep breaths before she explained in a toneless voice, "The mayor demands payment of his loan in full. And I have only two days to come up with the money plus interest. There's no way I can manage that."

"Couldn't you obtain a loan from a bank?"

Marie-Louise shook her head. She had tried that before.

"What about Count Wolfburg? I'm sure he'd be more than willing to help."

Again, Marie-Louise shook her head.

"Couldn't you sell some assets? Some antiques, maybe some land?"

She shook her head.

"What about the furniture?"

"I can't part with any of it. Each piece holds sentimental value, is connected with childhood memories, or memories of loved-ones. No, that wouldn't do at all."

"That leaves the land."

"Unfortunately, there is none. It has all been sold, except for the castle and the immediate grounds surrounding it."

Although Marie-Louise rejected the housekeeper's suggestions, they triggered the necessary impulse to look for alternatives. Perhaps the mayor was open to negotiations? Poor man! He had tried to help her, and now found himself in a position, possibly due to circumstances beyond his control, to demand payment to save his own business.

Out loud, Marie-Louise spoke her thoughts, "Writing me this letter was probably one of the hardest things the mayor had ever done in his life."

Hands on her hips, the housekeeper rolled her eyes. "If you ask me, I think he's a pretty sleazy character."

"Oh, no, Frau Zimmer! He's the nicest man; he showed me nothing but kindness and consideration."

"I'm sure it wasn't out of the goodness of his heart. He doesn't do anything unless he profits by it."

"I think you're wrong."

"Just be careful."

Before contacting the mayor, Marie-Louise made a list of all the alternatives she could think of. Making lists had become second nature to her ever since she decided to preserve Hohenstein. She gave a sad, little laugh and concentrated on her alternatives again.

Suddenly, a brilliant idea flashed into her mind. What if she sent her mother a telegram asking for one of those new automobiles? Anique wouldn't spend any money on Hohenstein, yet a motorcar for her only child was a different story. It might work. She could then take out a loan with the vehicle as collateral. Yes! She'd try that approach.

She'd have to talk to the mayor and arrange for an extension of his ultimatum, because it would take at least a week or more before her mother's check would arrive in the mail.

Marie-Louise took out paper and pencil and composed a letter to her mother.

In the middle of the letter, she stopped. What was happening to her? Had she lost her mind? How could she even consider doing something so deceitful? Sure, it might save Hohenstein, but would she be able to ever forget her dishonesty? Would she be able to live with herself, to respect herself, to look people straight in the eye? No. She couldn't go through with it! Not when she concealed the truth of her real reason for wanting transportation.

She thought of her proud Hohenstein ancestors in the picture gallery and knew they wouldn't look upon her with favor were she to dishonor their name. One day, she hoped, her portrait would hang there, too, and later generations would talk about her and her brave efforts to restore the family estate. That one day might never come, though, if she didn't come up with the money for the loan in a hurry.

She remembered the day when she had promised her ancestors in the picture gallery that she would preserve Hohenstein and make them proud, and she had worked very hard to achieve this goal. Should all her efforts have been in vain? Despite her resourcefulness and business sense, as Ullie called it, she might still lose her home unless she could come up with a plan to avoid this disgrace.

I must tell Ulrich. He can help.

When she walked across the courtyard to ask Jakob to harness the horses to the coach, she hesitated until she came to a standstill. How could she ask him to help her out of her present situation when he had made it very clear from the start that he wouldn't give her a loan? And how could she tell him that she had made an unwise decision, accepting a risky loan from the mayor? He had urged her to consult him before making any decisions regarding Hohenstein—and she hadn't.

Whistling for Kaiser, Marie-Louise took a walk in the forest. She needed to sort things out, come to grips with the situation, get familiar with every possible outcome, positive or negative. And what better place to concentrate on a problem than the tranquil ambiance of the old trees that never failed to whisper peace to her soul. Today was no exception.

The problem itself did not change, but a resolution formed in her mind that made her take courage. Why hadn't she thought of this before? She owned a business, a profitable business, and should be able to obtain a small business loan. The bank certainly couldn't refuse this time on the grounds that she didn't have enough income to make the payments.

Early the next morning, therefore, Marie-Louise went to the Commerce Bank, but although the bank director congratulated her on her success, he still couldn't grant her the desired loan due to the high risk nature of her business and the unstable political situation of the country.

Marie-Louise wanted to scream. Instead, she hung her head while tears of frustration wet her cheeks.

On the way home, she racked her brain for any options to secure a loan elsewhere. Dr. Walter might be in a position to lend her the money. He always said that they were family. No. She shook her head. She couldn't do that, not without talking to Tante Ambrosia first, and it wouldn't be fair to burden her with Hohenstein's problems right now.

Who else did she know who could possibly help? Well, there was Nick's father who had shown an interest in Hohenstein, but his interest was for an investment project and not for a money lending venture. He wanted to turn her home into a resort or spa of some kind, and that wasn't what she wanted. Besides, going through all of the negotiations would take too long, and she needed the money *now*.

Marie-Louise had Jakob turn the coach around. As a last resort, she wanted to talk to the mayor and find out if he was open for negotiations.

He said neither yea nor nay, but agreed to come to the castle the following evening.

As the time of the meeting approached, Marie-Louise paced from the parlor to the library and back and looked out the window for any sign of the mayor's automobile. When he finally drove up, she wrung her hands and heaved a sigh, then caught herself doing it, squared her shoulders and went to greet him.

"I'm sorry, Baroness, to cause you so much trouble," he opened the conversation.

Smiling slightly, she tried to hide her panic. "I guess that's the risk I took in getting that kind of a loan." She dug her fingernails into the palms of her hands until they hurt. Looking up, she confessed, "I wasn't able to come up with the money yet, of course, because I only had two days to find another lender."

He nodded.

Frustration built up within her, and she asked, "Couldn't you have waited with your letter until I came back from Falkenberg, to give me at least a week to come up with a solution?"

"Unfortunately, that was quite impossible."

Ashamed, she apologized, "I'm sorry for lashing out at you, but my nerves are on edge. You have always been a good friend to me, and I know you wouldn't put me on the spot like this if you weren't in dire straits yourself."

He straightened his tie and cleared his throat. "You mentioned negotiations at your visit. What did you have in mind?"

Thank goodness—he was open to negotiations. "If you would grant me one week, I'm sure I could come up with the money."

He shook his head. "That's out of the question."

Looking at her from under his bushy, gray brows, he asked, "Do you have any other suggestions?"

"I could offer you a partnership in my business."

"No, thanks. The restaurant business doesn't bring enough to make it worth my while."

"Not even if I transferred the business in your name?"

"Not even then, Baroness."

He sat in front of her, his arms crossed over his chest, and watched her like a cat did its prey.

Her chances to save Hohenstein moved further and further away, and panic clutched at her heart. Her gaze wandered around the room trying to find something, anything that would be of worth to the mayor.

"I could give you some of our antiques," she suggested.

"I'm not interested."

Exasperated, she finally asked, "What is it that you want, then?"

"I want Hohenstein."

As if someone had punched her in the stomach, she sucked in her breath. "Never!"

The mayor sat there and smirked, and at that moment, she thought his smile satanic and not at all fatherly. She turned away, the sight of him all of a sudden bringing a sick feeling to her stomach. Could it be that Frau Zimmer had been right in her assessment of the man's character? If so, why hadn't she seen behind his friendly veneer?

His oily voice brought her back to reality. "Never say never."

Leaning forward, she said in hushed accents, "Do you think Count Wolfburg would sit idly by while you snatch Hohenstein from me?"

"There isn't much he can do. I hold a note that you signed. You can't pay up, and I foreclose."

Her thoughts chased each other in quick succession. Wasn't there anything she could say to change the man's mind? She couldn't just let him take her home away from her. What about her father's stipulation?

With more bravado than she felt, she pointed out, "You can't foreclose on me because Hohenstein is tied up for several more years."

Another satanic grin. "That's right. Therefore, I brought a contract for you to sign, deeding the castle over to me as soon as you come into your inheritance, which is in six years, if I'm correct."

"That's blackmail." Glaring at him she hissed, "I should report you to the police."

"And let the world know that Marie-Louise, Baroness von Hohenstein can't pay her debts?" he sneered.

"You'll never get Hohenstein!"

He shrugged. "I will, unless you agree to my proposition."

"What proposition? I don't know if I want to listen to any more that you have to say."

He covered her hand with his fleshy one. "Hear me out."

With a sick feeling in the pit of her stomach, she eyed the mayor. "All right, what's your proposition?"

He cleared his throat, searched in his briefcase, and cleared his throat again. "If you can't come up with the money before midnight today, you lose Hohenstein."

When she didn't respond he continued, "It would be a shame after all the work you put into restoring it."

Although the old benevolence was back in his voice, Marie-Louise detected the warning signs this time. How could she have ever thought of him as being kind? Seeing him now, without the mantle of cordiality draped about his shoulders, she recognized his cunning and manipulative nature, and shuddered. Why did she have to get involved with him of all people? And why didn't she consult Ulrich before accepting the loan? She had been glad enough when the mayor had offered it to her at a time when she desperately needed the money.

She should have trusted Ulrich! Well, that was water under the bridge now. She had made a mistake, and would have to suffer the consequences. Perhaps the mayor would come up with an acceptable proposition. She'd do almost anything to save Hohenstein.

Pressing his point, the mayor reiterated, "Yes, it would be a shame to lose it all." He shook his head. "You can save Hohenstein, you know."

She looked at him, not trusting him. "How? Tell me how?"

"You work for me."

She had a hard time hiding her disgust. Working for him? What kind of work? She'd rather not ever see him again. Cautiously, she asked, "What would I have to do?"

The mayor steepled his hands and rested his chin on the tips of his fingers. "You'd live a normal life, go to all the social functions and gatherings of the noble upper class, and find out whose estates needed a *helping hand.*"

Marie-Louise sprang up. "You want me to spy for you! You want me to do the dirty work for you in circles you can't penetrate? You want me to help ruin others as you're trying to ruin me?"

"Tsk, tsk, tsk. Those are harsh words, Baroness. I haven't ruined you—yet. And I'm not going to ruin you should you decide to work for me. As a bonus, I'd even waive the amount of the loan."

"My services must be very valuable to you."

"No need to be sarcastic."

She sat down again. "Tell me one thing. What are you doing with all the castles you want me to push your way?"

"We're turning them into resorts.

"Who's *we*?"

"The Luxury Resort Company."

"And who besides you stands behind this title?"

"There are four of us."

"Their names, please."

He clammed up, but she repeated, "Their names."

He rattled off the names, which, of course, didn't mean anything to her.

Running out of patience, the mayor rummaged in his briefcase for an official looking piece of paper, neatly stuck in a folder. "Baroness, do you want to save Hohenstein or not?"

She sat at the table and rested her chin on her hand. Her mind worked overtime, but she couldn't come up with an acceptable solution to her dilemma. If only Ulrich were here.

"If you want to save Hohenstein, you'd better sign this contract." The mayor pushed the folder toward her.

"I need time alone to read over the contract and to consider the pros and cons."

"All right. I'll give you an hour."

"That's not enough."

"It'll have to do, Baroness. Either you sign, or we'll have to go the other route. I've brought a contract for that eventuality, too. But I'm sure, as intelligent as you are, you'll save your skin and keep Hohenstein."

"Fall in with your wishes, you mean?"

"Either way, I win."

"I'm sure you do." She couldn't help keep the bitterness out of her voice. With a resigned sigh, she got up and walked out of the library. Her step had lost its spring as she crossed the vestibule, opened the heavy oak door and stepped out.

What a mess she found herself in! In her hand, she held the power to save Hohenstein. Her job would be easy enough. Nobody needed to know of her activities. And she wouldn't even have to pay back the loan!

What about all the other families, though, who would lose their homes because of her? They probably loved their estates as much as she loved Hohenstein.

On the other hand, wasn't she responsible for Hohenstein? Let the others worry about their own problems!

Slowly, she walked down the worn steps, touched the railing as if caressing it, smoothed her hand over the spots on the wall where the stucco had crumbled, and directed her steps toward the old gatehouse with its fresh coat of paint and fancy scrolls she had worked on when Ulrich had come and had startled her.

She crossed to the stables that still housed Ulrich's team. Oh, the struggle she'd had trying to hitch the heavy horses to the coach! She'd never forget that afternoon.

Her gaze wandered up to the new roof. She could still feel the pride and sense of accomplishment after she'd worked out the barter with the roofer's wife and daughter. Necessity had been the mother of invention in this case.

Her next adventure had been her business, especially the café. It meant a lot of work but she liked it, and it had proved to be a gold mine. If only the mayor would have given her more time, she could have sold it. She would've come up with the money, if only . . .

Kaiser chose this moment to join the baroness and pushed his snout into Marie-Louise's hand.

"You're a good dog. What will happen to you if we lose Hohenstein? What will happen to me? Tante Ambrosia will marry Dr. Walter, which is good, so I don't have to worry about her." She walked a few paces toward the carriage house, and then stopped.

"What will happen to all the Hohensteins hanging in the gallery? Will they have to look down on strangers in the future? Or will they fall victim to a tourist industry? Will they be silent witnesses to masses of guests basking in the glamour of a time gone by? Or perhaps, they will be removed from the castle and sold at an auction?"

Marie-Louise shuddered. Her ancestors would turn in their graves, and she couldn't let that happen. Hohenstein was hers. She had the responsibility toward her ancestors to preserve it, and to pass it on to her posterity. *Oh, Lord,* she groaned, *what am I to do? Save my home, and force others to lose theirs?*

Weary, she leaned her head against the sun-warmed trunk of a tree. She wanted to keep Hohenstein, because she loved it with every fiber of her being, but she couldn't do what the mayor asked of her. She couldn't build her happiness upon others' misfortune. That wouldn't be right.

With a heavy heart, she looked around. The gatehouse and armory, the bridge, the stables, the carriage house and the main building. *My home,* she thought. *Goodbye.*

A lump formed in her throat. Her eyes burned but remained dry.

Upon entering the library again, she asked the mayor, “May I see the other contract you mentioned?”

He handed it to her.

She read the contract, but had a hard time seeing the letters because tears blurred her vision. With a shaking hand, she took pen and inkpot out of the desk drawer and signed her name. Her signature didn’t look as steady as usual, as a matter of fact, it could have been written by an old woman, as wobbly as it appeared. The mayor reached for the contract and stuffed it into his briefcase.

Marie-Louise had just signed her home away.

Chapter Twenty-eight

After the mayor left with a smug expression, Marie-Louise directed her steps toward the gallery. One by one, she looked at her ancestors, brave witnesses of a proud past. All of them contributed their share to the legacy of Hohenstein, which the youngest twig a few minutes ago put to naught.

I've let you down, but at least I didn't dishonor your name.

On a sob, she turned and made her way to the sitting room. Her hands touched the polished surface of a drop-leaf table, smoothed over the soft velvet of a *chaise lounge*, rested on the cool marble of a windowsill. All this, familiar and loved, would belong to strangers in the future. It couldn't be! It must be a bad dream she'd wake up from shortly.

The tears that wouldn't come earlier hovered on the edge of her lashes and blurred her vision. *Self-pity won't bring Hohenstein back,* she chided herself. If only Tante Ambrosia were here. Everything would be easier. At least, she'd have a shoulder to cry on.

Absent-minded, Marie-Louise straightened a pillow. How fortunate that Ambrosia was to be married. Not having to worry about her aunt's future took one big burden off Marie-Louise's shoulders. She knew that she would cope somehow. She'd return to Berlin to attend university there. Or perhaps she'd go somewhere far away, maybe even overseas.

The lump in her throat tightened. At least funding for her education was secure. What would she do between now and the start of the semester, though? Run to her mother? No way. She could look for a job, but she didn't possess any marketable skills.

She probably wouldn't be able to continue with the café and souvenir shop because the mayor probably would want her to vacate the castle immediately.

Another sob escaped her.

She could try to find a job working in an art gallery until the semester started.

She heaved a sigh, opened the French doors and stepped onto the terrace overlooking the park. How she loved these old trees that were almost as old as the castle itself, and had given shade to generations of Hohensteins before her. No place on earth could compare with her home! Her home that would soon be taken from her.

As another cry wanted to escape her throat, she quickly pressed her handkerchief to her mouth to stifle the sound.

She walked to the stone railing and looked down. Her senses drank in the evening sounds of birds flying to their nests, crickets chirping on the lawn below, and frogs croaking in the distant pond, and the smell of freshly cut grass mingled with the perfumed scent of roses wafted up to her. Oh, how she loved the sounds and smells of Hohenstein!

On the horizon to the west, a parting sun painted red edges haphazardly on the surrounding cloud flurries, while the others, further away, disappeared into obscurity. A soft breeze rippled through the leaves and urged the little lizard in the flower bed below to scurry a tad faster to his home under the stairs. Peace.

Peace everywhere, except in her heart. Her insides felt raw with grief. Her mind wrestled with the problem of her uncertain future. What would become of her?

She didn't know how long she stood on the terrace staring out over the park, but when the last rays of the sun disappeared and darkness descended, she went inside. Walking aimlessly from room to room, she finally stopped in front of the cabinet with the sheet music. Not really looking for anything in particular, she pulled out a volume of compositions by Franz Liszt and riffled through the pages.

Consolation, she read. That's what she needed right now. Perhaps the composer had faced tragedy in his life, too, and had resorted to music to ease his pain. If it helped him, it might help her as well.

She opened the lid of the beautiful white grand piano, arranged the music on the ornately carved stand, and seated herself on the bench with its petit point cushion. She played a few chords to limber up her fingers before she attempted to play in earnest.

A little timid at first, she soon lost herself in the music, at one with it and the deceased composer, whose heart cried out in agony *Why me?* but soon received the assurance that all would be well. The music ended with his humble submission to a Supreme Being, his soul looking up, trusting, not seeing the silver lining yet, but believing it would soon appear.

After the last notes died away, Marie-Louise sat silent, hands loosely clasped in her lap, head bent. She had found solace in the music. Although her heart still ached, she was now able to look beyond the moment, and direct her thoughts to more specific questions. How long could she stay at Hohenstein before the mayor pushed her out? Would he let her stay until her inheritance came due? And where would she go afterwards?

What would happen to her business? Would she be able to run it until she had to leave, or would she have to close everything right away?

She thought of Jakob, the loyal old servant. Where would he go in his old age?

Another thought occurred that almost took her breath away. What if Ulrich found out how foolish she had been to trust the mayor? She had spurned his request to come to him for advice before making any major decisions. Now she had to pay the price.

She couldn't keep the truth from him. He'd find out sooner or later.

Would he be angry? No, she decided, not angry. Disappointed perhaps—and hurt. Hurt, because she didn't trust him.

She remembered how, at first, she had suspected *him* of foul play. Oh, how foolish she had been! If she could but turn back the clock! Because of her blind rebellion against the dictates of her rank, she had tossed aside a man of genuine integrity, and turned to one of unscrupulous business practices.

Picturing the mayor's benevolent smile, now almost turned her stomach. She had fallen right into his trap. And that such a scoundrel should own Hohenstein made her ball her hands into fists. People like him should be behind bars!

She took a deep breath. Her home was lost forever. Tears stung her eyes as she hung her head.

Marie-Louise couldn't remember how long she sat on that piano bench commiserating her fate, when a movement in the background caught her attention. She turned, and when she saw her visitor, rose as if in a daze, and took a few steps forward.

"Ullie?" she whispered, not sure if he was real or a figment of her imagination.

When he raised his arm in salute, she wanted nothing more than to rush into his arms and tell him of her horrible nightmare. On second thought, however, she hesitated. Did she really want to admit that she had been foolish to trust the mayor? Could her pride endure another blow? She bristled at the thought, but realized that he'd learn the truth soon enough.

"Are you all right?" he asked, his voice tinged with concern.

No, she wanted to cry, but instead, nodded. The lump in her throat made speech impossible.

Raising one brow he regarded her skeptically. "Are you sure?"

She pressed her lips together but nodded again.

Why had he come to Hohenstein today—the blackest of all days? She didn't need an audience for her misery, and she was definitely not in the mood for small talk. Feeling her knees go weak, she held on to the piano for support.

"Don't you want to tell me what's bothering you?"

Swallowing hard, she fought for control. Finally, not looking up, she wanted to know, "Do you still have a position at the bank for me?"

After what seemed an eternity he answered, "Sorry. The position is already filled." Then he smiled. "There is, however, an opening for a personal companion if you're interested."

She stood frozen for a moment before she looked at him. How was she to understand his remark? Was he teasing?

His smile deepened. He opened his arms and, after a stunned moment, Marie-Louise pushed away from the piano and moved toward the haven of those arms as if drawn by a magnet.

Safe in his embrace, she leaned her head on his shoulder, closed her eyes and inhaled the familiar scent of Irish moss. For the first time that day, she felt secure. Her problems seemed to have left her shoulders and transferred to his. If she could but make this moment last forever!

As the tension gradually left her body, her mind started functioning again. She glanced up at him. "Did you say *companion?*"

He nodded. "*Personal* companion," he stressed.

"Did you mean what I think you meant?"

"You understood perfectly well, my love," he laughed, bent his head and brushed a kiss onto the tip of her nose.

She shook her head, "I'm confused."

"What is there to be confused about?"

"You are to be engaged pretty soon, in fact, you were going to announce your engagement at the upcoming summer ball."

"Not a bad idea, but I don't know if I want to wait that long."

"Please, be serious," she reprimanded. "Teasing about something like that isn't fair to your future wife."

He drew back to look at her. "What are you talking about?"

"A reliable source told me that you are to be engaged."

"A reliable source?" he said and wrinkled his brow. "It couldn't have been *that* reliable! And who would know what my plans were? Oh, I see. Did my brother visit you?"

She nodded. "Yes, he told me of your impending engagement, but why would he have said something like that when it wasn't true?"

He shook his head. "The only reason that I can see is, that he probably wanted to assure you of my love, and wanted to let you know that *you* were the chosen one."

"Well, I certainly didn't get *that* message."

"Obviously. And now I also know what was bothering you all this time, why you looked as if you wanted to cry when there was no reason for it that I could see. Did you really think that I was so lost to all decency that I would kiss you when I was promised to someone else?"

When she wouldn't look up, he put his finger under her chin and tilted her head up so that she had to look at him. "Silly girl, didn't you know that I loved *you*? That I love you more than anything in this world?"

"You never told me," she whispered.

"But I showed you, didn't I?"

"I thought it was just compatibility."

"Yes, I remember you told me that before." He tucked one of her curls behind her ear. "Now, how about my proposition?"

"Did you really mean what you implied?"

"Absolutely." He trailed feathery kisses on her eyes, her nose, her temples down to her mouth, and she moistened her lips with her tongue waiting for his kiss, but it didn't come. Instead, he lifted his head and his eyes crinkled, "I'm still waiting for your answer, Baroness."

At his question, she stiffened and withdrew her hands from behind his neck. Before this went any further, she had to tell him the truth about Hohenstein. He may not want to have anything to do with her after he heard of her folly. No matter how devastating the outcome, she had to tell him the truth *now*.

Drawing erratic figures onto his shirt front with her finger, she wasn't quite sure how to broach the subject. Finally she blurted out, "I lost Hohenstein."

He breathed a light kiss onto the crown of her head. "Let's not discuss this issue right now. I've something far more important on my mind at the moment."

Heat crept into her cheeks as he whispered close to her ear, "I've waited for this moment for a long time, but I knew I had to be patient. After I kissed you that first time, you were so angry with me, you never wanted to see me again, although you enjoyed the encounter."

She pulled away and pouted. "I did not!"

"Liar," he said softly drawing her close again. "Your response betrayed you. I wanted to teach you a lesson, and in the process you stole my heart. Making you admit your true feelings wasn't easy. I knew I had to be patient and win your trust before I could hope for more."

He tilted her chin up with one finger again until her lips were only millimeters away from his. "You were worth the wait, though, my love."

Marie-Louise felt the warmth of his mouth, and quivered in anticipation of his kiss and raised herself on tiptoes until her lips touched his.

Before he started his sensuous exploration, a wicked gleam entered his eyes as he murmured against her slightly parted lips, "No more rebellious thoughts about the esteemed rank of nobility?"

She could only shake her head and, blushing, abandon herself to the infinite pleasure of his kiss. It was warm and feather-light and teasing.

When they finally drew apart, Marie-Louise grew serious.

"Ullie, Hohenstein doesn't belong to me anymore."

Far from being shocked at her disclosure, he said, "That reminds me . . . I have something to give to you." He reached into his breast pocket and pulled out a folded piece of paper.

Exasperated with his inattention, she laid a hand on his arm. "Ullie, did you hear what I said?"

"Of course I did, but before you launch into a lengthy explanation, I want you to read this," and he handed her the paper.

Looking at him askance, she unfolded it, smoothed it out and . . . gasped. In her hands she held the very contract she had signed a few hours earlier, giving away Hohenstein. "How did you come by this?" she asked in a hoarse whisper.

"The mayor handed it to me."

"Don't tell me you're in on this scam?"

His eyes clouded over. "Marie-Louise, don't you know me better than that?"

"I'm sorry," she apologized. "I'm thoroughly confused. Why do you have this contract, and what am I supposed to do with it?"

"I told you before. The mayor gave it to me. And you can rip it to shreds, or frame it and hang it over your bed—come to think of it—better not hang it over your bed, because your bed will be our bed in the very near future. And I don't want to be reminded of the mayor's dealings."

Marie-Louise sounded stern. "Count Wolfburg, if you just proposed to me it was very unromantic!"

He grinned. "My family is not known for their flowery speeches, or for their earth-shaking proposals."

"So I've heard."

"Ah! Mother shared some of our family secrets with you."

"You bet."

"I knew it! I should never have talked her into inviting you to Falkenberg."

"That was your doing?"

He laughed, "Of course. The poor mayor tried so hard to lure you away from Hohenstein, long enough to land his *coup*. That's why he offered you his cabin in the Black Forest."

"Do you mean to tell me that you knew all along what he planned to do?"

"Not exactly. I knew he wanted to strike, and I helped things along."

"Why?"

"He was snatching estates away from unsuspecting families for quite some time before I found out. At first, I didn't know who stood behind the organization of the *Luxury Resort Company*, but I was determined to find out. When you, my love, returned to Hohenstein and needed money, I was certain you were a golden target."

"You used Hohenstein as bait?"

"I had to."

"How could you do that to me," she accused. "It could've backfired."

He squeezed her hand. "I had to do it to uncover those gold diggers. Please, forgive me. I would've never let them harm you or take Hohenstein away from you."

She struggled out of his embrace and, hands on hips, vented her feelings. "Do you realize what I went through these past few hours? What I suffered? How could you have been so sure that you could prevent a disaster?"

"I kept informed."

She took a few deep breaths to calm herself. "How did you keep informed?"

"Remember the interruption when you first visited me at the bank?"

"Yes, I remember."

"The man was a private detective, but he wasn't the only informant."

She stared at him. "And all that happened under my nose, and I didn't know!"

He smiled. "Another one of my informants was Frau Zimmer."

"Really? Why am I not surprised?" She remembered how Ulrich had insisted on sending his housekeeper to Hohenstein, but she had never suspected the woman to spy for him. Now she felt as if she was watching a jigsaw puzzle come together, she herself being one of the pieces.

"Who besides the mayor runs the Luxury Resort Company?" she asked. "He mentioned that there were four of them."

"There is the mayor of course, then the director of the Commerce Bank—"

Marie-Louise whistled through her teeth. "That explains why he didn't give me a loan. It wasn't for any of the reasons he mentioned."

"The third person is an investor from Freiburg, and the fourth is the county commissioner."

"That's terrific."

"They would've squeezed the life blood out of you, my lovely baroness."

She shook her head. "What about the railing along our moat? Who was responsible for that request?"

"That was the mayor's doing."

Marie-Louise wrinkled her brow. "I often wondered how the mayor knew immediately that I had returned to Hohenstein."

Ulrich nodded. "His wife told him."

"His wife? I didn't meet her until much later; actually I met her at a restaurant in Hinterzarten on my way back from the ballet in Stuttgart."

"You visited the Schmidt & Roth Company?"

"Yes, but I don't understand what that visit had to do with the mayor's knowledge of my return to Hohenstein."

Ulrich put his arm around her shoulders. "The mayor's wife is the Schmidt in Schmidt & Roth."

"Oh," she said.

"You see, the mayor needed you to return to Hohenstein so that he could snatch up the castle. However, he needed to find a way to bring you back. Get it?"

"You mean the problem with my tuition payment was staged to bring me to Hohenstein?"

"Yes. It was part of the plan."

She shuddered, "How awful."

After a moment, she remembered one of her earlier questions, and quizzed him. "You still didn't tell me how you took the contract away from the mayor. I'm sure he didn't just hand it over."

"Oh, yes, he did—after I confronted him with all the evidence."

"What evidence?"

"First of all, he didn't give you a week to come up with the money according to the contract."

"But the letter arrived while I was at Falkenberg."

"That's true, but the law requires that a certified letter be delivered when payment is requested, and the receiver has to sign on delivery. Sending the request by registered mail will not hold up in a court of law, and that was one of his mistakes."

Ulrich took her hand and guided her inside where he pulled her down to sit on the settee next to him. "Another flaw was that my 'spy' found plans of Hohenstein as a holiday resort already approved by the county."

"They had plans already drawn up before they even owned the castle?" she asked.

"That's right."

"What was his reaction when you confronted him?"

"At first, he denied the accusations, of course."

Head resting in her hands, Marie-Louise asked, "How did you know that the mayor visited me today?"

"Frau Zimmer sent Jakob with the message."

Marie-Louise was stunned. "All this was going on, and I had no idea."

He smiled. "Welcome to the adult world."

She sniffed. "They didn't teach us at school how to deal with crooks."

"Of course not," he said, "but I was very proud of you when you refused to work for him, rather sacrificing Hohenstein and yourself than dishonoring your name."

She shuddered. "It was a nightmare."

"I know, and I'm sorry for all the heartache you suffered. I wanted to rush to your side and protect you, but I couldn't. It was my duty to expose the Luxury Resort Company."

After a pause Marie-Louise wanted to know, "Would you have given me a loan if it hadn't been for them?"

He reached for her hand. "Of course I would have helped you, but unfortunately, my hands were tied."

She sighed. "Couldn't you have told me about that company? I'd have played along."

He gave her a peck on the cheek. "I couldn't risk you playing along too well. The mayor might have suspected a trap."

"What will happen to the mayor?" she asked.

"I'll report him to the authorities and warn all of our people."

"I don't have to worry about him anymore?" she asked.

"No, he's gone from your life for good."

She thought about that for a moment, before she said, "But I still have to pay back the loan."

"No, you don't. I gave him a check."

"From my inheritance?"

"No."

"You mean you paid the loan off with your own money?"

"Yes."

"Ullie, I can't accept that."

"Why not?"

"Because it's my loan, or Hohenstein's, and I'm responsible for it."

"Stubborn little thing! As your husband, we'll have all things in common, therefore, I can pay my wife's debts."

"I'm not your wife yet."

"All right, let's not be that particular about a few weeks here or there—you'll be my wife soon enough, and then you can access your inheritance."

He stood up and walked with her to the stone balustrade. Leaning forward, he smiled into her eyes. "Let's not talk about other people or money any more," he urged, his voice thick and husky, barely above a whisper.

She laughed softly. "Actually, you don't want to talk at all. You're more of an action-man."

"You've got that right," he murmured as his lips traced a burning trail along her jaw that sent streams of lava through her entire body. She closed her eyes and pressed closer to him, basking in the safety of his embrace. She had finally come *home*, home to the man who had captured her heart.

Acknowledgements

My heartfelt appreciation to my editors for their guidance and advice.

About the author:

Didi Lawson exchanged her town car for a pick-up truck and learned to operate a tractor when she and her husband moved from Arizona to a farm in Missouri where she now weaves her tales. Her love for writing started early in life when she entertained her friends with her stories, won prizes for her essays in high school, and wrote road shows and poems for the youth group in her church. She enjoys the outdoors, her children and ten grandchildren, and keeps an active social calendar.

About Xchyler Publishing:

At The X, we pride ourselves in discovery and promotion of talented authors. Our anthology project produces three books a year in our specific areas of focus: fantasy, Steampunk, and paranormal. Held winter, spring/summer, and autumn, our short-story competitions result in published anthologies from which the authors receive royalties.

Additional themes include: Losers Weepers (spring/summer 2015) and Worldwide Folklore and the Post-modern Man (winter 2016).

Visit www.xchylerpublishing.com/AnthologySubmissions for more information.

Look for these releases from Xchyler Publishing in 2015:

Blondes, Books and Bourbon, an anthology of short stories set in the White Dragon Black world of Jonathan Alvey, by R. M. Ridley. March 2015.

Vanguard Legacy: Fated, the conclusion of the three-book series by Joanne Kershaw. April 2015.

Everstar by Candace J. Thomas, Book 3 of the Vivatera series.

To learn more, visit www.xchylerpublishing.com.

Xchyler
PUBLISHING

Made in the USA
Charleston, SC
11 November 2015